That's enough, Alix!' he said sharply.

'I'm not playing games, Jake,' Alix whispered earnestly, believing he doubted the reality of her commitment. 'I'm not pretending, and I'm not going to lead you on, just to refuse. If—If it's what you want, then it's what I want, too.'

She tried to embrace him again, but Jake seized her wrists in a painful grip and tore them brutally away from his neck, thrusting her away from him so violently that she stumbled back and almost fell.

'I told you, stop it, Alix! It's *not* what I want!'

She stared at him, wild-eyed. 'But you said . . .'

'I said you were beautiful, and so you are. I didn't say I wanted to start an affair with you!' he snarled at her before she could protest further.

Alix felt her cheeks burn as a scarlet tide of humiliation spread over them. 'Why not?' she asked crisply.

He looked momentarily more discomposed than angry, and moved away, turning his back to her. 'Listen, Alix, if and when I want to take you to bed, I'll say so. I don't need gilt-edged invitations.'

'I wasn't making you an invitation!' she burst out furiously.

'Weren't you? You had me fooled. Where did you learn to behave like that? Here in Paris—or have things changed back in England since I left? What happened to that nice, respectable young lady who was so pleased *not* to have to go up to Robbie's room, even when she was wearing his ring?'

Ann Hulme was born in Portsmouth and educated at the Royal Holloway College—part of the University of London—where she took a degree in French. She has travelled extensively, and it was the fascination of the various countries in which she made her home— France, Germany, Czechoslovakia, Yugoslavia and Zambia—which made her begin to write. She now lives in Bicester, Oxfordshire, with her husband and two sons.

Ann Hulme has also written ten Masquerade Historical Romances. Recent titles include *Interlaken Intrigue*, *The Garden of the Azure Dragon*, *The Hungarian Adventuress* and *No Place for a Lady*.

THE FLYING MAN

ANN HULME

WORLDWIDE BOOKS
LONDON . SYDNEY . TORONTO

*First published in Great Britain in 1988
by Worldwide Books
Eton House, 18-24 Paradise Road, Richmond, Surrey,
TW9 1SR.
© Ann Hulme 1988*

*Australian copyright 1988
Philippine copyright 1988*

*ISBN 0 373 50786 0
09-8806-113972
Set in Monotype Times 10 on 11pt*

*Typeset in Great Britain by
Associated Publishing Services Ltd, Petersfield.
Made and printed in Great Britain*

CHAPTER ONE

'BRITISH WOMEN will follow their men to the front line!' trumpeted Miss Frobisher from the rostrum where, beneath a large Union Jack, she stood, flanked on either side by obedient acolytes. 'And when together we shall have won the War and driven the Huns back whence they came, let us see whether they will still dare to insult British womanhood by refusing us the vote.'

Alix Morrell turned this sentence over in her mind and wondered whether Miss Frobisher really meant that it was the unsuspecting Germans who were refusing British women the right to vote.

'They will not dare!' Miss Frobisher was growing slightly breathless, but was still perfectly audible at the back of the hall where Alix sat together with Jennie Frobisher. 'Ladies, the fight against the Kaiser may not yet be won, but the fight of the British women for justice *has* been won!'

'What do you think of my Aunt Emma?' Jennie whispered.

'I think she's terrifying,' Alix confessed. 'Like Boadicea, Joan of Arc and Good Queen Bess, all rolled into one. Mind you,' she added cautiously, 'I haven't heard Mrs Pankhurst.'

Jennie dismissed Mrs Pankhurst with a twitch of her shoulders. 'Aunt Emma can knock spots off Mrs Pankhurst any day!'

Miss Frobisher had finished, but the gathering of attentive ladies in the hall, peering up at her eagerly beneath the brims of their huge fashionable hats, remained silent, either mesmerised by the sight and sound of the speaker or afraid to clap lest it was not, after all, the end of her speech, and they should be left embarrassingly in mid-applause when she started again. Fortunately, Miss Frobisher chose to sit down and the two acolytes came to life and applauded heartily. At this signal the audience burst into its own enthusiastic tribute.

'Come on,' Jennie grasped Alix's wrist. 'That's our signal. They'll all be demanding their tea and buns before you know it,'

The two young women were by far the youngest in the hall. Most of the audience was married, respectable and mothers, so that it was hard to envisage them at the front line, as Miss Frobisher had urged. The girls made their way under cover of the applause to the tiny, dark and inconvenient kitchen attached to the main hall.

Alix, struggling to fill the heavy kettle at the chipped glazed stoneware sink, gasped, 'I still don't see why she has to use *us* as slave labour to feed her militant hordes.'

'That's what we're here for!' Jennie said cheerfully, piling currant buns on a plate on an ancient trolley, together with a pile of cups and saucers.

'Is that all the food there is?' Alix demanded, dismayed. 'One plate of sticky buns? Those women will demolish those in about five seconds.'

'It's not my fault,' Jennie objected, 'There's a war on. Sugar's rationed, and no one wants to offer to make cakes.'

There was a buzz of conversation from the main room, but the kettle was slow to boil. 'Oh, do come on!' Alix urged it. 'We'll never get all this over and out of the way in time. The dressmaker only brought my gown round this morning and I haven't had time to try it on, even. She's coming back at six.'

Jennie was silent, carefully dividing the buns between

two plates so that they should look more.

'Oh, Jen,' Alix said in gentle despair, 'you're not going to refuse to go to the Harrises' party?'

'What's the use of my going? As soon as the dancing starts, I shall have to go and hide in the cloakroom. It's all right for you; you've never been a wallflower in your life.'

'You won't get a partner by skulking in the cloakroom. Anyway, Robbie and Gerard and Philip Harris will all dance with you.'

'Robbie's your fiancé. He's only got so much leave and he doesn't want to spend it with other girls. Gerard will dance with Blanche—Blanche will make sure of that. Philip Harris is all right but we have absolutely nothing in common, and circling round a dance-floor in stony silence is worse than sitting it out with the chaperons. I'm for the cloakroom.'

'You're not,' Alix said firmly. 'I shall come and drag you out, and don't let me find you reading a book. You smuggled a book in there last time. Who ever heard of anyone going to a party, and hiding in the cloakroom to read?'

'I do it all the time,' Jennie said calmly. Together with Alix she struggled to lift the heavy tea-urn and set it on the trolley. 'Besides, it doesn't seem right—all that jollity. Every other family seems to be in mourning, and nearly all the young men have gone to fight.'

'We *all* feel that way!' Alix said fiercely. 'But Robbie and Phil are going back to France. We're all trying to make their leave happy. It's for them.'

Back in the main hall, the ladies with the fox furs and the large hats were milling about chattering and waiting for the tea, which was greeted with cries of rapture as Alix and Jennie trundled in the trolley. For the next ten minutes they were both kept fully occupied. As the mob thinned out and Alix stepped back with a sigh of relief, she became aware that Miss Frobisher's tall, angular figure, topped by a mauve toque hat, was at her elbow.

'How's that young man of yours, Robert Harris?' she demanded without preamble. 'When's he off to the Front?'

'The day after tomorrow,' Alix said, wishing Miss Frobisher were not quite so tactless. She strove to keep her own tone bright. 'It's so unusual, both Robbie and Phil being home on leave at the same time—that's why Lady Harris is giving a party for them. Philip goes back to his regiment next week. Robbie's in the Royal Flying Corps.'

'A flying man, eh?' Miss Frobisher mused. 'The world's changing, my dear. Man in the clouds and woman in parliament, eh?' Miss Frobisher emitted a braying sound, and Alix realised the last words were a joke. She smiled dutifully. 'What will it be like in five or six years' time, I wonder?' demanded Miss Frobisher rhetorically.

A cold finger laid itself on Alix's spine. She looked over her shoulder and saw the main door had swung open, letting in a draught. Jennie had just gone to close it. Alix shivered.

Miss Frobisher was also watching Jennie. 'My niece is a sensible girl; head screwed on the right way. Can't say the same for her sister. Silly flibbertigibbet, Blanche. Takes after her mother.'

Miss Frobisher departed abruptly, but Alix had understood, knowing the situation in the Frobisher household.

Accepted wisdom was that it was all right for a woman to marry 'up' and a man to marry 'down', But not the other way about. In practice, this theory had failed Jennie's mother, Maisie Frobisher, miserably. As a pretty, pert, sharp-eyed and sharp-witted Cockney chorus girl, she had captured a 'stage-door johnnie' of good family and somehow persuaded him to marry her.

Alas for her dreams of being a 'lady'. The chirpy little Cockney sparrow had become a nervous, unhappy creature in a cage into which she had flown of her own accord. Her links with her own background ruthlessly cut, she found herself among people with whom she had nothing in common and before whom she was constantly terrified of making some social gaffe. Her husband's family refused even to receive her. Stage-door johnnies do not make good husbands. When he had died, she had been left almost penniless and with two daughters approaching marriageable age, Jennie and Blanche.

Jennie was shy and awkward. But Blanche—Blanche had inherited her mother's early good looks, a flawless complexion, golden curls and guileless blue eyes. She was not clever, but she was sharp-witted in the way of generations of Whitechapel urchins from whom she was descended on her mother's side. And she was ambitious. Thus, Blanche should marry brilliantly and restore all their fortunes. Mrs Frobisher grasped at this possibility as a man drowning at a lifebelt. It meant, of course, bringing Blanche 'out'—and that cost money. Mrs Frobisher swallowed her pride and, flanked by her daughters, called on her husband's wealthy and eccentric aunt, Emma Frobisher.

Miss Frobisher, predictably, took one look at Blanche and snorted. But quiet, intelligent Jennie took her fancy straight away. Mrs Frobisher and Blanche couldn't understand it, as, humiliated and rebuffed, they heard Aunt Emma refuse brusquely to do anything for Blanche, but offer to pay all expenses if Jennie would go up to Oxford.

The fact was that the battle for women's suffrage was in sight of being won, and Miss Frobisher was free to turn her powerful personality to Women's Education. For Jennie, it had been as if a Fairy Godmother had granted realisation of a secret and apparently hopeless

dream. There was a certain price to pay by way of
dancing attendance on Miss Frobisher and supporting
her in her many feminist activities—hence trolley duty
at the suffragette meeting. But it was a small price to
pay for a chance to join the small select band of women
at university.

'You're happy, aren't you, Jen?' Alix asked affectionately, as the girls walked homewards.

Jennie smiled. 'Yes, I am.' Her eyes clouded. 'I hope
you'll be happy, too, Alix, and have what you want in
life.'

'I'll be all right,' Alix said awkwardly, 'when the war
is over and Robbie and I can get married.'

'It's having something to look forward to,' Jennie
said unexpectedly. 'Before Aunt Emma made her offer,
I had no future at all. Now I have a tomorrow.'

Jennie was given to saying sudden, odd things like
that, and not for the first time, Alix wished she hadn't.
The thought of 'tomorrow' frightened her. Much as she
wanted to marry Robbie, even that prospect failed to
encourage her as it should have done. They had been
engaged for two whole years, and it got harder and
harder to imagine that they would ever really be man
and wife.

A screech of brakes broke into her thoughts. The
ringing of a handbell heralded a van which came
careering down the road, with a boy of about fourteen
hanging out of the window and ringing a large bell of
the school playground type. He was yelling hoarsely,
'Zeppel—een! Air-raid! Take cover . . .' He was
enjoying himself immensely.

The van careered past. There were some people
running now, men and women with children in their
arms, but rather aimlessly, as if unsure what to do. The
two girls stood on the pavement, shielding their eyes
and staring into the sky.

'There it is!' Alix exclaimed, pointing upwards.

Above their heads, from behind a ridge of rooftops, the great, bloated shape drifted noiselessly and ominously into view. Alix thought it looked like a great fish, a porpoise or a dolphin, swimming silently along. Powerful, quiet and menacing, it was frightening, comical, ungainly and beautiful.

'What terrible things,' Jennie whispered. 'Do you think he's going to drop bombs on us?'

But the Zeppelin drifted on, most likely making for the docks along the Thames where his bomb-load could do more damage. Zeppelin raids were hit or miss affairs, destroying civilian targets in mistake for strategic ones, a prime example of the Kaiser's villainy and a source of endless fascination. The girls were not the only ones who, instead of taking shelter, had stopped in the open street to watch. Unnoticed by either Alix or Jennie, a man in Royal Flying Corps uniform had stopped in the doorway of a tobacconist's he was leaving, to stare up at the airship. He was watching it intently and with a critical frown, as if working out the mechanics of the structure. After it had passed, he pulled the inside from a cigarette packet and drew a sketch of the Zeppelin on it, the sort of precise sketch engineers make. Preoccupied, he missed seeing the girls pass him by. Jennie saw him, but hurried on.

At the end of the street they parted, to make their separate ways home. Alix lived with her mother's sister, Mrs Daventry, and her cousin, Gerard. Her own parents had died in a railway accident in France when she was twelve, but even before that, she had scarcely known them. Somewhere in the background had been old grandfather Nathanael Morrell, a successful Northern industrialist. A man of immense stature and personality, with flaming red hair which his grand-daughter had inherited, Nat Morrell had successfully quarrelled with all his family and most of his business acquaintances. His son, Alix's father, had been thrown out of the family home at twenty-one. He came South, to London, to seek his fortune. A handsome, capricious man, he had never sought to reconcile his differences with his father, and had compounded his disgrace by making an unsuitable marriage, to a frail woman of the 'milk and water' type—as old Nat was reputed to have commented dourly when the news was relayed to him in his counting-house.

There had been enough of Nat in his son to ensure that Edward Morrell made his own modest success in life, as an importer of wines. This caused him to spend much time travelling around vineyards. His wife, being delicate, had quickly declined into the self-imposed condition of semi-invalid, which necessitated taking the cure at select spas. Their one child, Alix, had been a difficult birth, and the doctor had decreed 'no more babies'. Contraception had not then been readily available or socially acceptable, and marriages upon which doctors passed this sentence came to an end as far as any physical reality was concerned. No more babies, no more anything. Edward Morrell travelled the vineyards of France, Italy and Spain, contenting himself with occasional forays into the more reputable brothels of the countries through which he passed. Ironically, his wife had joined him on a visit to the South of France, the first journey taken together in years, when the railway crash had claimed them both.

In a sense, it made little immediate difference to Alix. Her father's business and her mother's poor health had precluded either of them taking her along on their various travels, and she therefore continued to live as she had always done, with her widowed Aunt Ethel Daventry and cousin Gerard, in the large, red-brick, late Victorian villa. Its narrow windows restricted the light and made the large rooms gloomy, and its draughts necessitated huge and expensive coal fires in winter. When the wind blew in the wrong direction, the grates belched fumes rendering the drawing-room similar to a Norwegian smoke-house in atmosphere.

Yet it was a comfortable enough house in its way, run by a staff of efficient servants, and Alix had always been happy there. It was surrounded by well-kept lawns, and rhododendron bushes, in and out of which she and Gerard played cowboys and Indians until Gerard was sent away to school.

In the meantime, old Nat continued to fall out with his neighbours, his partners and any remaining downtrodden relatives. Finally, on his deathbed, he quarrelled with his solicitors, who had represented his interests for years. He accused them of incompetence, sacked them, engaged a new firm and drew up a new will. In it, for reasons known only to him and never to be divulged, he left the bulk of his considerable fortune to the unknown grand-daughter in far-off London, on whom he had never set eyes, and whose existence he had never formally acknowledged. At twelve, Alix had been an orphan whose father had left her a modest but respectable sum in trust. At sixteen, she was suddenly an heiress.

The sudden possession of so much money meant as little to her as the loss of her parents had done. She had never known old Nat, was not yet old enough to control the money herself, and the one thought which had leapt into her mind at once had been that there was now extra money for extra art tuition. For some time it had been clear that she had real artistic talent. She was allowed to have the extra art lessons, which encouraged her to dream of going to Paris and studying seriously. But here she ran into a brick wall of opposition.

The money was there, but the idea that a young girl should go to France, unchaperoned, and study art shocked Mrs Daventry to the core. It was quite out of the question. It involved, she said in a hushed voice, drawing, you know, unclothed models . . . and artists were notoriously loose-living. If Alix wished extra tuition here in England, that was quite in order. Painting was a very nice accomplishment for a young girl. But to be a serious painter, to talk of earning a living . . . The veto was final.

At the beginning of the War, Alix had met Robbie Harris at a tennis party, where she had been partnered by Gerard, now a qualified solicitor. He was a burly man, the typical former rugger blue, now putting on weight behind an office desk. He was well aware of this risk, and was predictably a fitness fanatic. Gerard was predictable in everything from his opinions to his clothes. An excellent tennis player, normally he hated doubles with girls because they didn't hit the ball hard enough and most of them couldn't run. But he would always partner Alix because, as she well knew, he had been in love with her ever since he had come down from Oxford and discovered that the freckled child with the carrotty pigtails, holland pinafore and black stockings had become a ravishingly beautiful young woman with a mass of auburn hair and green eyes which, when she was angry or frightened, seemed almost emerald in hue.

Alix was very fond of Gerard, but knew she could never fall in love with him. He'd always been like an elder brother, and his down-to-earth respectability irritated her. Sometimes, when she got up early and went out into the garden to paint—as she frequently did in summer, when the dew touched grass and flowers with silver—she caught glimpses of him standing at his bedroom window in striped pyjamas, breathing deeply and stretching his arms. It was an action which seemed to typify Gerard, like his other habit of raising his whisky glass and saying 'Chin-chin!'

Gerard was intelligent enough to know how she felt. Meekly he accepted his role of tennis partner, shoulder to cry on and escort, if no one else was available. He watched over Alix devotedly, dogmatic, pompous, honest and loyal, but had viewed the whirlwind romance with Robbie Harris with silent disapproval. Gerard was above selfish jealousy, Alix knew. He only wanted her to be happy. His disapproval of Robbie was rooted in something far more tangible. He thought Robbie not impervious to the fortune old Nat had left his grand-daughter. He and Alix had had their first and only serious quarrel about it.

'It's a horrible thing to suggest, Gerry! Am I to go through life wondering if every man is after my money? Robbie loves me!'

'A man would have to be made of stone not to love you!' Gerard was betrayed into exclaiming. He reddened in embarrassment, but went on obstinately and in what Alix called his 'lawyer's voice': 'It would be foolish to overlook the possibility.'

Mrs Daventry found Robbie charming, and had willingly agreed to him and Alix becoming engaged. But whenever marriage was mentioned, Aunt Ethel would begin to raise objections, pointing out it was war-time, Robbie away so much, things so uncer-tain . . . Alix suspected the hand of Gerard in this. Her aunt was of that generation brought up to consult the man of the house, and the man of the house was undoubtedly Gerard, with his wing collar, gold half-hunter and spectacles, which he would take off and polish when he wanted to gain time. Torn between a real liking for Robbie and a habit of listening to her own son's opinions, she wavered, and came down on the side of caution. Alix was now twenty-four, but that was still young enough to justify waiting a year or two.

Gerard was in the drawing-room, standing before the empty grate and scowling morosely into it, his hands thrust into his pockets. He turned as Alix came in, unpinning her hat and shaking out her red hair.

'Hullo, Gerry,' she said cheerfully, tossing the hat on

to the piano stool. 'You're home early. I've just seen a Zeppelin. I went with Jennie to listen to her Aunt Emma bidding British womanhood go to the Front and do its bit.'

'Have you?' Gerard said sourly. 'You're lucky anyone thinks you're fit to go.'

Alix's cheerfulness evaporated. 'Oh, Gerry, not again? They've turned you down again?' When he only nodded, she ran over to him impulsively and hugged him in commiseration. 'I am sorry, Gerry! I know how you feel about it.'

'I wouldn't mind so much,' Gerard burst out forcefully, 'if it weren't for the fact that I'm twice as fit as half of the fellows they accept! It's my confounded eyesight.' He broke off in exasperation.

'Not everyone has to go and fight, Gerry. It's not your fault. Everyone knows how hard you've tried to join up,' she consoled him.

'Not everyone!' Gerard said in a clipped voice. 'As I was walking up from the station, some woman I'd never set eyes on stepped out from nowhere and gave me this.' He slowly withdrew his hand from his pocket, and held open his palm. On it lay a small white feather. His hand was trembling and damp with perspiration, such as Alix had never seen in him.

She drew in her breath sharply. She snatched up the feather and crushed it in her fingers. 'Stupid, stupid woman! She didn't know you from Adam. How on earth could she presume to know why you're not in uniform? You shouldn't have accepted it.'

'Couldn't refuse,' said Gerard wryly. 'It's like serving a writ. Someone steps out and hands it to you. You automatically take it, and it's too late.' He turned aside so that she couldn't see his face. 'What makes it worse today, is that blasted party of the Harrises this evening. Every fellow there my age will be in uniform. Both the Harris brothers. They're even coming in from the Empire and Dominions to fight, like that Canadian crony of Robbie's.'

'Which Canadian crony of Robbie's?' she asked sharply.

Gerard looked mildly surprised. 'Didn't he tell you? He's invited some Canadian pilot he met a while back. Sherwood, the chap's name is. He's got the drawing-room manner of a bull moose, and every time he sees a woman a look comes into his eye which will have the chaperons running round like sheepdogs, herding all their fair charges into a corner, penned in for safety.'

Alix bit her lip. It probably had no significance that Robbie hadn't told her. But sometimes she felt there were a lot of things he didn't tell her. He was obsessed with flying, she realised that. Occasionally it seemed that his mind was occupied with little else. It was like having a rival for his love. Perhaps that was why he seldom discussed his flying. He sensed a kind of jealousy in her.

Recently, of course, they had talked about something else. It wasn't something she could discuss with Gerard or Mrs Daventry. Robbie wanted her to go to bed with him. He was tired of waiting for them to be married, and she understood that. But somehow she did not feel ready to commit herself to that extent. Certainly not while that barrier always remained between them. Robbie didn't deny there was a problem in their relationship, but believed getting into bed would solve everything. Some deep-rooted instinct, however, told Alix that it would only make matters worse. It would underline the transitory nature of their meetings. He would take her in his arms, only to leave her once again. The Royal Flying Corps always came first. He led a whole life away from her, a life as satisfying to him as any encounter with a woman. He'd tried to explain to her, once, what it was like to fly. It had shaken her, because a passion had been in his voice and in his eyes, just like that when he spoke to her of love, or kissed and caressed her. When he spoke about his machine, it was as if he spoke of a woman. It even had a girl's name—*Sara*. He'd named it after a cousin, he told her, and as much as he'd like to change it to *Alix*, to do so would be unlucky. He was surprisingly superstitious about everything to do with flying.

So she shared him with *Sara*. *Sara* was wood, canvas and wire, with an engine for a heart. But that heart beat, and *Sara* was just as surely alive as Alix was. He was *Sara's* lover, before he was ever hers.

Yet it was difficult to keep refusing what he wanted. He was disappointed, and accused her of not loving him. She couldn't explain to him how she felt about a flying machine called *Sara*. All she could do was to keep saying 'No'. It always seemed to lead to another quarrel. 'If you loved me,' Robbie would say petulantly, 'you would . . .'

He said this with such conviction that lately she had begun to think, 'Yes, I would, if I loved him,' and that led to the unthinkable—*perhaps I don't love him* . . . She never allowed this treacherous idea to surface openly. It did seem treachery. Robbie depended on her, counted on her loyalty when he was away at the Front. Not even in the furthest recesses of her mind must the idea take root and grow that she might just possibly have agreed to marry the wrong man.

Tonight, she was sure, he would ask again . . . She did not know how much longer she could keep saying 'No'.

CHAPTER TWO

ROBBIE WAS waiting for her in the entrance hall, lurking at the foot of the stairs. 'My God, Alix,' he said, 'you look lovely.'

She did look lovely. The nile green gown echoed the colour of her eyes, and her hair, in the artificial light, glowed like the embers of a fire. Young girls wore little jewellery, and unmarried ones did not normally wear pearls. But Alix wore her mother's pearls and against her creamy skin they took on a subtle, translucent lustre.

But he was beautiful, too, in the way the young, healthy, male is. The artist in Alix was always aware of it. The ancient Greeks had understood male beauty, and celebrated it in their statues of athletes and warriors. She looked at Robbie now, in his Royal Flying Corps uniform, his handsome, boyish face and engaging smile, and wondered whether she would ever finish the portrait she had begun the last time he had been home on leave. She had tried to work on it in his absence, but somehow it hadn't been possible. He had had time to come to the house and sit for her only once on this leave, and she had made little progress. It was as if the portrait mirrored the state of their relationship. It had run into difficulties, and was not turning out as planned.

Other doubts, too, had begun to assail her during his present leave. For the first time she had begun to wonder if she had not been foolishly idealistic in thinking Robbie did not care about her money at all. This particular doubt had been prompted one afternoon. A

garrulous neighbour, Mrs Bingley, had come to tea, and
Alix had chanced to overhear her say, 'The Harrises
were always a spendthrift family. Those boys have been
brought up with expectations beyond their means. Lady
Harris owes money to tradesmen all over the place . . .'
Mrs Daventry had cut in sharply at that, and reminded
Mrs Bingley that Robert Harris was engaged to Alix.
Mrs Bingley had squeaked, 'Oh, so sorry, I was forgetting', in a coy little voice that clearly indicated she
hadn't forgotten at all but was taking the opportunity
to be catty.

Mrs Bingley was the mother of a daughter known to
one and all as 'poor Harriet'. Poor Harriet was sickly,
with a 'chest'. The doctor was constantly being
summoned to the Bingleys to examine Harriet's chest—
no mean achievement, Robbie had once said unkindly,
since there was so little of it! Poor Harriet was present
this evening, trailing behind Mrs Bingley as usual. She
was pale-faced and lank-haired and dressed in an
unbecoming shade of mauve. The fashion was for
evening dresses with loose, bloused bodices, and
somehow this seemed to emphasise Harriet's flat chest.
She looked sullen and resentful, not at all in the party
mood, but who, dominated by a mother like Mrs
Bingley, large, red-faced and tactless, would look
cheerful?

'Poor Harriet is here,' said Robbie wickedly, 'with
the monstrous Mama.'

Alix's eyes were searching the room. 'I'm looking for
Jennie Frobisher. If she's hiding in the cloakroom again,
I'll have to go and drag her out. Robbie, can't you do
something to help? She is far too shy.'

'Well, I can't go barging into the ladies' cloakroom,
if that's what you mean,' he retorted. 'Anyway, I have
tried, I introduced her to Jake.'

Alix frowned. 'Who's Jake?'

'Jake Sherwood. He's around somewhere. He's a

Canadian pilot, a friend, who happened to be in London, and I asked him to come tonight. But your friend Jennie took one look at him and bolted. I think she was afraid he was going to ravish her.' He glanced round to see who stood near them, but they were well out of general earshot. 'Look, Alix,' he whispered urgently, 'I'm not going to stand here talking about other people. You know I leave the day after tomorrow. Lord knows when I'll get any more home leave. Not for months, probably . . .'

It was coming. Alix knew it, and knew she couldn't head him off. He was talking quickly and earnestly. He'd planned it all out. Later on that evening, after the supper interval, when everyone was slightly merry and not up to noticing who went missing, he'd slip out and up to his room. Alix should wait five minutes, and then go out through the conservatory and through the garden to re-enter the house through the french windows of the dining-room. From there, Robbie insisted, she could easily get upstairs without anyone noticing her, by the spiral back stair used by the servants. 'It isn't as if we weren't engaged,' he was saying, 'and going to be married anyway. You know how I feel about you, Alix, and if you loved me . . .'

The old argument was rehearsed again, but Alix was tired of it. She didn't want to say 'Yes', but she was tired of saying 'No'. And he was going back to the Front in forty-eight hours. Anything could happen, and they both knew it. Perhaps she was being unfair, and prudish and old-fashioned. A little wearily, she heard herself say, 'Oh, all right.'

She said it at the time to put an end to the argument, without really meaning to. But once she had said it, there was no taking it back again. Robbie's face lit up. 'It will be all right; no one will know.'

He was probably right, but as the supper interval drew to a close, Alix's heart began to feel like lead. She knew now, as she'd never known before, what was wrong in their love affair. She just didn't want Robbie in the same way as he wanted her. The physical longing just wasn't there. 'Perhaps I'm frigid,' she thought wretchedly. 'It's me, and when we get up there at last, in Robbie's bedroom, it will all be a miserable failure, and Robbie will blame me.'

Robbie, beside her, squeezed her hand and whispered in her ear. 'I'm going now. Wait five minutes and go out the way I told you. I've checked that the dining-room windows are unlocked, and there's no one in there.'

He was gone. How was she to spend the next five minutes? Standing here, looking like the lamb for the slaughter? Alix glanced around and saw Gerard, not far away. If Gerry knew, he'd be furious. He'd punch Robbie on the jaw and drag Alix home. But Gerard was fully occupied. Blanche Frobisher, a Dresden figurine in shell-pink, was gazing into his face with demure coquettishness. Gerard was polishing his spectacles, and even at this distance she could see he was perspiring.

Alix met the curious stare of Mrs Bingley. Poor Harriet was nowhere to be seen, having presumably managed to slip the leash for the time being. Mrs Bingley, with a sure instinct for scandal, was bearing down on Alix, a false smile painted on her plump red face.

'All alone?' she asked coyly. 'Where's your young man, then?'

Alix wanted to say loudly, 'He's gone upstairs to the bedroom to wait for me!' But she managed to smile weakly and mutter something about looking after other guests.

'So nice to see so many people,' chattered Mrs Bingley, 'So few parties these days. Such a shame for you young people. My poor Harriet . . .' She set off on a long

and involved account of poor Harriet's latest tribula-
tions.

It must have been a lot longer than five minutes
before Alix was able to detach herself decently from
Mrs Bingley. By the time she did, she had begun to
panic, thinking that Robbie would believe she had let
him down—lost her courage at the last moment, and
wasn't coming. She hurried across the room and
managed to get into the conservatory unobserved. 'Out
of the conservatory, and across the garden . . .' Alix's
mind was so taken up with her instructions that she
failed to look where she was going, and cannoned into
a group of potted palms, flushing out a couple who had
been hidden behind them. They stared at her guiltily,
and to her immense surprise, she saw that it was poor
Harriet, and Philip, Robbie's brother. Poor Harriet
looked very flushed, and quite pretty—and the front of
her gown was very much awry. Not only the doctor, it
seemed, had an interest in Harriet's chest.

Philip, scarlet and perspiring, exclaimed, 'Oh, hell,
Alix, you gave us the fright of our lives. We thought it
was the old dragon!'

'I'm sorry,' Alix stammered. 'It's only me. Do carry
on,' she added disastrously in her confusion.

'Have you seen Mother?' hissed Harriet anxiously.

'Yes, but she's talking to someone. She's not coming
out here, Harriet, I'm sure.'

As one person, Philip and Harriet responded, 'Thank
God!'

She left them, behind the palm trees, and bolted out
of the side door and into the blessed cool of the garden.
It was very dark, especially coming from the brightly-
lit house, and she tripped over some empty flower-pots
near the door, causing an unearthly clatter. That, in
turn, startled a prowling cat, which leapt out and
plunged away through the undergrowth, making Alix
give a little cry of alarm. Fortunately there was so much

noise coming from the house that she thought it unlikely
anyone would hear her. If Philip and Harriet had not
been so concerned with one another, they might have
wondered where she was going, all alone, in the middle
of a party. She hoped Mrs Bingley didn't find them.
She felt her way along the wall to the dining-room
windows. Robbie must be wondering where she was by
now, as she was so late for their rendezvous. She
reached the tall windows and stretched out her hand to
the catch.

But at that moment, to her surprise and alarm, a
hand inside the windows seized the handles and pulled
the glass doors inwards and open, and a man in RFC
uniform appeared, dimly lit in the embrasure, staring
curiously out into the moonlit garden.

'Oh, Robbie!' Alix gasped. 'You startled me. I'm
sorry. I was always going to come upstairs, honestly—
but I kept bumping into people.'

At that moment, the horrible, blinding realisation
struck her that this was not Robbie, but a total stranger.
Panic enveloped her, depriving her of reason and
composure, and without hesitation or reflection, she
turned and fled. She could not go back to the conservatory and blunder past Philip and Harriet again, so
there was only one direction she could take—further
into the recesses of the garden.

She plunged into a tangle of shrubs and flower-beds,
stumbling over unseen objects in the darkness and
catching her hair and dress on the outstretched limbs of
trees. She didn't know the garden well, even by daylight,
and by moonlight it was a jungle, a nightmarish fantasy
world of shadows, and an endless maze in which she
could run for ever until exhausted. She stumbled to a
halt, and as she peered wildly about, trying to make out
a pathway in the darkness, a hand came out of the
gloom and grasped her elbow firmly. She gave a sharp
cry of fear.

'Don't be so darned stupid!' said a curt voice by her ear. 'Come indoors. You'll get cold, and cut yourself on something.'

Alix gasped and whirled towards the speaker, but could make out only a dark, forbidding male form towering over her. 'Go away!' she whispered.

'I'm not going to hurt you,' his voice said impatiently. 'Here, let me guide you—you'll fall flat on your face,' he concluded ungallantly.

Ashamed and humiliated, she allowed herself to be half guided, half frog-marched back into the house in his rather ungentle grip.

He pushed aside the velour curtains and they both stumbled into the dining-room, lit by a single dim standard lamp in one corner. Her rescuer—or pursuer?— released her and turned to close the french doors and draw the curtains. Then he turned back, and she saw him properly.

Her first thought was, how could I ever have mistaken him for Robbie? This was a much taller man, a solidly built fellow, with a great deal of thick, light brown hair of the sort no amount of brushing and combing can ever tame, twisting this way and that in an obstinate disorder. Something in that lean face suggested that the man to whom it belonged did not take kindly to authority, either. It had the sort of independent, self-reliant informality that said to any man, 'I'm as good as you are, and if you think differently, you'll have to prove it.'

'Your shoes are muddy,' he said unsympathetically, as his grey eyes flickered rapidly over her, assessing her, too. 'Here, clean them up.' It was very much an order. He took his handkerchief from his pocket and handed it to her.

A burning tide of red suffused Alix's throat and face. She snatched the handkerchief and sat down to kick off her soiled evening shoes. How on earth could she explain to this man what she had been doing? Who was he, anyway? Then it came to her, of course, that he was the Canadian, the one Gerard had mentioned and Robbie had invited—a pilot.

'You could do with a glass of brandy,' her unpredictable acquaintance remarked, going to the sideboard.

'No, thank you,' Alix said hastily, pulling on her cleaned shoes. Her one desire was to get away from here, and him, as quickly as possible. She held the muddy handkerchief helplessly for a moment, and then threw it into the fireplace. He wasn't likely to want it back. 'I expect,' she said carefully, 'you are wondering where I was going.'

He glanced over his shoulder towards her, and amusement gleamed in the grey eyes. 'No, I'm not wondering. You told me where you were going.' Taking no account of her previous refusal, he put a small glass of brandy on the table in front of her. 'Drink it!' he ordered in his brusque way.

Alix drank a little, coughing, and pushed the rest away, to stare up at him defiantly. 'Well, what are you going to do about it?' she challenged.

The man shrugged. 'What do you want me to do? Come upstairs with you? My pleasure . . .'

Embarrassment turned in an instant to anger in Alix. In a coldly cutting voice, she said, 'I'm sorry. There's been a mistake. I find your remark extremely offensive.'

'Oh, I know,' he said easily. 'You weren't looking for me, more's the pity. But you were making a heck of a noise, and I thought some intruder had climbed over the wall. You can't blame me for coming to investigate. Why did you run?' She didn't reply, and he went on, 'There was no need. I'm very discreet and I don't tell tales, not on pretty girls . . . and I wasn't trying to insult you.' He rubbed a hand over his already untidy hair. 'I don't fit well into your social scene. I was brought up on what we call the wrong side of the tracks.'

'I can well believe it,' Alix snapped.

The laughter faded from the grey eyes, which were suddenly uncomfortably hard and direct. 'Now don't get me wrong, pretty lady. I'm not apologising for it! My folks were good people, and I don't apologise for them, or anything else.' He moved towards her, and she recoiled. 'Don't wrinkle that lovely nose at me,' he added gently, but it was a warning.

Alix said, in a choked voice, 'I know nothing about you. Why should I despise you? But I'm not going to be insulted just because you fancy yourself free to do as you wish. You owe me no explanation, either. I don't want to know anything about you.'

She stood up and went to the mirror over the fireplace to tidy her hair. She could see him reflected in it, standing and watching her from the other side of the room. He held a glass in his hand, and leaned against the sideboard, one elbow propped negligently on the top. 'Like a bar,' she thought in disgust.

A click from the doorway into the hall caused them both to turn towards it. It was pushed roughly open, and Robbie came in. She had almost forgotten him, but as she had earlier thought he would do, he had come searching for her.

He looked from one to the other of them, and said in exasperation, 'What are you doing in here, Jake?'

'Only stealing the brandy,' Jake said with a dry look at Alix, 'Not your girl.'

'Yes, I see you've met,' Robbie said in a defeated voice. His evening plans were ruined, and he knew it. They both knew it, and Alix could only feel relief, although she wished it had come about in some other way. 'This is Jake Sherwood, Alix,' Robbie went on, making a belated formal introduction. 'Alix Morrell, Jake; my fiancée. I told you about her.'

'Yes, you did,' Jake said, 'But not nearly enough. See here, my children, I'm not one to spoil anyone's innocent fun. I hear, see and speak no evil.'

'Oh, what's the use?' Alix cried out angrily to Robbie. 'It was a stupid idea and I was stupid to agree to it! You don't think, either of you, that I'm going through with it, *now*? I don't care whether *he*,' she pointed at Jake, 'is to be relied upon or not. I doubt it. I can't think why you invited him, for he's without manners or social graces of any kind. And as for introducing him to Jennie, you must have been mad!'

She pushed her way past them both and ran out, back to the noise and confusion of the party. In the hall, she bumped into Gerard, an anxious expression on his face.

'Oh, there you are,' he said. 'I was just coming to look for you. Where have you been?'

'Robbie wanted to introduce me to his Canadian friend,' she said awkwardly. 'I—I left them both in the dining-room, having a drink.'

Gerard looked relieved, the worried frown that had creased his brow smoothing and his whole manner brightening. 'Oh, that's all right, then,' he said. He paused. 'Although I don't see why Robbie had to take you away to introduce you to him.'

'Don't fuss so, Gerry,' Alix said wearily.

'Well, what did you think of Sherwood?' he demanded. 'I found him a rum sort of fellow. Touchy.'

'That's putting it mildly,' Alix commented bitterly. 'I thought he was . . .' She broke off. 'I thought he was extraordinary,' she concluded.

If she had known more about him, it might well have given her food for thought.

His father had been a carpenter, a hard-working, honest and self-educated man, with a dream. That dream had been centred on his son, a handsome, strong boy with an obstinate streak and a passion for all things mechanical. The boy spent his free time down at the goods-yards, watching the locomotives, asking a hundred pertinent questions of the engineers, begging rides in the cabs. He came home, and he took everything apart, from clocks and watches to his mother's washday mangle. Watching the youngster, the old man made a promise. Jake should have education. Jake should go through college and realise his ambitions. Jake should be somebody, some day—the man who gave the orders, and not the man who took them, as his father had been all his life.

The old man had died, worn out by hard work and the struggle to maintain a family, when Jake had been but fifteen. But his dream had not died. Jake's mother had seen to that. 'You're to go through college, son. It's what your father wanted, We'll manage somehow.'

And somehow the money had been got together, money to feed them both and money to finance his studies. His mother sewed and took in washing. He did all manner of work. He mended things for people, and they paid him willingly, saying, 'That boy can fix anything', and he went back to the goods-yards and signed on as casual labour.

They were hard men who worked down there, just before the old century turned. Immigrants mainly, a closed community of sweat and violent passions, grim determination and a peasant capacity for suffering. You worked there, with them, if they let you work there. The supervisor hired you, but those burly, swarthy men with the unintelligible accents, the checkered shirts and dungarees let you stay. They did not like interlopers, and these did not last long. They gained mysterious broken arms and legs when crates toppled over on them for no reason. But Jake was accepted. Jake was the kid they had seen grow up, who had hung around the locomotives and now worked his way through college.

A good boy, and with a widowed mother. Family, looking after aged relatives, the veneration due to Mama—that was something they all understood. From their modest pay-packets, nearly all sent money back to the old country, to some muddy village in the Bukovina or the Ukraine, where the old people lived, and would have starved had it not been for the remittances from the New World and the children they would never see again, but who never forgot.

Jake learned to fight down there in the yards. No sport of gentlemen, but the rough and dirty knuckle fights that took place behind the sheds and left men who moved too slowly disfigured permanently from the hobnailed boots which struck their faces as they scrabbled in the dust. They all liked Jake, but the boy had to learn to look after himself; and he did.

So he led a double life. The engineering studies were going well, and he took every opportunity to attend other lectures and slake an incurable thirst for knowledge and persistent curiosity. He went to art lectures, and knew the world's great paintings from picture slides and books. He went to concerts and listened to the music of the great composers. He sifted through the tattered books on junk-stalls and bought himself a library of the world's great literature for a few pence, and he read it all, from Dickens to Dostoevsky, from Balzac to Mark Twain.

Then his mother fell sick. She lay on the iron bedstead in the bare ward of the city infirmary and the doctors said nothing could be done. But money can buy back health. If you could pay for the medicine, you had a chance. Jake knew where to get the money.

In the back streets of the city, with lookouts posted for the approach of the law, took place the prize-fights: fierce, cruel bouts on which huge sums were wagered by men in clean suits and polished shoes, with soft hands. Jake knew how to fight. He'd learned in the yards. A good bare-knuckle fighter could make a tidy sum. Inevitably, he was found out. No one could explain away that number of black eyes and split lips.

'This college, Mr Sherwood,' the Dean said, his voice quivering with emotion, 'is not accustomed to have its students participate in vulgar fist-fights and bar-room brawls. Your attendance at future classes will not be required.'

His mother died. Jake packed his books and went across the border, into the United States. He went to Detroit, because there they needed men like him, to help to create the new industry springing up based on the automobile.

The day was fast approaching when every family would want to own its motor-car. Jake had engineering training, he understood design, he understood the men who worked on the factory floor. It seemed nothing could stop his rise to the top. He was making money and had nothing to spend it on but himself—and since he spent all his time in his office designing new and better motor-cars, it didn't get spent, but lay in the bank. Why not, someone suggested, invest in the new industry? Why just work for it? So he invested, and he made more money. He was thirty years old, and people whispered, 'In another five years, he'll be a millionaire.'

It seemed that he would embody not only his father's dream, but the American dream—the successful, self-made man, who had risen by his own efforts from the bottom to the top . . .

But in Europe, far away, a war was breaking out. It was going to be a different kind of war from any which had been fought before. Over there, they had a need for men who understood the new machines which were about to be turned out on to the battlefields. Above all, they needed men to fly.

He was young, successful and had no ties, and wasn't yet ready to say he had achieved it all. A desire for a new challenge smouldered in him. He looked up into the sky and saw that man had conquered it. He saw machines which flew . . .

CHAPTER THREE

WHEN ALIX awoke the next morning, she lay in bed and rehearsed all that had happened the evening before, and wondered how on earth she could have been so foolish as to get herself into such a preposterous situation in the first place. With or without Jake Sherwood, the evening would have been a fiasco. She would either have ended up in bed with Robbie, acting out a part she doubted very much she could have played at all convincingly. Alternatively, she would have been forced to tell Robbie the plain truth, that she didn't want his lovemaking.

'I couldn't tell him that . . .' she thought, and a cold little voice in her brain whispered in reply, 'This is the man you're planning to marry. What will you do when you're his wife?'

Robbie came later that morning to apologise. He hadn't known Jake would be in the dining-room and it wasn't his fault, he added in an aggrieved voice. It was his last day of leave, and he had obtained two tickets for *Chu Chin Chow* in town. They could go and see it, and have a meal.

Alix saw, as soon as he arrived at the house to collect her that evening, that he was decidedly out of sorts. Something else had happened, in addition to their catastrophically bungled tryst, something he hadn't mentioned before. In marked contrast to his usual cheerful, debonair manner, he slouched in one of the drawing-room armchairs, his cheeks flushed, his head thrown back and creasing up one of Mrs Daventry's

carefully embroidered antimacassars, his fair hair
flopping untidily over his forehead. There was a sullen,
tight set to his mouth and a tenseness to his whole
body. He was like an angry young animal, one which,
in the physical prime of life, has rashly challenged the
older, sedate leader of the pack and found, to his
surprise and hurt, that the chieftain has teeth yet, and
knows how to use them.

Yet, even sulking as he so evidently was now, he was
still an attractive figure in the RFC uniform, long, lean
and healthy, with that something which made the pulse
quicken at the sight of him. It would be difficult for any
woman not to fall in love with him, and Alix supposed
that she was no different from any other woman in that
respect. When she was away from him, the doubts
crowded in, but in his presence they seemed niggling,
unworthy criticisms.

All the same—here a critical frown crinkled Alix's
smooth brow—all the same, he hardly had the right to
sit there nursing his own grievances as if everything last
night had been her fault. A prickle of irritation swept
over her at his selfishness, his preoccupation with his
own viewpoint. It did not pass unnoticed by Robbie.

'You needn't glower at me,' he said suddenly in an
aggressive and ill-used tone. 'I told you that I didn't
know Sherwood, of all people, was going to be skulking
in the dining-room, getting plastered quietly all on his
own.' He hunched his shoulders defiantly. 'At least, it
was *only* Jake. It could have been worse. Jake won't
blab.'

'I'm not glowering at you,' Alix returned sharply.
'But if you're in a rotten mood, I'm certainly not going
to the theatre with you.'

Her tone told him that she meant what she said. He
sat upright and his manner changed. 'Look here, Alix,'
he said urgently, 'you don't think I'm after your blasted
money, do you?'

Startled, she exclaimed, 'No!' automatically and with sufficient conviction to make him relax slightly. Puzzled, she added, 'Why bring that up?'

'Because that pompous cousin of yours has been moralising away at me. He boned me late last night about taking you out of the party to meet Jake in the dining-room. Your absence, he informed me, could have been misinterpreted. I should be mindful of your reputation. Those are his words, not mine! Well, I couldn't tell him the truth, could I? I just had to stand there like a fool and listen to him. I couldn't deny it. If he'd known the whole story, he'd probably have taken off his jacket and invited me to "come outside"!'

Alix's mouth twitched. Robbie was so genuinely angry, and yet, in retrospect, the whole episode was beginning to show unexpectedly humorous aspects. So *that* was what had upset poor Robbie so. He had emerged, mauled, at Gerard's hands, the victim of a verbal tongue-lashing far worse than a punch on the jaw. She could imagine the scene: Gerry laying down the law, determined to preserve Alix's honour and reputation, and Robbie, unable to defend himself and obliged to listen as Gerry reduced him to the status of a callow, unthinking youth.

'It's not funny!' Robbie exploded now, furiously, seeing the laughter in her green eyes. 'It was damn embarrassing. Old Gerard thinks I'm an unprincipled fortune-hunter. How would you like it?'

Not a word of apology for the humiliation she had suffered. The mirth died in Alix's eyes. 'As a matter of fact,' she told him bluntly, 'at the time, last night, I didn't like any of it, at all! *You* were embarrassed? For pity's sake, what do you think I was? I thought Sherwood was *you*. I blurted out everything. Robbie, it was awful. And he's an awful man; he didn't even pretend he hadn't heard! He's no manners, and goodness only knows what sort of a background he has. He was helping himself to the brandy, and it wouldn't surprise me if he'd gone on to help himself to the silver!'

To her amazement, Robbie's ill humour vanished like a pricked bubble, dispersed in a flash, as he burst into gales of laughter. As Alix watched, mystified and annoyed, he wiped his eyes of tears of mirth, and spluttered, 'I must tell him that! Good Lord, Alix, the man's stinking rich. He's got so much money, I don't suppose he knows what to do with it. The idea of his putting the silver spoons in his pocket . . .'

'Well, I'm glad you think it *is* funny. Tell him, if you like, by all means!' Alix's red-haired temper burst out fiercely. She bit her lip, and eyed him thoughtfully. She had been about to ask what it was in Jake Sherwood Robbie had possibly found to like or admire. With a cold feeling seeping into her heart, she already knew the answer. Money. Robbie liked Jake, really liked him. But a part of the fascination Jake held for him was Jake's wealth—acquired by goodness knows what means. In the same way, Robbie loved *her*, but Gerry had been right all along: Robbie was a fortune-hunter, in the nicest possible way. Not an unscrupulous one, as he believed Gerard thought him. How insulted Robbie had felt by Gerry's accusation, because he himself saw nothing contradictory in his attitude. He did love her. But he was a man for whom money was an attraction in the same category as beauty, charm or wit. There was a kind of innocence about it all which it was difficult not to find totally disarming.

'Look,' he said now, leaning forward, his forearms resting on his knees and speaking in that attractive, boyish way guaranteed to melt the hardest heart. 'You're right in that he was helping himself to the brandy. He was probably pretty drunk, and won't remember a thing today.'

'He'll remember every word and gesture,' Alix said bitterly. 'That sort of person does.'

Robbie got up and came across to put his arms round her. 'Come on,' he coaxed. 'What does it matter?' He pulled her towards him and kissed her warmly, his arms tightening their grip on her, and filling her with an unreasoning panic. 'Don't be mad at me, Alix,' he whispered throatily. 'You know how I feel about you. Last night I really wanted . . . Well, Jake, curse him, showed up and spoiled everything, but don't let's quarrel about it.'

He wanted a response from her, a physical response, something he could sense in her body. Not this stupid panic, but an awakening desire equal to his own. Try as she might, she could not give it. Nor could she pretend. She closed her eyes. He always made her feel this way, as if she had failed him.

Almost wistfully, he said, 'You'll enjoy *Chu Chin Chow*. It's got the most fantastic costumes. You're an artist, you'll appreciate that. This is my last evening, remember. Let's not let anything else go wrong.'

Alix smiled up at him then, and impulsively put her arms round his neck, wanting to comfort him for the disappointment she knew he felt at her coldness. 'Nothing will go wrong,' she promised.

Despite everything, she did enjoy the show. Afterwards, Robbie took her to supper in a little restaurant near the theatre. Unmarried girls were not supposed to be seen dining out with young men, unchaperoned. That was considered 'fast'. However, in the extraordinary circumstances, and with due consideration of Alix's engagement ring, Mrs Daventry had been reluctantly persuaded to allow this one departure from the strict rule, providing they sat in the middle of the restaurant in full light, and didn't skulk in any ill-lit corners.

The restaurant was filled with uniforms, the air full of chatter and brittle laughter. There was a sense of determined gaiety, a resolve to forget the war and to live for this one moment. Yet despite this, and although they had agreed not to do so, they couldn't help but fall to talking of his departure the following morning.

'I'll get to the station somehow!' Alix promised fervently.

'You can't, darling,' Robbie said patiently. 'The train leaves at six-thirty sharp. There's no way you can get there so early, and anyway, it will be chilly and crowded. I don't mind.'

But he did mind, and she knew it. There was a note of resignation in the calm of his voice. She was going to fail him again. It was as if she must always fail him. She stared miserably at the shining crystal, the crisp, starched damask table-cloth and slightly wilting flowers of the centre-piece. If she didn't somehow manage to be at the station tomorrow morning, it would hurt him deeply. There was a blight on their whole romance that had been entered into with such optimism. Perhaps it was caused by the war, or the flying, or having waited too long. Perhaps, in her mind, the money was, after all, slowly but surely growing into an unsurmountable barrier between them.

Yet neither of them wanted to make the break. Robbie—whatever his true reasons, and possibly even he was not aware of these—was determined to marry her. As for her, how could she destroy the hopes of a man about to leave for the Front? A man going off to battle? The war, and his departure, prolonged their agony, and left them tied to each other in a hopeless tangle of confused emotions.

They had fallen silent, either side of the table, when Robbie exclaimed, 'Good Lord, there's Jake!'

It was the very last person she would have wanted to see. But there he was, an unmistakable figure, coming towards them in answer to Robbie's signal. As he approached, it struck her that Jake was older than most of the others. They were all so very young, the men in uniform, especially the flying men, some little more than boys. Even Robbie, at twenty-six, often joked that he felt like an old man among them. But Jake looked older than Robbie, at least thirty. It seemed late for a man to go and volunteer. Most had careers and commitments by then.

He wasn't alone. There was a girl with him, hanging on his arm. She was of the type Alix would have expected him to take an interest in, a brassy blond in a tight red dress, with painted lips and eyes faintly clouded by alcohol. She stood before the table, clutching Jake for support, and giggling tipsily.

'This is Tilly,' Jake said gravely.

Robbie, doing his utmost not to laugh, said, 'Please, won't you sit down, Miss—ah—Tilly?'

'Ta, don't mind if I do,' said Tilly, and collapsed onto a chair. 'Oops!' she said, as a wine-glass rocked.

The conversation was awkward, punctuated by Tilly's hiccups. 'This is a nice place, isn't it?' she said cosily to Alix, breathing gin into the atmosphere. 'I like my gentlemen friends to take me to *nice* places, with the toffs. I mean, they *ought* to pay for it, didn't they? My ma told me that—never give it away free, gal, that's what she said.' She fumbled with a packet of Abdulla cigarettes and managed to spill them over the table.

Jake avoided looking at Alix, but he couldn't fail to be aware of her scornful green eyes fixed on him. Robbie was talking rapidly, trying to turn the conversation. He mentioned leaving in the morning. Jake, it seemed, had another week's leave. Somehow the conversation progressed to the early hour Robbie's train left, and the fact that Alix would not be able to be there.

'Oh, that's okay,' Jake said suddenly. 'I can go and pick up Miss Morrell, and bring her to the station.' A smile touched his mouth. 'It's the least I can do!'

'Of course, you've got the Sizaire!' Robbie exclaimed, his voice and face brightening. 'Jake has a motor-car,

Alix, a Sizaire-Berwick. You should see it, it's a beautiful machine.'

Alix didn't want to see it, much less to ride in it. But it was the only way she could hope to be there. She listened as they fixed a time when he could come and fetch her. Robbie wrote down the address and drew a map on the back of the menu, which Jake folded and tucked into his pocket. Then he nodded casually to Alix, and sauntered off, Tilly tottering alongside him, her peroxided curls propped on his shoulder.

'That girl is drunk!' Alix said reproachfully. 'He ought not to have let her get like that—and he ought not to have brought her here!'

'Oh, he always has girls hanging round him,' Robbie said dismissively. 'I don't know if it's his unspoilt charm, or the car. Either way, they swarm like bees round the honey-pot. It's the same in France.'

'So I see!' Alix said stiffly, not to be mollified.

Robbie grinned at her. 'Well, they might not be *ladies*—but I don't suppose that worries him!'

It was a pleasant evening, and they decided to walk from the restaurant to the station. As they strolled along, arm in arm, Alix saw how people passing by looked at them. She noticed especially how some of the women looked at Robbie. There was one woman, in particular, who was getting out of a taxi, enveloped in a vast, expensive white fur. She was between thirty-five and forty, her face in the garish gaslight painted and distorted, yet not unattractive. She glanced quickly at them both and somehow dropped her spangled evening bag on to the pavement. Robbie stopped to retrieve it and hand it back to her with a smile.

'Thank you,' she said. Her voice was hard, like her eyes and smile, but appreciative. Her heavy-lidded, mascaraed eyes swept over Alix briefly, assessing her, before turning back to Robbie. She gave him a little smile, and then her escort intervened, fussily bearing her away.

'She dropped that purse deliberately,' Alix said brusquely.

'Good-looking woman,' Robbie said, 'for her age. Did you see those diamonds?' He glanced at her. 'Are you jealous?' He sounded hopeful.

'Of that harpy?' Alix shrugged, knowing she sounded annoyed, which was stupid. But the way the woman had looked at Robbie had angered her, because of the naked invitation in those hard, speculating, mascara-rimmed eyes. 'Brazen', Mrs Daventry would have called it. She would have called Tilly brazen, too, but Alix had rather liked Tilly, whose promiscuity was of the honest kind.

'I have this power over women!' Robbie whispered melodramatically into her ear. 'They hurl themselves, or their evening purses at least, at my feet!' He chuckled.

But Alix was staring at a hoarding on which a poster proclaimed that such and such a custard powder was already sweetened and would not make inroads on your sugar ration. She was frowning in concentration.

'You know, Robbie,' she said suddenly, 'I'm sure I've seen that woman's picture somewhere.'

The following morning was dry, but overcast and cool, an early chill in the air. Jake was punctual to the minute, and came indoors to be introduced to Mrs Daventry. Gerard had set off even earlier to Oxford, to see a client, and Alix was rather glad he wasn't there.

Mrs Daventry was obviously very impressed, partly because of the Sizaire-Berwick parked splendidly before the house in cream and black splendour, not unlike a Rolls-Royce at first glance—and partly because aviators were still a rare enough breed of men to be very impressive. Nor was there any denying, Alix admitted grudgingly, that Jake was a very handsome man, and no doubt even Mrs Daventry's matronly heart fluttered.

Alix needed to put a cloak over her new carnation silk ensemble to travel in the Sizaire, which was an open-top tourer. Jake set up the canvas hood, but even so it was draughty and she had to tie her hat on with a scarf. But Jake was prepared, and produced a rug, saying briefly, 'Put that over your knees,' so she was well protected against the rigours of motoring.

'It's very kind of you to help us like this,' she shouted above the engine noise, determined to be polite.

He shrugged. 'I thought you were going to refuse, back there in the restaurant.'

'Why?' she demanded defensively.

The car rattled and bounced over a rough piece of road, frightening the milk-roundsman's horse. 'Well, I'd like to think I was wrong—but I get the impression you don't like me very much.'

This frank statement was embarrassingly true, and Alix could find no way to answer it safely. She pretended the noise was too much for conversation, and as he seemed to be concentrating on driving, they both fell silent until they reached the station.

The wind blew coldly along the platform, crowded with many people. It was an infantry troop train. 'I've hitched a ride with the Army,' Robbie told her with a grin. He guided her round the piles of kit, and the groups where young women much like herself hung on the necks of husbands and lovers 'off to the Front'.

No one knew exactly where. No one was even supposed to know to which port the troop train was taking their menfolk to embark for France. The platform swarmed with khaki uniforms, polished Sam Browne belts and optimistic young faces. Among them were some faces more wary, belonging to men returning from leave, men who had been at the Front before, and knew. Besides, there was less enthusiasm now than at the beginning of the war. A glorious enterprise of

flamboyant patriotism had become a mud-caked stale-
mate of waste and frustration. Conscription had just
been introduced. Men were being killed at a faster rate
than volunteers could replace them. It was noticeable
that quite a few of the 'other ranks' had fortified
themselves with beer, and Alix suspected that some of
the officers had had a drink or two.

But a large number of these youngsters were the new
conscripted replacements, and perhaps for that reason,
someone had tried to re-create the fervent enthusiasm
that had marked the departures at the beginning of the
war. A band had been found somewhere and blew
noisily at the far end of the platform with patriotic
fervour, surrounded by red, white and blue bunting,
which reminded Alix of Miss Frobisher's suffragette
meeting. There were some well-dressed middle-aged
women here, probably members of some Home
Comforts for the Troops group. They were handing out
flowers to some of the young men. They probably
encouraged their daughters to hand white feathers to
total strangers, like Gerard.

The new ensemble she had chosen to wear was unsuitable in every way, but she had wanted to look her best
for Robbie, so that at least the picture of her he would
carry away to war-blasted Northern France would be
of colour and of life. All the same, she knew she looked
a little incongruous, standing there amid the stacks of
kitbags in a carnation pink silk tunic over an ankle-
length hobble skirt in the fashionable peg-top look. A
wide-brimmed straw hat trimmed with flowers crowned
her red hair, which she had parted in the centre and
smoothed to either side in wings, rolled into a long,
curving sausage from ear to ear at the nape of her neck.
The car journey had loosened long, curling tendrils
which hugged her bare neck. But, after all, the clothes
didn't matter. It was the faces everyone wanted to
remember, desperately trying to fix every little hair and

wrinkle in the mind's eyes for ever.

'You're the loveliest girl I ever saw,' Robbie said, as he stooped and kissed her, whispering into her ear, 'I wanted you to be here.'

'Come back to me, Robbie,' she managed to mutter in a choked voice, grasping at the rough sleeve of his jacket. Suddenly nothing mattered except that he should come back—not the squabbles or misunderstandings, neither the chasm in understanding between them, nor whether he counted on her money. People mattered, and life, and living.

Moments later, and it was time to part. As the train pulled out, Robbie leaned out of the window, cupping his hands round his mouth, and shouted, 'Cheer up, darling, it won't be long!'

The gathering noise of the train wheels had drowned out all words after that, and the band, now playing 'Auld Lang Syne'. Alix stood waving until it was out of sight, imagining she could still distinguish Robbie's hand among the forest of khaki arms signalling frantically from the window of every compartment. At last the train rocked round a bend and was lost from sight, and Alix was alone with others on a platform suddenly quiet, with smudges of soot on her carnation silk costume.

She had almost forgotten about Jake, and was quite startled to turn and see his tall figure in its RFC uniform standing just behind her. His hat was pushed to the back of his head somehow in a most un-regulation manner, and over his arm he had her cloak, which she had given him when they had arrived.

'You ready to go now, Alix?' was all he said, his grey eyes watching her carefully, probably for signs that she might break down.

She nodded, grateful that he had not said anything stupid, such as 'Don't worry!' and grateful, too, that she was not alone, that someone was there, even this steely-eyed, brusque-mannered airman she didn't much like. She even forgave his calling her 'Alix' in that familiar way. He was Robbie's friend, and he had been kind to them that morning. It wiped the slate clean, at least, of what he had done in the past to annoy her. After today, she wouldn't see him again, and it would no longer matter.

As they drew up at the house, she turned and asked him if he would care to come in and have a late breakfast.

He stared at her for a moment, then shook his head. 'No, thanks.'

'I'm sure my aunt would be very pleased,' Alix insisted. Because she didn't want him to accept, she felt obliged to insist. He probably knew it.

He was still staring at her in a thoughtful way. He was thinking that this beautiful girl with the hair like a sunset and the unhappy green eyes was unlike anyone he had ever seen. And she belonged to someone else. He liked women, but he'd always been too busy to set up any kind of permanent relationship. But, then, he'd never met a girl like this one. If he had, perhaps things would have been different. But she had a way of looking at him, with those marvellous green eyes, as if he'd crawled out from under a stone. He wasn't going to get to first base, that was pretty clear. Anyway, she was Robbie's . . . At that thought, a faint frown crossed his forehead. He wished there was some damn thing, anything, he could say to comfort her, but if any of them survived that living hell over there to the end, it would be a miracle. He wasn't in the way of making false promises or offering unfounded hopes, and certainly not to this girl, who was intelligent enough to know that he lied.

'I don't eat breakfast,' he said. 'And I have to get back.' He turned his grey eyes away from her, and fiddled with the driving wheel. 'I'm sorry about being in the wrong spot all the time—at the party, and again last night, with Tilly. I took her home after we left you—to the place where she lives, I mean—and left her there. I didn't take advantage of her being inebriated. I'd like you to know that.'

Alix flushed. 'I . . . Well, you did quite right.'

'What I really want to say,' he went on, 'is that I'm sorry I messed things up for you and Robbie.'

'Look, you didn't!' she interrupted. 'You didn't,' she repeated dully.

Jake jumped down and came round to the other side of the car to help her out. When she turned to him to say goodbye, and thank him, he said unexpectedly, 'I'll call, before I go back, in case you want me to take any message to Robbie.'

'Well, yes . . .' Alix faltered. She wished he hadn't such an unsettling attitude. He always seemed to catch her off balance. But he hadn't waited for a reply, in any case, but climbed into the Sizaire and drove off with a laconic wave.

CHAPTER FOUR

ALIX HOPED he hadn't meant his last words, and that they had been the sort of casual remark people make on parting without any real intention of following them up. 'I'll write . . . I'll call . . .'

But he was not the sort of man who made casual statements without meaning them. If he said he would call, he'd call.

All the same, she had not really expected him to do so, so when, a few days later, she came downstairs to hear Mrs Daventry exclaim, 'My goodness, Captain Sherwood, what a pleasant surprise!' a surge of annoyance rose in her. She had absolutely no wish to see the wretched man again. Try as she might, it was difficult to hide that everything he said annoyed her in some indefinable way. The man himself irritated her; so confident, so sure of himself. She suspected he had formed a very poor opinion of them all, and saw them as effete and overmannered.

'I don't fit into your social scene,' he had said, going on to make quite clear that he did not apologise for this omission. He despised their 'social scene', with its limited viewpoint and stilted conventions—it wasn't for him. He wanted no part of it.

As Alix entered the drawing-room, Mrs Daventry was twittering nervously, 'Perhaps you'd care for some tea, Captain Sherwood?'

Jake, looking faintly horrified, was declining this offer politely. Towering over Mrs Daventry's plump, diminutive figure, he dominated the drawing-room, handsome, even dashing in appearance, with his striking RFC uniform and slightly dishevelled air of informality. He was quite at ease. His grey eyes met Alix's over Mrs Daventry's head, and his wide, firm mouth softened into a smile. 'I said I'd call,' he reminded her pleasantly.

Alix stammered, 'How kind of you to come,' and hoped she did not sound condescending.

'I'm afraid it's Mrs Bingley's Bridge afternoon,' Mrs Daventry apologised, 'So I can't stay. But so nice to have met you again . . .' She departed, and they were alone.

'You don't like my coming here,' Jake said coolly. There, he'd done it again—put her on the defensive. Alix felt herself bridle.

'I didn't expect to see you, that's all. It's spared me having to go to Mrs Bingley's awful Bridge party, anyway. Won't you sit down?' she added formally, and sat down herself on the nearest chair.

He ignored the invitation and turned his back on her, very discourteously, to wander over to the piano, on the top of which stood a collection of family photographs in ornate silver or carved wooden Victorian frames. He picked them up, one by one, and studied each critically: Mrs Daventry as a young girl in a wasp-waisted evening gown with a bustle; the late Mr Daventry, in sepia, wearing a beard like a hearthrug, and placing one foot on a dead stag; Gerard and Alix at all stages of childhood, Gerard plump and serious, Alix freckle-faced, her long hair kept in order by a bandeau in the manner of Alice in Wonderland. When he had examined them all, Jake spoke, still with his back turned to her.

'You know, most of my adult life, I've lived on my own—in small apartments and so on. It seems odd, now, to see all these family bits and pieces around the the place. My mother had all this kind of thing at home, when I was a kid. When she died, some sort of relative of hers came down and took everything. I guess she took the photographs, too. I wish, now, I'd kept some of them.'

He said all this in a practical, matter-of-fact manner, in no way sentimental, but Alix found it strangely touching, a moment of unlooked-for vulnerability in this very self-possessed man. She felt herself relax, and somehow found herself telling him about her own parents, the train crash, her childhood here.

He listened in silence, and when she paused, asked, 'What do you do, now? All day?'

It was as if he accused her of idleness. There was that faintly disparaging note signalling a veiled insult. Alix's relaxed mood vanished in an instant, and the old antagonism returned. 'Why do you ask?' she said stiffly.

The grey eyes rested on her with an uncomfortable directness. 'You're young, educated, intelligent. This kind of life!' He hunched his shoulders in a scornful way and swept out a derisive hand which embraced not only the comfortable room with its discreetly expensive furnishings, but in some manner, her whole world. 'It's surely not enough, for you.'

'You mean, am I totally useless?' Alix said tightly. 'I told you once before that I don't have to listen to your insults. I don't know why you came here today—but you can get out, this minute!'

Cheeks flushed and her green eyes crystal bright with rage like chips from a mountain glacier, she stalked towards the door, with the intention of throwing it open dramatically for him to leave. But he moved too quickly for her, striding lightly and easily across the room to block her path and grasp her arm to halt her.

Beneath those strong fingers closing on her, every nerve in her body leapt into a tingling life, and with a shaking voice she demanded, 'How dare you! Take your hand from me. I'll call the maid!'

'No, you won't,' he said firmly, but to her immense

relief he released her arm. However, almost immediately he caused a fresh surge of confusion and anger to engulf her, by asking tauntingly, 'Well, then, if you're not useless, tell me why . . . tell me why you're not just another spoiled little rich girl!'

But he had gone too far, perhaps intentionally, wanting to goad her into a spontaneous, imprudent burst of truth.

'I don't give a damn what you think of me!' Alix blazed at him, little caring if this was the sort of language young ladies used or not. 'Who are *you*, anyway, to ask? And if wealth is such a crime. I'm surprised you've dirtied your hands with it. Robbie says you're a self-made millionaire.'

'Right and wrong,' Jake said casually. 'Self-made, but not yet quite a millionaire. But I will be.' His assurance took her breath away, and he smiled slightly at the astonishment on her face. But it was a mirthless smile that did nothing to soften the determined set of his features. 'I earned it; I worked for it. I slaved my guts out for it. I started with *nothing*. My mother and I lived in two miserable tenement rooms, and she killed herself working to help me get my education. Nobody else ever helped me, Miss Morrell. Nobody ever gave a damn. That's the first thing you learn when you're poor: nobody gives a damn, not really. Poor people aren't individuals, and they have no rights. They're an embarrassment to the prosperous, to be kept quiet with charity. Education, opportunity, these are things they have to fight for themselves! You're right to say I dirtied my hands. I did. I got right down there in the dirt and hauled myself up out of it again by my bootstraps!'

He fell silent, the echo of his voice lingering harshly in the room.

Pale, Alix said in a tense voice, 'I wanted to be an artist. They didn't allow me. Sometimes it's easier when you're poor. Then the only way is "up and onward".

No one steps in and says, "that isn't ladylike, and you'll embarrass the family. So stay at home and behave yourself and make a respectable marriage . . ." A woman isn't supposed to want anything else, you know. But I did want something else—and I think, in my heart, I still do.'

'Whose life is it, theirs or yours?' Jake asked bluntly. 'Why didn't you just tell them to go to hell and go ahead and do what you wanted?'

'You don't understand!' Alix burst out in frustration. 'They *love* me. I couldn't hurt them. It's so much easier for a man. When I said I wanted to go to Paris and study art, my aunt and my cousin reacted as though I'd proposed dancing the can-can in my underwear!'

Jake chuckled. 'Now that I should like to see!'

'I'm sure you would,' she told him calmly, in control of herself now. 'But not in a hundred years, Jake Sherwood.'

'So, tell me about being an artist. I assume you didn't just meekly give up painting altogether.' He raised his eyebrows enquiringly. 'Where do you do your painting?'

'H-Here,' she stammered. 'I've a sort of studio at the top of the house, in the attics.'

'I'd like to see it,' Jake said.

Reluctantly, Alix led the way upstairs. She was sensitive about her painting, and disliked showing it to people who had no understanding. People like Mrs Bingley, whose idea of 'art' was embodied in the so-called 'furnishing paintings' produced by the thousand to grace the interiors of houses like this one. She pushed open the studio door and stood back defiantly to allow him to enter first, as her guest, and intruder, into this, her own and very private sanctum.

The unfinished portrait of Robbie stood on the easel, facing the door. The light from the overhead window, which had been set into the roof especially to help her, struck it at an angle, so that the head seemed just to have turned to see who entered, the frank blue eyes questioning the new arrivals. Jake stood before it for a long time in silence.

'How long have you been working on it?' he asked her at last.

'Ages,' Alix sighed. 'I'd hoped to get it finished this time he was home on leave, but he could come and sit only once. I tried yesterday to do some more work on it, but when he's away in France, it's as if a kind of shutter comes down on it and I can't seem to make it *alive*. Do you understand?' She stole a cautious, nervous glance at him and waited in trepidation for his reply.

'Sure I understand,' Jake nodded. He looked at the unfinished painting of that slight, handsome, English figure. She had caught Robbie's way of looking at people, ingenuous, honest, no guile in the frank blue eyes. What she hadn't caught was the other side of Robbie's character, more calculating and egotistical. Perhaps she hadn't painted it because *she* didn't see it. The portrait made him uneasy, not for what it revealed of the sitter but for what it betrayed of the painter. She was so vulnerable, and she didn't realise it. Women like that often ended up badly hurt. He hoped Robbie . . . Damn Robbie!

Abruptly, he said aloud, 'You're good.'

She was good, very good. As they had climbed the attic stairs, he'd still half-imagined he'd find a row of insipid paintings of flowers and kittens, the sort of thing well-brought-up girls churned out *en masse*. But he should have known better, and realised that Alix wouldn't waste her time on trivia of that sort.

They clattered down the narrow stairs and then down the broader, carpeted staircase to the main hall. There he collected his cap.

'I'll be going!' He turned the cap in his strong, capable hands with the heavily scarred knuckles. Alix felt her eyes drawn to the white streaks of knitted skin on the suntan. Had he smashed his hands against something? 'Do you want me to take a message—to Robbie?' he prompted.

Alix started, and dragged her eyes from her fixed contemplation of his hands. 'Oh, only that I'll try and get the portrait finished—before he comes again.'

A slight flicker of amusement gleamed in the depths of his eyes, and he held up his scarred hands and said, 'Fist-fights. Does that shock you?'

'I can't imagine men fighting like that,' Alix said honestly. 'It seems barbaric.'

'Whereas modern warfare is so civilised?' He was mocking her now.

'You think me foolish,' she said quietly.

He shook his head. 'No, I don't think you foolish at all. I think you're very intelligent, and a talented painter. Robbie is very lucky. I do mean that. I wouldn't say it to you if I didn't mean it.'

Alix felt herself blush. 'I'll walk out to the car with you,' she offered.

The Sizaire-Berwick, beautifully polished, stood on the gravel drive. 'It's my pride and joy,' Jake declared, proudly patting the bonnet.

'What will happen to it while you're in France?'

'Oh, I'll ship it over,' he said casually.

'Take it with you?' Alix stared at him, astounded.

'Why not?' He grinned at her. 'You know, pretty lady, everything I say upsets you. I rile you, and at the best I puzzle you. But if a man—or a woman—wants to do something, he, or she, should go right out there and do it. That's what I said earlier—and I stand by it.'

Impulsively, Alix said, 'Yes, you're right! Of course that's how it should be! Why shouldn't you take the car to France?'

Jake laughed, his lean cheeks creasing and the fine skin at the corners of his eyes crinkling. It was contagious, and Alix began to laugh with him, while he watched her.

She was beautiful when she laughed. No artist could have wished a better model. There was so much life in that lovely face, so much intelligence and a heart-breaking fragility. This large red-brick house, so solid and respectable, with its rhododendron-lined gravel drive and high laurel hedges, was like a protecting womb. For all he had taunted her earlier, he hated to think she might one day be forced to leave it behind and face all the cruelties and deceptions of the world outside, alone. Robbie was no good as a shield. He was the kind who leaned on others. But who would be the right man for this lovely, laughing, auburn-haired young woman, a very living portrait of unfulfilled promise? Not himself, that much was for sure, Jake thought wryly. That couldn't work out. Robbie, at least, belonged to her world. He, Jake, didn't. He was an interloper from a different culture. He might just as well have stepped out of some Time Machine, a totally alien creature.

Alix stopped laughing and bit her lip, confused. When she glanced shyly up at him, he was looking down at her with that thoughtful expression she had seen in his grey eyes before.

'I guess you won't like this,' he said, 'but I'd like to kiss you. May I?'

He did not allow her time to react but stooped to bring his face close to hers. Her hair smelled of lily of the valley. He had meant to kiss her lightly and chastely, on the cheek. But the scent of her hair, and the nearness of her, made his skin tingle and swept away this modest intention like a frail twig thrown into a rushing weir. His arms closed round her slim, supple body, dragging her into his embrace, and his mouth sought out hers, crushing it in a powerful claim for possession.

Alix gasped, and her heart leapt wildly. She wanted to cry out, but was unable to speak. Her senses whirled about her and the world danced madly. Her hands tightened involuntarily on his shoulders and she pressed against him as if her body no longer belonged to her, but was already his . . .

Then she remembered. They both remembered—and stepped back, away from each other, releasing one another simultaneously, as though some electric force had flung them apart.

Alix stumbled back, out of his reach, her green eyes fixed on him wildly. Slowly, as if not fully conscious of the action, she lifted her hand to touch her throbbing lips with her trembling fingers, before whispering, 'Why did you do that?'

Jake shrugged. 'I don't know,' he muttered hoarsely. It sounded a feeble answer, but it was the simple truth. He didn't know. He hadn't intended it. 'I didn't mean to'—he rubbed his hand over his tousled mop of light brown hair, '—but I'm not sorry. I'm sorry if it upset you, but I'm not sorry I did it.' He thrust out his chin truculently, defying her to object.

Alix, suddenly angry, burst out, 'You *should* be! You're Robbie's friend, and he trusts you! Anyway, people here, the sort of people *I* know, don't behave like that. You've only just met me!'

'Now just a moment!' Jake said evenly, and something in his voice, a warning note, stopped her flood of reproaches. 'In the first place, I told you before—I'm not one of "your" set, your sort of people. I don't fit in, and it wouldn't suit me. Secondly, have you thought that Robbie also trusts you? You could have fought me off, you know. I didn't notice any struggles.'

'Look,' Alix said with difficulty, 'I think you have altogether the wrong idea about me. Perhaps it's understandable, because the very first time we met, well, it was in what's usually called "compromising circumstances". But I don't normally behave like that, slip out of parties to keep rendezvous in bedrooms. It was just a silly, spur of the moment, idea and I'll be honest—I wasn't sorry you came along to spoil it. I was relieved.'

He seemed startled. 'What about Robbie?' he demanded. 'He wasn't so happy. He was hopping mad—not at you, at *me.*'

'Why? It wasn't your fault. Anyway, as for what's between me and Robbie, that's private and none of your business.'

'Do you love him?' Jake asked. He sounded genuinely curious to know.

Alix looked away from that level, probing gaze. 'Yes, of course I do. I'm going to marry him. We've been engaged for—for ages.'

'I can never understand a long engagement,' he said brusquely. 'Either you want to get married or you don't. Why wait?'

'People do wait.' She could hear the defensive note in her voice. 'People do have long engagements; it's quite an ordinary thing.'

'An ordinary thing?' He opened his eyes wide, and a sudden grin stretched his lean cheeks. 'Now that is a romantic way to talk about it.'

'Shut up!' she flared angrily, her cheeks vying with her hair in colour. 'I don't care what you think! I do love Robbie, and I'm going to marry him.' She was shouting now at him, defiantly, and unable to control her voice.

'So, congratulations, that's fine. As you said, Robbie's a friend of mine. Why should I object?' he stared at her challengingly, and then relaxed, and patted the Sizaire. 'Jump in; I'll take you for a spin. Isn't there some kind of tea-shop or whatever around here?'

'I don't want to go anywhere with you. I wish you'd just leave!' she threw at him.

'All right, I'll apologise for kissing you. Does that help? You ought to accept my apology; it's very bad manners not to. You should know that, brought up in such nice society. And what about hospitality? Here I

am, a stranger. I don't know anyone. Come and sit and
talk to me in a nice public, crowded place, where I can't
kiss you! I won't even hold your hand, and I'll have
you back here in under an hour.'

'If you want company, go and find your friend Tilly!'
she told him sharply.

'Believe me,' he said wryly, 'she has no conversation.
All her talents are concentrated in one very human
activity. If I wanted that, I'd go and find her. But all I
want is some company.'

Alix sighed, and glanced back at the house. The
maids would have seen them standing out here, talking
for so long, and they would be wondering what was
going on between them. They might even have seen him
kiss her. She couldn't stay here any longer and, mule-
headed to the last, the man refused to go away. She'd
never been in a situation like it, and she'd certainly
never met anyone like him.

'All right,' she said stiffly. 'I'll go and get my hat. But
only for an hour, do you hear?'

The High Street tea-rooms were crowded at this time
of the afternoon, and she wished she could have thought
of somewhere less popular. But perhaps it was better to
be here, in a crowd. There was safety in numbers, and
she really didn't want to be cornered with him in any
discreet little half-empty place. The chatter of voices
filled the room, and the tinkle of cutlery and clatter of
plates. The harassed waitress guided them to a table by
the wall and dragged out a chair.

'Here do?' she demanded impatiently. 'You can see
the orchestra. It's nice. They start playing in a minute.'
She dashed away, the notebook tied to her apron belt
swinging, to answer a summons from another table.

'We're going to hear the band,' Jake said amiably.

'It won't be a band; it will be a piano, a violin and
something else, and it won't play anything written later
than nineteen hundred. No rag-time, if that's what

you're expecting,' Alix said curtly.

Jake leaned his elbows on the table and smiled at her. She wore a hat with bands of cream tulle swathed about the crown, and a wide flat brim. Beneath it, her auburn hair burst out in rebellious curls, framing her flushed face. Her green eyes sparkled like emeralds, and he could see the pulse throbbing in her white neck.

'Do I scare you?' he asked suddenly. He frowned, as if the idea annoyed him.

'No!' Alix looked startled. 'I just think you're very rude and—and thick-skinned. You don't listen to any objections I make. You knew I didn't want to come here.'

'But you came' he pointed out.

The waitress came back before she could reply. 'Tea-for-two? Eclairs-is-all-gone-but-scones-is-nice. Real-cream-today.'

'Just the tea,' Alix said firmly.

'I don't drink tea,' Jake objected. He smiled beguilingly up at the harassed waitress. 'Do you think they'd make me a cup of coffee in the kitchen?'

Beneath his smile, her brittle professionalism dissolved and she blushed like a sunset. 'I'll ask, but 'spect they will—you being in uniform.' She threw him an arch look and trotted away.

'My, my,' said Alix vengefully, *'don't* we bowl them over!'

'I'm not making progress with *you.'*

'I'm not available,' she said crossly.

'True, I forgot.' He shrugged his broad shoulders. 'Next time someone kisses you, other than Robbie the perpetual fiancé, struggle a little. It keeps the record straight.'

'Don't think that I won't walk out and leave you here,' she told him calmly.

The orchestra—a piano, a cello and a violin, as Alix had predicted—had assembled and began to play a selection of melodies which, in their rendering, became almost indistinguishable one from another.

'Can I ask you something?' Alix asked, on an impulse.

He raised his eyebrows at the curiosity in her voice. 'Go ahead.'

'Well, it's very patriotic of you to come over here and fight, as you have done. But what made you do it? I mean, you seem older than some of the others, most of them. I don't mean to be rude,' she added.

'No offence taken. I'm pushing thirty-four. I'm not especially patriotic, not in the jingoistic way you mean. I just wanted to fly.'

Flying. What was it about flying that made it such a magnet for them all? They were all the same, the flying men. They coaxed their fragile wood, canvas and wire chariots into the air, performed prodigious deeds of valour in them, and frequently crashed them. Battered, bleeding and bruised, they crawled out of the wreckage, through a tangled cat's-cradle of struts and wire, cheerfully determined to do it all again the next day.

Jake, who had been watching her troubled face, asked softly, 'Is that what you don't like, the flying? I'm a pilot. That's wrong?'

'I don't understand it,' Alix whispered. She looked across the tea-rooms. They were blurred, the gesticulating, chattering customers like so many marionettes, performing behind a veil, their voices seeming to come from a million miles away. She had lied to Jake in saying she loved Robbie enough to want to marry him. She did love Robbie, but not in that way, and not that much. To marry him would be wrong. But Jake must never know that, and neither must Robbie—not just now. To abandon Robbie in war-time was impossible. As long as the war lasted, the fiction of their engagement had to last. There must be no suspicion implanted in Jake's mind that she hadn't meant every word she'd said. If he ever suspected the truth, somehow, some day, he'd reveal it to Robbie. Not intentionally, perhaps—but by some slip of the tongue, some oblique reference. Not only that, but the engagement acted as a brake on Jake's own behaviour. He might steal a kiss. He might flirt with her mildly. But so long as she was engaged to Robbie, it would stop at that—and she didn't want it to go any further.

Something brushed her cheek lightly, and she started. Jake withdrew the hand he had stretched across the table. 'What's up?' he asked. The grey eyes were unusually gentle and sympathetic. 'You were miles away, and you looked as if you had all the sorrows of mankind on your shoulders.'

'I worry about Robbie, I suppose,' she said, looking down, ashamed to meet the honest gaze that seemed to penetrate the innermost depths of her soul.

Jake, in his turn, fell silent, feeling the same helplessness he had known at the station, that total inability to give her any comfort. Seeing her tragic, pale, beautiful face, like a carved marble Pietà, he felt an urge to put his arms round her again, this time to whisper, 'Hold on to *me* . . .' He shook his head. 'Watch out,' he told himself. 'Keep a clear brain. You don't need to get involved with this girl. She isn't interested, and you're too old to be burning your fingers, hankering after forbidden temptations.'

The waitress brought the tea and the coffee, and they sat drinking it in silence. Alix found that her hand was shaking, and she had to put her cup down in the end and leave it unfinished.

'You want me to take you home now?' he asked her, pushing away his own empty cup.

Alix smiled at him ruefully. 'I'm sorry, Jake,' she said contritely, because she was really sorry. 'You wanted company, and I've been rotten company. You really shouldn't have bothered to bring me. I've had nothing to say to you. That's not because I was standing on my dignity. It's because there's nothing we can talk about.'

'No, there isn't,' he agreed soberly. 'You're Robbie's girl, and you don't want to sit here with me. Just like you said, we're different. Different backgrounds, different points of view, different ideas.'

That didn't mean that there were not a dozen things he wanted to say . . . and a couple he'd like to do. Behind that cool, lovely and untouched exterior of hers there lurked the first hesitant beginning of a fire. It needed the touch of a lover to bring it into life. But if he told her *that*, she'd very likely be shocked rigid.

He signalled for the bill. 'Come on, let's get out of here. That band is destroying my eardrums. Listening to it, it's worse than flying at high altitude.'

They walked back down the street to where he had parked the car. The High Street was always crowded, and the nearest spot he had been able to find was by a little park. Locals always called it School Park, although that wasn't its name, because it stood alongside the redbrick Infant School, which boasted two entry doors neatly labelled Boys and Girls.

'Why can't they both go in the same door?' Jake asked, pointing.

'The boys would pull the girls' plaits and untie their aprons,' offered Alix by way of explanation.

Jake said impishly, 'They still do that when they're grown, or something like it.'

It wasn't much of a park, just a square of grass, some wooden seats, a couple of flowerbeds and some swings in one corner. There had been children on the swings, but now they ran away, laughing and shouting, leaving the empty swings bouncing on their chains.

'Come on!' Jake exclaimed, grasping Alix's hand tightly. He hauled her after him towards the abandoned swings.

'What on earth are you doing?' she gasped, stumbling along beside his tall figure as he strode out briskly.

He thrust her unceremoniously on to the seat of a vacated swing, 'Hold on, I'll give you a push.'

Alix gripped the chains on either side and put her feet straight out in front of her, to clear the ground. 'If the park-keeper sees us, he'll tell us off!'

'We'll run. What do you say: he's an old man and we can run faster than he can?' Jake pulled the swing back by the chains and released it with a hearty shove.

Alix flew through the air, the rush of wind catching her skirts and sending them fluttering around her knees, and blowing her hat askew. 'Stop it, Jake! Don't push the swing so hard!' Despite her protests, she was enjoying the movement and couldn't help laughing. Back went the swing, creaking noisily, and forward with a swoosh, Alix's feet pointing into the air. '*Stop* —you're quite mad! And you're making me as crazy as you are!'

'It's time somebody did!' called Jake's voice unrepentantly above her head.

The swing careered wildly, twisting. Alix shrieked, let go of the chains and fell off the seat backwards, to land in his arms.

'All right?' he asked, clasping her firmly, both arms wrapped round her arms and upper body.

Alix looked up into the face grinning down at her. 'This is all wrong,' she thought. 'I never feel this way with Robbie—so—so light-hearted. When Robbie takes me in his arms, I want to escape. But now, in this man's arms, I feel so happy. What is going wrong with me?'

Jake's grey eyes were looking down at her enigmatically. 'I wish you weren't Robbie's girl.' He suddenly sounded very serious.

'But I am . . .' Alix whispered ('and I wish I weren't', leapt unspoken into her mind).

'Sure.' His tone was brusque now. He stood her up on her feet like a marionette. 'Your hat is crooked.'

'I'm not surprised!' She put up both hands and straightened the tulle hat. 'Is that all right?' She tilted her face and stared at him enquiringly.

Her face was flushed from exercise and her green eyes sparkled. She was panting a little, and he thought, 'I'd sure as hell like to take a tumble in the sheets with her . . .'

'*Oy!*' shouted an aggrieved voice. They both looked up and saw a gnarled, elderly figure in a park-keeper's uniform hobbling aggressively towards them. 'Can't you read? Not to be used by kids over twelve, them swings. Break the ruddy chains!'

'Now run!' Jake ordered, and they raced helter-skelter out of the park, hand in hand and laughing.

Behind them, the old man was shouting furiously. 'Worse than ruddy kids!'

They seemed to get home again very quickly. Jake turned into the drive with a flourish and drew up. He jumped down and came round to help her out. Alix let go of the brim of her hat, and held out her hand to him, though the formal little gesture seemed out of place now. A barrier had vanished between them that couldn't be put back again.

He glanced down at it briefly, a neat little hand, small and white, all the nails trimmed, but one of them had a thin green mark under it—paint. It made him want to laugh, but he didn't.

He took the offered palm in his, and said, 'Well, it's been a pleasure, Miss Morrell. Keep up the painting!' By rights, he ought now to release her hand, but he didn't, and she didn't attempt to remove it from his grip.

Alix heard herself say, a little tremulously, 'Next time you're on leave, if you're in London, call and see us— won't you? Or even, or even, if you have time to come again, before you leave . . .' Her voice trailed away and they still stood there, holding hands, unwilling to break the human contact. She felt angry with herself for having wasted the time in the tea-rooms. She could have talked to him if she'd really tried. Suddenly, now that they were parting, there were so many things she wanted to ask.

He pressed her fingers, and let go of her hand at last. She watched him jump athletically into the Sizaire, but as the awakened engine roared into life, she felt an unexplained panic at the thought that she might never see him again, and shouted desperately, 'Jake!'

But a spray of gravel showered the air from the screeching wheels and smothered her cry. He drove off, without a backward glance, as if he hadn't heard.

CHAPTER FIVE

IN FACT, that wasn't to be the last she saw of him, that
summer of 1917. His visit, however unwished it had
seemed at the time, had left Alix feeling curiously
unsettled, as though something had been begun, but left
unfinished. She found herself roaming about the house,
unable to concentrate on any task, even to paint. She
would stand, staring critically and often discontentedly,
at finished work with which she had been rather satisfied
before. She tried looking at the paintings Jake had seen
with his eyes, wondering how he saw them. Her work
had never really been exposed to the critical gaze of an
outsider. Gerry and Robbie and her friends would
always offer an opinion, but they were too considerate
of her feelings to pull anything to pieces. It was no way
for an artist to grow, and Alix knew it. She needed
Jake—or someone like him. As it was, his presence
seemed in some way to have remained imprinted on the
atmosphere of her studio, watching, as though she
wanted *his* approval, more than any other.

Alix remained nervous and tense, as if there was a
thunderstorm brewing, though the sky stayed clear and
fine. The weather was so good that week that some
hardy souls were going down to the beaches to disport
themselves in the new bathing-costumes, which Mrs
Daventry insisted on seeing as unbelievably indecent,
because they only just covered the tops of women's
thighs.

It was early evening, and Gerard was shut up in his
study preparing a brief for the morrow. Mrs Daventry

sat in the drawing-room, placidly engaged on a piece of tatting, and Alix prowled from room to room, like a cat that has been shut in, when it wants to go out and be a tiger in the shrubbery.

'Oh, do sit *down*, Alexandra, and read or—or something!' Mrs Daventry observed at last. 'Whatever is wrong?'

'I don't know,' Alix said. It was true, she thought; she didn't understand what was wrong with her. Or perhaps, deep down inside, she did—but couldn't bring herself to admit it, because it was so frightening, and must be unthinkable. She leaned on the window-ledge and stared out into the front garden, her chin cupped in her hands. The evenings were already starting to draw in now, and it got darker markedly earlier. The light was fading, and Mrs Daventry had already cast a thoughtful look or two at the standard lamp, as her fingers nimbly moved the tatting-shuttle to and fro.

Suddenly the purr of an engine and a crunch of gravel sounded outside. Alix's heart leapt into her mouth, and she knew at once it was Jake—and that subconsciously she had been waiting for him. There was no way she could have known he would come, only something inside her had remained obstinately expectant, as if it knew that he would return.

She turned and ran out of the room, ignoring Mrs Daventry's cry of 'Alix—where are you going *now*?' She pulled open the front door and ran down the drive, coatless in her thin gown.

The Sizaire was parked outside the gate, the engine still ticking over, half-hidden by the laurel hedge. The uniformed man sitting at the wheel seemed to be sunk in thought, as if unsure what to do. Perhaps he was as surprised as she was to find himself there. As Alix came up, breathless, he looked up and after a moment said, without any formal greeting, 'I didn't know whether to come up to the house or not.'

He leaned across and pushed open the car door, and she clambered into the passenger seat beside him. Without another word, he drove slowly off, a little way down the road, and parked at the back of the churchyard, where a leafy lane ran off down through a patch of trees. The lane was called Lovers' Lane, like a thousand others up and down the country. People walked their dogs there, but the lovers, if any there were, preferred the deserted peace of the long grass between the tombstones of the churchyard.

Jake switched off the engine and leaned back, stretching his arm across the back of her seat. It was getting truly dark now, here beneath the trees. The churchyard was beginning to look a little ghostly, and small dark shapes flitted eerily across from the belfry to the trees, wheeling and diving.

'Bats,' thought Alix, adding in self-reproach, 'bats in the belfry—that's what I must be, or I shouldn't be here, and feeling like this.'

The yew trees rustled in the evening breeze, and she shivered. Jake asked, 'Cold?'

'A little. I forgot to take a coat. I heard the car—and I ran.'

He smiled slightly, and said 'Oh?' He put his arm round her, and she moved comfortably into the warmth and protection of his broad shoulder. 'I didn't know whether to come,' Jake said, after a moment. 'My leave is up. I go back tomorrow.'

'From which station?' she asked in a tense voice.

'No, don't come and see me off. You've gone through that once this week, and I don't want to put you through it again.'

They were both silent for a while after that, because they were both thinking about Robbie, whom they both cared about and neither of them could hurt.

'When will you get leave again?' Alix asked, a little tremulously.

She felt him shrug. 'I don't know. I might not come
to London, anyway. It might be better if I didn't . . .'

The darkness was settling around them. Jake raised
his hand and ruffled her hair lightly. 'Funny thing . . .'
he said.

Alix whispered, 'Yes, it is.' After a moment, she
blurted out desperately, 'I don't know *why* . . .'

'No, neither do I,' he answered soberly.

He bent his head and kissed her gently as she turned
her face towards his. It was dark now, not the blackness
of winter nights, but the luminous purple of summer.
The little bats swooped merrily around their heads,
catching insects, and a rush of large wings told the
passing of a newly-awakened owl just setting out on his
nightly hunting. Jake could still make out Alix's face,
even though the features were smudged and the outline
imprecise. Her mouth was soft against his, her lips
parted, unresisting, so that his tongue brushed against
her even little teeth. She put her left hand against his
chest, but didn't push him away. He asked quietly,
'What is it? Are you frightened?'

'Yes, a little,' she confessed. Inside her, everything
seemed in a turmoil, her heart leaping about in wild
excitement and the pit of her stomach churning.

He smiled in the darkness, and took hold of the small
white hand pressed against him. But as his fingers closed
on it they closed, too, on the hard metal setting of her
engagement ring. Remembering her flight through the
Harrises' garden, he asked, 'Were you ever in bed with
Robbie?'

'No,' Alix hesitated. 'He—He keeps asking. I know
how he feels, but it's just, he keeps going away . . .'
She couldn't explain it to Jake. She couldn't tell him
the simple truth, and say, 'Robbie has never made me
feel the way you do.'

'Going away,' Jake was thinking. 'I'm going away,
too. Nothing's permanent, not for a fighting man.' But

for the women it was different. They had to sit it out at home, day after day. It turned any lover into a sort of bandit, appearing over the horizon, seizing his prize, and galloping off in a cloud of dust.

'With anyone else?' he was prompted to ask her, following up his previous question.

'No.'

Jake released her hand and cupped his fingers round her face. He put his mouth close to her ear and whispered huskily, 'Then I'd like it to be *me*. I'd surely like to be the first.'

He felt her shudder in his arms and heard her utter a dry, sobbing breath. He could take her now, just like that, and she wouldn't offer any resistance. The urge within him was so strong that he almost allowed himself to ask, 'Let me?' The words were already forming themselves and hovered in his mouth, so that his tongue already touched the back of his teeth to make the sound of 'l'.

But he didn't. It wasn't, he thought ruefully, because it wasn't what his body wanted right now, or because he'd never made love to a girl in a car seat before, parked in some darkened, deserted spot. A different sort of girl, of course, which compounded the problem. He was like a man who, having only ever dealt with the fake article, is amazed and bewildered to find a real gemstone lying in his hand.

He didn't ask, because he knew she was uncertain and mixed up, her defences in disarray, and did not herself know what she wanted. There was a good chance that, in her confusion, she might say 'Yes', and if she did, it would mean a whole lot of trouble later and they'd both be sorry. He wanted to make love to her, but he didn't want either of them to regret it, afterwards, souring the memory.

She would regret it, because she was the sort of girl brought up to be afraid, as if fear and guilt could be made to equal innocence. He would regret it, because he still cherished a few old-fashioned scruples, and they turned on loyalty. Robbie wasn't just a friend, but a comrade-in-arms and a man who had already gone back to the Front. Jake knew what it was like over there. He knew the odds stacked against the flying men. Among all that chaos, that destruction, that sheer waste and ever-present uncertainty, there had to be something to hold to. You had to be able to trust the men who shared the Mess with you—even if you couldn't trust any other damn thing. He could still bend over Alix and whisper 'Do you want me to?' and she might, just might, answer, 'Yes'—and it would be the same as if he took up a machine into the clouds and shot Robbie down out of the clear, blue sky.

Alix shivered again in the crook of his arm, not just because the evening air was cool, but because her nerves were strung like guitar strings, vibrating at the touch of his hand, to every movement he made, every breath he took. She knew that although she had not answered 'Yes' to the unspoken question that hovered on his lips, her body, responding to impulses of its own which she couldn't control, had already done so—and he must have sensed it. She could lie to him, but her treacherous body, yielding to his embrace, would not. She could only beg silently: 'Please don't—I'm not strong enough . . .'

But he was stronger than she was. As she trembled, he took his arms away and struggled out of his tunic, which he draped round her shoulders in a comforting gesture bringing warmth. The warmth of his body, transferred to hers, like a gift. Before he did, he took the cigarettes and matches out of a pocket, and now he lit one.

The flame flickered up, briefly illuminating his face. He drew on the cigarette, the red glow gleaming in the darkness, and sat smoking in silence for a while. He was getting the question out of his system. At last, he asked quietly, 'You're still going to marry Robbie?'

'Yes.' There was a note of pain in her voice. 'Yes, I am. He . . . I must . . .' She broke off.

She heard Jake give a little sigh. Then he said brusquely, 'You're probably right. He's one of your circle, after all. He'll give you the sort of life you're used to.'

They both sat in silence until he had finished his cigarette and tossed the stub into the darkness, the faint red glow describing a trailing rosy arc through the night and falling to earth like a tiny shooting star. He started the car up again, and drove back to the house. Alix got out and returned his tunic. Her heart felt heavy, and although it was chilly, she didn't care. A chill seemed to have fallen over her whole world, and her body was dull, and ached for what it could not have. She stood, hugging her bare arms, and waiting for him to drive off.

'No,' he said. 'You go into the house.'

'Why?' she asked, puzzled.

'Because I'd rather you walked away from me. Don't stand and watch me go away from you. It's unlucky. Flying men—we're all superstitious, you know.'

Alix turned and walked slowly up the dark gravel drive. Behind her, in the night, she heard the purr of the engine and the scrape of the tyres, as he drove away.

During the days that followed, Alix immersed herself in her painting, discovering, as so many others have, that work is a wonderful cure for low spirits, anxiety or uncertainty. She stood before the portrait of Robbie and told herself sternly that the entire problem it presented was a mental *bloc*, a kind of 'artist's *bloc*' akin to 'writer's *bloc*'. The way round it was to start working on the picture, and the work itself would provide the clue.

It was a fine theory, but in practice it proved less than satisfactory. The painting fought back—or at least, that's how it seemed. Certainly it appeared to have taken on a malignant life of its own, like the celebrated portrait of Dorian Grey. It didn't age, as that notorious likeness did, but it remained obstinately incomplete.

She had always found it difficult to work on it when Robbie was away. Now it was worse, because when she closed her eyes and tried to see Robbie's face, another face swam up out of the recesses of her memory. She could only open her eyes and stare up at the skylight and the empty firmament above, and wonder what they were both doing now, over there in France. Had Jake taken the Sizaire across the Channel, as he had said he would? In the end, she decided on another tactic. She put the portrait at the far end of her bare attic studio, out of the way, and started work on something else.

Shut away in the studio at the top of the house, she had the comforting sensation of being mistress of her situation. This was her domain, her private world. If anyone came in here, it was as a visitor. People always knocked on the door, even Gerard. He came up every day, on his return from the office, and asked, 'How's it going?' After he'd been given the relevant reply, he'd say, 'I was going to have a drink before going off to dress for dinner. Come and join me?'

'I'd like to, Gerry, but I want to get finished for today,' was her stock response.

Eventually he found a way of countering it. He said, diffidently, 'Oh, well, I'll bring you a glass of sherry up here . . .' When he did, he brought his whisky and soda too, with an apology. 'Shan't be in your way, shall I? I'll just sit over here.'

Then he'd sit in the old armchair with the stuffing coming through the holes in the upholstery, which had once graced the nursery. Gerard would settle down, and as if to a preset routine, sigh and lift his glass in salute. 'Chin-chin!' he said amiably.

Once upon a time that habit of his had annoyed her, but now she didn't mind, and laughed and teased him gently about it. At the same time, the sight of his solid, comforting presence sprawled out in the ancient chair, his spectacles pushed up out of the way on top of his head, led her to speculate about Gerard's future.

He was, she knew, thirty-six, and professionally very successful. Socially, he was the mainstay of the tennis club, and as Boat Race time neared, he went back to the scenes of his student days and cycled along a towpath, shouting at the sweating crew. But it seemed to her that it was high time Gerard settled down with a family of his own. She'd always tried to be scrupulously honest with him about the way she felt, and she did not really believe he still entertained any hopes of settling down with *her*. But the only other woman on the horizon appeared to be Blanche Frobisher, and that was because Blanche was, as Mrs Daventry had observed disapprovingly, 'throwing herself' at him. Blanche's determination to be Mrs Gerard Daventry was by now so obvious, Alix thought, that surely Gerry must see it too. If he did, he gave no sign of it. He was always very polite to Blanche and Jennie's mother, Maisie Frobisher, which not everybody was. But he seemed more tolerant of Blanche than taken by her.

'All the same,' Mrs Daventry said snappishly, 'it wouldn't be the first time a girl has worn a man down until he gives up and marries her!' Then she had added, 'I dare say Blanche is quite a nice girl, but I can't say she's the sort of girl I'd have chosen for a daughter-in-law—and as for that dreadful vulgar mother of hers . . .' Poor Maisie, the dubious reputation of her gaiety girl days clung to her like a shadow.

Nevertheless, Blanche was beginning to sense eventual victory, and even felt secure enough to call at the house without her mother in attendance, usually on the pretext of seeing Alix. This, although Alix had never been a close friend, as she was of Jennie.

Blanche chose to make one of these visits one particular afternoon when Alix was alone in the house except for the staff. She had been expecting Jennie, and had told the parlourmaid, Jessie, to bring Miss Frobisher straight up to the studio. Jessie, not distinguishing between the Frobisher sisters, promptly showed Blanche into the studio, where Alix was busily at work.

'I was passing by,' Blanche said mellifluously, 'so I thought I'd call in.' She perched on the arm of the old chair and turned her round, blue, china doll's eyes on Alix. She was wearing a blue dress, fully four inches above the ankle, with a natural waistline and a long, straight bodice beneath the fragile georgette which her soft little bosom made to tremble invitingly. She wore no corset. She was small in build, with child-like slender limbs, and tiny hands and feet. She liked to dress in shell-pinks and turquoises, and Alix sometimes thought, uncharitably, that she looked like the sugar doll off a highly decorated iced cake.

Blanche hitched up her georgette skirts and crossed her shapely legs, swinging one foot to and fro. As a tactic, it might have reduced Gerard to a frenzy of spectacle-polishing, but directed at Alix it was faintly ridiculous, and even Blanche seemed to realise it. After a moment, she slid off the armchair, like a bored kitten, and set off to roam about the studio, looking for something to amuse her.

Alix watched with growing irritation, for, just like a kitten, Blanche had a tendency to meddle mischievously with anything that took her eye and roused a moment's curiosity. The curiosity never did last longer than a minute or two. Blanche picked things up and put them down—but never back in the right place. She took tops off paint-tubes and failed to screw them back properly.

If a colour intrigued her, she squeezed blobs of it out on to the nearest flat surface, and never cleaned it up. She knocked over a jar containing brushes, and jammed them back in carelessly and upside-down. She stood in Alix's light. Yet, as the sun fell through the skylight on to Blanche in her short, flimsy dress, so obviously worn over the minimum underwear, her blond curls and smoothly rounded contours, it struck Alix that here was a Botticelli nude. 'What a body . . .' she thought professionally, adding a reservation that it would have been nice to have seen some evidence of a brain in the dainty head.

'Blanche!' she exclaimed, exasperated at last. 'Paint is very expensive! I do wish you'd stop squeezing the tubes like that!'

Not only did she squeeze the tubes, but she squeezed them in the middle, which was even worse.

Blanche gazed at her with her round eyes. 'Does it cost a lot? But you don't have to worry about that, do you? I mean, you've got plenty of money—of your own.' She dropped the tube she had been holding carelessly, near the palette on which she had been playing with the colours, combining patches of vermilion and burnt umber and squirls of white. She looked around. 'You're clever, Alix, aren't you? Being able to do all this. Like that picture of Robbie.' She pointed to the portrait. 'It looks just like him. I can't do anything. I had piano lessons, but I can't play.'

'I'm sure there's something you must be good at,' Alix said wearily, and even as she said it, her glance fell again on that slender, provocative and graceful form and she knew what that something was. Blanche was born to be a mistress. In Renaissance Italy, a prince would have kept her and had her painted reclining on a silken bed with a pet dog running about the floor, and servants in the background. In Paris of the 1840s she would have been one of the great courtesans, a

Lady of the Camellias. But here she was out of her time
and out of her place, lost in middle-class suburbia.

Just at that moment, Jessie came to say that a
message had arrived for her. Alix excused herself, wiped
her hands and went to deal with it. She was probably
gone no more than ten minutes, but as she re-climbed
the stairs, she had a premonition that she ought not to
have left Blanche alone in the studio. Hastily she pushed
open the door and almost ran into her sanctum.

Blanche, standing before Robbie's portrait, whirled
round, her cheeks aflame. She held the tube of vermilion
in her hand.

'Oh, Alix,' she gasped. 'I am *so* sorry! I was fiddling
with the top, it wouldn't go on—and I must have
squeezed the tube by accident. It just squirted out . . .'

Across the portrait lay two long streaks of red, and
one large splodge. Alix grabbed the turpentine and a
cloth and muttered, 'It's all right, Blanche, I can clean
it up!' She pushed her way past the girl. 'Only *do* get
out of the way, can't you?' Her suppressed anger flared
up.

'I am sorry . . .' Blanche said in her mellifluous
voice, but she sounded really scared. She watched Alix
set to work to repair the damage. 'Perhaps I'd better
go.'

'I think perhaps you had!' Alix said grimly, and
Blanche retreated precipitously.

Alix had just about finished cleaning up all the mess
Blanche had made, when Jennie arrived. Finding her
friend dishevelled and angry, she asked immediately,
'What's wrong?'

Alix rubbed the back of a paint-streaked hand over
her perspiring forehead. 'Oh, nothing. Blanche was here,
and she fiddled around with everything and managed
to smear paint all over Robbie's portrait. I got it off.'

Jennie paled. She put down the books she was carrying
on the armchair, and began to take off her gloves

slowly. Abruptly, she demanded, '*Could* she have done it accidentally?'

Alix looked up in surprise. 'How do you mean?'

Jennie looked miserable. 'I mean, was it an accident? Did you see her do it?'

Alix frowned. 'What are you getting at, Jen? I wasn't here when it happened, but she was playing about, squeezing the tubes, before that.' She hesitated, remembering the nature of the paint-streaks on the portrait. 'It was rather odd. If paint had squirted out . . .' She broke off, remembering suddenly that it was Jennie's sister they were discussing.

'It's all right,' Jennie said in a defeated voice. 'I *am* sorry, very sorry, Alix. She—She does things like that.' She looked up, and met Alix's astonished gaze. 'I know she's my sister, but that's why I feel so badly about it. When we were small children, you know, she'd always destroy anything I did, Plasticine models, sand-castles, anything. Sometimes she still does the same sort of thing. Some weeks ago, I was working on an essay, and I left it on my desk. When I came back, she'd spilt ink over it. *That* was an accident, she claimed. And I'm sure she tore some pages out of my books. She denied it, but no one else . . .' Jennie shook her head. 'I shouldn't have told you, but if she's going to start behaving like this in other people's houses . . .'

'Have you mentioned this to your mother?' Alix asked hesitantly.

Jennie gave her a look that spoke volumes. Blanche was Maisie Frobisher's idea of how a young girl should be, and Maisie's hope for the future. Any criticism would have been vehemently rejected. Very quietly, Jennie said, 'I think Blanche is—ill.'

A chilly little silence fell in which a sudden flurry of raindrops pattered against the skylight. It had been growing darker as they talked, and now the light was too poor to work by. Alix took off her painting-smock and hung it carefully on the hook behind the door.

'Do you mean, mentally?' She tried to keep her voice casual. It was such a terrible thing, too terrible to contemplate, but when she saw the misery in Jennie's face, she knew she meant exactly that.

'I don't mean she's *mad*,' Jennie said hastily. 'Only— Only in some ways she's like two people, not one person. Two minds in one head. You know she can be charming. Then, without warning, she can be totally different, spiteful and vindictive.' Jennie smiled a little sadly. 'I know if no one marries Blanche, I'll end up having to look after her. She couldn't look after herself, you know.' Calmly, she went on, 'Mother can't understand academic women, of course. She thinks I'm unfeminine. But, the other day, she said she supposed if I went to Oxford I might be able to get a really well paid job afterwards, and "help out". Keep the whole family, was what she meant.'

'You have a right to a life of your own!' Alix protested.

Jennie shook her long brown hair. 'No, I haven't. I've Mother and Blanche to look after. I'll always have Mother and Blanche to look after.'

'But supposing you want to get married?'

Jennie laughed. 'I'm not marriageable—ask Mother!' She stopped laughing. 'But it's especially horrible that Blanche spoiled Robbie's portrait,' she said soberly.

'It's not spoiled,' Alix assured her truthfully. How to spoil something already flawed? The whole portrait was a tribute to a monumental mistake.

A thick, swirling, malicious fog had settled over the area and kept them grounded for two whole days. They all hated it. Enforced inactivity chafed at a man's nerves and manifested itself in a variety of ways. All of them tended to grow short-tempered and critical, which led to quarrels and general discord, so no one was very happy on this particular morning.

Robbie and Jake had commandeered the two chairs at either side of the smoky iron stove which heated the Mess. Robbie was crouched over a writing-pad balanced on his knee, writing a slow, careful letter to Alix. Jake seemed to be asleep, his long legs stretched out, making it necessary for other people to walk round or step over his feet.

Finally someone did trip over his outstretched feet and cursed him roundly. Jake woke up and moved. He glanced at Robbie and stretched his arms above his head. 'Haven't you finished that letter yet?'

'I've written everything I can think of. Now I'm down to "today it's very foggy" . . .'

'Sounds a hell of a love-letter to me,' Jake said critically.

'May be it isn't one,' Robbie muttered briefly. He closed the writing-pad with a snap. 'It's all over and finished, you know. She just can't bring herself to tell me, let alone to break off the engagement. I've known it for ages. I ought to have made it easier for her to break away, but I kept thinking we could sort things out somehow. Well, we couldn't. When I go home next, I'll have to offer to release her from her promise. I should have done it on this leave. But I didn't want to let go.'

Jake stirred slightly in his chair. 'When this war is over . . .'

'It's never going to be damn well over!' Robbie interrupted fiercely. 'It goes on and on for ever, like one of those fiendish punishments the old Greek gods used to dream up on Olympus when they had it in for mankind.'

'Heck, you can't do it!' Jake exploded. 'Suppose you're wrong about Alix? If you offer to let her break the engagement, it's the same as telling her to break it. It's the same as breaking it yourself. It's saying you don't want to marry her any more. You can't do that to *her* . . .' He seemed to realise that his voice was growing louder and more forceful, and fell silent.

'Something's got to happen,' Robbie said obstinately. 'It can't go on like this. Anyhow, it's not as though I'm leaving her alone, without support. She'll be all right. She'll marry that stuffed-shirt cousin of hers, Gerard.'

'No!' Jake exclaimed vehemently, and drew in his breath. 'I mean, just think about it, will you? You owe her better than that.'

'I do care about her, you know!' Robbie said defiantly. 'You needn't try and make me sound like a prize cad!'

'I'm not trying to do any such thing. But you're such a damn idiot, you don't seem to realise . . .' Jake broke off. 'You'll end up like me, with nothing to go back to after the war.'

Robbie snorted. 'You'll go back to making money!' He glanced curiously at the man next to him. 'What *will* you do, after the war, anyway? When you go back to Canada.'

'Start a passenger-carrying air company,' Jake said calmly. 'The railroad has had its day. People will want to fly from place to place.'

Robbie expelled his breath in a long, low hiss. 'You think on the grand scale! You ought to be back at HQ with the ruddy generals.' But a new note had entered his voice, despite the banter, akin to envy. 'You fellows who know how to get into things which make money, you'll always be all right. I wish I knew how you did it,' he concluded, a little sullenly.

'It's called "work".'

'Not my style. If I do marry Alix, we'll have to live off her money. I haven't got any. That pompous ass, Gerard, thinks I'm a fortune-hunter, you know.'

'Are you?' Jake asked mildly, but with an uncomfortably direct look at his companion.

'I told you I care about her!' Robbie snapped. Resentfully, he added, 'It would have been nice, though, to end up with a wealthy wife.' He leaned back lazily, and an impudent grin spread across his attractive, boyish countenance. He looked younger than his twenty-six years.

Jake thought, 'The women feel sorry for him. He calls up the maternal instinct. Even Alix fell for it.'

Something in Jake's face must have warned Robbie, because he burst out aggressively. 'It's not a crime! You needn't scowl at me like that. People do marry for money, you know, all the time. Alix is a fine girl, beautiful, talented, and rich. In heaven's name, you can't blame me for trying to hold on to all that if I could! But at least give me credit for knowing when I'm beaten, and let me retire gracefully!'

Jake contemplated him, thinking, 'You miserable little parasite, perhaps she would be better off without you, at that!' After he had thought this, he was sorry, because he liked Robbie and got along well with him. And if Robbie—with any faults he might have—was what Alix wanted, then Jake was not going to let Robbie fail her. A quarrel now wouldn't help matters. He jumped up out of his chair and went to peer through one of the windows. 'It's clearing,' he said unexpectedly. 'I'm going up, to take a look around.'

'I'll come with you as your observer,' Robbie offered.

'No need, I don't need a chaperon!' the man by the window retorted brusquely.

'Perhaps you do,' Robbie argued. 'Don't pitch into me, if I tell you that you should see the M.O.'

'I'm perfectly fit!' Jake's grey eyes glittered at him.

Robbie held up a placating hand. 'All right, you're fit. But your concentration is shot to pieces. Look, you're not the only one . . .'

Struggling into his heavy leather flying gear, Jake muttered, 'Shut up, can't you? I don't need a nursemaid.

Stay there and finish your goddam letter. I won't be gone long.'

As he strode out towards the hangars, he knew Robbie was right in one respect, anyway. He wasn't as sharp as a man needed to be, up there in the air. He was too old for this life, thirty-four now. They all looked upon him as an old man, and sometimes, recently, he felt it. He knew how it had come about. He was dog-tired, so tired that he could no longer relax or sleep properly, just cat-nap, half his senses always on the alert, like a jungle beast. That's what war did to a man. It turned him into a creature of the jungle. He began to think and act like an animal. Jake's own mental and physical exhaustion were the result of two years' operational combat flying. It had taken a pitiless toll of him, consisting, as it did, of too much flying in icy temperatures, the pressure of altitude in open cockpits, oxygen shortage, combat fatigue and shock—life in a theatre of war.

As the machine climbed above the cloud, he began to think about Alix. It wasn't any of his business, but Robbie ought not to talk of ditching her like that, even if it was all dressed up in fancy talk of 'releasing her from her promise'. But if Robbie were right, and Alix did secretly want to be free? Alix, free . . . Even if she were, it would make no difference, not now.

Jake's mouth set tightly and he leaned forward and tapped the compass. Damn thing was stuck again. He craned his neck over the side of the cockpit and looked for landmarks below: a main road, a railway line, anything. All he saw was a mish-mash of intersecting trenches, some abandoned, some moving like ant-heaps. There were some trucks travelling single file on some sort of road down there and he must still be over Allied lines. He hadn't been flying long enough to have passed over No-man's-land.

He was beginning to experience the sensation of

release flying always brought him. Despite that, he felt
his mind beginning to drift again and pulled himself
back to the present with a determined jerk. He *was*
tired, mentally ragged, slow in his reactions, and ought
to see the M.O., as Robbie had suggested. If he hadn't
been so angry with Robbie over Alix, he might even
have listened to him. But he had a fear of being
grounded, and that fear kept him from confessing his
weakness. When he couldn't fly, unused energy seemed
to be bottled up inside him. Unable to get out, it worked
away, wearing him out from within. In the past he'd
got rid of some of it by going out and picking up some
girl, those brief, bought-and-paid-for amorous encoun-
ters acting as a kind of safety valve. But lately . . .'

The biplane banked and soared, and the pilot forgot
everything in the sheer thrill of flying. The air currents
played on the landing wires so that they vibrated like
harp-strings and sang, serenading him with a strange,
ethereal music full of discords and unexpected
harmonies. So long as he could fly. Nothing else
mattered, so long as he had that. If ever the day came
when he could no longer fly . . .

Jake pushed away this thought. Gradually, from out
of his subconscious, Alix emerged to occupy his mind
again. He tried to push the image away, but it insisted
on returning, Alix with her crown of auburn hair and
eyes which smouldered at him when he made her angry—
which it seemed he habitually did. But not always.
There was a memory, too, of her slim, pliant body in
his arms . . . What wouldn't he give to hold her like
that again.

The image and the feelings it inspired vanished
suddenly and were replaced by a prickling of the hair
on the nape of his neck, some sixth sense warning of
danger. He looked quickly around. Good God! He must
have been falling asleep. There they were, just below
him, a whole formation of Albatrosses, more than

obvious with great black crosses painted everywhere—and he hadn't spotted them! He wheeled away hastily, making for the nearest cloud cover.

But at least one of the German pilots had spotted *him*. He peeled off from his companions and came in pursuit, seeking sport and an individual confrontation. For some minutes they manoeuvred round, each seeking to gain an advantage over the foe, chasing in and out of the clouds. Then, just as suddenly, the Albatross was gone.

Although Jake circled warily for a while, the Hun had definitely taken himself off and rejoined his pals. Perhaps he had just got bored, but it was more likely, he knew, that the formation of Albatrosses had some specific objective and had had no time for him, contenting themselves with having driven him off. He was more worried about those German fighters than he liked to admit. They had been cruising along so serenely—as if they knew they were in their own airspace.

A sudden dull thud echoed in Jake's ear and his machine bucked like a rodeo bronco. Then it did it again. The 'Archie' was coming up all around, and any lingering doubts he'd had about where he was were dispelled. He was lost, and over enemy territory—that's where he was! There was a sharp crack as something hit the instrument panel. Altimeter and inclinometer leapt wildly and then stuck. He didn't know where he was, how high he was—or even if he was flying level. A giant hand seemed to reach out, grab him physically and shake him, and he knew he'd been hit, somewhere near the hip-joint, probably. As often with serious injury, the initial reaction was numbness rather than pain.

He had time to be thankful that Robbie wasn't with him, because Alix waited for Robbie. No one, thank God, waited for *him*.

Then he was hurtling down, bracing himself for the

impact and the final darkness. At that moment he
smelled the fuel. Looking down, he saw it, leaking from
the holed tank and splashing round his flying boots. He
began to pray then, as he had not done since his mother
died. He whispered the words aloud. 'Please, dear God,
let it be immediate. Don't let me burn . . .'

It was one of those long, breathless, late summer days.
Alix had been all morning in the garden, painting a
watercolour of the house. She was disturbed by the
maid coming across the lawn to her.

'Lunch will be served in a quarter of an hour, Miss
Alexandra, and the post come, so I brought it out.'
Jessie had recognised Robbie's handwriting and
produced the letter almost surreptitiously, as if she
arranged a forbidden tryst. She was of a romantic
disposition, an avid read of the works of Ethel M. Dell,
and she thought young Captain Harris 'ever such a nice
gentleman'.

'Thank you, Jessie,' Alix said with a smile, setting
down her brush. She tore open the envelope and pulled
out the sheets covered with Robbie's erratic scrawl. The
shock came at the beginning of the second sheet.

. . . Jake Sherwood has been missing a week, and
we have to suppose he was shot down. Jake was a
fine pilot and would have nursed his machine home
somehow if he could have done so. Equally, had he
ditched safely, he would have made his way back to
base by hook or by crook. In fact, he was a fine
man, and a good friend, and I shall miss him.
'Gladiator, make no friend of gladiator!' as the old
Romans rightly said. We seem to have lost so many
good fellows. I know you didn't care for Jake when
you met him in London, but if he was a rough
diamond, he was a thoroughly reliable comrade-in-
arms, and someone who had given up a great deal
of personal success in order to come over here and

fight. Everyone here is very down in the mouth about
his loss . . .

Alix folded the letter carefully and put it into the
pocket of her painting-smock without reading to the
end. She could finish it later. Automatically she rinsed
her brushes and closed up her paint-pots. The garden
colours, so bright in the sunshine a moment before,
seemed to have grown suddenly dull in hue, as if a
cloud had appeared and passed before the sun, which
had suddenly lost its brilliance, up there in an empty
sky.

They all loved the sky, the flying men. Jake as well
as any of them, she supposed. And, in the end, their
true love claimed them. .

To sit through lunch was agony. Gerard was home,
which was unusual at lunchtime. He leaned over the
table and whispered, 'Everything is all right, old girl,
isn't it?'

'Everything's all right,' she replied in a flat voice,
because that was easier than trying to explain. Explain
what? A passing acquaintance, a man she scarcely knew,
someone she had nothing in common with and whose
manner and words had confused her, would henceforth
be no more than one more gilt name on a roll of honour
somewhere. Did anyone mourn him? From what he had
said to her, it had seemed he had had no family. Yet
the death of this stranger made her feel as though some
part of her had been wrenched out and had gone down
with him.

After lunch, wanting to get out of the house, she
walked over to the Frobishers'.

Unfortunately Jennie was absent, assisting Miss Emma
Frobisher, but Maisie Frobisher and Blanche were at
home, engaged in cutting short the hems of old dresses
to make them look like the new fashions. They bundled
the needlework away as the one slatternly maid employed
in the house showed Alix into the 'best parlour', as Mrs

Frobisher insisted on calling the drawing-room.

It was an overcrowded little room, upholstered in fading chintz and crammed with an incongruous assortment of ornaments. There were quite a few good Chelsea pieces, not one of them quite whole. Each had a crack or a chip, or a mended limb. There were also a number of modern, inexpensive knick-knacks, of crude manufacture and sentimental design. These last were Maisie Frobisher's own choice. The Chelsea pieces had belonged to her husband's mother, and Maisie kept them on display—even though she privately thought them old-fashioned—because she knew they were the right kind of thing to have about the place.

Patting her henna-ed curls and fiddling nervously with the paste pearls about her neck, Maisie assured Alix that Jennie wouldn't be long, and begged her to stay to tea. Blanche sat on one side and watched carefully. She looked very like a lifesize animated version of one of the Chelsea figures, with her retroussé nose and voluptuous pouting lips, her flawless porcelain complexion and her overall air of knowing innocence, like a naughty child. Like a wilful, bad child, she was watching Alix warily. Some weeks had passed since her attempt to spoil Robbie's portrait, but she could not be sure whether it had yet been forgotten or forgiven. She was wondering whether she had 'got away with it'—or whether Alix might mention the incident before her mother. Mrs Frobisher was quick to dismiss such tales of Blanche's spite from Jennie, but from Miss Morrell, such a story could not have been ignored.

'She's afraid I'm going to tell tales,' Alix thought, seeing the expression on Blanche's face. 'Silly girl.' Her eye fell on an open magazine which lay on the threadbare sofa beside her, the sort of pictorial magazine that reported society events and gossip, the kind of thing which fascinated Maisie Frobisher. It was an old copy, and Alix fancied she had seen it before. Indeed, she *knew* she had seen it before, because there, right in the centre of the right-hand page and looking straight up at her, was a photograph of the woman in the taxi.

'I knew I'd seen her picture!' Alix thought triumphantly. The woman obviously liked furs, for here she was pictured in an expensive blue fox stole worn over a tailored costume. Beneath the elaborately trimmed hat, the eyes stared out, hard, knowledgeable, mascara-lined. She read the caption to the photograph: 'Mrs Henry Lyndhurst, widow of the discoverer and manufacturer of Lyndhurst's Health Tonic, was among the guests at a charity bazaar in aid of the war effort . . .'

'What are you looking at, Alix?' Blanche's sweetly chiming tones asked.

'Oh, nothing. Only this photograph, which caught my eye,' Alix said hastily.

'Which one is that, then, dearie?' asked Maisie Frobisher with interest. 'Oh, that's Mrs Lyndhurst, isn't it? Her husband was a millionaire, you know. Of course, he wasn't her first husband. Her first was a gambler, and shot himself . . . Ever such a scandal, it was. I remember it; it was in the papers. He was accused of cheating, you see. Anyway, after that, she married Henry Lyndhurst. He was already quite an old man, and being married to her just about finished him off!' added Maisie with a cheerful vulgarity which would have had Mrs Daventry freezing like ice.

For once, Alix was obscurely grateful both for Maisie's obsession with the lives and doings of the rich, and with her garrulous chatter, which meant she had to do nothing but sit and listen. As Maisie's voice flowed on, she tried to concentrate on it and not to keep thinking of that falling aeroplane, the tearing of materials and crack of wood, the comrades back at the base, staring up into the empty sky and knowing that one more of their number had flown away into the clouds never to return.

'She'll be my age,' said Maisie unexpectedly, still pursuing the topic of Mrs Lyndhurst. 'I knew her first hubby, you see. Well, I didn't exactly know him, but he used to come backstage and chat up the girls. I'm talking of when I was in the theatre.' Her thin, white hands fluttered moth-like over her tinted hair.

Blanche shifted uneasily on her chair, but Maisie was not to be stopped. 'I don't think he was much good.' She paused, and a shadow passed over her faded looks, preserved by artificial aids into a travesty of their youthful prettiness. Neither had the stage-door johnnie she had married proved 'much good'. What man ever was? 'That's how it was in those days,' she said aloud, obscurely. She brightened. 'Seen my album, have you?'

'Mother!' Blanche began sharply, but Mrs Frobisher had already gone to the bureau and produced a green leather scrap-album.

She seated herself by Alix and began to turn the pages. 'This is me, just eighteen. Pretty, wasn't I?'

'Yes, very,' Alix agreed, looking at the gaiety girl with the wasp waist, tilted Grecian bend stance and mass of curling hair. But she was thinking that Mrs Lyndhurst was probably forty-three or four, a little older than Alix had judged from that brief glimpse through an open taxi door. A wealthy widow, with a liking for younger men.

'Here's my name on the programme,' added Mrs Frobisher proudly. 'Not every girl got her name on the programme, I can tell you. The chorus was just the chorus. But this is me, in the small print, "With Miss Maisie Labelle". Of course, my name wasn't really Labelle. It was Fitchett. But you couldn't go on the stage with a name like Maisie Fitchett, so Maisie Labelle I became! It's French, you know, and means "the beautiful". The stage manager thought it up.' She

beamed proudly at the yellowed programme and
smoothed it out with her thin fingers on which the rings,
which were so obviously coloured glass, twinkled.

'I'm sure Alix doesn't want to know all that, Mother!'
Blanche said loudly.

'Please, it's very interesting,' Alix protested, truthfully
but without enthusiasm. The album encapsulated the
'naughty nineties' and its vibrant, rakish theatre life.
She would have liked to study it in detail, but not now.
Not with the weight of Robbie's letter on her heart.

Mrs Frobisher closed the album regretfully. 'Of course,
you wouldn't understand what it was like, Alix dear. I
mean, born into money, like you were. When I was
fourteen years old I worked trimming hats, ten, twelve
hours a day. If the work was there, you stayed in the
shop till it was done. And if it wasn't there, you didn't
get paid, and you went hungry!'

At that moment Jennie's voice was heard in the hall,
and Blanche sighed audibly in relief. Mrs Frobisher
returned the album to the bureau a little sadly. Jennie
came in and greeted them all. She looked tired and
exasperated, though her eyes lit up with pleasure at the
sight of Alix sitting on the worn old sofa.

'You look all in, Jen,' Alix said in concern. 'I could
have come and helped with whatever it was.'

'Oh, Aunt Emma likes to have Jennie around,' said
Mrs Frobisher briefly. 'To my mind, the old girl is half
crazy—all that women's rights and I don't know what.
What woman ever had any rights, I'd like to know? It's
a man's world, this is. You girls will find that out, mark
my words.'

'We've won the right to vote, to be members of
parliament!' Jennie protested, flushing.

'You've won nothing!' Maisie told her daughter
fiercely. 'I've seen your suffragette ladies marching with
their banners! All women with money and time to go
off and take part in such nonsense. Who's cooking the

old man's dinner and minding the baby while they're marching? Some other poor devil of a woman who hasn't got time to think about her rights! Those women haven't *won* the vote. They were given it by men who have so much they don't mind losing a bit. But you go down Whitechapel way and look about you. If a woman there was to tell her man out loud in front of everyone she was his equal or his better, he'd black her eye. And why? Because he doesn't have anything to give! All he's got is his pride and his right to be king of the roost. He's not going to let any woman take that away from him. Old Emma knows a lot of things, but she don't know anything about men! When a man's got nothing else, he's only got his *pride*, you remember that!'

'I just wish Aunt Emma weren't so enthusiastic,' Jennie explained with a rueful grin.

'Why should you complain?' Blanche said sulkily. 'Look what she's doing for *you*!'

Her mother gave her a warning glance, and Blanche felt silent. But Miss Frobisher's refusal to help Blanche had obviously not been forgotten or forgiven, and Alix realised that Blanche, beneath that china doll exterior, nurtured a burning resentment.

Tea was served by the slatternly maid. The tablecloth was darned and two of the cups had handles stuck on with glue. The cake had obviously been made 'to last the week' and was dry and crumbly, and the tea was of the grade sold by grocers as 'kitchen'.

It was with gratitude that Alix saw the tea-things cleared at last by the maid, by now even more untidy and slapdash, clashing all the china together so that it was a wonder any of it was whole. But she and Jennie were able to retire to a quiet corner, and she was able to tell her what she had not told Mrs Frobisher and Blanche, that Jake was missing and presumed killed.

Jennie was silent for a while. 'It's always terrible news,' she said at last quietly. 'I am sorry—even though he was a frightening man.'

'Frightening?' Alix exclaimed in surprise.

Jennie flushed. 'Yes, there was so much energy in him, seething like water boiling in a pot, and he was—ruthless. Didn't he alarm you?'

'No,' Alix said slowly, 'he didn't alarm me. At first, he annoyed me, because he was so sure of himself and so rude. Now, I think that was because he was a stranger, and a little shy, and we were none of us very nice to him. At the end, I—I rather liked him. I wish I could have known him better.' She looked up and caught Jennie's astonished expression. 'Of course,' she blurted out, 'being posted as missing, presumed dead, isn't quite the same as people *knowing*, for sure . . . but they all suppose he must be . . .'

'He was a dangerous man!' Jennie said fiercely. 'And if you were truly beginning to like him, Alix, then I'm glad he's dead. I hope he never comes back—not into your life, ever!'

CHAPTER SIX

JAKE WAS enveloped in a velvet blackness. He felt that he was buried alive, suffocating, trapped. Sometimes the blackness was split, and he saw a picture, startlingly clear. The pictures were unconnected, patches of animation piercing the veil of encroaching oblivion, and meant nothing—except pain. They were accompanied by a pain such as he had never experienced before, and he began to dread them, those moments of clarity, because they brought back that pain again. He wished that whoever or whatever was causing this would stop doing it, stop waking him up, and let him go to sleep, quietly, where it didn't hurt.

At the same time, something inside him warned him that to go to sleep now would be to sleep for ever. He stood on that shadowy frontier between life and death, and both sides beckoned. If he took a step out into the darkness, it would swallow him up, and he'd never find his way back because there was no return, no way back from that far country.

Then he saw Alix standing on the bright side of the frontier. The sun was shining on her red hair, so that it sparkled with golden lights. She didn't speak, but held out her white hand towards him and begged him with her eyes to hold on tightly to her, and he would be safe, she would drag him back from the lure of the darkness on the other side. But he mustn't let go . . .

Jake surfaced, as from the bottom of a deep, black well, floating to the top like a swimmer in a thick, oily sea. As when a diver rises through the water from some great depth, the sea becomes more and more translucent, so that Jake at last reached daylight and air, and opened his eyes.

A mist of pain still enveloped him, and through it he saw the slender figure of a woman bending over him. He murmured aloud, 'Alix?'

The woman spoke. 'I'm sorry, monsieur. My name is Monique, not Alix.'

In a weak voice, but stubbornly, Jake said, 'I *saw* Alix . . .'

The woman caught her breath. She bent her head close to him and urged, 'Monsieur, you must try and listen, try and understand what I say. Do you hear me?'

'Yes . . .' he muttered crossly, because he felt she had somehow stolen Alix away.

'Will you let go of my hand, monsieur? You hold it so tightly, you hurt my fingers.'

He was awake now, and conscious. He obeyed her with a little difficulty, managing to relax his grip. She withdrew her hand, but patted his comfortingly before she took it away completely. He could see her now, in a hazy way. She had dark hair. She wasn't Alix, and a bitter disappointment touched him. He shifted his position, and immediately such a shaft of agony transfixed his body that he groaned aloud, and the woman exclaimed, 'Don't try and move!'

A myriad dancing lights whirled before his eyes and gradually dispersed. Reason and training were taking over. He was badly hurt, and mustn't move. Jake became aware of a wetness, warm and unpleasant, and knew he was lying in his own blood.

The woman saw his eyes clear again, and bent forward. 'You are safe here. The Germans won't find you. But I must get you a doctor.'

'No!' Jake croaked. Despite the pain and dancing stars, he put out his hand and grasped her wrist. Contact with a doctor meant risk of discovery. Discovery meant a prisoner-of-war camp, probably in Germany. He was drifting further away, further from Alix.

'It's unavoidable, monsieur, but I know a man. He's an old man, but a good doctor and won't betray us. Try and rest. I've sent someone to fetch him.'

Later the doctor came. By then, Jake had fought his way to a tenuous consciousness because he wanted to know what they were going to do with him. Weak and immobilised as he was, they could do what they liked and he couldn't stop them. But he could protest, and above all, he had to know. The consciousness kept threatening to elude him, but now he knew how to stay awake. All he had to do was to move, just a little. Then the pain came back, and that woke him up all right. It was agony, but it was the price he had to pay. Every time that sea of blackness welled up he tried to wriggle his toes, and all hell broke loose in his body and his brain. It did the trick.

The doctor said his name was Berthier. He examined him, apologising courteously for hurting his patient.

Jake whispered, 'My legs are still there?'

He knew well enough that legs hurting didn't mean legs still attached to the body. He'd seen plenty of men in hospital with amputated limbs, who complained of pain and even itching in limbs which were no longer there.

Berthier understood and said soothingly, 'Yes, yes, monsieur!'

Afterwards, Jake heard Berthier and the woman discussing him softly in whispers, of which isolated, disjointed fragments penetrated the throbbing pain set up by the doctor's careful probing of the wound.

'. . . a hospital . . . impossible . . . I must operate, or he will die . . .'

'Like hell I will!' thought Jake obstinately. But he knew that he was already dying as he lay there, the blood seeping out of him, and unless something reversed

the process, the moment would come when even pain
couldn't drag him back from that seductive dark land,
waiting for him out there.

Berthier came and bent close to Jake's ear. Still
unfailingly courteous, he explained what Jake already
knew. He added more, and then came to the deciding
point. 'We dare not take you to a hospital. Nearly all,
even the French civilian ones, contain German wounded.
To hide you in one for a long time would be far too
risky. Of course, if you wish to be taken to the Germans,
they will give you hospital treatment, but as a
prisoner . . .'

'No!' Jake snarled at him.

'The alternative, monsieur, is that I operate—here. I
have performed such operations, but not for a great
many years. I have not good facilities here, and above
all,' he paused, 'I have no anaesthetics. Would you be
able to bear it?' His tone rose anxiously. 'You must
decide quickly. You lose blood—soon you will be too
weak.'

'Yes,' Jake insisted hoarsely. 'Yes! Do it!'

He didn't want to die. He wanted to live and see Alix
again, somehow, somewhere, some day. No price was
too high.

After that, they poured a great deal of brandy down
him. It was probably a very good brandy, but he was
in no state to appreciate it. It made him feel muzzy and
slightly sick. He couldn't understand what they said any
more, and he couldn't speak to them coherently, but
mumbled and muttered nonsense. He was back in that
muddled half-world, but he knew that if only he could
find Alix in there somewhere, hiding amongst the strange
shapes and objects conjured up by his bemused brain,
it would all be all right.

They lifted him up now, and carried him down some
stairs and into another room. It caused him so much
pain that there wasn't a place for anything else. He was

wrapped up in his suffering, as in a blanket. He was very drunk, and the smell of brandy suffused the atmosphere. When the doctor began his task, it seemed to Jake, in his delirium, that he heard someone screaming, and then he realised that it was his own voice shrieking as the knife cut through the mutilated tangle of muscle and flesh. Very faintly, in the distance, a voice exclaimed, 'Watch out, he's going—we'll lose him!'

He wanted to shout at them, 'No!' But in his agony he cried out just once, desperately, '*Alix . . .*' before he passed mercifully into unconsciousness.

The war was drawing to a close, but without diminishing in savagery or lessening its demand for sacrifices of blood. Among the last victims it claimed Philip Harris, who imprudently put up his head above a trench and was picked off by a sniper in a German dugout less than a stone's throw away. But in November it really was truly over. The guns fell silent, and the red glow faded on the horizons of northern France as the fires which had burned for four long years flickered and were finally extinguished.

Robbie came home, but not for another year. At first he served with the allied forces occupying Germany, and then he was posted in the North of England. After still more delay in his demobilisation, he eventually returned, in a civilian suit, towards Christmas 1919.

His homecoming was naturally overshadowed by the loss of his brother, for whom a bright new plaque had been cemented on the wall of the local parish church. He came back, too, to a general feeling of lassitude and a curious sense of 'let-down', because a way of life which had lasted four years and in which war had dominated the tiniest facet of daily living had disappeared, and people, bewildered and disoriented, groped their way back to normality.

Besides which, he had no job, although Lady Harris,

by dint of lobbying anyone of influence she knew, had managed to secure him the modest offer of a clerical post in the accounts department of a company manufacturing—of all things, Robbie said in disgust—a patent health food. He was not anxious to accept the post, and hoped something better would turn up.

The good resolution he had entertained in France and discussed with Jake, of how he would offer to release Alix from her promise, had long since been abandoned. Frankly, from his point of view, such a thing would be highly impractical now. It was all very well a fellow offering to do the decent thing, if he had his own money. Robbie considered ruefully that he hadn't 'a bean'. He needed Alix's money, at least until something turned up to enable him to make his own fortune. With the optimism of his kind, he firmly believed something *would* turn up. With equal sang-froid, he envisaged them fairly happily married. Why not, for pity's sake? They'd had their sticky moments during a courtship unnaturally prolonged by war, but that was the fault of the war, not of either of them. After all, he cared about her more than he'd ever cared about any other girl, and he didn't see why she shouldn't care about him. It wasn't as though there were anyone else. Robbie considered and discounted Gerard. Gerry Daventry was a good fellow, but a crashing bore, and no girl in her right mind, let alone someone like Alix, would possibly prefer Gerard to him—so Robbie concluded with little false modesty. Hell, he was twenty-eight, physically fit, had come out of the war with a pretty good record . . . It wasn't as though he was offering her nothing in return.

He had been home a little over a month, and they were into the New Year of 1920. It had snowed, and he and Alix had been out for a walk on the common. The shouts of children filled the crisp air as they cavorted about in the snow, red-faced and exhilarated. Watching them, Alix remembered laughing children running from abandoned swings in a park, and glanced at Robbie. She had to tell him, she had to tell him now, today. For too long she had pretended the moment wasn't right, but listening to him talking now optimistically of the future, their future, she knew she dare not delay a day longer. She had to tell him she wanted to break off the engagement. If she left it any longer, it would be too late and she would have to go through with the marriage. It was a thought that every fibre of her being rejected.

Robbie, chattering cheerfully, did not seem to notice how silent she was as she trudged through the snow layer beside him. At last, unable to bear it any longer, Alix stopped abruptly in the middle of a flat patch of unbroken snow, and said loudly, 'Robbie, please! I've *got* to tell you something.'

A sober, wary look entered his blue eyes as he surveyed her pale face, ghost-white and tense beneath her tam-o'-shanter beret, which she had pulled down over her red hair against the cold.

'I wanted to tell you before,' Alix began, her misery echoing in her voice, 'and I have to tell you now. I—I can't marry you. I'm *sorry*. I've known it some time, but during the war, when you were in such danger, I couldn't tell you. All this past year, I've waited for an opportunity, but opportunities for things like this don't come, you have to make them. There's no easy way I can tell you, and it was wrong of me to put it off for so long. If I've hurt you, Robbie, I never meant to. It's just—just impossible. Please try and understand . . .' Her emerald eyes gazed up at him, begging him to try.

A dull flush crossed his face, and he thrust his hands into his pockets and hunched his shoulders, as flakes of snow fluttered down on them, the cards of his cardboard castle tumbling about his ears. To his eternal credit, he rallied and took it well. She was clearly very upset and trying not to cry, and he owed it to her not to make things worse. He would have argued with her if he'd thought there was half a chance, but one look at those despairing green eyes told him he'd missed his opportunity. The arguing should have been done long ago. There was a time he might have won the battle—but it was long gone by.

'If I said it knocked me all of a heap,' he told her wryly, 'it would hardly be true. I've thought, for a long time, you weren't keen. Ever since that last party we had here, when Phil and I were home on leave together, and Jake Sherwood came—do you remember? It was all going wrong then, wasn't it?' Alix nodded dumbly. 'You know, it's odd,' he mused. 'Phil's dead, Jake, too . . . I'm the only one of those who were in uniform that night to come back. I don't know whether they weren't lucky, Phil and Jake, in their way. Things aren't, well, turning out as we all thought they would do, after the war, are they?'

'Oh, Robbie!' she exclaimed wretchedly. 'I'm sorry—but I can't help how I feel.'

'I'm not blaming you, Alix,' he said quickly. 'I didn't mean that. I just meant, well, we were all so optimistic. But life seems to have become empty, somehow. It sounds strange, but I *miss* the war. I—I was somebody, then.' He shrugged. 'Mother grieves over Phil. He was always her favourite.'

Inwardly, he was thinking, 'Damn—I shall have to take that wretched job, now. If we could have married, Alix's money would have tided me over for a bit until something better came along. Oh, well . . .' He was still young, and there were other girls. Not nearly so good-looking, of course, or desirable. But there must be a plain one somewhere, with a bit of money, who'd be only too willing—and something would turn up.

They walked home slowly past the laughing, snowballing children and barking dogs. At the gate,

Robbie turned to her and asked, as it occurred to him to do for the first time, 'What will *you* do now, Alix? Now that you're free of me. Will you marry poor old Gerard?'

'No,' Alix said quietly. 'I'm not going to marry anyone, now.'

'You'll have to make some decision,' Robbie told her. He grinned and shook his head. 'I can't see you accepting genteel spinsterhood with nothing but a bevy of cats for company!'

Alix broke the news to Mrs Daventry and to Gerard that evening. Gerard did not trouble to hide his relief. 'I never cared for the fellow, although I'd have accepted him for your sake, Alix. I dare say there's no real harm in him, and he's got a fine war record, but the fact is, the fellow is a born sponger. Flying about in the sky and playing ducks and drakes with his and the other fellow's life—that suited him fine. But a steady job, nine to five? No. He doesn't have it in him.'

But Mrs Daventry, for the first time in her life, came into open and forceful conflict with her son and took quite the opposite point of view.

'How could you *do* it, Alix? How could you behave like this to that poor boy? After all he's been through! How could you just throw him over? You have behaved extremely badly, and I hardly know how to express my feelings adequately.' Her bosom heaved in agitation. 'I am ashamed of you, and I feel ashamed myself. I brought you up, or thought I had done so, to know your duty. Your duty now was clearly, *quite* clearly, to stand by Robert Harris. I can hardly find it in myself to forgive you.'

Alix paled before this unexpected onslaught. 'You're quite unjust, Aunt Ethel! Do you think I did this lightly? Robbie is twenty-eight and *not* a boy, and he understands quite well that I haven't "thrown him over". I've wanted to tell him for the past year, but I couldn't find the right moment. All I have done now is to speak openly of something we both already knew.'

Mrs Daventry changed tack. 'Very well,' she said stiffly. 'But you are nearly twenty-six yourself, and if you imagine that you will one day be married, you might consider that there are not so many eligible men to be had now. Have you thought of that? You have been very selfish, and you have been foolish.'

Mrs Daventry was doing no more than state something which had become painfully obvious to all. As the joyous celebrations of victory died away, a whole generation of young middle-class women looked at one another, and the unspoken question in their eyes, was, 'What now?'

What indeed, for them? They had been brought up to marry, run a home, to be the devoted wife at the shoulder of a successful husband. They did not know how to work, and were untrained for any profession. They had sat out the war waiting for the young men to come home—and the young men had tragically not come home. There was no one for them to marry any more, and they had suddenly to rethink their whole lives.

Jennie Frobisher was going up to Oxford. 'I'm the lucky one,' she said soberly, 'because I didn't have anyone to lose, and I was always intending to go to university if I could.'

Harriet Bingley ran away from home and went on the stage. It caused a minor furore and scandal. Mrs Bingley announced gloomily that she was sure poor Harriet had been obliged to sacrifice her virtue. One knew all about the theatre . . .

Alix, hearing this, reflected that if Harriet's virtue had fallen, it was likely to have done so, long before, to Philip Harris—that same Philip whose body now lay mouldering in a foreign churchyard. Jake, on the other hand, had as far as Alix knew, no resting-place . . . he had simply disappeared.

For them all, 'tomorrow' had disappeared. They had gone beyond tomorrow, into a new world.

But to no one was the harsh reality of the situation more trenchant than to Blanche Frobisher, who heard the news that Alix had broken off her engagement to Robert Harris with dismay, bordering on panic. Wildly, she turned on her sister.

'Don't you understand? Can't you see what it means to *me*? Now that Alix has thrown over Robbie, she'll probably marry Gerard. He's her cousin, and you know how it is in families like that! But what am I to do? You'll come down from Oxford and have a brilliant career and probably end up as a lady member of parliament, now that women are to go into parliament. Alix has her own money, *and* Gerard. What about me? What am I to do? I'm not clever. I haven't got any money. I *have* to get married! It's all I can do! If I don't, I shall stay at home for ever with Mother, getting poorer and poorer, till I'm old and fat and plain and no one cares! Don't you understand?' Her voice broke hysterically, and her pretty, china doll's face was distorted in frustration, rage and fear. She rounded on her sister furiously. 'If Aunt Emma had given me half of what she's spending on *you*, I could find a husband easily. Now Alix will take Gerard, and you have had all the money. It's not fair! You and Alix, between you, have taken everything from me!'

But, unknown to Blanche, Alix had already made her decision and knew what she was going to do. In the spring, she began to make her plans reality. She went up to her attic studio and began to sort through her paints and brushes. The unfinished canvas of Robbie was still there, but would never be finished now. It was a part of her life that was over and done with. She would wrap up the painting and send it over to Lady Harris.

Intent on what she was doing, she had not heard Gerard come in, and was startled to turn and see him watching her. He walked across and sat down beneath the skylight window, looking large, awkward and obstinate. He said, 'You mean to leave, don't you?'

'Yes,' Alix told him, her voice quivering very slightly. 'I'm going to Paris. I'm going to study painting, as I always wanted to do. With luck, if I get some proper training and experience, I might be able to get a job as a commercial artist. I'm not good enough for anything else, no Rembrandt! But I have some talent, and I believe I can make it work for me.'

'You don't need to work,' Gerard said stuffily.

'Yes, I do. I can't just sit here twiddling my thumbs. Even poor Harriet has made it as an actress, so I ought to be able to do something as an artist.'

'I can't stop you, can I?' Gerard said heavily.

'No, Gerry, my mind is made up.' She saw the expression on his honest, plain face, and added in a burst of exasperation, 'I'm not going to the dogs, Gerry, or throwing myself into a life of sin! I mean to *work*.'

Gerard's face reddened. 'Damn it, Alix, you owe me an explanation! Something better than "I want to paint"! I know you, my dear, better than you think. There's something else, something you haven't told Mother, and I doubt very much you've told Harris. But you owe it to me to tell *me*!'

Alix flushed, but put down the brushes in her hand, and said quietly, 'Yes, I do owe it to you, Gerry. The fact is . . .' She hesitated. 'Do you remember Jake Sherwood? The Canadian who came here, and was . . . lost?'

Gerry nodded, but he looked puzzled.

'Jake was a strange person,' she went on slowly. 'He made me realise that I could never marry Robbie. You see, I didn't truly feel as though I *belonged* with Robbie. Jake . . .'

'Are you trying to tell me,' Gerard interrupted with barely concealed anger, 'that you fell head over heels in love with that—that backwoodsman? Well, I suppose he had a wild colonial charm and was a great ladies' man . . .'

'Stop it, Gerry! I'm not saying anything of the sort. I didn't fall in love with him. I just—just felt differently after I knew him. He made me see myself differently, and my relationship to others. He told me something I've never forgotten. He said, "If a man or a woman wants to do a thing, he or she should go right out there and do it!" He was right. I want to paint, and I'm going to do it.'

'I see,' Gerard said, his voice shaking with emotion. 'So, after he'd cast these pearls of homespun wisdom upon the air, he drove off and became a hero. Well, he couldn't fail, could he? The man who had everything! And sealed it all with a glorious death.' He was fighting to control his voice and himself. Alix had never seen him so openly agitated. 'I can't compete with a hero, Alix,' he said at last, more quietly. 'I couldn't have competed with Sherwood when he was alive—and I certainly can't compete with him now that he's dead! That's the trouble with heroes, they're immortal. They're always young, virile, gallant and triumphant. Girls love them when they're alive, and go on loving them after they're dead. A fellow like me, dull, stuck in a law office, has no chance against all that.' He looked down at his hands. 'You never loved me, Alix, except as a cousin. But I . . . You were always very dear to me, and my feelings haven't changed. You're twenty-six. You've a lifetime ahead of you. I don't want you to go off chasing rainbows, because I don't believe there are any crocks of gold at the end of them, only heartbreak. I'm doing well. I'm not a poor man. If you wanted to be a professional artist, I wouldn't object. You do understand what I'm trying to say, don't you. Alix?'

Alix walked over to him and put her hands on his burly shoulders. He looked up at her, and a lump formed in her throat. 'Yes, I do know, Gerry, and I thank you. You're probably the finest person I've ever known. But I couldn't marry you, either. It wouldn't be right, any more than it would be right for me to marry Robbie.'

'You did fall in love with the fellow, didn't you?' Gerard said softly.

'I don't know whether I did, Gerry. I hardly knew him, and most of that time we were either at loggerheads or just sitting silent trying to think of something to say to one another. Perhaps, after all, we never did manage to say any of the right things. I think regretting what you haven't said must always be worse than regretting anything you have said. But don't worry about me. I know I'll be all right.'

'If you need us,' Gerard said 'you'll let us know? I mean, *Paris* . . .' His voice trailed away in disbelief and he hunched his shoulders, a picture of despondency. 'Anything could happen!'

CHAPTER SEVEN

THE PARIS of the early twenties, into which Alix plunged determinedly, vibrated with a feverish life which even the extravagances of the nineties could hardly have equalled. The city burst with people and with ideas. Everyone wanted to forget the four years of horror and the blasted plains of Flanders and Champagne to the north. Women shortened their skirts even more, threw away their corsets and bobbed their hair. Make-up, once the sign of the fast woman, became every woman's mark of sophistication. The restaurants and the cafés of the Champs Elysées were filled with the elegant and the fashionable, all living with an intensity unthought of before, seized by a frenzy of energy and gaiety as they tried desperately to make up for the lost years.

Probably the city had never been more cosmopolitan. Many people were finding their way to France. In Britain, in the wake of the war, prices were high and, after an initial boom, times were getting difficult. For many, it made sound economic sense to go abroad, and why not to France? These new expatriates replaced some noticeable absentees who once would have graced the continental scene. The young Prussian counts and barons, and the English gentlemen sowing their wild oats, these had died in the hell of the trenches. But the Americans came, rich with money from their mighty new industries. And, of course, there were the Russians . . . arriving by the trainload without a penny in their pockets.

Fleeing before the Bolsheviks, they tumbled into the

Paris they remembered from their affluent and secure days. Only now they had no money and were refugees, clinging to a lifestyle they could no longer afford, and maintaining themselves in a dozen ingenious ways. Married men sold their wives' jewellery, and the unmarried ones earned their keep sometimes in the boudoirs of the bored financiers' wives at Neuilly and the Faubourg St-Honoré. Untrained for any work, many of these young Russians knew how to drive a car—so they became taxi-drivers. As most of them were former White cavalry officers, they sent their taxis careering through the traffic with all the dash of a cavalry charge, and being aristocrats, they treated all other road-users and pedestrians with a cheerful scorn. They took a particular delight in making the bourgeoisie jump for its plump lives, and were known to drive round and round with pretty young ladies who unwarily hailed their cabs, while they steered with one hand and attempted to pay gallant addresses to their fares at the same time.

Into the quarter of Montparnasse swarmed the writers of half the globe, to sit in the smoke-filled cafés and discuss the novels they were going to write—and some did write. But Alix made like a homing pigeon for the artists' quarter of Montmartre, atop the steep hill overlooking the smoky city Baron Haussman had laid out for Napoleon III.

She was a little shy at first, believing she might be viewed as an oddity, but she needn't have worried. In that patchwork community of artistic Bohemia, no one was odd. At first she took a room in a modest *pension*, but soon she received the offer of a small flat in a twisting cobbled little alley running off the Place du Tertre. It had two tiny rooms and a dark kitchen and minute lavatory. It had no bath. It crouched at the top of a ramshackle building, above a bakery. The wooden floors sloped, and the walls were papered with a faded, torn flowery paper probably dating from the eighteen-fifties, when Montmartre had been a village to which the pleasure-seekers of Paris came, because being outside the city limits, it escaped the city by-laws. But from the flat's windows could be seen the white Byzantine domes of the basilica of the Sacred Heart, so close it seemed she could stretch out a hand and touch them. It was a little lonelier here than in the *pension*, but she relished its privacy, her own little kingdom.

In the Place du Tertre, aspiring and impecunious artists exhibited their work, hoping to sell to tourists. Alix did not need the money, but she did need to know if anyone would buy her work. So she took her courage in both hands and went down one sunny morning, with three or four views of the district, and managed to sell one. The fillip to her confidence was enormous. After that, she went down from time to time, when she had enough work to display. One morning, having little to put on show, she added in an interior, a view of a room in her flat, which she had set herself to put on canvas one rainy day.

As she sat on her little folding stool, watching the people stroll about looking at the paintings, she became aware that someone was staring at her work. Looking up, she saw a man with the olive skin of the Midi, a shock of wild black hair, a cigarette clamped in his teeth, an expensive hand-tailored suit which he managed to wear with all the elegance of a scarecrow in its cast-offs, and his tie under one ear.

He pointed at the small canvas of the interior. 'You did that?'

'Yes,' Alix admitted, rather embarrassed. 'It's in my flat.'

He put his hand in his pocket, and for one moment she hoped he was going to produce some money to buy it, but instead he took out a small white card and handed it to her. 'I'm an interior designer,' he said. 'I need someone who can paint me an imaginative interior. Come and see me.' With that he was gone.

Alix read the name printed on the card: Paul Daquin. She took it home and stuck it up behind a mirror, but for some reason she was shy of accepting his invitation, and the card stayed there until the autumn.

Now the leaves began to fall on the great boulevards. The children ran shrieking away from their nurses and danced through the red and yellow heaps. The flowers were gone from the beds in the Jardin du Luxembourg and the lovers no longer sat under the trees.

Paris emptied, as the people fled like swallows at the approach of winter, seeking the sun of the South. There was an emptiness, too, in Alix's heart, but work, she believed, would fill it. She took down Paul Dacquin's card from the mirror, and went to his studio.

When she arrived, she thought at first some dreadful accident must have occurred, because pandemonium reigned. Afterwards, she found out that it was always like that. Daquin, in his shirt-sleeves, stood in the middle of the floor, yelling at a typist with bobbed hair and long beads, who screamed back at him and finally threw all the sheets of paper on her desk up the air and stormed out.

Daquin stared at Alix. 'Who are you?' He raised his strongly marked eyebrows in his thin, olive face, which made him look like a painting by El Greco.

Tentatively, she reminded him. It was not possible to say whether or not he remembered. He grabbed her wrist and hauled her unceremoniously into an adjoining office in the middle of which stood a standard lamp. It was, without doubt, the ugliest lamp Alix had ever seen. It had a carved wooden base, picked out in gilt, a peach silk lampshade luridly banded with green velvet, and a gold-tasselled fringe.

'Look at that,' Daquin ordered her.

'I don't like it,' Alix said.

'Chère mademoiselle, I do not require you to like it. It belongs to a fat pig who went into the war a poor man and came out of it a rich one. He has no taste, and too much money. He bought that monstrosity for his mistress. He wants a bedroom designed around it. You can design one for me.'

'But surely . . .' she began in protest.

'My dear Alix, who are we, you and I, struggling artistic souls, to question the whim of a fat bourgeois who wears, mark you, spats! Bring me something by tomorrow.'

She was so angry, and the task seemed so impossible, that she went home, pinned a sheet of paper to a drawing-board and three hours later sat back, looking at something which resembled, if anything, the wilder fancies of the Prince Regent at Brighton.

When she took the design back to Daquin the next day, he was on the telephone. He took the paper, glanced at it, and said, 'It looks like an Arab brothel.'

'I've never been in an Arab brothel!' Alix said coldly.

'I have,' he retorted mildly.

Two evenings later, he appeared without warning at the flat. 'You are a genius! The client is of settler stock from Algeria. It reminded him of his misspent youth, and he loved it. I've come to take you out to dinner.' He smiled at her like a handsome gypsy, his teeth white against his Mediterranean complexion.

After that, she executed several designs for Paul, and he paid her generously. Otherwise he was the most exasperating and impossible man to work with. He was always shouting, and was appallingly rude to his clients. He worked long hours without a break and with no sense of the passage of time. He had to be told forcibly that it was dark and everyone wanted to go home, please. He'd been married once, but, Alix was not surprised to learn, his wife had divorced him. He did not seem to regret her departure. 'She was colour-blind, anyway,' was his one remark on the subject.

But one thing he understood very well. He understood the clientèle for whom he created expensive and lavish interiors of extraordinary vulgarity. Beneath that wild exterior and tactless manner ticked a shrewd business brain. Respectable businessmen bathed in his reflected Bohemian glory, envying him, and society women loved him to insult them.

'*Il couche avec . . .*' the typist said to Alix, with a shrug of her shoulders. 'He sleeps with them. The husbands pay for the designs and he seduces their wives . . .'

The typist, Juliette, worked loyally for Paul, while hating him fiercely. Why, Alix didn't know. Behind his back, Juliette always referred to her boss as '*le beau sabreur*', in a reference to his supposed prowess in the bedroom. Alix sometimes wondered whether Juliette hated Paul so passionately because at some time past they had been lovers. Or whether she hated him because they hadn't.

Her accusation that Paul enjoyed the favours of his lady clients might well have been true, but although Alix dined several times with him, he never talked to her but of business and new projects. If dinner for two was supposed to be a romantic occasion, it seemed to have slipped Paul's mind. Wryly, Alix admitted to herself that she knew why. He thought she was a struggling artist. He didn't waste his talents as a lover on struggling artists. He kept those for rich women, and if ever he found out that she had a private fortune, that would be the day she would need to fix a double lock on her bedroom door. But as long as he didn't know, she was safe.

When she had been younger, Alix had sometimes speculated romantically as to why old Nat Morrell had decided to leave his fortune to her. As an adolescent, she had supposed it had been an act of remorse. Now,

older and wiser, she began to suspect it had been a last
act of revenge. The money had poisoned her relationship with Robbie; it could yet destroy her working
relationship with Paul. Only Jake—but there was no
Jake any more. As for Paul, she realised he was
unscrupulous and possibly the most amoral man she
had ever met, yet she liked him. She did not then know
how dangerous he was, or how cruel.

Street cleaners swept up the leaves and it grew too
cold to sit on street corners and paint. One wet afternoon, Alix set off down the steep, uneven slopes of
Montmartre for the inner city and the great Louvre
museum. She loved to wander among the fine paintings.
It made her conscious of her own limitations as an
artist, but even so, she felt a kinship with the creators
of the great canvases.

This was not the tourist season, and the galleries were
almost empty. She wandered through one after another
and came to rest before a large oil of a Napoleonic
chasseur of the Imperial Guard. He sat confidently
astride his rearing charger, the tassels of his elaborate
uniform flying, as if nothing could prevent his galloping
towards a glorious destiny.

'Why do we always see war as glorious, no matter
what horrors are unleashed?' she wondered. 'Gods and
heroes—that's what people imagine.'

She became aware that she was not alone in the
gallery. She turned aside from the magnificent figure in
the painting and her gaze fell on a man sitting on one
of the benches a little further down and staring at the
paintings hanging on the opposite wall. He looked a
tall man, even seated, and fairly young, and there was
something extraordinarily familiar about him, something
which sent a strange, nervous tingle running up Alix's
spine and made her skin prickle. She thought she must
be dreaming. Here, surrounded by the painted ghosts
of the past, she had conjured up another ghost, a figure

which always haunted her, and now sat as in life at the end of the long, empty room, so silent, so still, with all those painted eyes watching from the canvases.

She forced herself to walk slowly towards him, really believing with the first few steps that the figure would dissolve and disappear. But he remained there before her, real and solid, flesh and blood, and as she came up, he looked up at her, the grey eyes narrowed in that old familiar appraising way.

'Hallo, Alix,' he said huskily.

'Jake . . .?' she whispered, hardly able to force the word through her constricted throat. The gallery rocked around her, the pictures dancing on the walls. 'Jake, it *is* you . . . You're *alive!*'

He was real. He wasn't a figment of her imagination, a wishful embodiment of an unfulfilled dream. He was Jake, the same, and yet subtly different. He began to smile up at her, but then the smile faded abruptly, and he asked anxiously, 'Robbie?'

'It's all right,' Alix assured him quickly, answering the unspoken question in his voice and grey eyes. 'He came through all right. But poor Phil didn't. You remember Robbie's brother? He was killed, right at the end of it all. It was a terrible blow to Lady Harris . . .' She paused and added awkwardly, 'We—We didn't get married, Robbie and I, after all. You were right about long engagements.'

'*You* broke it off?'

Alix felt a mild twinge of annoyance that he could suppose it possible that Robbie, who, for all his faults, had been brought up to be a gentleman, might have been the one to request release.

'Of course it was me!' she said crossly and ungrammatically.

But that was Jake, the old Jake. Even at a time like this, when both should be so pleased to have found one another again, he had managed to find something to say which upset her. 'You don't change, Jake,' she thought, and sighed. Happy though she was to know he had survived, she found herself thinking: 'He's a born survivor. Men like him always come through. I should have remembered that.'

But, at that same moment, her eye fell on the stick propped against the bench on the other side of him. It was a stout stick with a rubber tip; not the sort used by the fashionable, but the sort used by the lame. He had survived indeed, but not, after all, unscathed.

For a brief, horrible moment, she wondered if the legs were completely useless. He'd made no attempt to stand up and greet her, something she had subconsciously accepted as a simple lack of manners till now. But could the truth be that he'd been brought here and dumped on this bench to be called for later, like a package? 'Please, God, no . . .' she thought, offering up a childish prayer with a child's hope of it being instantly granted. 'Not Jake, he couldn't accept it . . . He couldn't live like it.'

Jake had seen her glance and the expression on her face. Defensively, he growled at her, 'It's the hip. It's weak. I'm not a complete cripple, if that's what you're wondering. I can walk, but damn slow. Sometimes, without warning, the hip gives out altogether and I go down like a skittle. Getting up and sitting down are the worst, so you'll excuse me if I don't have very good manners, and jump up and down on your behalf!'

Relief surged over her. 'All right,' she said calmly, and sensed the anger seep out of him at her matter-of-fact acceptance of his infirmity. She sat down on the bench beside him and folded her gloved hands in her lap. 'What are you doing in Paris?'

He was, he said wryly, convalescing. 'That's what they tell you to go and do when they can't do any more for you.' An eminent French surgeon had operated on his injured hip six months earlier and made some slight improvement. But he would always walk with a limp. 'Because it wasn't treated properly in the first place, when I injured it.' The pain, so they had assured him, would go away eventually.

Jake did not say how bad the pain was. Alix suspected it was very bad. He had the look about him of a man who had been seriously ill. His skin held a hospital pallor, a tinge of grey, and there were lines of suffering about his mouth. In the same way as she had offered up her childish prayer, she wished she could comfort him in a spontaneous and loving childish way, putting her arms round him to show him how sorry she was. But that would be misunderstood and, she suspected, not very well received.

So instead she began to tell him about her painting and her modest success in designing for Paul. For some reason, she felt slightly embarrassed at mentioning Paul to Jake, although afterwards she could not think why. She didn't describe Paul, and referred to him primly as 'Monsieur Daquin'.

Jake listened to her, not only with interest but intelligently. It surprised her that he should be interested in art, or might choose to spend his time in an art gallery or museum. It seemed a long way away from motorcars and flying machines. But he knew what he was talking about, and as they chatted together, Alix felt herself relax. She was glad she had found him again, not only because she knew he was alive, but because she suddenly realised how lonely she was in Paris. He was a friend. He knew the people she knew, and she hadn't to explain everything to him. He understood her.

'Why don't you come to lunch?' she asked on impulse. 'Tomorrow. I'm no cook, but there's a good *charcuterie* near the flat. I can put together some salad.'

'I'd like that fine,' Jake said.

Then she remembered she lived at the top of a steep cobbled street on the heights of Montmartre, and she wondered how he would manage to get up there if he were seriously disabled.

'I got back from the war!' he said sharply, when she attempted to explain all this. 'I can get as far as your apartment!'

Then he said something only Jake would say. The irritation at her fussing faded and enthusiasm lit up the grey eyes. 'Did you know that one of the first successful trial runs of a motor-car was made in Montmartre?'

Alix, thinking of the steep streets, said, 'Probably a good place for it.'

He arrived the next day with a bottle of Nuits-St-Georges, a long stick of bread and a delicious-looking pâté in a decorated pot. 'I took a cab up here,' he told her, in answer to her question. 'Driven by one of those crazy Russians.'

'You didn't have to bring your own food,' Alix told him reproachfully. 'Here, let me take all that.'

He surrendered his armful of groceries with some relief and limped into the little flat.

'It's awfully small,' she apologised.

'Am I drunk?' he asked her. 'Or does the floor slope?'

He grinned at her, a cheerful anarchic sort of grin, and a feeling swept over her she knew she could only describe as joy. Impetuously, she burst out, 'I'm so glad you made it, Jake! So glad you came back out of that— that shambles of a war. I don't care if it was the "war to end all wars", it destroyed everything we had.'

'You have to start over,' Jake said quietly. 'If you can.'

There was a terrible emptiness in the way he spoke the last words. They stood there, in the middle of the sloping floor of the little room, and stared at one another over a paper bag of mundane groceries. Two people seeing each other again after a long time, seeking to see what had changed and what had remained the same. They were survivors, both of them. But they had survived scarred. The scars weren't all outward, they were inward. They had both changed.

Alix thought he seemed so much nicer a person somehow. Not so brash. Heaven alone knew what a dreadful time he'd been through.

Jake was thinking she was as beautiful as ever. But she had gained a new maturity and an inner strength. She had been a lovely, wilful girl, and now she was a graceful woman who had grown in understanding.

They set out the table together. He moved quite nimbly around the room, despite the sloping floor and his infirmity. Probably he wanted to show her he was no useless invalid. Alix had a shrewd idea that so much activity caused him pain, but he wouldn't admit or show it. He was too proud, and much too obstinate.

The two of them sat over their little meal, and they talked. They talked at first of others, of people Jake had met in London. He asked after Gerard, which surprised her, because she had not realised he'd spoken much to him. In fact, he seemed to remember everybody. He even remembered poor Harriet.

'She went on stage,' Alix informed him. 'She changed her name to Gloria something-or-other, and she's done very well. She's appearing in a West End show now, I believe, in a body-stocking and spangles, and very little else, I gather.'

'As I recall,' Jake said mildly, 'she *had* very little else. The sight of Harriet in a body-stocking must be about as erotic as a lamp-post. What happened to the little dark girl, the one Robbie introduced to me?'

'You mean Jennie. She went up to Oxford.'

'She always looked at me as if I was about to do something dreadful,' Jake said. 'You, on the other hand, always looked at me as though I'd already done it.'

Alix blushed. 'I didn't know what to make of you,' she admitted. 'You were different.'

'So were you . . .' he said quietly.

A curious feeling swept over Alix and she began to fiddle nervously with her wine-glass. 'What happened to you, Jake? Robbie wrote that they all thought you'd been shot down and killed.' She remembered that awful day, and the letter, and the darkness cast across the sun. 'Can you talk about it?' she asked him hesitantly.

'Sure, I can talk about *that*!' he said enigmatically. He told her about his last flight, and the burning machine plunging earthwards. 'I'd begun to think I wouldn't get out of it,' he said frankly, 'but when I saw the flames, it gave me extra determination. I'd seen men burn, you see . . .' He fell silent for a moment, the grey eyes clouding with memory.

'My only hope of landing was to cut the engine and glide. But, without the instruments, I misjudged. I was lower than I had reckoned. From out of nowhere I saw a hillside coming up towards me, and an old man in a French peasant's blouse standing by a cart and waving his arms at me frantically. It was odd how clearly I could see him. Then I ploughed into the hillside and the whole damn machine disintegrated about me. The landing wires snapped, and the wing struts, and the wings folded. The undercarriage collapsed. I was knocked out. I don't really know what happened. All I do know is that when I came to, I was in a bed in a strange house.'

Alix broke in, 'But . . .' but he could not have heard her.

'It seems the old peasant had watched me crash and come running over to pull me out before the Huns got there. He also saved me from being roasted alive. He told me how, just after he'd managed to drag me up on to his cart and was driving away, the whole machine went up in flames. "It was beautiful," he said to me, "like a firework display, monsieur, on a saint's day." Not much fun if you're the firework! So, he took me to the house of a genuine countess, a person of some importance, who lived near by. She was a real aristocrat to her fingertips, and a French patriot to the core. The Germans treated her very politely, she said—and I bet they did! They wouldn't search her house without cause. It was secluded, in its own grounds, and her staff were trustworthy. So I was safe. In any case, the Germans probably thought the pilot was trying to get across country to our lines. The problem was my injured hip, because I couldn't be taken to hospital, and there was a lump of metal lodged in it. The next day she fetched an elderly retired doctor who lived locally and could be trusted. He did his best, but he'd qualified in 1866 and hadn't practised since 1898! However, he'd been in the Franco-Prussian War as an army surgeon, and he hated "*les Boches*". The old fellow did his best for me, including an improvised operation on madame la comtesse's kitchen table, with me fortified with excellent brandy from her cellar in the absence of any anaesthetics. They tell me I nearly died.'

Jake shrugged. 'I was months hidden in that house, and despite everything, a day didn't pass when I didn't think I might be discovered.'

Alix was silent as she thought of the barbarity and sheer agony of that kitchen operation. No anaesthetics, nor proper surgical instruments—just some antiquated tools the elderly surgeon had left over from youthful campaigning with the armies of Napoleon III. What had he used for antiseptics or sutures? The whole operation had probably been performed by the light of an oil-lamp, and by a man of eighty. It didn't bear thinking about. Jake had said he'd nearly died. It was a miracle he had survived. But Jake was a survivor, even of that mid-nineteenth-century surgery in makeshift conditions.

'To be shut up in that house for so long,' she said slowly, 'and not knowing what was happening, or how the war was going . . . What did you do? What did you think about?'

'I thought quite a lot about you,' he said softly. He saw her look away and mistook her reaction. More briskly, he added, 'And I read a lot—she had books.'

Alix stood up and began to clear the table things away, refusing to let him help. There was little to do anyway. She stacked everything in the dark kitchen and went back into her cramped little living-room. Jake was standing by the window looking out at her beloved view of Sacré-Coeur.

'They built that church,' he said soberly, 'to celebrate the ending of a war. The Franco-Prussian one.'

She put her hand on his arm. It was an instinctive gesture, wanting to communicate with him, not just by words, which let you down, but by touch, which says so much without words. He turned to look at her, a question in his grey eyes that she did not quite understand. Then he picked up the hand she had put on his sleeve and, holding it gently, asked, 'What about you, Alix? What have you been doing when not painting, or drawing designs for Daquin?'

'Walking a lot, or I did in the summer. I go to the galleries. I can always learn from the great masters.'

He looked down at the slim white fingers he held in his. 'No man?'

'No!' she said quickly. 'Only Daquin, and he's an employer and doesn't talk about anything except work.'

'Is he married?'

'Not now,' she admitted awkwardly. 'He's divorced, I believe.' To underline that Paul meant nothing to her, and because her ear caught a false nonchalance in her words that she knew Jake could not have missed, she added, 'I think he has some kind of an affair with his secretary, or did have. They quarrel a lot, shriek at each other. But when I go into the room they usually stop, so I think they must have been lovers, once.'

'No one can hate that much who hasn't once loved just as fiercely, is that it?' Jake smiled.

'Something like that.' She looked up into his face. 'And—you?'

He struck his stick on the wooden floor. The rubber tip made a dull thud. 'I'm *hors de combat*,' he said abruptly, as if he wanted to cut off this avenue of conversation.

'I bet . . .' Alix thought inelegantly.

But Jake limped away and was suddenly making moves to leave. He picked up his hat and, still leaning heavily on his stick, turned to face her by the door. 'How time flies when you're having fun,' he said drily. 'Sorry, Alix, I've got to go now.'

'So soon?' Alix exclaimed, startled. A pall of depression settled over her. He'd had enough. He was beginning to get bored with her and her conversation. Reminiscences of old times get wearisome after a while, if you can't build new and fresh bridges between you. But when she looked at him again, she saw how pale he was, and changed her mind as to his sudden wish to leave. Little pearls of perspiration marked his forehead and, as she watched, he lifted his free hand and wiped the back of it across his brow. 'He's overdone it,' she thought remorsefully. 'He's overtaxed himself, and I let him do it.'

'Thanks for the lunch,' he said.

'I'll come down the stairs with you . . .' Alix offered hastily.

The staircase was narrow and crooked. Like the room's floor, its treads of age-polished wood sloped into the well of the house. If there were ever a fire in this building, it would have flared up and disintegrated in minutes, leaving them all stranded on the upper floors. It was a thought that occasionally struck Alix, but now she could only think what a hazard it presented to Jake. Climbing it was one thing, going down a much more difficult task.

'There's no need!' he said, almost angrily, as she moved towards him, putting out her hand. 'I told you I'm not a damn cripple, just slow and awkward.'

'The stairs are awkward, too. If I take your arm on one side . . .'

'For God's sake, Alix!' he yelled at her in a sudden burst of rage, so violent it made her start back instinctively in alarm. 'Let me alone, will you? I don't want your help!'

'Go on by yourself, then!' she retaliated, her voice shaking slightly.

Alix listened as he stumbled out of the door and began the treacherous descent. There were thirty-four treads. She had counted them many times. Alix began to count them now, in her head, numbering off each one safely negotiated. At seven, he paused, and then he began again. When he paused, everything inside her seemed to stop with him, even her heart seemed not to beat. He was on the move again and now must be on the mezzannine, turning to begin his way down to the floor below.

The crash of the fall shook the entire ancient building. Someone was shouting in French, very loudly, and doors were opening on the floor below as people ran out. Alix flew like the wind out of the flat and hurtled down the staircase.

Jake was halfway down the second flight, propped against the wall, one leg crooked up in front of him, the other stretched out. His face was twisted in pain, and his eyes tightly shut. His stick was continuing its journey downstairs on its own, sliding bump-bump from tread to tread, till it slipped through the wrought-iron balustrade that guarded the edge of the staircase and clattered down to the unseen depths below.

The people in the flat on this floor had come out to see what had happened. The man was in his shirt-

sleeves and collarless, and his wife still holding a
saucepan in her hand. A child appeared behind them,
slipped under his father's arm and ran down the stairs,
past Jake and Alix.

Jake was whispering, 'Hell—hell—hell . . .' over and
over again, in a sort of litany, as if the pain could be
exorcised in this way.

The man in shirtsleeves said, '*C'est un américain* . . .'
He leaned forward and bellowed into Jake's white face,
'*Rien cassé?*'

Jake shook his head slowly from side to side. 'No,
nothing broken . . . Okay . . .' The words came
halting and hoarse, half whispered and half muttered,
welling up on a sea of agony.

The man shrugged and ushered his wife back into
their flat. The child came clattering back up the stairs,
carrying Jake's stick. '*V'la, m'sieu!*' He presented it
proudly to the prostrate form on the staircase.

Alix took it quickly and thanked him, and the child
disappeared into the flat in answer to a shrill call from
his mother.

Alix sat on the step above Jake and waited until he'd
got his breath back. 'You'd better come up again and
have a glass of something. I've no brandy, but there's
some wine left. Or I'll make some more coffee.
Here . . .' She grasped his arm.

'Get your hand off me!' Jake snarled, and twitched
his sleeve out of her grip. 'Get the hell out of it, Alix,
and leave me alone. I can manage!'

Pure anger flooded over her, partly as his surly
rejection of her offer of help, and partly born of relief
that he had not broken any bones and had got his
breath and voice back.

'Like blazes you can manage!' she said crisply. 'Don't
be so difficult! I warned you about the stairs, but you
had to be obstinate. Unless you want to fall again,
you'll have to let me help you.'

He opened his eyes at that, and growled, 'Help me then, if you're so darned set on it! Be a blasted nurse-maid! That's all I need, isn't it? Some woman in a starched white apron giving me orders. You'll be cutting up my food for me next.'

'I know it hurts!' Alix said sharply. 'But I think your pride is hurt more than your backside. So stop being so stupid and let me help you up.'

Somehow she got him to his feet and handed him his stick. 'No, down!' Jake ordered fiercely, when she would have led him back up to her flat. So they continued haltingly downward and managed to arrive at the street door without further mishap.

Out on the pavement, Alix said, 'I'll go and find a taxi. Stay here.'

'I'll walk to the Place du Tertre!' His mouth set into a thin obstinate line.

'Jake, you don't have to prove anything to *me*.' Alex begged. 'Or, if you are proving anything, you're proving that the crack on your head you got in your plane crash addled your brain! You're being cantankerous and stupid—and childish!'

Jake's hand shot out and gripped her shoulder in a tight, painful grasp. 'Listen to me, Miss Morrell,' he said, breathing heavily. 'I appreciate your help and concern. But I don't want it. And I don't want your little homilies, either. Meeting like that, in the Louvre, it was a disaster! You had thought I was dead, and I'd thought you were happily married to Robbie. It would have been far better for us both to have stayed that way, safe in our own delusions. I didn't want to see you ever again, Alix. I wish to hell that I hadn't been in that gallery yesterday. Get out of my life, and stay out, can't you?'

There was nothing she could reply, and Alix said nothing. She stood, as if frozen, in the street, wanting to cry, the hot tears of shock and humiliation pricking at her eyelids, and knowing she wouldn't, couldn't, cry now.

Jake took his hand from her shoulder and added, more gently, 'Sorry, but that's how it is.'

The gentleness was worse, far worse, more than an insult. It was an injury. It wounded in the spirit and in the flesh, as though he had plunged a knife into her heart.

Two girls were coming down the street towards them. One drawback—from Alix's viewpoint—to living in Montmartre was its disproportionately high population of ladies of easy virtue. They mostly came out at nightfall, like some rare species of night-blooming orchid. These two were ambling idly along in the daylight. The weak autumn sun lent no colour to their pallid, sharply pretty faces. Their bodies had a transitory bloom of youth, already fading. A badly nourished childhood, early promiscuity, abuse of alcohol and irregular hours were corroding their youthful beauty as rust bites into neglected metal. They were old while being young. In a year or two, every attraction would be gone and they would seek the evening shadows as a precaution.

But now they still had enough beauty left to emerge boldly in the candid light of day. As they passed Jake and Alix, one of them ran a brief, dispassionate, professional eye over Jake. But the other girl looked at Alix and smiled sympathetically, twitching her thin shoulders. Alix was clearly having trouble with her man, and getting the worst of it. The girl understood all about that. There was something conspiratorial in the brief little smile she gave. For a second or two, they were sisters.

At that moment an empty taxicab appeared, cruising down the road on its way back into central Paris. Jake flung up his arm and hailed it. He scrambled inside, and said, 'So long, Alix—be good.' And he was gone.

The tarts had gone, too. Alix stood in the empty

street and rubbed her arms, shivering in the late afternoon cool. Perhaps he'd meant every cruel, biting word, driving her away like an unwanted dog. Perhaps, his pride humiliated, he'd only struck out at her like a trapped wild animal. She had no idea where he lived, or if she'd ever see him again.

'Well,' she thought, turning to go back indoors, 'If you need me, you know where to find me, Jake Sherwood.'

She climbed slowly back up the twisting staircase and regained her flat. The partly full bottle of Nuits-St-Georges still stood on the checkered table-cloth. Aloud, she said fiercely, 'And, in the meantime, you can go to blazes!'

CHAPTER EIGHT

IT WAS NOT very often that the offices of Lyndhurst's Health Tonic were graced by a visit from their founder's widow, but today was such a day.

'She comes only when she wants to make trouble,' one of the members of accounts department observed gloomily. He peered down through the unwashed window at the yard below, where the woman in the fox fur stole and fashionable costume was standing by her limousine. She was surrounded by an obsequious court of senior management, 'all bowing and scraping', said the observer sarcastically.

Robbie, bored, wondered whether he could get away a quarter of an hour earlier tonight. He swatted a fly with a rolled-up memo and asked, without interest, 'Who?'

'Old Ma Lyndhurst. The fair Edith. She's down there in the yard, dispensing rock-hard charm and veiled threats.'

Robbie, for want of anything better to do, got up and wandered to the window to join the cynical observer of the scene below.

'Well, I'm damned . . .' he breathed softly. Whirling round, he snatched up his jacket from the back of his chair and, before the startled eyes of his colleague, bolted out of the office and hurtled down the stairs without a word of explanation.

Before he entered the yard, he paused long enough to smooth his hair and straighten his tie. Steady now, look natural . . . But let her remember me, he prayed, do let her remember . . .

Edith Lyndhurst's sharp eyes saw him almost at once, and he knew she *had* recognised him. He approached the group boldly. Senior management looked shocked and slightly nonplussed. Robbie ignored them all, reserving his shy, boyish smile for her. But would she choose to ignore it? He saw her whisper some question to the area manager, and caught the man's reply. 'Harris—in our accounts department.'

'Have we not met before, Mr Harris?' Edith asked him graciously, as he came up.

She had decided to admit him to the magic circle. His heart lifted and began to beat rapidly. He felt as he'd done in the old days, patrolling the open skies and spotting his adversary idling along below him, unconscious of his presence. 'Play your cards right, old son, and you're home and dry!' he thought.

'We have met, very briefly,' he told her diffidently. 'More a chance encounter, really. I hadn't expected you to remember me.'

'Oh, I remember you,' she said, 'very well.' Her voice had a crystal clarity to it that somehow failed to be musical. It wasn't unpleasant, but a shade too hard, and lacked spontaneous warmth. Now she was hesitating, and he held his breath.

Edith Lyndhurst appeared to make a sudden decision. She opened her black leather purse and took out a small visiting-card and a gold pencil. Hastily she scribbled something on the back of the card and handed it to him. 'I'm giving a cocktail party tomorrow. Perhaps you'd care to come? If you're free, naturally.' The word 'free' was very slightly emphasised. She didn't mean free for one evening, she meant unattached. 'I've written the time and the address.'

Robbie took the card, his fingers perspiring a little. He was aware of the gaping, blank faces of senior management watching this amazing scenario unfold before their dumbfounded gaze.

But she hadn't waited for his stammered thanks. She climbed into her car, showing a glimpse of shapely calf in a sheer silk stocking, and the uniformed chauffeur shut the door briskly, giving Robbie a supercilious look.

'Another ruddy gigolo,' thought the chauffeur. 'She'll eat this poor devil alive.'

Robbie timed his arrival at her party carefully, not too late to be rude, but just late enough to make her wonder if he was, after all, coming. It was a carefully preserved Regency town house in Chelsea. Outside, classical good taste prevailed. Inside, it was modern, luxurious, vulgar, and redolent of wealth. A butler greeted him at the door. A footman in livery showed him into the drawing-room in which a crushed, solid pack of ambulatory wealth shouted at each other across an atmosphere thick with alcoholic fumes and cigarette smoke. As he entered the room, he saw Mrs Lyndhurst's eyes rest momentarily on him, and then she turned back to the man with whom she was talking. Robbie felt a small glow of triumph. He was right: she had begun to wonder.

A white-jacketed waiter appeared with a silver tray of drinks, and Robbie took one absently. Carefully he turned away from his hostess and began to chat to a plump lady in black with little rows of jet pendants quivering on her massive bosom. After a moment, he became aware of a heady perfume and the presence of someone at his elbow, brushing against him.

'How nice that you could come, Captain Harris,' Edith murmured. 'Are they looking after you all right?'

He raised the half-finished drink in his hand. 'Absolutely splendidly, thanks.'

'There are some things to eat somewhere,' she said vaguely. 'Smoked salmon and caviar, if Bertie . . .' She glanced scornfully towards the man with whom she had been talking. 'If he hasn't eaten it all. He is an awful pig.'

'Poor old Bertie,' thought Robbie, amused. 'Given his cards.'

Edith didn't speak to him again during the party, but he was not surprised when, towards the end when people were beginning to leave, she murmured in passing, 'Do stay, if you can. I've just a few friends to supper.'

'Supper' was an expensive meal, and probably his month's salary would scarcely have covered the cost of it. But he knew his role. He stayed to the last. When everyone else had gone and they were alone, Edith went to the marble fireplace and stood with her back to him, a well-corseted, elegant figure in a low-waisted saffron gown, a gold slave bracelet twined round her bare upper arm. Her tinted hair was carefully marcel-waved, her skin flawless, but with that uncomfortably over-cleansed and over-preserved look which is the result of regular facial treatment at the hands of professional beauticians.

'What happened to the red-haired girl?' she asked casually. She took down a cigarette-box and extracted a black Russian cigarette, setting it in an ivory holder.

'We broke up,' Robbie said. He stood up and went to light her cigarette, and saw her smile as she bent her head and the flame illuminated her face. 'Bitch . . .' he thought, but without rancour. 'It's awfully nice of you to have asked me along tonight,' he said aloud in his frank way. 'I wish there was some way I could thank you.'

The heavy-lidded eyes flickered briefly over his slim figure. 'Well, perhaps there is, at that.' She smiled, and blew a small cloud of aromatic tobacco smoke into the atmosphere. 'Give me a quarter of an hour,' she said.

She was not foolish enough to allow any lover to watch her undress. Professional beauticians and good dressmakers can do a great deal to beat back the years, but cannot stop the body losing the elasticity of youth.

He wasn't to see her struggle out of her foundation garments. He was only to see the finished product in a white satin négligé.

While he waited, Robbie helped himself to another drink, already feeling a right of occupancy in this splendidly vulgar, lavish house. He'd known all along why he'd been invited here. He didn't mind. It was something he did well—and the desire was not on one side only. He wanted her.

The bedroom was, predictably, a cluttered mess of drapes and pleated satin cushions, fringed lamps, cut-glass powder-bowls and china statuettes of leggy girls hanging on to leashed greyhounds. Significantly, it held only one small mirror, and that on a dressing-table.

'I had a Frenchman come over and do the whole house for me,' Edith said, unexpectedly. 'From Paris. He called himself an interior designer. He was—very good.'

'I'm very good,' Robbie whispered into her ear.

Even so, she was surprised at the passion of his lovemaking. She'd had young lovers before, but never one like this, who really seemed to want her. Afterwards, she propped herself up on one elbow on the crushed satin pillows and bent over his tousled, handsome form stretched out beside her, so like a healthy young animal.

'You know,' she said softly, 'some people would say I was much too old for you.' She caressed his forehead gently with the tips of her well-manicured fingers.

'They'd be wrong,' he told her. 'You excite me.' He grinned up at her conspiratorially. He meant it. Every inch of this room, and every inch of her, spoke of money, and the power it had. It affected him like a drug. He'd always felt this way about money. He saw she was smiling down at him a little mockingly, and wondered if she'd guessed.

Her nails were bright scarlet, long and pointed. She

ran one over his lips, down his chin, across his chest and rested her hand on his flat muscular young stomach. 'You know, my beautiful boy, I could make you very happy.'

'You already have,' he told her huskily.

'That's not what I mean, and you know it's not what I mean. What's one night's tumble in the sheets, even as well done as this? You're right, my sweet, you *are* good. I—I have a lot of friends. But sometimes I get very lonely.'

Robbie put his hand over hers which lay on his stomach. He could feel the rising urgency of his body and he pushed her hand downward so that her touch hastened it.

'On the other hand,' she whispered, 'I could make you thoroughly miserable. Do you want to take that risk?'

'Yes . . .' he almost croaked, reaching for her.

'Foolish boy,' she said indulgently.

It was a week before Alix heard anything from Jake. Then a letter came. It was hardly a letter, really, more a note. It said laconically: '*I've bought a painting, and I'd value your opinion. Please come.*'

'You've got a nerve, Jake Sherwood,' she said, but she felt a glow of happiness. It was an olive-branch. He wanted to be friends again.

His flat was in a discreet, residential area, a broad avenue of solid nineteenth-century blocks. He lived on the first floor, but there was an electric lift. No winding, treacherous staircase here. A maid or housekeeper of some sort opened the door, an elderly, sturdy figure in a black overall. She led Alix towards the door of the salon, and as they approached it, Alix was startled to hear music drifting through the panels. Someone on the other side was playing the piano, and playing it very well.

'*C'est monsieur* . . .' said the maid stolidly, in reply
to her question. She put out a hand to the door-handle.

Alix exclaimed, 'No, wait! I'll announce myself.'

The woman's face showed no reaction. She simply
left Alix to it. Very, very gently Alix turned the handle
and softly opened the door.

It was a long, airy, well-lit room, sparsely furnished
with good early-nineteenth-century pieces which
harmonised with the architecture of the rooms. It was
furniture well and lovingly made by craftsmen, which
Jake, a carpenter's son and himself a designer of
beautiful and functional objects, appreciated. Full-length
windows gave on to a balcony and the shining grand
piano stood at one end in a shaft of autumn sunlight.

Jake sat before it alone, playing for his own pleasure.
His fingers moved over the keys with a light, sure touch.
He had a true musical ear, a sense for the phrasing of
the music and an ability to bring out the tenderness and
passion in the melody.

Alix waited until he had finished and then walked
over to the piano and rested her arm on the top. When
he glanced up, she said quietly, 'That was beautiful.
Most people keep a piano for a decoration. I didn't
know you could play so well.'

'You mean you didn't imagine in your wildest
moments that I played at all,' he returned drily. 'I saw
you, with your mouth hanging open, over there by the
door.'

'It was not! I was surprised. You'd never said, so I
thought . . .'

'You thought, Miss Morrell, that I was some kind of
illiterate backwoodsman from out in the sticks
somewhere.'

'You certainly act like it sometimes,' Alix said sternly.

He had the grace to look down, away from her
accusing green eyes. Carefully he lowered the lid of the
piano and then said, a little awkwardly, 'I thought,

when I sent you the note, that you mightn't come.'

'Serve you right if I didn't. You were horribly rude to me. I correct that—you were just horrible!'

'Yes, I know.'

He didn't have to tell her he was sorry. She knew he was. Nor had there ever been any doubt in her mind that she would come, for all he had hurt her badly and she was well aware that it could, and probably would, happen again. How many times can a person take being rejected, shouted at, driven away, before the final break comes, the straw which snaps the camel's back? She had no idea. But she was here because she loved him, and that made all speculation or argument superfluous. As long as he needed her, she would come. He didn't know that, and it was as well that he didn't.

Alix took off her hat and dumped it unceremoniously on top of the piano. 'Well, where's this fabulous painting?'

Jake smiled at her, relief in his grey eyes. 'Over there, by the wall. It's not the only one I've bought. I've bought several. It gets to be catching.' He reached for the stick leaning against the piano and scrambled awkwardly to his feet.

Alix turned her head away so as not to watch his struggles, and asked casually, 'Are you all right, after that fall?'

'I'm fine. All I have is a lot of bruises in places where, dear young lady, you may not gaze upon them.' He hobbled briskly past her to the far side of the room and picked up a canvas wrapped unglamorously in brown paper.

'This isn't going to turn out to be some fat, pink, lascivious nude masquerading as "Venus Surprised", painted by a follower of Boucher, is it?' she asked suspiciously.

He looked hurt. 'No, it is not. I don't go round collecting dirty pictures. It's by Renoir.'

Alix, moving towards him as he began to unwrap the picture, paused and exclaimed incredulously, '*Renoir*? You bought a Renoir, just like that?'

'Not "just like that". I had a dealer keep an eye open and to call me when the right picture turned up. Of course, it's not one of Renoir's best. It's a late picture, painted a few years ago when he was already an old fellow and his hands were crippled. I've bought several other, really modern, paintings. No one wants them just now and prices are low. It's the time to buy . . . You'll see, they'll appreciate in value when people realise what they are.'

'You're not an art lover, you're a businessman,' Alix said crossly, and, she knew, unfairly.

'Why can't I be both? Why are the English so darned snobbish about being successful in business?'

'I don't know.' She laughed. 'Something to do with eighteenth-century notions of a gentleman not soiling his hands in trade, I expect.'

'Soiled his hands in virtually everything else, I'll bet.'

He had unwrapped the painting and propped it up on a chair. It was a small canvas of a young girl in a dark blue gown holding a tangled spray of field poppies, the bright patches of red striking a contrasting note against the mottled blues, greys and greens of the background and the girl's gown, but echoed in auburn streaks in her hair.

'Poor old chap's technique was shattered by his useless hands. He had the paint-brush tied to his fingers,' Jake said. 'But he still had it in him, and he had to get it down on canvas, no matter what it cost him. I can understand that. I know how he felt. I like this picture better than his earlier ones, where he had full control and could do what he wanted.'

'I like it too,' Alix said slowly. 'But perhaps it doesn't mean to me what it means to you.'

'It means a lot to me, and all kinds of things.' He

frowned at the canvas. 'Like those poppies in the girl's arms. Poppies grew all over the battlefields. From the sky, we could see fields of red. They reminded me of the old tale of the dragon's teeth. You remember, Jason and the Argonauts? Some king or other, Jason's enemy, sowed the ground with dragon's teeth, and from every tooth sprang an armed man. It was as if every poppy sprang from a dead soldier hidden in the earth . . .' Jake touched the canvas lightly, his fingers resting briefly on the girl sitter's auburn hair. 'And this, the red lights in her hair, made me think of you.'

He turned and looked down at her. The hat had not been able to prevent the autumn winds from playing with her hair. Untidy copper-red tendrils framed her face, and the cold air had lent a pink flush to her cheekbones which had not faded away. She was all the colours of autumn, everything a painter might have sought on his palette. Reds and browns, coppery pinks and the steady evergreen of her widely spaced emerald eyes.

'Dear heaven,' he whispered throatily, 'you're so damn beautiful, it hurts . . .'

He swept her up towards him, crushing her in his embrace and pressing his mouth down on hers hungrily, like a starving man.

This was everything which had never been before. She had never felt this way with Robbie. This was what had been lacking: the desire, the urgency, the throbbing of the body's pulses and complete abandonment of self. She wanted Jake, she wanted this man. Her arms slid about his neck, drawing him down on to her, as her body moulded itself against his, her urgency seeking to communicate itself to him with the inescapable message of her desire.

She knew he had read the message, and waited for his response. But it was not what she had expected. He muttered something she did not catch beneath his breath, and abruptly pushed her aside.

'That's enough, Alix!' he said sharply.

'I'm not playing games, Jake,' Alix whispered earnestly, believing he doubted the reality of her committment. 'I'm not pretending, and I'm not going to lead you on, just to refuse. If—If it's what you want, then it's what I want, too.'

She tried to embrace him again, but Jake seized her wrists in a painful grip and tore them brutally away from his neck, thrusting her away from him so violently that she stumbled back and almost fell.

'I told you, stop it, Alix! It's *not* what I want!'

She stared at him, wild-eyed. 'But you said . . .'

'I said you were beautiful, and so you are. I didn't say I wanted to start an affair with you!' he snarled at her before she could protest further.

Alix felt her cheeks burn as a scarlet tide of humiliation spread over them. 'Why not?' she asked crisply.

He looked momentarily more discomposed than angry, and moved away, turning his back to her. 'Listen, Alix, if and when I want to take you to bed, I'll say so. I don't need gilt-edged invitations.'

'I wasn't making you an invitation!' she burst out furiously.

'Weren't you? You had me fooled. Where did you learn to behave like that? Here in Paris—or have things changed back in England since I left? What happened to that nice, respectable young lady who was so pleased *not* to have to go up to Robbie's room, even when she was wearing his ring?'

'How dare *you*, of all people, speak that way to me?' Alix exclaimed. 'On that occasion, if you recall, you offered to replace Robbie, and you didn't even know me! How dare you criticise me now? Why, you moralising, conceited, ill-mannered . . .' Words failed her. 'What do you think? That I go around throwing myself at men? Well, I don't. I never have—and I'm not going to start now, least of all with *you*! Thank you for letting me see the painting, and goodbye!'

She grabbed her bag from the chair and stormed out. She fancied he called out her name, but she didn't care. Ignorant wretch. To think she'd been so foolish! To interpret a kiss as meaning he truly wanted her, and most of all, to let him see, in an unguarded moment she would rue for the rest of her days, that she had wanted him. Her punishment for her stupidity had been to be more or less told she was a tramp. 'And, and by that—that *mechanic*!' Alix thought furiously. 'That machine-besotted, self-educated, money-making social climber!'

The harsh, snobbish, untrue words, while she recognised them for what they were, nevertheless afforded her a crumb of comfort. She went home, and swore never to speak to him again, or see him, ever.

In fact, 'again' proved to be a week. Paul Daquin had a new project under way and had co-opted Alix's help, which meant working Paul's erratic hours. One evening, she left the studio late, ate a hasty omelette in a little café near the building and finally made her weary way to Montmartre in the darkness. It was cold, and the street lights imperfectly stabbed at the gloom. The earlier rain had made the cobbles beneath her feet wet and uneven, and in the poor lighting, dangerous. It seemed as if no one would voluntarily choose to be out and about on such a dismal night. Despite that, the ladies of the streets were at their customary chilly stations in the doorways. Some of them recognised her by now as a local resident, and one or two voices even greeted her politely, '*Bonsoir, madame*!' from darkened recesses, with an incongruous charm. They always called her '*madame*'.

Alix climbed the stairs and let herself into the flat, to find, to her surprise, that a light was on. Jake was sprawled out on her rickety sofa, in his shirt-sleeves, fast asleep. He must have been there some time, and had spent part of it rummaging in her tiny kitchen, because he'd found a bottle of table wine and drunk half of it. His discarded jacket was draped over the back of a chair. The partly filled bottle and empty stained glass stood on the floor.

Alix picked them up and took them back to the sink, and returned to stare down at him in a mixture of annoyance and frustration, into which crept, despite herself, a distinct and unworthy sensation of moral victory. He'd known she wouldn't come to him, not this time, not a second time, after his appalling rudeness. This time he'd come to her. But the sense of victory was short lived and soon regretted, replaced by sadness. That fine, strong man whom she had met in war-time, and who had opened up for her a casement on to a whole new horizon, had entered the time of peace as an embittered, lonely cripple. Even in slumber he looked white and tired, his face strained and marked by the ceaseless presence of pain.

But Alix resolutely hardened her heart, stooped and shook his broad shoulder. He opened his eyes.

'How did you get in here?' she demanded.

Jake pushed himself up on his elbows and squinted at her. 'Concierge let me in.'

'She had no right to!' Alix said crossly.

'She could see what I am . . . *mutilé de guerre*. She lost two brothers in the war, did you know?'

Startled, Alix admitted, 'No, I didn't. Well, I suppose it was all right to let you in. But that still doesn't explain why you're here.'

Jake was looking about him, as if something was missing. 'Where's the rest of the wine?'

'*My* wine is in *my* kitchen. You are on *my* sofa, and I'm still waiting to find out why.'

'Because I climbed up here, from Pigalle, up all those

confounded steps. It nearly killed me. I was all in when I got here and dog-tired. I just fell asleep, waiting for you.'

Alix's anger evaporated. 'I was working late with Daquin. He has a new client. Why couldn't you take a taxicab, for goodness' sake? Stay there, I'll make us some coffee.'

She went back to the kitchen and took down the cups. Jake appeared in the doorway, pulling on his jacket. She ignored him, and his attempts to tidy himself up, resolutely concentrating on her coffee-making, although out of the corner of her eye she could see him fiddling with his tie and rubbing his hands over his unruly brown hair.

'I suppose you've come to apologise, Captain Sherwood?' she asked calmly.

'Yes, if that's what you want,' was the less than satisfactory reply.

'What I want? It's what you should do! Haven't you *any* manners? And I don't want to hear your apology.'

'Make your mind up,' he growled.

Alix pushed past him with the tray, and he limped after her back to her tiny sitting-room. He'd left his stick by the sofa, and supported himself on the short journey from the kitchen by holding to the furniture, in a way which almost broke her heart in two.

Keeping her face averted from him, she put down the tray and repeated wearily, '*Why* didn't you take a taxicab?'

Jake fell back again on the sofa with a sigh of relief. 'I did, as far as Pigalle. Then I walked, because it took longer. I wanted to come, but I was in no hurry to get here. I thought I'd get the door slammed in my face, but as it happened, you weren't here.'

'I ought to throw you out,' she said, trying to sound fierce, and failing.

'Alix . . .'

There was something in his voice, sober and tense, that caught her attention and made her look up sharply.

Jake looked down, away from her gaze, and took a cup of coffee from the tray. The cup rattled in the saucer, spilling its contents. 'I didn't mean to yell at you the way I did. That wasn't fair, and I didn't mean what I said.' He shrugged. 'Not what you thought I meant by it, anyway.'

'Then you shouldn't have said it,' Alix replied resentfully. 'You made me sound like a tart, like one of those girls out there in the street.'

A faint wan smile sketched itself on Jake's lean and drawn features. 'You wouldn't know how to be like them, Alix. Look, what happened was my fault entirely. I kissed you. I shouldn't have done that. You misunderstood.'

'Yes, I did,' Alix exclaimed, her frustration spilling out again. 'I thought you meant something by it. I thought it was how you felt.'

'It doesn't matter how I felt. What matters is how *you* felt.' He hesitated and set down his coffee untasted. 'I hadn't expected you to feel that way about me, and I . . . There's something I have to tell you.'

'What? That you like to make all the overtures? That it isn't nice for respectable girls like me to have any physical feelings? Ladies don't—well—just *don't*, is that it?'

'No, it isn't! What man wants to make love to an immobile, unresponsive martyr? But it's no damn use your wanting me, Alix. You're wasting your time. I'm no use to you. I'm all washed up, nothing, just a shell!'

'Rubbish!' she said forcefully. 'If you don't want me, say so. But don't blame being lame. You have an injured hip that is very painful and awkward, but it's not totally disabling, and it doesn't make any difference to what you *are*, to me! Good Lord, you dragged yourself up all those steps this evening! If you wanted to take me to bed, it wouldn't . . .'

'Wouldn't stop me?' he supplied, as she broke off.
'No, it might make me clumsy. But something else stops
me.' Without warning, he leaned forward and snatched
at her shoulders, shaking her violently as she struggled
for breath in an onset of panic, because he looked so
wild. 'I *can't*, Alix! *Understand*, for crying out loud!' he
shouted at her. 'I'm trying to tell you, but you don't
seem to realise what I mean. I'm not being noble and
decent, or trying to protect you against yourself! I'm
not worrying about your reputation, or mine, or whether
I have to drag myself around on a stick these days. I'm
telling you the truth—that I can't, not any more . . .'

It was so quiet in the pleasant, untidy little room
when he fell silent and the sound of the words faded. It
was so horribly quiet, yet not empty. Grief filled the
room, grief and agony and frustration and injured
pride—all the suffering of a man from whom the essence
of his manhood has been taken.

Alix felt as if paralysed, unable to move or speak.
She had not thought of this; it had never remotely
occurred to her, not crossed her mind for a fleeting
second. At last she managed to swallow, forcing the
saliva past the constricting lump in her throat. 'Is it—
because of being shot down, and the wound . . .?'

He shook his head, and rubbed his hands over his
face, which gleamed with perspiration. The white scars
on the skin of his knuckles stood out starkly. 'No,' he
muttered, 'No, it . . .' He broke off and finished curtly,
'What the hell does it matter to you, anyway?'

Pale-faced, she cried out, 'Of course it matters to me!'

She realised then just how much *he* mattered to her,
and just how much she did love him, how deep it ran,
that love of which she was so newly aware. He had
walked back into her life, almost a stranger, and yet
one she knew so well. She couldn't let him go out of it
again, ever. She needed him as much as he needed her.

He was hurt and lonely and filled with hate and rage against himself and the world. He was trapped in a prison, and without her he would never break out of it. And as long as he was in that prison, she was trapped in there with him.

After a moment, she managed to ask in a fairly cool and practical voice, 'But you've sought medical help? Is there anything physically wrong?'

'No!' he said sharply. 'I'm quite complete, if that's what's on your mind. It's nothing physical. The doctors tell me it's psychological. That's a fancy modern medical term for anything they can't explain. Oh, they give excuses—strain, stress, exhaustion, shock . . . "The war, Captain Sherwood, the crash . . ." They're so damn bland about it. They assure me everything will be all right in time. Just like the damn hip will be all right in time. How much time, that's what they don't tell you! I'm thirty-six years old, Alix, and I'm impotent—that's the word for it. People make jokes about it, but it's not funny when it happens to you. I've ceased to exist.'

'Stop it, Jake!' she ordered him fiercely. 'You *have* to believe the doctors! You have to believe it will be all right.'

She knew she was shouting her words into the wind. It was the one affliction all men dreaded, and of all men, Jake was one of those least able to face up to the feared disability when it had struck. She remembered Jake, as he'd been in London, during the war . . . brash, confident, determined, successful. A man with a love of flying, of expensive fast motor-cars and cheap fast women. Alix remembered Tilly.

Yet she had not wanted to sound sharp or unsympathetic with him, so she added gently, 'Look, I'm sorry, and I can understand you're impatient . . .'

His grey eyes were like flint as he interrupted her speech. 'The last thing I want or need, Alix,' he said harshly, 'is any damn pity. And the last person whose pity I'd want, is yours.'

He turned away and collapsed back on to the sofa. He looked exhausted, the lean face haggard with spent emotion. Alix could see the whiteness of pain round his mouth and the sweat rolling off his skin. She felt a kindred despair in herself, for her inability to help. Too inexperienced herself in matters sexual to help him over such an impossible hurdle, and too physically weak or untrained to offer even simple help with the 'getting up and sitting down' which he had told her were the worst.

But they weren't the worst. The worst was what he had just told her now.

She sat for a while, trying to gather her shattered thoughts, trying to piece together some picture of what this calamity must mean to him, and have meant to him since he'd discovered it. How had he discovered it? In some fatal, failed and humiliating encounter with a girl like Tilly?

Alix couldn't ask him that. Instead, she asked, 'When you came over here to Europe, did you . . . did you leave a girl behind, at home, in Canada?'

She'd never asked him this before. It had never crossed her mind. But with her terrible new knowledge, it occurred to her now that, if he had, it might explain why he'd lingered in Europe so long after the ending of hostilities.

'I'd left Canada to work in the States,' Jake said in a flat, empty voice. 'I—well—sowed my wild oats, I guess. But there was never time for anything *more*. I felt towards my work the way some people are with drink—dependent on it, addicted. It sounds strange, stupid even, to me now, but when I wasn't working, I really fretted. It's bad when you get like that.' He paused briefly, and glanced up at her. 'Do you mind if I have a cigarette?'

'No, of course not. Wait a moment.' Alix jumped to

her feet and found some cigarettes in a crumpled packet on a table.

When he'd lit one, he leaned back, marginally more relaxed, and said, 'So the answer to your question is, no, I didn't. No one in particular. All the girls I knew will be married by now, I suppose. Most of the fellows my age, too. But there would be no point in my going back and marrying anyone, would there? Well, I was never much the marrying kind . . .'

Jake tapped out the ash, his eyes fixed on the ashtray. 'I'd like to go back to Canada. I had plans—once. But I can't go like this.' He looked for his stick, his voice growing brittle, finding it beneath his hand, propped against the sofa. He brandished it, so that it only just missed Alix's ear as she leaned forward to rescue the ashtray and she ducked, the stick whistling over her head.

'Veteran returns!' he declaimed, in the manner of the newspaper headlines of the day. 'Local boy back from the war—leaning on a stick and no damn use to anyone, man or beast—and certainly no damn use to any woman!'

'Stop it, Jake!' Alix caught at the stick and dragged it out of his hand.

'Why?' He stared at her belligerently. 'Why the hell should I? It's true. *You* know it's true. You're the only person who does know, apart from the doctors.' He shrugged and added soberly, 'So sorry I can't oblige you, Alix. Honestly, I should have liked to.'

Alix flushed. 'You'll get over it!' she said furiously, hating the defeat in his voice, so uncharacteristic of the man she remembered.

'*Will* I? And, in the meantime, what do I do? Keep trying and failing? Have you any idea what that's like? No, you haven't . . .'

Alix jumped to her feet and began to pace restlessly

up and down the room, unable to sit still and racking her brains. She had to say and do the right thing. To make a mistake, to say the wrong thing, now, would be irretrievable and fatal.

At last, in as level a voice as she could manage, certainly sounding far calmer than she felt within, she said, 'There are other things, you know, in a relationship.'

'Such as?' he asked sarcastically.

'Comfort, friendship, having someone there you can rely on to understand, talk to about things which mean something to you both, shared interests.' She remembered the Renoir, rising from its clutter of brown paper. 'Having someone there who cares about you.' Alix began to stumble over her words a little, in sudden embarrassment. Forcing it back, she went on, 'Sex isn't everything. My own parents' marriage was dead as far as *that* went, after I was born. I was a "difficult birth", a breech baby or something. Anyhow, she, my mother, nearly died, and they were told, no more babies. They travelled about a lot, separately, after that. But they stayed *friends*. They still cared about each other, even if neither of them cared much about me. Perhaps they blamed me. They used to write long letters to each other. I don't know what my father did for sex. I suppose he frequented ladies of easy virtue. I can't imagine him keeping a mistress in style in St John's Wood; he wasn't that kind of man, much too hard-headed. Whatever it was, it was all done terribly discreetly. Not a breath of scandal. The point is that my Aunt Ethel always said of my parents that they had a "very good marriage". She really meant it. It *was* a good marriage in many ways. They were friends. They respected one another. They didn't quarrel. It—It worked, in a sort of way. Lots of married couples were far *un*happier.'

'If I had a marriage like that,' Jake said dourly, 'I'd blow my brains out. So would *you*, Alix,' he added, and his grey eyes rested on her in that uncomfortably direct way she knew so well. 'So don't give me any more rubbish about chaste, platonic arrangements. Okay, your parents were friends, no fights, no squabbles, hell! They didn't have anything to fight about! That's not caring! That's giving up, accepting failure and making the best of a bad job. May be they'd have loved to have a really tough fight and be able to go off to bed afterwards and make up. Did you ever think of that? In the bedroom, that's where it's all at. So what's a few spats? A few hard words and hurled dinner dishes? It gets the blood pounding around, anyway.'

She couldn't answer him, much as she wanted to, and sat staring miserably at her hands.

'I'm like an engine no one can get working,' Jake said slowly. 'It can be the most expensive engine in the world, but if it doesn't work, it's for the scrap-heap. When I was a youngster, I worked in the goods-yards with the Ruthenians. We called anyone from Eastern Europe a Ruthenian, regardless of whether he was or not—well, it was a real man's world down there, Alix. It carried no freeloaders. You had to prove you were fit for it every day of your life in some way, drinking, fighting, whoring. A thing like—like this, which has happened to me, it would have been unthinkable to them. It *is* unthinkable, until it happens. You thought I was dead until you saw me in the Louvre that afternoon. Then you said how glad you were to find me alive. But *I'm* not glad to be alive! I'm not alive. You were right the first time. You thought me dead, and I *am* dead, Alix!'

CHAPTER NINE

ALIX AWOKE the next morning and remembered that she had a nine o'clock meeting with Paul at his studio. She sat up in bed, stretched her arms above her head, and then drew up her legs and wrapped her arms round them, resting her chin on her knees. Going to work, putting her energies into designing yet another preposterous interior for one of Paul's wealthy clients, seemed totally meaningless in the face of what Jake had told her the previous evening.

'Though Jake would say it's not my problem, but his,' she thought. Her eye fell on the alarm clock and she saw with horror that she had failed to set the alarm bell the previous night and the hands stood at eight twenty-five. She moaned, 'Oh, no . . .' and scrambled out of bed, dragging off her silk pyjamas. She struggled into the first clothes to come under her hand in the wardrobe. Her face barely washed, no make-up, and the comb dragged ruthlessly at speed through her auburn hair, she grabbed a folder of sketches and raced downstairs. She set off for the centre of Paris, lamenting that she lived so far out, and knowing she would be late.

There was, of course, a fair chance that Paul would also be late, and she might yet arrive before him. If he'd been attending some party or other the previous night, as often happened, he would almost certainly not appear before eleven, even if that meant keep a whole string of appointments waiting. She often wondered how he managed to get away with it. Why didn't people just take their business elsewhere?

They didn't because, when Paul finally deigned to put in an appearance, he always managed to charm them. 'Dear madame,' he would say, bowing elegantly over some bejewelled hand. 'I overslept . . . You understand . . .'

A hint of roguish smile, the gleam in the dark eyes, a hand brushing back the tousled dark hair, and the lady inevitably succumbed, coyly wagging a finger at him. 'You are a rascal, Monsieur Daquin!'

For the men, he repeated the same words, but in a totally different tone. 'My dear Baron, I do beg your pardon. I—overslept, ah, *you* understand?'

The conspiratorial hushed voice, the appeal to a fellow man-about-town, and the mildest home and family loving client cleared his throat and hastened to assure him, 'My dear fellow, of course, of course! Say no more . . .'

Paul's car, a huge, flamboyant, red Hispano-Suiza, was not parked in its usual spot, so Alix breathed a sigh and slowed down, regaining her breath in order to climb the stairs to his first floor studio and office. Nobody waited in the anteroom, so he had not, for once, missed any appointments. She pushed open the door to the office and walked briskly in.

It was quite empty except for the secretary, Juliette, who was hunched over her desk, hugging herself tightly. She was wearing a black jacket covered in ornamental beadwork, and her long thin arms looked like the legs of some spider, clasped on its prey. It was almost as if she devoured herself. Her eyes, fixed unseeingly on Alix, were wide open, unnaturally large, the pupils strangely dilated. She was swaying slightly, rocking to and fro, and moaning softly.

Alix let fall the folder of drawings in her hand and they scattered, unheeded, across the office floor. 'Juliette?

What's wrong? Are you ill?'

Juliette frowned at the sound of Alix's voice and her arched, plucked eyebrows wrinkled in an effort to concentrate. Her garishly painted 'cupid's bow' mouth worked soundlessly for a few moments in her pale face. Then she whispered, 'That *salaud*, that bastard, that filthy pig!'

'Paul?' Alix asked, knowing that it could only be Paul to whom Juliette was referring so abusively.

'He promised me . . .' Juliette muttered. Her eyes seemed to focus at long last on Alix's concerned face bending over her. 'Don't let him into your life, Alix. Don't let him into even a corner of it! He has a black, evil heart . . .'She unwrapped her black spider's arms from about her own shoulders, and flinging out her hand, grasped Alix tightly by the forearm. 'You have to run away, Alix, *now!*'

'What on earth are you talking about?' Alix asked, frightened, despite herself, by the searing intensity in the girl's voice.

For a second Juliette looked as though she was going to weep, but then she shook her head and rocked back in her chair. In a movement as unexpected as it was violent, she seized an ink-bottle and flung it straight across the room. It struck the opposite wall, shattered, and left a blue-black stain spreading across floor and wall.

'He promised me!' she shouted fiercely.

Before Alix could do anything, Juliette's mood changed abruptly yet again. She began to giggle, quietly and with no apparent cause. It made Alix's flesh creep.

Then there was a movement behind her, and Alix heard a man's voice swear softly. Spinning round, she saw it was Daquin, who had come up unheard. His handsome, olive-skinned face was hard and pitiless. Revulsion was printed on it as he looked down at

Juliette. He might equally have been looking at some unpleasant sight on an anatomist's dissecting-table.

'Paul!' Alix exclaimed urgently. 'She's ill, what can we do?'

His lip curled scornfully. 'The little bitch isn't ill.'

'You don't think she's drunk?' Alix exclaimed incredulously. 'She can't be, not at this early hour of the day.'

'Drink? No, drugs,' he returned brusquely.

'W—What?' Alix gasped.

He shrugged his shoulders. 'I warned her that the next time it happened I'd throw her out, and I will. Stay here—I'll go and get a taxi to take her home. It's all right, she's harmless, just gibbering.' He threw a last disdainful glare at the girl and strode out.

When he came back, he stood over Juliette and snapped his fingers as if summoning an animal. 'Come on!'

With disbelief, Alix watched the fiery-tempered secretary stand up obediently, like a zombie, and follow Paul out, swaying a little.

He must have put her in a taxicab. He looked a little ruffled on his return, but he was a master of the situation. He lit a cigarette and stuck it in the corner of his mouth. 'Now!' he said briskly. He stopped to scoop up the spilled sketches from the floor. 'What have you brought me?'

'What did she mean, Paul?' Alix asked quietly, but very determinedly. 'She kept saying that you'd promised.'

He shrugged, deftly sorting the sketches into order. 'How should I know?'

'She must have got the foul drugs from somewhere. Was it from you? Is that what you'd promised her? A fresh supply?'

At her cool, probing question, he looked up, at last, from the sketches. 'Don't be stupid, Alix,' he said gently. 'Do you think I'd risk everything I have for that little tramp?' He put down the sketches and took off his jacket, hanging it higgledy-piggledy on the corner of a chair. Dragging the gold cuff-links from his shirt wrist-bands, he pushed them into his trouser pocket before rolling up his sleeves. Then he took off his tie. It was his usual preliminary before sitting down to work. Juliette had claimed that Paul had a drawer full of gold cuff-links in his flat, all presents from enamoured lady clients.

He sat down now at the desk vacated by Juliette and spread out the sketches. 'I don't mess about with drugs, Alix. I'm an old-fashioned sinner, women and wine . . . and I'm not too bothered about the wine, just sex. And now we've sorted *that* out, do you think we might do some work? It's what I pay you for.'

Juliette never returned to the office. Another girl took her place, efficient and placid. She had kohl-rimmed eyes like the vamp of the cinema screen. Paul nicknamed her 'Theda Bara'. She always called him 'Monsieur Daquin', very properly, and when he shouted at her, didn't answer, but stared at him with faintly puzzled, black-rimmed eyes.

Paul never mentioned Juliette again. She might never have existed. But from that day on, Alix began to see Paul differently. Possibly he'd been right to dismiss Juliette, but that dispassionate excision of her from his life seemed abnormal. He wasn't even angry. Like a surgeon amputating an infected limb, Alix thought, he feels nothing.

For the week following the departure of Juliette, Paul kept Alix busy on the new designs; so busy that she hardly had time to contact Jake. They had one hurried lunch together in a crowded riverside restaurant overlooking the Ile de la Cité.

'I was hoping you'd come and visit my art dealer with me,' Jake said ruefully. 'You can tell me what to buy.'

'No, I can't. If it's a question of taste, your taste is what matters, not mine; and if it's a question of investment, well, you're the businessman.'

'It strikes me,' he said bluntly, crushing his napkin into an untidy heap on the table, 'that you're quite a businesswoman yourself.'

Alix's green eyes surveyed him challengingly. 'I thought you'd approve. I hadn't expected *you* to say it was all right for a man to go out and earn his living, but not a woman.'

'I didn't say it. As far as I'm concerned, women can do whatever they want,' he said firmly. 'But I'm not sure I didn't prefer the old Alix.'

'I am the old Alix.' She sounded nettled and a little hurt, not liking to hear him criticise her, not over this. In a way, her whole new career sprang from what he had said, and everything she was doing was done for him. She wanted him to say, 'Well done, Alix', but so far, he'd obstinately refused to do so.

Jake smiled at her. She'd cut her hair, but not as short as some of the modern women's hairstyles, which he thought mannish and unattractive. Her hair floated in a tangled haze of auburn curls like a nimbus. When the sun struck it, gold lights seemed to sparkle in its depths like a glorious sunset. She was frowning a little, he could see, at his last remark, wrinkling her nose at him. He knew what she wanted of him—some sign of encouragement—but he was loath to give it. He did admire her for what she'd done, and for her success, but it underlined that he, now, had less to offer her than he'd ever had. And that had always been precious little. He'd been like a boy trying to catch a butterfly in a net, wanting the beautiful creature, but only able to destroy it if it ever fell into his hands.

Jake felt dull anger churning inside him, the old bottled-up energy that couldn't get out and which women and flying and fast cars had once assuaged. He wished he could meet with Fate face to face and demand to know what he'd done to deserve this. What dreadful crime had he committed that the Daughters of the Night should persecute him like some modern-day Orestes? He forced himself to smile again at his companion.

'You'll get lines on your forehead, scowling like that,' he told her.

'Tell me . . .' she leaned across the table towards him earnestly. 'Don't joke. Tell me truthfully, am I getting all hard-bitten and tough?'

'God, no!' he said, startled. 'Perish the thought. But you are getting very tied up with this fellow Daquin and his peculiar idea of earning a living.'

'It isn't peculiar. People want that sort of thing.'

'Anyone who has to be told what colour to paint his own house, and can't choose his own furniture, is a pretty poor fish.'

'Rubbish, they're just too busy.'

'*You're* too busy!' he grumbled.

Alix put her hand over his. 'I'll be free next week, and we'll have a proper lunch, taking our time. I promise.'

Jake's long lean fingers closed over hers. 'Alix,' he said patiently, 'I'm not asking you to waste more time on me, just to give yourself more time for yourself.'

'I have time, only not now. I've got to go.' She scrambled to her feet.

'All right, all right! Give me a chance to pay the goddam bill!'

'I'll pay it,' Alix offered brightly. 'I'm earning.'

'No,' Jake said firmly, 'you will not. I may be totally superfluous in every other respect, but please allow me the solitary male consolation of picking up the check!'

That evening Alix was late getting back to the flat. Too tired to think of going out to eat, she cut herself a sandwich, made a cup of coffee and put both on a tray. It was as she was carrying it into her little sitting-room that she heard noises on the staircase and a loud, strangely familiar, voice. It was speaking correct grammatical French, rendered almost unintelligible by an atrocious Anglo-Saxon accent. It asked for Miss Morrell's apartment. Shortly after there came a knock on the door, and when she opened it, a burly frame filled the doorway and a voice said in relief.

'Ah, there you are, Alix. Damn peculiar place you've got here.'

'Gerry!' Alix cried, throwing her arms round him and dragging him into the flat. 'Where have you sprung from? Oh, sit down, let me make some more coffee. Where are you staying?'

He sidled in like a large penguin in his dinner-suit, and stood on the sloping floor looking hopelessly incongruous and at the same time immensely dignified, as if his ice-floe had broken adrift. 'I've been trying to find you all day, Alix. When I called here this morning, some woman said you'd gone "to work".' Gerard snorted. 'She gave me a telephone number.' He produced a piece of paper with Paul's office number laboriously pencilled on it by the concierge, to whom Alix had given it for emergencies. 'I rang up, and got some fellow who was damn rude—but swore he'd give you the message.'

'Paul,' Alix said resignedly. 'He didn't. Well, never mind, Gerry. Sit down and I'll get that coffee.'

'As a matter of fact,' Gerard said diffidently, 'I came to ask you to come and dine with us. I've got a taxi waiting.'

'Us?' Alix stared at him. 'You haven't managed to coax Aunt Ethel across the Channel?'

Gerard reddened. 'No . . .' He took off his spectacles and in his old, familiar habit, began to polish them with a large white handkerchief. 'Fact is, Alix, I'm married. I'm on a sort of a late honeymoon trip. We thought we'd surprise you. I hope you'll be pleased. You were always friendly with the Frobishers.'

Alix sat down abruptly on the nearest chair, and said, 'You've married Blanche . . .'

It had always been on the cards, and, goodness only knew, Blanche had worked hard enough for it. But even so, that Gerry had 'actually gone and done it', as Alix thought colloquially, really took some few seconds to absorb and digest.

But Gerard was staring at her in amazement. 'Blanche? Lord, no . . .!' His undisguised astonishment and the horrified tone in which he denied the suggestion, spoke volumes. 'Not Blanche; Jennie! Jennie and I are married.'

Of course. Somehow it seemed obvious now. Why had she never thought of it before? 'I'm so pleased!' Alix exclaimed enthusiastically, kissing him. 'It's—It's perfect!'

Gerard said, 'Ah . . .' and shuffled his feet on the floor. 'Are you coming, then, Alix? The girls are waiting at the hotel.'

'Lord, Gerry, how many wives have you got?'

He grinned. 'Only one. But Jennie felt . . .' He'd stopped smiling. 'We had a bit of trouble with Blanche: Jennie will explain. Anyhow, as it's a late honeymoon trip, not a proper one, Jennie thought we should bring Blanche along. It seemed rather mean to leave her behind. Mother thought it a nice Victorian touch, too.'

Jennie and Blanche were sitting together in the cocktail lounge of the hotel. Jennie seemed to have blossomed.

She looked more confident, prettier and, Alix thought, as she embraced her friend, very happy. Even her ivory satin evening gown was worn with a new assurance.

Blanche looked much as she had always done. The Dresden prettiness was still there, attracting quite a few interested glances from male guests in the lounge. She had bobbed her blond hair fashionably, and it had been ruthlessly marcel-waved into regular troughs as rigid as tramlines. But it was a style which suited her tinsel prettiness. She sat swinging one crossed silk-stockinged leg provocatively and smoking a cigarette, aware that all eyes were on her.

Alix thought, 'Blowed if I'd bring Blanche along on *my* honeymoon!'

It was getting late, and Gerard hustled them all into the dining-room like a rather worried sheikh with an unruly harem. He called them all 'you girls', collectively. He'll call us that, thought Alix charitably, when we're all at least forty, except for his wife, whom he'll probably call 'the little woman'. Darling predictable Gerry, as unchanging as the laws of Nature.

'We were married three months ago,' Jennie said, 'but we couldn't get away at once. The fact is, I'm standing for parliament, and there was all the business of getting chosen to contest the seat. It's been a hectic time for us all, and this two-week trip to Paris is sort of stolen time.' She grimaced ruefully.

'I say, Jen,' Alix said, impressed. 'I bet old Aunt Emma is dancing a jig over that.'

'Um, she does approve, I think!' Jennie replied with a twinkle in her eye. 'But I couldn't have done it without Gerry to back me up with tons of moral support. It's been difficult, because everyone assumes that any woman who does get into parliament will be occupying herself solely with improved maternity care and child welfare, all approved feminine matters. It's an uphill business, persuading hard-headed political men that a woman can have an informed opinion on anything else.'

'How did you get chosen? Was some sitting member retiring?'

Jennie said, very carefully, 'No, I'm standing as a socialist.'

That made sense, too. But Alix glanced thoughtfully at Gerry, blandly dissecting his sole *bonne femme*.

'Oh, I know my husband isn't going to vote for me,' Jennie said calmly, intercepting the look. 'But it doesn't matter. He respects my views. Poor Gerry had a rough time when it first got out. One or two people, purple-faced old diehards at his club, said it was a confounded disgrace that he couldn't control his wife, and wanted to blackball him. But we're gradually riding out the storm.'

'When are you coming back to England, Alix?' Gerard asked bluntly.

Alix fidgeted with a piece of bread, and mumbled, 'I don't know.' She was blessedly released from having to elaborate on this by the arrival of the meat course.

In fact, her return to England was something she hadn't even considered. When she had come to Paris originally, it had been an open-ended arrangement with so much depending on how successful she would prove. But now that she had met Jake again, it occurred to her that she couldn't leave, not now. Not while Jake remained in Paris. She was going to have to tell Gerry and Jennie about Jake's reappearance, and it wasn't going to be easy.

After dinner they set off for the coffee lounge, but Blanche excused herself abruptly.

'I'm going back to the cocktail bar. They have a band in the evenings, and there's a dance-floor. Someone will ask me to dance. It's all right, Gerard, I'm quite safe. I'm not going to get picked up by some lounge lizard.

I won't leave the hotel, I promise.'

'Let her go,' Jennie whispered to the obviously reluctant Gerard.

When Blanche had departed, hips swaying invitingly in response to the lure of the dance-band saxophones, Gerard said bluntly, 'I don't like her going off unescorted like that. Damn it, it's not—not proper!'

'If you don't let her go, she'll sit here and sulk,' Jennie said calmly. She turned to Alix. 'You might as well know that we had a dreadful time with Blanche. When Gerry started calling at the house to see me, Blanche and Mother would insist he was coming to see Blanche. When Gerry and I actually got engaged, Mother was at her wit's end, having always considered me her ugly duckling. Blanche flew into an awful temper and accused me of terrible things.'

'I have never,' said Gerard obstinately, 'at any time in my entire life, given any indication that I had any intentions regarding Blanche. I'm a solicitor. I deal with breach of promise cases. I've seen more girls like Blanche sobbing in my office, declaring some chap had ruined their prospects and wanting to sue him for everything he had, than I could count. I'm hardly likely to have said anything stupid to her. Good Lord, as if I would! I never even thought of her.'

Gerard might know all about the law, thought Alix sadly, but he didn't know women. He was looking flushed and embarrassed now, perhaps feeling he'd spoken too freely. Jennie looked troubled. Blanche was a burden she was resigned to having to bear, but to ask her husband to share this burden was not something she felt it was honest to do. Alix understood Jennie well enough to realise this. Jennie was going to have to make a decision, and it was going to be a hard one. Alix, too, had a difficult decision to make, and she made it now.

She set down her coffee-cup and said brightly, 'Do

you remember Jake Sherwood? He was a friend of Robbie. He was shot down at the end of the war and we all thought he was dead. Well, he isn't. He was terribly injured . . . But he's convalescent, and in Paris.'

Dead silence greeted her announcement. She saw Gerard and his wife exchange glances.

'Well,' Gerard said with Olympian calm, 'I'm glad the fellow came out of it all right. I can't say I'm overjoyed to hear you've been seeing him.'

'I don't know what you mean by "seeing him",' Alix said, a little sharply. 'We've had lunch a couple of times. I'm busy working for Daquin, these days. It hasn't left me much time for anything else.'

'Good,' Gerard said simply.

'Look, I know you didn't like Jake, either of you . . .' Alix looked from Gerard to Jennie. 'But *I* like him, and he needs me.'

'Good God, Alix!' Gerard exploded. 'Why must you always involve yourself with lame dogs? You always end up getting hurt. Look at Robbie Harris. Anyone with half an eye could have seen what *his* interest was.'

'That's very rude of you, Gerry, but I'll excuse you on the grounds of cousinship. I know you always thought Robbie was after money.'

'And I was right, too, wasn't I?' Gerard thrust out his jaw pugnaciously. 'Seeing how he's behaved since!' He saw Alix's puzzled look, and added, 'You won't have heard, perhaps. He married recently, and is now the third husband of a notoriously flighty and very wealthy widow quite a bit older than himself.'

'Mother says eighteen years older,' Jennie supplied. 'Mrs Lyndhurst, the president of the company he was working for.'

There were people who always got what they wanted without difficulty. Things just dropped into their laps. Mrs Lyndhurst had wanted Robbie that evening when they had first encountered. Now she had him. But perhaps Robbie, too, had got his heart's desire at last.

Aloud, Alix said carefully, 'If she's older than he is, perhaps it doesn't matter, if they're happy with each other. At least, Gerry, you can't say Jake is after my money. He has his own money.'

'You're making a mistake, even so!' Gerard said fiercely. 'I knew it was ridiculous, allowing you to come to Paris on your own. Well, this does it. You're coming back to London with us.'

'Sorry, Gerry, but I'm not,' Alix heard her own voice declare resolutely. 'I'm staying here, and looking after Jake.'

Jennie asked in her cool, disconcerting way, 'Is that what *he* wants?'

'I honestly don't know the answer to that, Jen. Possibly he doesn't. But it's what I'm going to do, whether he wants me or not.' Alix met Gerard's eye and forestalled the explosive speech she saw forming on his lips. 'Before you say anything, Gerard, come and see Jake with me. You'll see *why* I can't just leave him. He needs me, and I want to be with him. Even if you don't really understand, and even if you can't accept it and think I'm crazy, at least you'll know why I've made the decision I have. Please, Gerry? You're supporting your wife even though you're not entirely in agreement with what she's doing. You supported me when I left home and came to Paris, even though you hated the whole idea. Don't take your support away from me *now*. I need it now, more than I ever did. And yours, Jennie, although I know you never cared for Jake. You're both my friends—my dearest and oldest friends. If you love me, please try, both of you, to support me now.'

Alix wasn't expecting the visit to be an unqualified

success, but at least she hoped it wouldn't disintegrate into disaster. All the same, she had to acknowledge a distinct feeling of butterflies in her stomach as the taxicab decanted Gerard and herself before Jake's apartment. It was a cool, clear day, but bitterly cold, with an icy wind cutting around street corners, bowling dust and débris before it along the pavements and pinching maliciously at noses, lips and ears.

The meeting did not start well, the two men greeting each other with stony formality. Jake, perhaps because he was host, showed marginally more warmth. But Gerard seemed to be twice as pompous as usual, and stiff to the point of near total woodenness. He watched Jake limp awkwardly towards him, and shook his outstretched hand unenthusiastically, before clearing his throat and saying expressionlessly, 'Good to see you again.' Then he turned aside in a sudden brusque movement, pulling out his handkerchief, and took off his spectacles to polish them energetically.

Jake met Alix's eye and raised his eyebrows wryly. She bit her lower lip nervously, thinking, 'Gerry's embarrassed at seeing Jake's struggles.' But that was before she took a quick, surreptitious glance at Gerard's flushed face and was astonished at the expression on it. It did not show embarrassment, but anger, mixed with frustration and despair. His features were set into rigid lines, his lips pressed tightly together, the pulse in his throat throbbing visibly above his stiff collar.

Alix realised with a pang of dismay that in her anxiety to convince Gerard of Jake's need of her, she had omitted entirely to consider what Gerard's feelings might be on meeting a man whose injuries marked him, as clearly as a row of medals would have done, as a war hero, a patriot, a man who had done his duty. For Gerard—the man who had not fought in that ghastly inferno, whose services had been refused, whom officialdom had declared 'unfit' to defend his country, and into whose hand a stranger in a crowd had once pressed a white feather—it was almost too much to bear. What would Gerard not have given for a chance to offer an equivalent sacrifice?

Now she watched Gerard put the handkerchief away, settle his spectacles in their rightful place, and say stiffly, 'We had no idea, my wife and I, that Alix had seen you again.'

'Alix told me you're married,' Jake said agreeably. 'I remember Miss Frobisher, as she was then, when I met her. How's she liking Paris?' He was limping towards the sideboard and the decanters. 'Drink?' He glanced over his shoulder.

Gerard debated, and Alix held her breath, believing he was going to refuse, before he replied gruffly, 'Whisky, please. I'll have a dash of water in it, if you've no soda.'

Alix heaved a sigh of relief, and seeing Jake's grey eyes glance in her direction, shook her head. 'Nothing for me.' But she went to take the whisky he poured out for Gerard, because he was apt to spill things in his uneven progress.

As he handed it to her, Jake murmured, 'Old Gerry thinks I'm the conquering hero. If he knew the sordid truth, he'd know he has the advantage over me.'

Trust Jake, ever shrewd, to spot instantly the cause of the underlying awkwardness of the situation, and to reduce it to basics.

They sat round in an ill-at-ease group. Gerard raised his glass and said 'Chin-chin!' but absently, as if his mind was elsewhere. He sipped at the whisky and set it down. 'Of course, this is only a brief holiday visit for me. Nevertheless, I'd hoped, despite the lack of time, to dissuade my cousin from pursuing this career in design she's embarked upon.'

'Oh?' Jake returned a little coldly. 'Why?'

Gerard reddened. 'It may be in order, where you come from, for young women of decent family to go haring off on their own and to live in odd places, but neither my mother nor I find it suitable for Alix to be doing it.'

'Alix is a very capable person,' Jake said swiftly, before she herself could protest. 'And Paris is the most civilised of cities.'

'That's neither here nor there!' Gerard snapped. 'There's no need for her to *work!*'

'Forgive me,' Jake said mildly, 'but some people might say—though I'm not one of them—that there is no *need* for Mrs Gerard Daventry to go into politics. Politics have never been anything but a tough and dirty business; no place for the squeamish or faint-hearted.'

Gerard's complexion had darkened to a rich, ruby hue. The pulse in his neck was fairly leaping about, and Alix wondered, with some concern, whether he was going to have an apoplectic fit. 'What my wife does, she does with my support and the protection of my name! Behind her she has husband, family and family home. Alix has none of these, here!'

Alix wanted to burst out that having Maisie Frobisher and Blanche behind one could hardly be counted reliable support, but she understood the point Gerard was making, and objected vigorously, 'Don't be old-fashioned, Gerry. I can design for Paul without needing an armed bodyguard.'

'I've never met the fellow,' Gerry said aggressively, resorting to his whisky, 'but nothing I've heard about him from you encourages me to think he's the right sort of company for you.'

'And what about *me?*' Jake asked him. 'Am I suitable company for Alix?'

'As a man who has held a commission in His Majesty's services, I should hope *your* conduct is to be relied upon!' Gerard almost snarled.

'Oh, you bet it is,' Jake said, without humour. He twisted awkwardly in his chair. 'Alix has told me quite a lot about Daquin, and I'm sure she can handle him.'

'I don't care for the way you express that!' Gerard charged resentfully. 'My cousin was brought up in a society in which women are accorded an automatic respect. She was not taught, or expected, to "handle" a situation, especially of the kind which I understand *you* to mean.'

'Stop squabbling!' Alix interrupted loudly. 'And stop, both of you, talking about me as if I wasn't here! Thank you for your support, Jake, but I can stand up for myself.'

A grin twitched at the muscles around Jake's mouth, and he said gravely, but with a sudden roguish twinkle in his eye. 'Yes, I know that.'

'You'll forgive us.' Gerard set down his glass heavily. 'But I feel it's time we took our leave, my cousin and I. We've left my wife and her sister at the hotel, to their own devices, and should be getting back.'

He jumped quickly to his feet, and Jake, taken unawares, was obliged to scramble up awkwardly with the aid of his stick. The hip, with malicious timing, chose that very moment to make one of its more spectacular collapses. It gave way, buckling uselessly with a vicious stab of pain. He swore colourfully, lurched sideways and plummeted to the floor in a crash of glass and furniture, and a heady smell of whisky.

Both Gerard and Alix ran to help him, where he lay sprawled on the carpet. Gerard got there first, but Jake struck away his arm angrily and shouted, 'Leave me, damn it, can't you?'

Gerard hesitated, looking up anxiously at Alix for guidance.

She gasped quickly, 'Let me. I know how. He doesn't

need support so much as steadying. It's the hip . . .'

She stopped and grasped Jake's shoulder, and after a brief struggle he was reinstated in the chair, his face white and drawn, his hair falling untidily over his brow and his grey eyes fixed in rage, pain and misery. He was still swearing, quietly and with great concentration, which caused a grim expression to settle on Gerard's face, replacing the concern that had been there. He picked up the broken glass in an automatic, safety-conscious gesture, and muttered, 'What now? Do we fetch a doctor, or what?'

'No, he's all right!' Alix heard herself exclaim fiercely, as she moved to place herself between the two men, shielding Jake from Gerard's view. Her face was flushed, and her gleaming green eyes briefly reminded Gerard of a bristling, protective mother cat defending her young.

Séraphine, the housekeeper, appeared silently with a dustpan and brush and began to sweep up the remaining fragments of shattered glass, restoring the upturned occasional table to its position and achieving, by the brisk normality of her movements, a relaxation of the tense atmosphere.

'Go on, both of you,' Jake ordered a little breathlessly, but with authority. 'Go back to the hotel. Leave me. I'm fine.'

As they descended to the ground floor in the rattling lift, Gerard, his eyes on Alix's pale, set face muffled in the fur collar of her coat, said, 'I take your point, Alix. But there's such a thing as biting off more than you can chew. He's an independent blighter, and he's on a short fuse. It's all bottled up in there. He won't forgive us, you know.'

She looked up sharply. 'For what?'

'For being there when it happened. For seeing him make a fool of himself like that.'

The lift came to a halt with a jolt and clank of metal.

'He didn't make a fool of himself!' she said fiercely, as they stepped out. 'He couldn't help it.'

'That's the whole point, my dear; he couldn't. He was helpless. Confound it, of course the man feels a fool!' Gerard said doggedly and with unexpected harshness. He took her arm as they stepped out into the sudden blast of chill wind sweeping the street. 'And face up to it, Alix. The man isn't one of *us*. He doesn't think like us, react like us, go about things as we would. Oh, he's got sterling qualities, I don't deny, but he's a rough diamond. Don't be fooled by an acquired interest in collecting works of art, and a veneer of sophistication. The Caesars, the Borgias and the Bonapartes did the same. Early upbringing and natural inclination always comes out. Have you noticed those smashed knuckles? He didn't get those scars in the war. He got them brawling. That's the way he grew up; not reasoning with the other fellow, just trying to break his jaw! Believe me, he's a man's man and only really at home in a man's world. If you want to find men like him, go and look in stableyards, garages, bars and billiard-rooms! War suits them. In war-time they're to be seen at their best. With women, they're generally to be seen at their worst.'

'He's just different, a self-made man!' she said defiantly. 'You make it sound like a crime.'

'I admire the fellow's courage and business brain,' Gerard said bluntly. 'But he'll break your heart, Alix. He'll shatter it like that whisky tumbler, into a dozen fragments, and perhaps I won't be there to pick up the pieces, when he does!'

CHAPTER TEN

BLANCHE WOUND up the phonograph in the little hotel sitting-room and began dancing to the tinny jazz music issuing from it. Her pearl-drop earrings bounced to and fro as she kicked up her heels and waved her hands, but the rigid marcelled tramlines of her hair budged not a fraction. Where she knew the words of the songs, she sang them, in a plaintive, little-girl voice. Otherwise she just sang, 'tum-tum-tum', and occasionally interspersed it with 'boop-de-boop'.

When she saw that her sister had come into the room, the gaiety and animation faded from her flushed face. She lifted off the phonograph needle and threw herself sulkily into a chair.

'I should have thought,' Jennie said mildly, 'you would have been out, looking at Paris, not cooped up in here. The weather's quite pleasant.'

'I've been out,' Blanche dismissed the suggestion. 'I walked along the rue de Rivoli and had coffee under the arches and looked in the windows. But I haven't any money, so what's the use? I walked all round that big square near there, the one with the column in the middle with things carved all over it.'

Jennie sighed. 'Well, then, we'll have some tea. Gerry's gone with Alix to see Captain Sherwood, so we're all on our own.'

'Oh, yes,' Blanche said dreamily, folding her hands behind her head. 'So Alix has met an old flame again.'

'He isn't an old flame!' Jennie retorted in a crushing voice. 'He was a friend of Robbie Harris.'

'Phooey! He's a single man, isn't he? So what if he was a friend of Robbie? Robbie's married now. Alix isn't, and Jake Sherwood just *happens* to be in Paris.' She lit a cigarette, ignoring Jennie's obvious grimace and her move to open the window. 'I remember Sherwood. He came to a party at the Harrises'—during the war. He was very good-looking, and lots of, you know, oomph.'

'I'm sure I don't know what oomph may be,' Jennie said serenely, taking charge of the tea-things which had arrived.

Her admonitory tone angered Blanche. A spiteful note entered her voice and a diamond-bright glitter her blue eyes. Her round, pretty face suddenly contrived to look sharp and pinched. 'Don't pretend to be so innocent! You took us all in with that act for years. Bookworm Jennie, who wouldn't say boo to a man . . . until you decided to take Gerard away from me.'

'Don't start that again,' Jennie said wearily. 'I didn't, and you know it. You've no reason to feel so sorry for yourself.'

'I've got good reason!' Blanche muttered. 'You've had everything. Look how Aunt Emma took a fancy to you, because you favour Father's side of the family. She always said I was "just like Mother"—which was another way of saying she thought I was common. I could have dropped dead in the gutter, and Aunt Emma wouldn't have contributed a ha'penny towards a wreath. Gerard was my only chance of getting away. For years I put up with it all, Mother fussing round and pinning every hope on me, and old cats like Aunt Emma sneering and snubbing me. Now what am I? The unmarried daughter, left at home with Mother, who grumbles all the time how she scrimped and saved for me and I wasted all my chances. *What* chances?' Blanche cried out bitterly.

'I'm not arguing with you, Blanche. You're in one of your moods. I'm more worried about Alix just now. I do hope she isn't going to do anything stupid.'

'Like jump into bed with Sherwood, you mean? I bet she already has.' Blanche got up and went to a mirror. She licked a fingertip and carefully drew it across her plucked eyebrows, consciously restoring the Dresden prettiness. Obviously the subject of Alix bored her. Blanche quickly became bored with any conversation of which she was not the central theme. 'Alix can look after herself,' she said carelessly.

'I used to think that, too,' Jennie sighed, 'but now I'm not so sure. Gerard's worried.'

The spiteful look returned to Blanche's face, and her eyes gleamed with malicious, mocking laughter. 'Perhaps you'd better hope Alix *has* fallen for Sherwood, Jen. Or your loving husband might spend more time worrying about his cousin than his new little wife!'

Jennie looked up, and at the expression in her sister's face, Blanche drew back, and shrank into her chair, frightened. 'Blanche,' Jennie said quietly, 'if you ever try to make trouble between me and Gerry, I'll cease to have anything to do with either you or Mother, for ever. You know what that means, don't you?'

Blanche looked sullen. She did, indeed, understand only too well what her sister's threat meant. Jennie, with her increasingly widespread connections, and Gerard, solid, prosperous and respected, made it possible for Blanche to enter into a society which would be closed to her otherwise. Blanche was pretty; but pretty girls abounded. Good society admitted—officially—only those who had money or connections. Pretty girls with no money and no one to speak for them were rightly seen as adventuresses, and rigorously excluded. They were consigned to the demi-monde, where life was sweet for a few years, but rapidly soured as their looks faded.

Blanche didn't like Jennie's friends. She felt ignorant in front of them. They discussed topics which not only bored her profoundly, but left her totally at sea, unable to contribute a single sentence. But they lived in large, detached houses, and most had a private income or were 'well up' in the professions. They drove motor-cars and holidayed in the South of France. The women enjoyed generous dress allowances and a great deal of personal freedom. They were never required to so much as boil an egg in the kitchen. Somewhere, in that wealthy, self-assured and secure throng, Mrs Frobisher was confident there must be a husband for Blanche. Blanche had been well warned by her ambitious parent, before leaving for France, that she must do nothing to upset Jennie and Gerard, because she needed them.

But Blanche was bored. Paris bored her. The hotel bored her. The company of her sister and brother-in-law both bored and irritated her. She slipped away from them whenever she could and, despite her assurance to Gerard, was only too happy to be picked up by any hotel-lounge gallant who would buy her a drink and provide a brief spell of entertainment in one of the bedrooms. Blanche liked men, not for their conversation or their achievements, but for their essential masculinity. They admired her, and she enjoyed their admiration, and the touch of their hands on her skin. Most couldn't wait to lure her upstairs for one of those interludes of furtive, hurried lovemaking. She enjoyed every minute of it, from their fumbling, hasty attempts to unfasten stubborn dresses with sweating fingers to the moment of possession when, panting and moaning, they lost control of themselves completely.

Needless to say, Maisie Frobisher had no idea of Blanche's activities in this respect. She would have been rightly horrified. Nothing would have ruined Blanche's chances of marriage more quickly than even a hint of scandal. Nor would Gerard or Jennie have stood for it for a moment. Blanche would have been packed off home immediately, were she discovered.

At first, outwitting her mother, Jennie and Gerard had amused Blanche. But increasingly she had come to resent that she was not free to do as she wished openly. Jennie, with her political career, was doing what she wanted, and even Alix—towards whom Blanche had always nurtured a deep, burning jealousy—was free to come to Paris, paint and involve herself with any man she fancied, even Sherwood.

But Alix had money. So did Jennie, now, thanks to her marriage, together with the added protection afforded by her married status. Only she, Blanche, was hampered by a host of petty restrictions and considerations, by her lack of fortune and her unmarried state.

Her diamond-bright blue eyes narrowed and her full, pouting rouged lips twitched nervously as she stared at Jennie. Jennie—who had stolen the husband who should have been *hers* . . .

With a movement so swift it seemed almost too fast for the human eye to follow, Blanche threw herself forward, snatched up the pot of hot water from the tea-tray and hurled full in her sister's face.

Only experience and lightning reactions saved Jennie. She had been forewarned, just fractionally in time, by that glitter in Blanche's eyes and the twitching muscles round her mouth. She threw herself to one side and most of the water splashed over the chair and floor. But some caught Jennie's sleeve, soaking it from shoulder to wrist.

Jennie leapt up with a gasp, and swabbed at her wet clothing with a napkin, while Blanche, half elated and half frightened at what she had done, crouched on the edge of her chair like a cornered animal.

'You'll *never* do anything like that again!' Jennie said

harshly. 'Do you hear me?'

Blanche hunched her shoulders, and glowered.

'I'm going to change my dress. Ring for the maid and tell her the pot was accidentally knocked over.' Jennie turned and walked as composedly as she was able into her bedroom, where she stripped off the wet dress and dragged a fresh one from the wardrobe.

Blanche had followed her, and sat on the bed, watching. 'I'm terribly sorry, Jen,' she said mellifluously in her little girl's voice. 'I didn't mean it, honestly.'

Even though she was used to Blanche's sudden changes of mood, Jennie was taken unawares and stopped buttoning her dress to stare at her sister. Blanche looked as docile and innocent as a well-behaved child. Jennie had not been frightened before, but she felt fear now, fear of that mind through which a vein of wickedness seemed to run, like a flaw in a jewel. She made no reply, but brushed her hair with a shaking hand, and walked out.

Left alone, Blanche sat for a few minutes on the bed, gazing thoughtfully at the twin pillows. At last she got up and went to the wardrobe, which Jennie had left open in her agitation. Jennie's dresses hung in a neat row, the ivory satin evening gown at the end. Blanche unhooked it and slipped it off the hanger. She held it up in front of her, before the cheval glass, turning this way and that to admire the effect, and humming a dance tune under her breath.

To the empty room, she said aloud, 'This is a wasted dress on you, Jen. It's so pretty, like me—and you're so *plain* !'

Then, slowly and deliberately, she took the soft material in both hands and ripped the gown from bodice to hem.

Alix and Gerald parted at the hotel, Alix politely

refusing an invitation to dine with the Daventrys, chiefly
in order to avoid Blanche's open curiosity. She walked
off quickly alone, before Gerald could protest. For a
while, she roamed aimlessly among the thinning crowds
of late afternoon shoppers, unwilling to go back
immediately to her tiny flat, and her mind churning
with the decision she had made and wondering how to
communicate it to Jake. How would *he* take it? Probably
badly.

Somehow, following some automatic instinct, she
found herself standing before the building that housed
Paul's studio and office. She sighed, and reflected that
she had, in any case, to collect some sketches she had
left there. Normally, this late on a Saturday, the office
would be closed, but she had a key, given her by Paul
in his usual casual way, so that she could go at any
time and work there, if she wanted. But when she had
climbed the stairs (it was an old building and had no
lift), she found that the key was not needed. The main
door to the studio suite opened to her hand, and the
inner door to Paul's office stood ajar, indicating that he
was working his usual erratic hours. Further confirma-
tion was given, if any were needed, but the aroma of
the scented Turkish cigarettes he smoked.

Paul, a dishevelled figure in shirt-sleeves and waistcoat, his hair unkempt and a 'six o'clock shadow'
darkening his chin, was standing on the far side of the
office, by the window, holding one of her sketches in
his hand and studying it intently. The cigarette, caught
negligently between his index and middle fingers,
smouldered, sending up a curl of blue smoke. Alix,
surveying him critically, felt a momentary understanding for those women who found his rakish and
ruthlessly self-interested personality attractive. They
would get hurt, but as children play with fire, so they
came back, time and time again, lured by the burning

coals and heedless of the flame. He and Jake were in many ways similar. Yet Jake wouldn't hurt anyone, she thought, not unless that person tried to hurt him, and he wouldn't discard people who had been loyal to him, as Paul would do.

Paul seemed to become aware of her standing in the doorway, and glanced up with no sign of surprise at her presence. He indicated the sketch in his hand, and said, 'You're a very good artist, you know, and a first-rate designer', just as if they were continuing a conversation begun some minutes earlier.

'I came to collect those,' Alix told him. She put down her bag and held out her hand for the sketch he held.

'I was thinking . . .' He stubbed out the cigarette in a glass ashtray on the window-ledge, already overflowing with half-smoked stubs. 'I'd like you to do more work for me than you do now. I've one or two really big contracts just within my grasp. But the fact is that I've more work than I can handle; you know that. I'm having to do too much running around to sit and design anything myself. Jul—' He hesitated imperceptibly, and changed what he'd been about to say to, 'My other secretary was good at dealing with suspicious architects and argumentative clients. Theda Bara is competent enough, but only if I write it all down for her in large block capitals first, and she's got the personality of a plate of noodles. Besides, she's in love. Not with *me*! Don't look at me like that! With some overweight youth who wears cheap suits. The girl is useless. But you, Alix, could deal with the clients for me, as well as take on some of the design work I do now. You've worked with me long enough to know the sort of thing. You make the right impression on people, you have chic, looks, education. You're a good businesswoman. What do you say? We could go out to dinner now, and talk it over.' He took his watch from his waistcoat pocket and glanced at it. 'Give me time to clean up and shave. I keep a razor here.'

Alix took the sketch gently but firmly from him, put it together with the others and tied up the folder carefully, to gain time. 'Give me a while to think it over. Anyway, I can't have dinner with you now, this evening. I've . . .' She sought an excuse. 'I've promised Jake I'd go back there.' It was a lie, but she couldn't be bothered with Paul, not just now.

'I thought you went there this afternoon with that brother you were telling me about,' he said resentfully, scowling.

'Not brother; *cousin*. Paul, you never listen to anyone! Yes, I did go with Gerry, but I've still promised to go back.'

'This cousin of yours . . .' Paul stared hard at her. 'What's he doing in Paris?'

'He's on his honeymoon.'

Paul grimaced, and said, 'Poor devil . . .'

Alix gave him an admonitory look and, gathering up her folder, left the office before he could return to his argument over more work.

In fact, it was a good offer he was making her, from the point of view of her career. But just now she had Jake on her mind. Perhaps that was why she'd lied about going back to Jake's flat. It was where, subconsciously, she wanted to go. She *would* go there. Waiting would not make easier what she had to say to Jake. Alix hailed a passing taxicab.

Jake hadn't expected Alix to return that night, and was sitting at his desk in the corner of the salon, working. He looked up in mild surprise as she entered, and she crossed quickly to him and automatically grasped his shoulder to stop him getting unnecessarily to his feet, although, in all fairness, he had made no move to do so.

'What's that?' She peered over his shoulder at the desk. The surface was covered with a sea of papers covered with complex-looking calculations, and a large map. Alix stretched out her fingers and touched it.

'Oh, a project I've had in mind for some time. It was an idea I had during the war. I still think it's a winner—but events stopped me putting it to the test, and now . . .' He hesitated and shrugged. 'Every so often I get out the draft ideas and rework them. That's a railroad map of Canada and the United States, incidentally, coast to coast.'

'Why do you need that? To transport things?'

'Transport "things" is what it's best designed to do, in *my* view. To transport people, we now have the aeroplane. It means designing bigger machines, of course, intended for passenger carrying. In the meantime, small aircraft lie about unused in every hangar on every aerodrome now; war casualties like me.'

'A commercial company carrying passengers?' Alix asked incredulously.

'Why not? The trouble over here is that they think in small distances. After all, some people live in countries the size of backyards. Every time they move, they bump into a frontier. But in North America, South America, Australia, Russia—you can cross a continent and never touch an international frontier. And people want to cross those continents now, Alix, as never before. Think of the time and the inconvenience saved by flying.' The enthusiasm died in his voice and he pushed the papers aside. 'Well, it's an idea.'

'You'll need a commercial artist, like me,' Alix said suddenly, and he looked up into her green eyes and pulled a face at her.

'I'm serious!' she insisted. 'I mean you'll need a

company emblem, and staff uniforms, and new offices which will want a really *new* décor, because it's a new kind of business. Even the aeroplane interiors . . . I mean, after all, you're going to transport people, not cattle. Even the colour of the seats matters.'

'It does?' he raised his eyebrows.

'Of course. Some colours are restful, and some enervating—and, Jake, I'd *love* to do it!' Her voice and eyes glowed with unfeigned enthusiasm.

'Hmm.' He was doodling on a spare scrap of paper, absently drawing spirals with a pencil and staring at her thoughtfully with shrewd grey eyes. Abruptly he stopped and pushed away the papers into an untidy heap, tossing the pencil down. 'Perhaps. I'll sleep on it. Anyhow, we won't talk about it now. What are you doing here? I thought you were going to dine with Gerry and his wife, and her sister?'

'I couldn't face Blanche,' Alix admitted. 'She stares at me, and asks endless questions. I'm glad Gerry didn't marry her. I was always afraid that he might. She was frightfully keen, and, I have to admit, I do feel a little sorry for her, because she must be upset.'

Alix was totally unprepared for the forceful and lengthy response this called forth from Jake. Slapping the palms of his hands on the arms of his chair to emphasise his words, he declared himself not in the slightest surprised that Gerard had declined to marry Blanche. His language was colourful and frank. What man in his right mind married a girl like Blanche? Gerard, Jake continued, ignoring Alix's obvious wish to interrupt, was a lawyer and supposed to impress people with his sound judgment. Did she honestly imagine a situation in which Gerard invited favoured clients home to dinner, just to find Blanche leaving lipstick traces all over the gin glasses and giving everyone free views of her stocking-tops?

It was probably all true, but Alix found herself thinking that it was cruel, and wishing he hadn't said it. But Jake was a man who said what he thought. There was a tough and uncompromising side to his nature which made her think, 'Perhaps I was wrong, and he *is* like Paul, after all.' Yet Jake was different from Paul, a more complex man, capable both of great sensitivity and extraordinarily harsh judgments such as he'd delivered now.

With a little shiver, she wondered if there had ever been a moment, right at the beginning of their acquaintance, when he'd been on the verge of dismissing *her* with that same callousness, seeing her as no more, perhaps, than a pretty decoration. 'Prove to me that you're not just another spoiled little rich girl', he had once challenged her. She'd managed to pass that test, but she asked herself now, uncomfortably, whether, like the Battle of Waterloo, it hadn't been a damn near-run thing.

Out of loyalty to Jennie, she tried, now, to defend Blanche. It was a mistake.

'I've met dozens of girls like Blanche,' he said curtly, 'mostly working in bars and selling their time and company. So has Gerard, you bet. Come on, Alix!' With this impatient exhortation, Jake twisted awkwardly on his chair. The hip, stuck in one position for too long, had become numb, refusing to respond to messages from the nerve-centres. Wrenched fiercely now into a new position, it responded to being awakened by a savage stab of pain. Jake pulled himself out of the chair, picked up his stick and began to limp up and down the room.

Alix had become used to this. He did it when he had sat still for too long and that incapacitating numbness had set in, which led to his being unable to stand at all or falling at the first attempt to walk. She stood up and began to walk with him, turning up and down the room, with her arm linked through his, exactly as though they were in the park.

'Nice day,' Jake said conversationally, giving her a wry, sideways grin.

Alix was relieved to see him make an effort to put his bad temper aside. 'How do you think Gerry himself looked, this afternoon?' she asked.

'Like prosecuting counsel! He doesn't like me too much, does he?'

'He doesn't like any man who is a friend of mine,' Alix said, with a twitch of her shoulders. 'He didn't like Robbie.'

'Well, he doesn't have to worry about me. Your virtue is safe, tell him.' Jake's stick struck against the leg of the table.

'He wants me to go back to England with them.'

Jake hesitated only imperceptibly before asking calmly, 'And is that what you're going to do?'

Her heart sank. It was going to be more difficult than she had anticipated. Talking him round to her viewpoint was going to prove a monumental task. But he did need her, whether he was prepared to admit it or not, and the belief spurred her on to recklessness.

'No. I told him, and Jennie, that I'm going to stay here, and look after you.'

They stopped by mutual accord at the end of the room by the piano. It was dark outside now, but the shutters of the balcony windows had not been closed and the evening noise of the Parisian traffic, dominated by agitated hooting, drifted in with the pale glimmer of the street-lamps. On the piano was a lighted, glass-stemmed lamp, which cast its iridescent glow over them both and over the Renoir, which Jake had hung on the wall behind them. The girl with the armful of poppies seemed to watch them with sympathetic curiosity.

Jake took his arm from Alix's, and said gently, 'It's not what I want, Alix. We've been through all this. I'm not ungrateful. But you're young and beautiful and full of life, and talent. I'm just a wreck. I'm not going to let you do it.'

Suddenly, surprising both herself and him, she burst out, 'You're just like Gerard, like *all* of them! You all know what's best for me, and just by coincidence, what's "best" happens to be what *you* want!'

Jake was staring in amazement at her blazing emerald eyes, sparkling with green fire, and at her impassioned face. Before he could speak, Alix plunged on, deliberately riding roughshod over any objection he might make. 'All I have heard from you since we met again is how *you* feel and what *you* want! How about asking me what *I* feel, and what *I* want?'

There was a long silence, and the echo of her voice died away slowly, the words losing themselves in the shadowy corners of the room.

'All right,' Jake said, his face and voice devoid of any expression. 'What do you want, Alix?'

'I want to stay here and look after you. I dare say you don't like the expression "look after", but that's it, that's what I want to do. When I'm away from you, I worry about you. I also think you've become too wrapped up in yourself and maudlin. You need someone here, with you all the time, to—to make you snap out of it. And I want it to be me,' she concluded doggedly.

'Move in here?' he asked sarcastically. 'Gerry would blow a gasket!'

'*Yes*, move in here. Of course, I could just come and live here without any formality. But as people don't know of your—your impotence—I agree, it would present to the world a situation that Gerry and Jennie and Aunt Ethel, all people who love me, would find hurtful and distressing. They'd think I'd gone to the dogs, living with a man. So, for their sakes, I'd prefer us to go through some sort of civil ceremony first. The French do that kind of thing awfully well. You know, the mayor in his tricolour sash, speeches, and so on. Civil ceremonies are respectable in France. Not as in England, where they usually mean divorcés and bigamists.'

'I told you, once,' Jake said in a low, dangerous voice. 'I don't want that kind of a sham marriage—and neither do you!'

'There you go again!' Alix stamped her foot in her frustration, and at this archetypal expression of feminine exasperation, a faint smile touched the corners of Jake's angry mouth, softening its aggressive line. 'You're telling me what *I* want. Well, Jake Sherwood, I'm telling you *myself* what I want. I'm perfectly capable of being my own spokesman!'

'Spokeswoman,' Jake corrected helpfully.

'Spokeswoman, then! The wedding ceremony would only be to keep Gerry and everyone happy.'

'I see. You're proposing to me, are you, Miss Morrell? Female emancipation has obviously got further than I thought! I'm very flattered.'

'Don't be whimsical, Jake!' Alix stormed at him. 'I've never flattered you, ever!'

'No,' he said quietly, 'you haven't. Promise me one thing, Alix. I have to insist on it, and you have to keep the promise.'

'What is it?' she asked in trepidation, because he looked so serious.

'Come here, stay here, boss me around, go through any kind of ceremony you want. But *never* do to me what you did to Robbie.'

Startled, Alix whispered, 'What was that?'

'Pretend. You pretended with Robbie. You kept that darned engagement going long after it was dead. Don't

do that to me. The day you decide you want "out", tell
me. We'll get an annulment, and go our separate ways.
Whether you meet someone else, a proper man who can
take you to bed, or whatever the reason may be. It
doesn't matter what. But the day it's all over, *tell* me.
Tell me the truth as you always have done, Alix. I
swear to God, I couldn't stand it if I thought you were
lying to me!'

'I'll never lie to you, Jake,' she whispered. 'I promise.'

Because Alix wanted Gerard and Jennie to be present
and they were returning to England at the end of the
week, the wedding ceremony had to be arranged in a
great rush. But, privately, she thought it better that
way. It gave everyone less time to argue or reconsider,
let alone to change their minds. Gerard and Jennie were
reluctantly supporting her. Jake had agreed to going
along with the idea. She, Alix, now that she had taken
the plunge, was in a feverish haste to get formalities
over and done with.

From time to time, chiefly in the sleepless small hours
of the night, an unwished voice inside her head whispered disturbingly that her haste was, maybe, because
she feared to consider that she might just have made
another mistake. She didn't doubt her feelings for Jake,
as she had done for Robbie. But she was far from
certain just what were Jake's feelings for her.

'*I* love him!' she said defiantly and a little miserably
into the darkness.

'*He* has always loved fast motor-cars and flying
machines, speed and freedom,' replied the voice cruelly.
'Can you be a substitute for all that? He never wished
a sham marriage; he said so. Are you ignoring him at
your peril? Will he grow to hate you?'

But the wedding morning dawned fine and clear, a
cool but sunny day. Alix had invited Paul to the

ceremony. He bought her work, and Jake had expressed an interest in meeting him. On a purely practical level, Paul would provide a luncheon partner for Blanche afterwards. Paul had received news of the proposed wedding, and his invitation, with a predictable grimace.

'I can't see why you want to do it, Alix. Marriage offers no benefits that I can see, and I've tried it!'

'Something tells me you're not a typical case,' Alix told him sternly.

'Are *you*?' he countered swiftly and shrewdly.

She was sharply reminded that, whatever else Paul might be, he was no fool. He already sensed something odd about this marriage, and he was not beyond working it all out for himself, given the tiniest of clues. She and Jake would have to be wary of Paul.

She avoided his question by replying, 'Don't be late, for goodness' sake. You know what a bad time-keeper you are.'

Probably more out of mischief than any wish to oblige, Paul wasn't late; he was early. The first sight Alix saw as she got out of the taxi was his gangling figure atop the Mairie steps, already in place to greet the arriving bridal party. He looked exceptionally tidy, wore a carnation in his buttonhole and carried a small box wrapped in silvery paper and tied up with white satin ribbon.

Alix sighed with relief. Gerard was also anxious to meet Paul. Gerard did not appreciate Bohemian raffishness, and she had feared Paul might just turn up (as he'd been known to do), half an hour late, with his tie under his ear and wearing odd socks.

Alix had given great thought to her own wedding ensemble. She finally settled on a cream georgette dress, as the day was so mild, beneath a light cream wool coat trimmed with lynx fur, a head-hugging hat restraining her rebellious auburn curls.

'You look lovely, Alix,' Gerard said soberly, kissing her. 'Are you quite sure about all this, my dear?' he whispered into her ear.

'Quite sure, Gerry. I promise you I've thought it all out.'

These last words had been tempting Fate, who always has a trick up her sleeve. Fate chose to play her joker's card immediately.

Jake and Paul stared at one another, and then Jake said slowly, 'We've surely met before? During the war . . . You were one of the French pilots who came over to our mess on Christmas Eve of 'seventeen.'

Paul's expression cleared and his eyes lit with enthusiasm. 'Ah, yes, of course—the Canadian. I remember you! We were all very drunk that night, and we went down to the village and found some girls . . .'

He became aware of the frozen faces of the other guests and broke off hastily, with a disarming smile. 'Sorry, Alix. On his wedding day, one shouldn't recall a man's bachelor misdeeds.

'Can we not go inside?' Gerard asked stiffly. 'The girls ought not to be standing about out here on the pavement.' As they climbed the steps, he demanded *sotto voce*, 'Who the devil is that fellow?'

'Paul Daquin—I work for him.'

Gerard said, 'Hah!' wrathfully. 'He was the blighter I spoke to on the 'phone.'

The wedding ceremony was mercifully short. Jake looked very distinguished, Alix thought, and rather serious, almost as if she were really going to be his wife and not just his nurse-companion. He was leaning on his stick quite heavily, but the hip didn't fail him, and if he was in pain, he didn't show it. She felt her heart quite swell with pride at the sight of him. He was a very handsome man, of commanding presence. He made Gerard look stodgy, and Paul, even tidy, looked as though he would have been more at home on a racecourse.

All the same, the discovery that the two men knew each other had come as a shock. Even more of a shock was the other discovery, that Paul had been in the war, and as a pilot. He'd never even remotely mentioned this episode of his life. Had other things simply mattered more to him? Or was this a memory so painful that he'd blocked it out? She realised that although she knew Paul quite well, she knew absolutely nothing about him really. She knew how he was in character, but not what had made him like it.

Now, however, was not the time to think about that. Alix smiled nervously at Jennie as they all lined up on the Mairie steps so that Gerard could take a photograph. They all shuffled about obediently in response to Gerard's commands, arranging themselves in a self-conscious group, while he barked, 'Closer together—no! Bride and groom in the front . . .' as though they were a flock of rather dense sheep.

'Tell him to hurry it up, for God's sake!' Jake muttered, and Alix realised with a start that he was in agony.

But Gerard ordered, 'Hold it!' and the camera clicked at last.

Jennie was looking quite elegant if a little serious in a pearl grey costume of which the skirt buttoned at the side, and a hat with a large feather transfixing the brim. Blanche was dressed unseasonably in shell-pink, which lent a rosy glow to her porcelain complexion. She smiled winsomely at Paul as Gerard arranged the photographic group, her golden curls gleaming in the sunlight. Paul was attracted, Alix could see that, but there was an enigmatic expression on his face. Alix felt a stir of unease. Blanche was a practised flirt, but Paul a hardened and experienced roué. He was one of life's takers, never a giver. If Blanche thought Paul was going to fall under her spell, she was heading for a bitter experience.

But Alix was now more worried about Jake, whose temper was beginning to fray. He eyed Blanche irritably, and muttered. 'She looks like a damn china doll.'

'Hush,' Alix hissed. 'She'll hear you!'

With expressions of general relief all round, they retreated to the restaurant where they were all to lunch at Gerard's invitation. He had constituted himself '*in loco parentis*', as he put it. 'Bride's father usually foots the bill for this sort of thing, so it's up to me, as bride's only relative present.'

It proved really quite a jolly little luncheon, but a strange one, too, as Alix afterwards reflected. They were like a set of negotiators round a table, sounding each other out and constructing tentative alliances and setting out terms, all under a cloak of conviviality.

As they sat down to lunch, Paul pushed a lock of dark hair out of his eyes, and presented his mystery box to her with a flourish. 'Wedding present!'

'Thank you, Paul!' Alix was surprised. She unwrapped the box and discovered an exquisite antique silver inkstand, an enchanting little glass ink-pot with a silver lid, and a little knife for trimming quills.

'First Empire,' Paul said, 'as used by the Empress Josephine.'

'This is a beautiful object, Paul,' Alix said slowly, genuinely touched, not only because he had thought to give them a gift in the first place, but because he had obviously taken much time and trouble to find something he knew she would like very much to own.

'For a beautiful lady!' He smiled at her charmingly.

Under cover of the distraction, Jake leaned towards Jennie, seated on his other side. 'You don't look too happy,' he said bluntly. 'I've been watching you. You've got disapproval of this whole affair written all over your face. What's your objection?'

Jennie flushed, but returned his look calmly. 'I thought the bridegroom was supposed to have eyes only for the bride?'

'That's a smart answer,' he said, 'but you're a very smart lady. You disapprove of me, don't you?'

'Alix is my oldest friend,' she said quietly. 'And a very vulnerable person. She would never hurt anyone deliberately, and I don't want to see her hurt. I don't know enough about you to tell what sort of a person you are, so, if you don't mind, I'll suspend my judgment till I see how everything turns out.'

'Yes, you are a clever woman,' Jake said slowly. 'But it isn't all in books, you know.' He gave her a dry look.

Despite all this, it was a cheerful party which sat late over the table, toasting the newly-weds in champagne. Blanche had drunk rather a lot, and was giggling and chattering to Paul. When the gathering broke up, Alix was not surprised to hear Paul say, 'Mademoiselle Blanche has not seen Paris. I am a Parisian. I consider myself responsible for putting this omission right. I have your permission?'

He asked this question of Gerard, very politely, with a little military bow.

'Paul's playing everything by the book,' Alix thought uneasily. 'What is he up to?' Immediately she felt ashamed, because he had behaved exceptionally well, been very nice to everyone, and given her an expensive and rare present.

So Paul handed the dimpling Blanche up into his Hispano-Suiza, and they drove off together.

'Where are we going first?' Blanche asked demurely.

He glanced at her and grinned rakishly. 'I thought we might start with my apartment.'

Alix had been to Paul's apartment only once, and promptly pronounced it to be an extension of his office.

It was littered with papers, sketchfolders, architects'
estimates and business accounts. But, of course, Alix
hadn't been in the bedroom.

Blanche didn't know it, as she stood in the middle of
the room and surveyed it curiously, but Paul also
conducted a great deal of his business in here. The
bedroom, was, in consequence, luxuriously appointed,
with a huge white fur rug thrown over the bed. The fur
rug impressed Blanche deeply. She thought it looked
just like a setting in a cinema film, and only lacked a
sultry-eyed vamp. She imagined herself playing the
vamp, and smiled delightedly. Again, she was not to
know that it *was* exactly like something the silent screen
had dreamt up, because Paul intended it so. A number
of wealthy lady clients had played the vamp on this set.

Blanche slid out of her clothes with a suggestive ease
that made Paul smile a little cynically. He wasn't her
first lover, and he wouldn't be her last, and she was
looking forward to the afternoon. The champagne they
had been drinking made her feel relaxed and pleasantly
amorous.

'Champagne,' Paul murmured wickedly to her,
'improves anyone's performance, even mine!' His hand
slid over the smooth skin of her thigh.

Yet she was not prepared for the arrogance with
which he took her, and gave a little cry. But he whispered, 'Not yet . . .' and she fell silent until a little later
when, moaning softly beneath him, she gasped
'Don't . . .' But she didn't mean it, and he didn't stop.

When they had finished making love, Blanche lay
back on the pillows and sighed. To the alcoholic goodwill
was added a feeling of general satisfaction, and it made
her talkative. A better judge of male psychology than
she would have realised that this was not the moment
to talk but to keep quiet. But Blanche, habitually
concerned only with what went on in her own mind

and body, didn't trouble to think that the bright, gossipy chatter which had amused Paul prior to physical union might simply irritate him afterwards.

Now she watched him get out of bed and tie the belt of his silk dressing-gown. He took a cigarette from his gold case on the dressing-table, but he didn't offer her one. As he lit his, Blanche asked a little petulantly, 'Can't I have a cigarette?'

'Of course,' he said in an offhand way. 'In the silver box on the bedside table.' He nodded to indicate it.

Blanche pouted, rolled over on to her side, and helped herself. He did, however, come back to the bed to light it for her.

'Don't take too long over that,' he said briefly. 'The good Gerard will be expecting me to bring you back, safe and sound, before long.'

'Gerry's not worried about me,' Blanche said. She leaned back against the quilted satin bedhead and expelled a curling upward spiral of blue smoke. 'It was always Alix he was keen on.'

This caught Paul's attention. He sat down on the edge of the bed and looked at her questioningly.

'Oh, he was madly in love with her for years,' Blanche said. 'Still is, the poor chump. He married Jennie only because Alix wouldn't have him.'

Paul drew on his cigarette, and asked casually, 'Why did Alix not want the respectable and devoted Gerard? He has money.'

'Phooey, not as much as Alix has! Alix is an heiress, you know.'

Had Blanche not been so tipsy, or so stupid, she would have sensed the change in the atmosphere and in Paul's demeanour immediately. 'No,' he said slowly, 'I didn't know it.' He stubbed out his cigarette, unfinished, and eyed Blanche speculatively. 'Is she very rich?'

'Oh, goodness, yes, rolling in it,' Blanche said vulgarly,

a touch of viciousness briefly invading her voice. 'She had a terribly wealthy old grandfather, who was very eccentric. When he died, he left everything to her.'

'Jake is a fortunate man, then,' Paul commented, a note in his voice not so very different from that which had sounded momentarily in hers.

'He doesn't need *her* money. He's practically a millionaire himself. He made a lot of money in the motor industry, just before the war—and still does. He owns companies and things,' she added vaguely.

Paul's expression was anything but vague. 'So, together they are worth a great deal of money?'

'Enormously rich. Her own money *and* Jake's—Alix must be one of the wealthiest women in Paris!' Blanche said jealously.

Paul said softly, 'She'd certainly be one of the wealthiest *widows*, if anything were to happen to him . . .' But he said it in French, and Blanche didn't understand him. '*Ma chère ,*' he said to her now, briskly. He stooped over her and lightly kissed her naked breast. 'You have a beautiful body—but put some clothes on it. I have to take you back. Gerard will be pacing up and down in front of the hotel!'

'You're not frightened of my brother-in-law!' she taunted him.

'No—but I'm a busy man with an office to run. I've got work to do, so get yourself dressed. You can shower, if you want, in there.' He indicated the bathroom door briefly and turned his back on her.

'Just a minute!' Blanche exclaimed, pushing back the fur rug and scrambling out of the bed. 'Don't just order me out, like that!'

'I haven't. I told you I'd take you back to the hotel myself.'

Blanche pouted, dissatisfied. Then she changed her tactics and looked up at him appealingly. 'I don't go back to England for another two whole days. Can we meet again?'

Paul stared down at her with a coldness which filled her with dismay. 'What for?' he asked simply.

Her pretty face twisted. She swore at him and leapt towards him, her blue eyes glittering and her sharp little fingernails clawing at his face. 'You rotter, you can't treat me like that! Not like a—a common prostitute!'

She found her wrists seized painfully in a steel grip, as Paul caught her and hurled her back roughly so that she sprawled inelegantly over the white fur rug.

'I said, get dressed!' he ordered her harshly. 'Or I'll throw you out on to the pavement naked, and your clothes after you!'

Blanche spat at him.

'*Chérie,*' he said softly. 'You are not a prostitute, perhaps, but you are, most certainly, very common.'

Alix and Jake sat silently over the dinner-table as Séraphine, the housekeeper, cleared the last dishes away.

'Does she mind my coming here, do you think?' Alix whispered, as the woman went out.

Jake raised his eyebrows in mild surprise. 'No, why should she? So long as you don't invade her kitchen.'

There was little fear of that, Alix thought. She'd never been taught to cook, and could only make omelettes. Hadn't some Napoleonic general, when his attention had been drawn to the large number of casualities on a battlefield, remarked that one could not make an omelette without breaking eggs? It didn't stop there. It didn't stop with dead bodies, and bereaved relatives. The true price of battle was men like Jake, and the women who loved them were the ones called upon to pay it.

Such a strange wedding night, and harder to face— for both of them—than she had thought it would be.

After she had gone to bed, alone in her own room, she heard Jake's piano. He played for quite a while, the music echoing through the night, until it suddenly broke off in a cacophony of jarring chords and wrong notes.

CHAPTER ELEVEN

CHRISTMAS APPROACHED, and the rain came down. Alix stood at the window and watched the rivulets trickle down the panes. Outside, leafless trees, black with water, stood wet and glistening, like sentinels. Puddles formed in dips in the pavement and the gutters ran like rivers in full spate, so that the drains could not cope and flooded the roads. The motor traffic sent up great muddy sprays to drench passers-by, and all the cafés had taken their tables and chairs inside for the winter.

She remembered Christmas in England, when she and Gerard had both been small. How they had loved the Christmas tree, festooned with tiny candles. Aunt Ethel had always been terrified of lighting the candles, in case the whole thing went up in flames. But eventually, after much pleading by both children, the candles were solemnly lit for five minutes, on Christmas evening, with Jessie the maid standing by with a bucket of water, just in case.

Alix sighed and turned to lean against the window, arms folded, and watched Jake, who sat at his desk, dealing with the day's correspondence. He hated paperwork, but dealt with it in a fiercely methodical fashion because otherwise, he said, he wouldn't deal with it at all. Since moving in, she had sometimes acted as his secretary, and had been amazed at the diversity of his business interests. One thing had led to another, he told her. 'I've been lucky.' He had, in fact, been shrewd.

Today, however, he hadn't needed her help. She

studied him, his tousled, light brown hair, grimly determined profile and strong, capable hands. He'd been
reading that one letter in his hand for at least five
minutes. It was a handwritten letter on expensive
notepaper. Alix could see the writing, ornate yet firm.
It began tidily, but gained increasing abandon as it went
along, the gaps between lines becoming wider, the words
scrawled. It was a woman's handwriting, and belonged
to someone who, beneath a calm, organised exterior,
hid some emotional upset. She felt a stir of unease.

Jake looked up and saw her eyes on him. He leaned
back in his chair and rubbed a hand over his hair so
that it looked even more dishevelled.

'You wouldn't want to go away for Christmas, I
suppose?'

Alix, startled, asked, 'To the sun, you mean?'

'Well, no, although we can do that, if you want.' He
picked up the letter from the desk and scowled at it.
'We've received an invitation. You remember the
Countess, my war-time rescuer? I wrote to her and told
her of our marriage. Now she's anxious to meet you.'

Alix said, 'Oh . . .' and moved away from the
window to stand behind his chair. Resting her hands
lightly on his shoulders, she asked dubiously, 'Do you
want to go?'

He lifted one hand to pat hers, on his shoulder, and
muttered, 'It seems churlish to refuse.' He paused and
then glanced up at her. 'Her husband will be there.'

It was a totally unexpected remark. Surprised, Alix
exclaimed, 'I didn't know there was a Count, too. You
didn't mention him.'

'That's because he wasn't there during the war. He
owns a newspaper that was violently anti-German, even
before the war. He stayed on in Paris all through the
war, and his wife sat it out in the family château behind
enemy lines. I thought, if you wanted to go, we could

drive down. You drive, don't you? I don't fancy a train journey. By car, we can stop and I can get out and limber up.'

'Gerry taught me to drive,' Alix said doubtfully. 'But where do we get a car?'

'We have one, the Sizaire. I still have it, even though I can't drive it nowadays. The hip objects.'

He saw how astonished she looked, and explained that he had brought the car to France as he'd told her he intended. The Sizaire had been garaged in a farmer's barn at the time of his last, doomed, flight. After the war, he'd returned to ask what had happened to it and found it still there. 'Under a tarpaulin. Mice had nested in the engine and a few chickens had laid eggs on the seats, but it was in a surprisingly good state.'

The Sizaire was now, apparently, garaged nearby. They went out later in the day, when the rain had stopped, to inspect it. It was in immaculate condition. Someone—Alix suspected Jake himself—still took great care of it. The ivory and black bodywork gleamed, and the leather seats had been kept polished.

Because she had only driven Gerry's 'Tin Lizzie' before, she was a little doubtful about managing this shining monster. But Jake would have none of her doubts and fears. He explained all its beauties and intricacies to her, his face and voice alight with enthusiasm. Then, while she sat in the driver's seat and watched, he took off his jacket, rolled up his sleeves and delved under the bonnet.

He was so obviously and blissfully happy. He whistled a little tune as he worked, and his hands became covered in grease. He twisted and fiddled with everything, talking to the engine as if it were an old friend. Anything to do with machines brought out the best in Jake. The aggression, the defensiveness, all vanished. Here he was in his own world, the one he understood and which understood him. Here no one criticized his drawing-room manners, no one asked what his father had done for a living. Man and machine met as equals and, secure in their environment, shut all else and all other people, out. Alix was an outsider, a onlooker. She couldn't share the mystic harmony between man and machine. Working on the engine seemed to give him some physical pleasure. It was like a love affair, and she was a third party coming between the lovers.

Eventually he stood up, wiping his grimy hands on a bundle of cotton waste, and smiling happily. 'She'll take us down there and bring us back, with no problems at all.' He saw Alix's pale face, and asked contritely, 'Sorry, are you cold? It is a bit chilly in here. I get carried away and don't notice it.'

She forced her frozen lips into a smile. 'It's all right.'

It wasn't all right. He had looked happier messing with that engine than he'd looked at any time since she'd met him again. He certainly looked happier than he'd done on his wedding day. Alix felt a dull jealousy of the Sizaire burn in her heart. How stupid, to be jealous of a machine. Yet she had been jealous of a machine once before, of the biplane called *Sara* which had filled Robbie's thoughts.

Now she felt that Jake wasn't married to her, he was married to this motor-car. This beautiful, lovingly cared-for heap of metal, rubber and leather represented the love of his heart, and Alix took second place.

It was still raining the day they drove down into the country. Fortunately, the Sizaire behaved very well in Alix's hands and even Jake said approvingly, 'You're a good driver', which was praise indeed. He was in considerable discomfort himself. The canvas hood leaked a little, but it was the sitting, and the motion of the car, which caused the hip to play up. He must have known it would be like this, and she wondered at his determination to make the journey.

Eventually they were forced to stop at a roadside café so that he could get out and walk about to ease the stiffness. The weather was still bad, and Alix ran through the rain into the little café, and sat down at a window table.

It was really a workmen's *estaminet*, full of burly men in blue blouses enjoying '*un p'tit verre*'. The air was thick with the pungent blue smoke of tobacco. They looked up as she came in, and surveyed her stolidly. They looked neither hostile nor welcoming, but had simply closed ranks against her. She was a stranger, a foreigner and—because they could all see the Sizaire parked outside—she was a rich bourgeoise, something they regarded with suspicion and contempt.

Alix tried not to notice, but she felt horribly out of place and wished Jake had come in with her. Instinctively she knew that had he come in here alone, he would have made himself accepted within minutes. He knew these men and how their minds worked. But she would always be an outsider. When she had first met him, in England, he'd been an awkward stranger in her world. Now she was an interloper in his.

The *patron* came up to ask what she wanted. He was a thick-set man, unshaven, with chest and arms like a gorilla and smelled of perspiration. She asked for two cups of coffee, and he grunted and went away, leaving her wondering apprehensively who did the washing-up.

Through the window, she could see Jake limping up and down alone in the rain, forcing the hip to come back to life again. Suddenly she became aware that they were *all* watching him. They probably thought he was mad, walking up and down out there in the pouring rain. The low murmur of conversation had died away, and the whole roomful of men sat, silent and mystified, and watched Jake's perambulations up and down the pavement.

The *patron* returned with the coffee and Alix, red with embarrassment, felt impelled to explain, 'My husband *is* coming inside. It—It's an old injury, and he has to keep moving.'

The man nodded and said *'Ah, oui?'* as if it were of no interest, and went away without further comment. Finally Jake limped in and sat down heavily opposite her, his face, hair and clothes wet through. He pulled out his handkerchief and dried his face before picking up his now cold coffee. 'It's fine now,' he assured her, and she knew it was a lie.

Unexpectedly, a slatternly girl appeared from the back regions and set a glass of cognac on the table beside Jake. 'Compliments of the *patron*,' she said briefly.

They were men of the same breed as those with whom he'd worked all those years ago in the goods-yards. They understood physical toughness and the lonely fight against physical pain. They understood that a man goes on, even when his back is breaking, because he has to, not because he chooses to. Jake hadn't spoken a word to them, but they knew him by instinct, and understood. They accepted him, and the whole atmosphere in the café was changed in an indefinable way. When they left, they were given several farewell nods, as if they'd been regulars.

Soon after they set out again, the roads became worse, and pitted with potholes. The deepest had been filled in with cinders, an inadequate repair, and the Sizaire lurched and bumped till Jake swore aloud. To either side of them lay ruined buildings, showing that they were passing across the former battlefields. Here the guns had thundered two years earlier. Now little informal cemeteries dotted the countryside, marking where the dead of battle had been buried hastily. Plans were under way to establish proper war cemeteries, but there were still plenty of odd graves about, grouped in irregular clumps of a dozen or so. Some markers had names scratched on them; some just said simply 'An English Soldier'. Others, even more stark, read *'Inconnu'*—'Unknown'.

'Perhaps it's not beautiful,' Jake said soberly, 'but at least it's peaceful—and quiet. I remember it when that ghastly crimson glow hung over it. I used to stand in the evenings, outside the Mess, and look towards the lines. On the horizon, as it got darker, there was always a creeping finger of red, as if everything was burning, and the fires would never go out, like the fires of hell. In the morning, sometimes, I'd fly over the area, and see the burned-out houses below still smouldering, and the fire gaining hold somewhere else.' He pointed through the driving rain at a low, black hillside. 'That's where I crashed. The house is quite close.'

'Jake,' Alix said nervously, 'the Countess thinks we— we're like other husbands and wives, doesn't she?'

'Don't worry,' he said briefly. 'She won't bed us down together. In that sort of house, husbands and wives always get separate accommodation!'

Moments later he touched her elbow and pointed to a turning ahead on their right. 'Here!' Alix turned the wheel and they drove through an imposing pair of stone gateposts and up a long gravel drive, the stones crunching beneath the wheels.

In France, all kinds of large houses are called *châteaux*. Some are real castles or palaces, some country manor houses. This one was a large, rambling stone building of great antiquity with pepperpot turrets and windows popping out of the roof at all angles. As a place to hide a wounded, hunted man, it could surely hardly have been bettered.

The rain had lessened to a fine drizzle as they descended from the Sizaire to stand before the main entry. Suddenly a voice hailed them loudly, and turning, Alix saw an old man in a blue peasant's blouse and a shapeless beret scurrying across the ground towards them like a large spider.

'It's Maurice!' Jake exclaimed. 'The old fellow who dragged me clear of the Camel and brought me here.'

'It's you, *capitaine*?' The old man grasped Jake's hand and peered up at him.

'It's good to see you, Maurice,' Jake said, pumping the old man's hand. 'This is my wife.'

Maurice twisted his head to one side and scrutinised Alix. His little black eyes were sharp and suspicious. She had intended to smile at him, but the smile faded at the hostility in those shiny black eyes, so like a lizard's. Jake was welcome here: she was not.

'Madame is waiting,' The old man said, jerking his head towards the house.

At that same moment, a low, melodious woman's contralto, said, 'Jake?'

Jake had never described his Countess to Alix, but she had somehow built up a picture of Jake's rescuer as an elderly, formidable dragon of aristocratic bearing and the manners of a former generation. Now the sight of the woman on the steps waiting to welcome them sent a physical shock through Alix, as though she had touched a live electric wire.

The Countess was in her late thirties, one of those elegant, ageless beauties, simply and expensively dressed, her clothes bearing the unmistakable stamp of Parisian 'chic'. She smiled at them, showing even little teeth, and held out a slim, white, beringed hand. 'Come inside. Do you want to drown out there? Such weather!'

'Hallo, Monique,' Jake said softly, and stooping,

kissed the smooth cheek she presented to him. 'You look well.'

Alix, unpacking upstairs, dragged things out of her case and threw them angrily on to the bed. He might have warned her! He could have at least described the Countess. She felt she had been tricked. Had she known, she would have insisted they take rooms in a local hotel, no matter how primitive. In fact, had she known the truth, she would never have agreed to this journey at all. Jake had made a fool of her in front of that poised and beautiful woman. The Countess must have seen the stupefied amazement on Alix's face. Jake had betrayed her trust in him. And she had trusted him, utterly, never doubting he would be as honest with her as he had asked her to be with him.

The worst of all was her suspicion, growing in certainty by the minute inside her like a malignant cancer, that this was how he had first discovered his impotence, in Monique's bed. It had all the hallmarks of a classic eternal triangle, this situation. The man hidden here for so many weeks, the husband absent in Paris for the duration of the war, the lonely, beautiful wife . . .

Alix had not met the Count yet, but she had begun to see him as a kindred being, duped as she had been. He was travelling down from Paris by train, Monique said, and would join them at dinner. Alix sighed, and stared disconsolately at her scattered clothing. Monique had told her to leave everything for the maid to unpack, but she couldn't face going downstairs yet. She began to open drawers and cupboards and fling items inside indiscriminately.

As Jake had predicted, they had been given separate, but adjoining, bedrooms. A door led discreetly from her room directly into his. Alix stopped hurling her underwear into the drawer of a walnut chest, and glowered at it. With a rapid step, she crossed the floor and turned the key in the lock, just in case he decided to wander in with husbandly informality. But why should he? They had been married two months, and she had never set foot in his bedroom nor he in hers. Theirs was a marriage of convenience, of outward show. Yet, on her side, she had undertaken it with all the commitment she would have given to a real marriage of flesh and blood. She had deluded herself that she could make a reality of pretence, when the truth was that not only had Jake not wanted a sham marriage—he hadn't wanted any marriage at all.

It was so hard to bear. She had forced herself, with such effort, to accept that he might never love her as she loved him. But she had never seriously believed his heart had been given to someone else.

'I had a right to know!' she whispered. 'And you had no right to treat me so callously.'

She went to the drawer and tried to bring some order to the muddle she had created. The serpentine-fronted chest had two small drawers at the top and three longer ones beneath. It was a pretty piece, probably early nineteenth century. The whole house was full of antiques, furniture and paintings. These old-fashioned pieces were currently out of favour, and Paul's clients mostly demanded modern furnishings. But one category of client didn't. These were the self-made, social-climbing 'arrivistes', wanting to persuade the world that they came of old, distinguished families. They filled their fine new houses with the discarded relics of others, a jumble of periods and styles, the sole requirement being that the article should be old and expensive-looking. Because of what they represented, Alix knew that these old pieces would see out the popularity of the new furniture and come into their own again.

As for the paintings, her own interest, those she had seen so far had been mostly family portraits of indifferent quality. But who knew? In these old houses there frequently lurked, forgotten in some dusty corner, a begrimed Poussin or overlooked Watteau. Some of these old aristocratic families lived with a small fortune hanging on the wall of a spare bedroom, and neither knew nor cared. Paul would have given his eye-teeth to see this house, she thought.

Alix changed into a jade green dress which she knew suited her, brushed out her red hair carefully and went downstairs to join Jake and the Countess. She knew they were in the salon, because she could hear Jake's voice through the white and gold rococo door panels. It sounded animated, and Alix felt a dull dread grow inside her at the thought of breaking in on their tête-à-tête.

Monique must have moved nearer to the door, for suddenly her voice sounded clearly, only a few feet away. 'And you are married? I confess I was surprised, but of course Henri and I were both delighted.'

'Henri might have been,' thought Alix mutinously. 'I'm not so sure Monique is telling the truth.' She had not caught the words of Jake's reply, but Monique was speaking again.

'And she is an artist? I admire that so much.' There was a pause, and then Monique said in a drier tone, 'But I am afraid she doesn't like *me*, your Alix.'

'Nonsense!' Jake replied sharply and more loudly this time, so that Alix could hear it. 'She doesn't know you. She's—shy. Give her time; she'll come around.'

Oh, *will* I? thought Alix rebelliously. She had no wish to hear any more. She had already paid the penalty of eavesdroppers. Jake, her husband, discussed her with another woman. She turned and bolted in the first direction presented, through the dining-room where a

startled servant was laying out the family silver and the
Sèvres dinner service, and out through a pair of glass
doors on to a terrace.

It had stopped raining at last, but it was cold, and
dusk was closing in rapidly. Alix rested her hands on
the stone balustrade and stared out across the gardens
slowly fading from view in the gloom. They seemed
extensive. Directly below was an arrangement of
geometrical flowerbeds in the traditional French style,
divided by gravel pathways. At the far end, too dark
now to be made out clearly, seemed to be a coppice or
small wood. Perhaps it had once been an orchard and
allowed to go wild and become choked with growth. As
she watched, some large bird, probably a wood pigeon,
flew into it and vanished, settling for the night. Probably
few people disturbed the birds that inhabited this
forgotten corner of the grounds.

At that moment, her fragile, restored peace of mind
was itself disturbed by a light footstep behind her.

'Why, there you are, Alix my dear. Won't you come
inside? It's so cold out here.'

Alix turned and managed to present a composed
appearance to Monique, framed in the doorway. 'I'm
not cold. I came out for some fresh air.'

Monique hesitated. 'My husband has just arrived
from Paris. Won't you come and meet him?'

Alix walked steadily after her, back into the house.
Jake was still in the salon, talking to a stranger. He was
leaning on his stick and she could see he was in some
difficulty. The journey had led the hip to play up badly,
but as she watched him limp jerkily across the room,
she hardened her heart against any sympathy. She didn't
feel sorry for him. She would never feel sorry for him
again. To do him justice, he'd never asked for pity.
Perhaps he knew he deserved none.

Monique said quietly, 'My husband, Henri.'

The stranger turned and bowed politely towards Alix. 'Madame Sherwood? It is an honour . . .'

He must have been well over sixty years of age, probably nearly thirty years older than his wife, a slender, silver-haired man with a thin, ascetic face and deep-set, intelligent eyes. Beside him, Monique, despite her black dress, looked like his daughter. Alix noticed that she was twisting the diamond ring on her finger nervously. Despite her self-possessed air, this sophisticated woman was a bundle of nerves.

An old husband, away in Paris, a handsome young pilot hidden in the house . . . It must have been inevitable.

It was late before they all retired to bed that night. As they parted company in the chilly corridor, Jake said in his direct way, 'You've been very quiet all evening.' His grey eyes watched her face. 'What's wrong?'

Alix flushed, and shivered in the draught. She folded her arms tightly, hugging herself, and muttered resentfully. 'They are *your* friends.' In a burst of candour, she added, 'You should have told me that Monique was such a young woman!'

'Does it matter?' He frowned, perplexed.

Of course it matters! Alix wanted to shout. Aloud, she said, 'It made me look so foolish, when we were introduced. She—She was so elegant and poised, and I stood there, open-mouthed, like a simpleton.'

He gave a hiss of exasperation. 'Is that why you've been sulking? I'd have told you, if I'd thought you'd find it so important. Women's minds work in such a peculiar way—I never gave it a thought. Poor Monique thought she'd offended you in some way.'

Was the explanation really so simple? Was all her suspicion, after all, a flight of fancy on her part? Alix muttered, 'It's cold here—goodnight.' She hurried away

from him, down the long, cold corridor to the modern
bathroom which had been installed at the far end of it.

When she came back to her own room, she could
hear Jake moving about next door, the sound travelling
through the panels of the communicating door. He was
stumbling awkwardly against the furniture and swearing
to himself. At first she thought resentfully, 'I'm not
going to ask if he needs any help.' But, after all, her
whole avowed intention in marrying him had been to
look after him. Alix drew a deep breath, gave a tap on
the door, unlocked it and went through.

The room was in a dusky half-light, lit only by the
bedside lamp which flickered erratically. Jake's naked
figure stood by the bed. He was wrestling with the lid
of a jar of embrocation and muttering under his breath
because it was jammed closed.

Alix stopped on the threshold. As an artist, she wasn't
unfamiliar with the male nude, and said to herself, 'I
ought not to be embarrassed, for pity's sake!' But she
knew that it wasn't embarrassment she felt—that
churning in the pit of the stomach, the tingling aware-
ness of every pore of her skin and the trembling, half-
trepidation, half-anticipation, which seized her limbs
and made her knees like jelly, her hands tremble and
her palms perspire. It was the oldest instinct in the
world, the readiness of the female to be taken physically
by the male of her choice.

She thought sadly, 'We hide inside our clothes. They
help us to pretend. But it's no use my pretending that I
don't want Jake to take me in his arms, that I don't
want to lie beside him on that bed—because I do. I
thought it would be all right, and I could live with him
without that, and it wasn't as important as people make
out. But I was wrong, and it is everything. Without it,
there is nothing.'

Jake looked up and saw her standing pale-faced, by

the door. 'What are you doing here?' he demanded
sourly.

There was something defiant in the way he looked at
her. She had wondered if, when he noticed her presence,
he would do something to cover himself up, but he
hadn't. It was as if he taunted both her and himself:
you wanted to know if I really was like other men, after
all, and I am—to all outward appearances. But that's
the irony of it all. My body had taken against me, and
plays malicious tricks. It either won't or can't do what
it's designed to do, and I am growing to hate it, as
much as it hates me.

Alix muttered, 'I came to see if you needed any
help . . .' Her voice sounded thick and awkward, as if
she had a sore throat, and the sound stuck in it.

'With this?' He held up the jar. 'Damn useless stuff!'
Jake hit the lid a sharp blow with the flat of his hand.
'It's supposed to ease the ache . . .'

The lid of the jar shot off unexpectedly and landed
with a clatter on the bedside table. 'Oh, what the heck,'
he said wearily. 'I can't be bothered.'

The noise of the falling lid, and his failure to achieve
even this simple, everyday mechanical action of opening
a jar, gave her a kind of confidence and broke the
frozen spell that held her by the door, afraid to enter
any further.

She pulled herself together, and forcing herself to
speak in a practical voice, said, 'You can't apply it
properly yourself, anyway. Let me do it.' She held out
her hand, and it shook only very slightly.

She wondered if Jake noticed, because he half turned
away and growled, 'I'm not sure you should even be
here!'

'I'm your wife!' she said vehemently—and suddenly
knew that, despite everything, despite the unfulfilment,
the unquenched longing, it was true. She was his wife,

legally married to him, and neither Monique nor anyone else could change it. 'Lie down so that I can get at the hip,' she ordered.

Jake hesitated for a moment, then muttered, 'All right,' and did as she bade.

She had not been prepared for the extent of the scar tissue, and her carefully assumed composure deserted her for a moment. 'That old doctor,' she whispered, horrified. 'I know he operated in the kitchen, but what on earth did he use? Kitchen knives?'

'Probably,' Jake smiled wanly. 'I was awash with brandy at the time, too drunk to know what he was doing.'

Alix sat down by his long, lean body and began to massage the embrocation into the hip with slow, careful movements. He'd suffered so much, and she had been so angry with him earlier. How could she have been so angry with a man who had gone through all this? Besides, she would always forgive him anything. She loved him that much.

'Finished!' she said aloud, and retrieving the lid of the jar, replaced it with unnecessary care.

Jake rolled over and sat up, pushing the pillows into a support for his back. Like a stripped Greek athlete, he had broad shoulders and narrow hips and very little body hair. Leaning back now in repose, the pain eased, his naked form had a power, grace and dignity which made her hope she could at least sketch him one day. But, at the same time, that physical longing was taking possession of her again, and she looked away because she didn't want him to see it in her eyes.

His voice said quietly and a little mockingly, 'You know, that's very effective . . .'

Alix started and asked foolishly, 'The embrocation?'

He smiled and shook his head and replied drily, 'No, *your* rubbing it in like that.'

Alix felt her face and throat burn as she realised what he meant. For a brief moment she felt almost angry. Probably he thought she was aware of it, and that her whole purpose had been a contrived ploy destined to arouse him. She pushed herself up from the bed, but Jake's hand closed on her elbow, restraining her, and she sank back.

'Alix . . .' He leaned forward slightly. 'It's not that I don't *want* to. Of course I do. Some nights, when I don't sleep, and it's very quiet, I can hear you tossing in your bed next door, and I lie awake, and I confess I think about nothing else but you, and how it would be, *could* be, if only . . .'

'My door has never been barred,' Alix whispered in a hoarse little voice. 'You could have come.'

'Yes, I know.' He stretched out his hand and touched the lapel of her dressing-gown. 'Take it off?'

With shaking fingers, Alix untied the belt and slipped the dressing-gown off her shoulders, and then, because she understood what he meant, she pulled the silk nightgown over her head and dropped it on the floor by the bed.

He sat staring moodily at her naked body for a moment, and then ran his fingers lightly over the outline of her breast and said, 'I know you suspect that I'm indulging myself in a sort of sulk, because I can't do what other men do. But it's not just a question of virility, or of proving one's manhood, it's more than that. You see, perhaps for women love is an emotion which rules the heart, but for a man—most men—it rules the loins. That's where he feels it, not up here,' he touched his chest, 'but down here . . . Being able to make love to the woman he's attracted to, being able to possess her body, it's part and parcel of the whole damned thing and can't be separated from it. That's why he mustn't fail, do you see? If he does, it's not just the denial of a pleasure, or an embarrassment, it's a denial of the whole emotion within him, of everything he feels. It makes him feel as though, whatever he's said to that woman before, he's lied. Without it he can't love anyone, not if he can't tell her with his body. Do you see? That's why I've never come to your room, Alix.'

Alix said shakily, 'You've had other women, before you met me, and perhaps even after you met me. Did you love them, the way you've described?'

He shook his head. 'No. That was a quite different need. There wasn't any love in it—not what women call love. It was a need, and a sort of release. A man doesn't have to be in love with a woman to get into bed with her. Sometimes it's just a purely mechanical reflex. You don't have to worry about those other women, Alix. You don't have to be jealous, or whatever. They didn't count for anything then, and still don't. What I was telling you just now, that matters.'

She whispered, 'I understand.'

'Perhaps.' He sounded doubtful. 'You know, that first evening we met, you were so mad at me when I offered to take Robbie's place. But that wasn't because I thought you were easy, it was because I saw you were rather special, and I thought perhaps we could have had something rather special together.'

'Can't we still?' she asked a little forlornly.

Jake shifted uneasily on the pillows. 'I don't know. Maybe there's only one way to find out, at that.' He pressed his hand against her bare knee. 'Stay here tonight, with me, now?' he whispered huskily.

He was her husband, and this was the first time she'd ever seen him undressed, or sat naked before him, or even been in his bedroom while he was there. And it was the first time that he'd ever asked her into his bed. Alix could not trust herself to speak. She pushed back the sheet and slid into the bed beside him.

He moved over slightly to make room for her, so that her naked skin touched the warm place in the bedclothes where he had been reclining. He rolled over and slid his arm round her. There was no heating in this cold room, but he was perspiring, and his damp bare skin clung to hers with an adhesive quality, and she could feel how tense the muscles were beneath.

As he had predicted, the injured hip did make him clumsy, and though she tried to disguise that his awkward approaches made her apprehensive, he himself was bitterly aware of it. He swore softly to himself beneath his breath and she sensed the fragile confidence draining away from him already.

Alix whispered, 'Switch out the light', hoping the darkness might help them both. He stretched his arm across her to the bedside lamp and plunged them both into an all-embracing blackness. In it, she could hear Jake panting and swearing and getting tied up in the sheet. Alix caught at his arm, and hissed, 'It's all right . . .' knowing he was about to explode with rage and frustration.

'No, it damn well isn't!' he snarled at her. He threw himself back on the pillows beside her, and she knew he was struggling to overcome this initial humiliation and start again.

'Alix?' he said quietly now. 'It would be easier if you came here, to me . . .'

Alix whispered, 'Yes, of course . . .'

Given his disabled hip, it would have made more sense if they had tried this position in the first place, Alix thought, as she slid her leg across his thighs. But as she stooped over him, he added anxiously, 'It still might not . . .'

'It doesn't matter, Jake!' she interrupted. 'I don't mind, even if . . . Whether it's all right or not, I don't mind *trying*. If it doesn't come right this time, then I don't mind trying again. But it *will* be all right, you have to believe it.'

But it wasn't. Jake thrust her away from him with a kind of muffled sob and lay on his back in the darkness, silent. His frustration, misery and anger seemed to fill the air like demonic wraiths, destructive yet themselves indestructible, tearing him apart.

Alix felt her own frustration and wretchedness build up inside her, dominated by a sense of her own inability, as if the impotence were shared between them and she were as responsible as he. She wanted to help him, but she didn't know how. There must be something she could do to enable him to overcome the imaginary, yet real-to-him, barrier that existed in his mind. She didn't know enough about lovemaking. She was a hapless victim of her own respectable upbringing. Mrs Daventry, reluctant but feeling herself compelled by duty to explain the nature of marriage to her young niece, had described lovemaking as a predominantly male undertaking which men initiated for unmentionable reasons of their own, and women suffered, rigid in mind and body, because that was Woman's Lot. There was nothing in that obscure lecture, delivered in hushed tones, which would have been of the slightest help here. Even at fourteen, Alix had realised that Mrs Daventry's explanation fell far short of the true nature of things. Now, she knew that it had been a disaster.

She ought, perhaps, to try and find some older woman of the world with sufficient experience to advise her. But how to ask advice about such a thing? Jake would never forgive her if she betrayed his secret.

At least, perhaps, she could try to comfort him in his despair. She put out her hand and touched his bare shoulder, but he flinched beneath her fingertips and muttered hoarsely, 'Just go away, Alix, will you?'

Alix got out of bed and went back to her own room. Her bed was cold and unwelcoming, and in the distance, down in the coppice, an owl hooted.

CHAPTER TWELVE

ALIX AWOKE just as a steely grey winter dawn was breaking. It was Christmas Day, but it hardly felt like it. There was a noticeable absence of seasonal goodwill and jollity in the atmosphere. She took out the present she had bought Jake—a book on French painters of the seventeenth century—and put it on the top of the walnut chest. She had wrapped it up carefully before leaving Paris, after inscribing the fly-leaf with a message which had read horribly impersonally. But it had to be impersonal, because 'To my darling husband' would hardly have been appropriate.

Alix pushed open the wooden shutters. The garden glistened damp and bare, with empty flowerbeds and rotting leaves choking the gullies at the sides of the gravel paths. The little coppice stood dark and unfriendly, as if it harboured strange and unexpected things. In such a mysterious little wood Hansel and Gretel had found the Gingerbread House. Foolishness, Alix thought, to entertain such fanciful thoughts about a few neglected trees. But, on an impulse, she decided to go and investigate it.

She dressed quickly in warm clothes and went downstairs. A solitary elderly woman in a pinafore was dusting out the dining-room. She looked startled to see Alix, but greeted her cheerfully and obligingly opened the glass doors on to the terrace for her.

Outside, the early morning chill struck much colder than she had anticipated. She thrust her hands into her pockets and ran down the terrace steps on to the gravel path and began to walk briskly towards the wood. Her feet crunched on the wet gravel. It was so sodden from all the rain that the weight of her footsteps acted like pressure on a sponge, forcing the ground to disgorge the soaked-up water and staining her shoes with black, wet patches.

At the edge of the coppice, she came unexpectedly upon a large dog-fox on his way home after a night's foraging. He stopped and stared at her in surprise, his winter coat coarse and patchy ginger and grey, his sharp little white muzzle and shiny black nose pointed up towards her. 'You're such a handsome fellow', Alix told him, and he turned and trotted away on his slender black-stockinged legs, his long brown brush slipping noiselessly into the undergrowth where he would lie up for the day.

Many years ago, the coppice had been an orchard, but the fruit-trees no longer brought forth any bounty. They had grown large and wild. Tall grass and weeds grew knee high about the gnarled trunks, and black-berry bushes had taken root and proliferated, barring the way with their prickly stems. Alix peered into the tangled undergrowth and decided against entering after all. There was something so cold and hostile about it.

Just then a wood pigeon, such as she had seen the previous evening, flew up with a tremendous clatter of wings, and she stepped back with a cry of alarm, her heart leaping painfully.

'What are you doing here, madame?'

Alix spun round. The old man, Maurice, stood a little way from her, a hunched figure, as gnarled as any of the aged trees of the abandoned orchard. He hobbled a little closer and peered up at her with his head tilted in a birdlike way. She was repelled again by his shiny little eyes that glittered at her, and found herself taking an unreasoning dislike to him. She should have felt grateful, since this was the man who had rescued Jake from death. He was watching her now, very closely, and, as on the previous day, it seemed to her in an unfriendly way.

'It is very damp, madame. You will catch cold.' His voice creaked like old wood. He had shown obvious pleasure at seeing Jake on their arrival yesterday, but, just as obviously, he was not pleased to see her, and certainly not here.

'I was just going back,' she said defensively.

He nodded. 'That's good, madame. The early morning air, it's dangerous, you know.'

Because she felt he was virtually telling her to 'be off', a kind of obstinacy settled on Alix. She said brightly, 'You saved my husband, during the war.'

He grunted. 'Flying machines! Such things! When I was a boy, we would have thought any man mad who said war would be fought in the air. But the old master, he was a balloonist. You understand me, madame, a balloon?' He made wide gestures with his arms to indicate a hot-air balloon rising.

'Yes, I know what a balloon is, but who was the "old master"?' Alix asked, puzzled.

'Why, the father of madame—the father of madame la comtesse!' He looked surprised, even shocked, that she should not know this. 'The *château* belongs to *her*,' he went on. 'He had no son, the old master, and everything became hers. It is her family home. Four hundred years—even during the Great Revolution her family remained here. No one bothered them. The people loved them and protected them.'

'And you, Maurice, have you spent all your life here, working for this family?'

'All my life, madame, except in the other war, when I was a young man and went to be a soldier.'

'The other war?' For a moment, bemused, she did

not grasp his meaning.

'The war of eighteen-seventy, madame.' He shuffled his feet. 'They packed us into railway-trucks like cattle, and sent us to be butchered like cattle, by the Prussians. The Emperor came,' he added unexpectedly and a note of pride echoed in his cracked voice. 'The Emperor came to review us!'

'Napoleon the Third?' Alix was interested now.

'The same, with the moustaches and the little beard.' Maurice scratched at his own stubbly chin. 'And the beautiful, haughty Spanish wife. Poor fellow, he came to review us because he was afraid to go back to Paris. They wanted to hang him from a lamp-post in Paris!' Maurice chuckled evilly, as if such a thing would have been amusing.

Disliking him even more, and wanting to be free of his company, Alix said briskly. 'I must go back.'

'Yes, madame, yes.' He came right up to her, still hunched and blinking up at her in his birdlike way. 'Go back, madame,' his voice creaked harshly. 'You can do no good here, poking into things, being curious, it does no good! Go back to Paris, madame!'

She was so angry that she couldn't bring herself to answer him. She turned on her heel and marched, head held high, back into the house.

Jake had bought her a silver bracelet inset with turquoise. They exchanged their Christmas gifts and wished each other 'Happy Christmas' in a formal way. She tried to tell him how much she liked the bracelet—which she did—but he did not seem to want to listen, and walked off before she had finished her sentence. Last night had upset him. He wouldn't talk about it, and she wondered uneasily if he blamed her for the failure.

To complete their reunion, Monique said, old Dr Berthier, who had operated on Jake in secret during the war, had been invited to lunch. 'He goes out very little now,' she explained. 'Eighty-two, you know. His mind is still sharp and he likes to know everything that goes on—but he tires easily.'

In fact the doctor proved a remarkably spry-looking old gentleman with a goatee beard and gold pince-nez. He was dressed in a very old-fashioned way in a frock-coat, but to put him in modern clothes, Alix thought, would have been totally inappropriate. He was a former dandy of the *'belle époque'*, an old *boulevardier* who had not lost his charm and the elegant style of a generation almost disappeared.

'In his day', the Count whispered to Alix, 'Berthier was quite a fellow! A great man for entertaining actresses. But a brave man, too. In the war of eighteen-seventy, he volunteered to serve as an army surgeon, and became a legend for his dedication in caring for the wounded in the worst of conditions.'

There was something about this fine old gentleman which made Alix take to him immediately. He was an old-style family doctor, a man to whom you could tell anything. A note of hope entered her heart, and after lunch she sought him out. The old gentleman was ensconced in the library, quietly enjoying a cigar. When she began to apologise for disturbing him, he wouldn't allow her to finish, but broke in to exclaim, 'Ah, there you are, my dear! Come in, come in!' Just as though he had been waiting for her.

Alix sat down by his side before the library fire, and told him how pleased she was to meet him and to be able to thank him for all he'd done for Jake.

He waved his cigar, dismissing it all, and said cheerfully, 'He's a strong man, your husband, difficult to kill!'

'Dr Berthier,' Alix said hesitantly, 'there's something I'd like to talk to you about. I hope you don't mind. I really don't know anyone else I can ask.'

He eyed her pale face and then glanced at her hands, tightly clenched on her lap. Tapping the ash from his cigar, he asked, 'This is perhaps the same matter as your husband discussed with me earlier?'

'Did he?' Alix exclaimed, surprised.

'Ah, yes. Some small problem in the matter of love, I understand.'

It was nicely put, but Alix said with a bitterness which surprised herself, 'Jake doesn't see it as a small problem. It's ruining his life!'

Dr Berthier disposed of the remains of his cigar and gazed appreciatively at the ash. 'Smoking is very bad for you! As a doctor, I am obliged to recognise the fact. But at my age it does not seem so very important. When you are old, other things too seem less important, but *not* to the young, I know. I can remember!' His shrewd old eyes twinkled at her.

'The problem that troubles your marriage is one which people are reluctant to discuss. For that reason, many people believe the condition is almost unknown. But, believe me, that is far from the truth. It can happen at any time, and for several different reasons. In your husband's case, I am sure it is the result of physical exhaustion and mental shock. His war experiences and the strain of daily combat, his crash, the operation I was forced to perform in such unsuitable conditions, being hidden here so long, finding himself lame, walking with the aid of a stick . . . Is it a surprise that a human body, faced with so many problems, finds it can no longer cope? Simple, natural actions become extraordinarily difficult adventures. The body goes "on strike".'

'I think I understand,' she said slowly.

'So, your husband tries to make love one day—and finds he cannot. He is already, physically and mentally, in a state of delayed shock. Can you imagine what such a discovery must do to a man who has always regarded himself as young, virile, aggressive, successful—a man mentally, physically and—forgive me—sexually, very active? At first he cannot believe it. He tries again. He fails again. Now he must believe it, but believe what? In his horror and shock, his mind leaps from one extreme to the other. He loses all confidence. He convinces himself that his sexual ability is permanently impaired. He is afraid to try again, in case he fails again. And when he does at last find enough courage to try again, he is so afraid of failure that—he fails. So it goes on, in a vicious circle. Failure breeds lack of confidence, lack of confidence breeds failure. Then, in this case, he does something very unusual for a man in such circumstances. He marries. I don't enquire your reasons for this marriage. Perhaps, madame, you saw yourself looking after this wounded hero, this splendid human animal unexpectedly vulnerable, and devoting yourself to him entirely. That always sounds attractive, my dear, but in reality it is a very dangerous thing to try and do!' Berthier shook his head and smiled at her reprovingly. 'Now he finds himself married to a very beautiful young woman selflessly giving her life to caring for him. It is not a pleasant situation for a man, especially such an independent man, to be in. He is both appreciative—and resentful. To his other worries is now added a sense of responsibility. He fears she is going to waste her young life, and he does not want that. He wants, in some manner, to make it all worth while.' Berthier paused. 'What he wants, more than anything, is to give her a child.'

Alix gasped, and stared at him wildly. 'A child? Jake's never said . . .'

'No,' Berthier said calmly. 'Not to *you*, perhaps. But you understand that he is more than ever desperate to succeed, and his despair is complete, because now, when he fails, he fails in the arms of the woman he would most wish to possess.'

'You're telling me I was wrong to marry Jake,' Alix said miserably. 'What can I do?'

'Wait,' Berthier said simply. 'Encourage him to be successful in other ways. Confidence is built up of so many things. What your husband needs is a success, a triumph, to do something all the world can see is a victory. The opportunity will come, never fear.'

The shrewd little old eyes rested on her again, uncomfortably sharp and direct. 'And he has to believe you love him. He must trust you implicitly.'

Alix left the doctor in his chair, settling down for a nap. She did not know what to think. She did not know exactly what Jake had told the old gentleman, nor if the doctor had correctly understood him. But, as Monique has said, the doctor was still sharp and still interested to know everything that went on. There was no reason to suppose he had misunderstood Jake. A child . . . Jake wanted a child . . .

She felt tired and depressed, almost ill, and for the first time began to doubt whether she had the will and the strength to struggle on. Before, whenever she'd felt like giving up and walking out, it had been because Jake had made her angry. When the anger died down, her resolve had been still there, intact.

But now she began to ask herself if her whole decision had been wrong. Had Gerry been right? Had Jennie? Had they all, because they were less than enthusiastic about Jake anyway, been able to stand back and see the situation with dispassionate clarity and judge it more shrewdly than she could? She had been standing too close, and loved too much. She had been blinded by her own longing to remain with Jake and her fear of losing him again.

Yet she *had* lost him. She had wanted to help, and

she hadn't helped. In failing, she had driven him further away. Every time he looked at her, he was reminded. Living under the same roof, the tiny everyday incidents of domestic intimacy drove the reminder home with the force of a sledge-hammer. A discarded lipstick in the bathroom, her hairbrush with shreds of red hair entangled in the bristles, those things were more than just the clutter of everyday life together: they were mute witnesses of nights apart.

During the rest of the day she tried to find an opportunity to talk to Jake, but he clearly either feared to be alone with her or blamed her for the fiasco of the previous night, and was angry with her. After dinner, he sat down to play chess with the Count. Monique was listening to Berthier. Alix said that the wine had given her a headache, and went up to bed early. As she passed by the chess-players, the Count half rose and made her a little bow, bidding her goodnight. Jake only looked up and stared straight at her with antagonistic, steely grey eyes.

She had been in bed for about a quarter of an hour, holding an opened but unread book in her hand, when there came a tap at the door. She dropped the book, her heart leaping up in hope that it would, after all, be Jake—sorry for his churlishness. She called nervously, 'Come in!'

But it was Monique who opened the door and stood hesitantly, asking, 'May I?'

'Yes, of course,' Alix told her, a little coldly.

Monique closed the door carefully and crossing the room, sat down on the edge of the bed. She was still a beautiful and elegant woman, but when one was very near to her, as Alix was now, a whole network of fine lines could be noticed criss-crossing her white skin. Life had not been kind to this gracious woman. Somewhere along the line, enthusiasm had died and hope had been blighted. Acceptance had come, but only after much suffering. Alix felt a new and unexpected movement of sympathy, of kindred spirit.

She said awkwardly, 'I'm so sorry I left the party. I hope it didn't look very rude.'

'Of course not, Alix dear.' Monique touched Alix's hand with her slim fingers, on one of which the diamond ring glittered. 'I came to see how you were. Do you need anything?'

'No, thank you.' Only Jake, and he hadn't come—wouldn't come. Didn't want to come.

'Alix . . .' Monique began. 'I know you don't like me, and I suspect you think Jake and I . . . But you are wrong, quite wrong. It was never like that.'

Alix felt her face burn, and she said foolishly, 'Oh?'

'You are not happy together, you and Jake,' Monique said sadly. 'I am truly sorry, because Jake has suffered so much. When he was here, during the war, and so badly injured, we all thought he would die. *You* were the reasons he didn't die, Alix. You were always on his mind. He clung to you, your image, the thought of you. It brought him strength.'

Monique pushed back her dark hair in which one or two grey streaks were beginning to show. 'When he was convalescing, I used to come up here and sit with him and talk. You were the entire subject of his conversation, and he never tired of it. Sometimes he'd ask me, "Am I boring you?" And I would always smile and say "No", because I knew how much he needed to talk about you. It was the best medicine he could have had, the hope that one day he'd see you again. When he wrote to tell me you two were married, I was so happy. I thought that at last Jake had what he'd wanted all along. But when you both came here, I saw at once that things were not right, that something was very badly wrong. I don't ask what it is, Alix, but I do beg you, please, don't give up. Jake didn't give up, when he was injured, because of you. Will you hold on now, Alix, because of *him*?'

Alix said wearily, 'Is it always worth trying to keep a marriage together even if it isn't one, and you're both paying a dreadful price?'

Monique gripped her hand. 'Yes!' she urged. 'Yes, it is, if in your heart there is nothing in the world you want more!' Her grip relaxed slightly. 'Perhaps you think, because my husband, Henri, is so much older than I am, that ours is a marriage of convenience only. That isn't so. I've always loved and admired Henri, but it has often been difficult. We never had any children. If we had, perhaps it would have been easier. As the years went by, he often used to say to me that I should have married someone younger, of my own age. He has felt it very keenly, that he was so much older. Not, of course, when we were first married, because it was less obvious then. But time is not kind. That doesn't mean that I have regrets. I can tell you with complete honesty that if some magical force took me back to my youth and said: "You can have any man you choose—take!" I would choose Henri again. Marriage is not easy, Alix, and it's never what we expect. But if two people really belong together, how can any obstacle force them apart?' She leaned forward and kissed Alix's cheek. 'You will feel better tomorrow, my dear.'

'No, I won't,' Alix thought dully, but didn't say it, and smiled dutifully.

Jake came up to bed late, at nearly midnight. Alix heard him moving in the next room, and then came a light knock on the door between their rooms. He was coming to see her, after all. But she suspected it was Monique's doing, and felt only resentment instead of the hope she had felt earlier.

He came in, and pulling up a chair by her bedside, asked defiantly, 'How are you now?'

'Not too bad,' Alix said. 'Did you come because you wanted to, or because Monique sent you?'

'I don't take orders from Monique!' he said sharply. 'I had every intention of calling in on you—but the chess game ran on, and then I waited for old Berthier to go.'

Jake looked down at his own strong, sinewy hands, clenched so tightly that the knuckles, with their criss-cross of old scars from his street-fighting days, gleamed white through the skin. 'I'm sorry if I was a grouch all day, and I'm sorry about last night,' he said grimly, as if determined to get some unpleasant obligation out of the way.

'You don't have to *apologise*, for heaven's sake!' she cried out fiercely.

'Yes, I do. Because I let you down. I know you wanted me to make love to you. As it was, all that happened was that we both finished upset and disappointed. I don't say it was any fault but *mine*.' His voice, which had been cool and dispassionate, suddenly broke off. He put both hands over his face and whispered brokenly through them, 'I'm sorry, Alix. I bloody can't, and I never shall.'

Alix threw back the sheet and scrambled out to clasp her arms round him and hug him to her tightly, possessively, wishing she could take his despair and throttle it. 'Don't do that, Jake, don't—*please!*' she begged. 'It isn't anyone's fault! Don't cry, my darling, don't—you never did that before . . .'

Jake muttered, 'Oh, hell . . . No, I never did, not since I was about six years old, anyway. I'm all right now, Alix—it's okay.'

He pushed himself away from her embrace and repeated, 'Really—it's all right now. Get back into bed.

You'll catch cold. This house is like an icebox.'

She scrambled reluctantly back between the sheets and watched him pull himself together, rub the moisture off his eyelids and generally turn back into Jake as he usually was. He even managed to smile at her, and that made her want to weep in turn, so she swallowed hard, and said sternly, 'You are *not* to get so down about it, do you hear? You are not a lesser person than you would be, otherwise. You are the same, and it doesn't matter so much to me, if we can't. You are *not* to give up. I won't let you.'

'Yes, Alix,' he said mockingly. They had touched the depths of despair together. That left only one direction to go, and that was upwards, so that they both experienced an over-reaction which made them light-headed as they rose from the nadir of personal disappointment. 'God, you're fierce,' he said. 'Didn't you tell me you used to go to suffragette meetings during the war?'

'Only to make the tea.'

Jake nodded, and she laughed.

His grey eyes ran over Alix's slender form lying on the pillows. The fine powder-blue satin of her night-dress, swelling and dipping in soft folds and hummocks, only hinted at that beautiful, unattainable body. How long, Jake wondered to himself, before another entered Alix's life? A lover who would succeed where he had failed, and who would capture first her body and then her heart. Last night, in her arms, he had made a fool of himself in the bitterest way possible, and he swore that never again would he let himself be drawn into a repeat of that cruel fiasco.

Yet, surely, she would find the need for someone, some day, and he was as helpless as he had been lying here wounded during the war, to prevent it. He felt he could see the as yet unknown lover, as a shadowy form which already haunted him and had become a constant companion, like a familiar spirit. Someone, somewhere would stretch out a hand and take from him the wife who was no wife. He hoped that, when it happened, he would find the strength to bear the bitter knowledge, that he would not hate her for her betrayal, that anger itself would not prevent him from letting her go.

No one, not even Alix, understood the anger that burned within him like an unquenchable fire in his breast. No one knew how much hatred and despair fermented in him and built up its unbearable pressure, which would one day no longer be contained. Old Berthier had been comforting and encouraging, but the doctor was an old man. He remembered the fire in the blood, but had forgotten what it was like to fear the flames.

'*Flames!*' Jake suddenly said aloud, without quite knowing why. He saw Alix turn a questioning look at him, and was forced to explain, awkwardly, 'When I crashed, I could smell the leaking fuel, and I was waiting for the flames. Even before they came, I could feel their heat, and remember the others who burned . . .'

A shiver ran over Alix, as though a supernatural hand had touched her. Her heart began to beat rapidly and painfully, and the blood to rush in her ears with the discovery of knowledge. Forcing herself to think carefully and coherently, and not to let herself be blinded by the sudden ray of light piercing the darkness, she whispered, 'But you didn't burn, Jake. The flames came later, after Maurice had pulled you clear.'

The fear of the flames. All their present misery was tied up with that moment of pure horror, that terror of the flames and their searing destructive power. The anticipation of that imminent total disaster had laid an iron hand on Jake's mind and refused to relinquish its paralysing grip.

She leaned forward and grasped his hand tightly in

hers. 'But you *didn't* burn, Jake! You only thought you were going to perish in the flames. You were afraid of something which didn't happen!'

Jake's grey eyes were clouded, and he shook his head irritably, as if some insect buzzed annoyingly about it.

Hardly daring to breathe, and terrified of saying the wrong thing, she urged with bated breath, 'It happened to other people, Jake, but it didn't happen to *you*!'

'I dream about it sometimes,' he muttered hoarsely. 'Less now than I did. At first, I dreamt about it a lot, when I was hidden in this house. I'd wake up in a cold sweat, and I could smell that leaking fuel and hear the wooden frame crackling in the heat. Sometimes I switched on the light and read till morning, because I was afraid to go back to sleep. Can you understand that?' He frowned at her.

'Yes, Jake, I can. But it's over and done with—all in the past!'

He stared at her for a moment, and then pulled his hand roughly from the clasp of her fingers, and snarled, 'Like blazes it's all in the past! I'm still fighting *my* war, Alix. War took my life and messed it up, and left me the broken pieces.'

The harsh sound of the words faded. Jake's face was set in hard, unrelenting lines. 'I told you I was sorry, and I am. But I won't put either of us through that again.'

He was referring to last night's bitter failure. But something far more important and significant had just happened, which pushed that fiasco into pale memory. Fate had put into their hands, at last, a key. It unlocked a door in Jake's mind. But as poor Alice had found, when she had tried to follow the white rabbit through the garden door into Wonderland, to use the key was by no means easy.

CHAPTER THIRTEEN

ALIX WANTED very much to communicate her new
discovery, as she saw it, to Dr Berthier before they
returned to Paris. In some ways, she was afraid to talk
to him again because he had sown such a seed of self-
doubt in her mind. But the doctor had done so deliberately, to shock her into taking a new look at their
situation. Certainly her mind was a turmoil of fresh
ideas, as she set out to walk to his house on the edge
of the village the following afternoon.

It was cold, but sunny, and outside in the fresh air
she felt better, almost optimistic again, her emotions
swinging from the depths of despair in which they had
temporarily languished to an equally extreme buoyancy,
which she knew in her heart could not last.

It was a tall, narrow house standing behind a high
garden wall, its wooden shutters painted pale grey, the
tiles of its roof a greenish hue. The black-clad and
ancient housekeeper let her into a hall smelling highly
of wax polish and coffee, and said the doctor was 'with
his books'. This was soon explained. The old man was
a bibliophile, an avid collector of early editions. He
received Alix in a study lined with ancient tomes which
exuded an odour of dried leather and yellowing parch-
ment. Once again, when she attempted to apologise for
disturbing him, he swept away her excuses and professed
himself delighted to see her.

'An old fellow such as myself receives few visits from
beautiful women! My dear, sit down, try to overlook, I
beg you, these somewhat gloomy surroundings . . .'

He waved a wrinkled hand affectionately at his tightly
packed bookcases.

Alix told him what had passed between herself and
Jake the previous evening. He listened carefully, nodded,
tapped his fingers together and said, 'Hm—hm . . . it's
possible—yes, possible . . . The mind anticipating an
event, it happens.' Quite unexpectedly he looked up, his
old blue eyes surprisingly sharp. 'And you, madame,
you enjoy good health yourself?'

'Very good,' said Alix, startled. 'I'm never ill.'

'Ah!' he held up an admonitory finger. 'What is *ill*?'
When she looked confused, he took pity on her and
went on. 'You sleep well?'

'Yes . . .' She hesitated, and prompted by a natural
desire for honesty and frankness, admitted, 'Not as well,
sometimes, as I'd like. I suppose I worry about Jake.'

'You have headaches? You are depressed? Nervous?
Irritable? Sometimes you feel ill although you say to
yourself, I am healthy?'

This was so exactly what she often felt that she felt
herself blush. 'Sometimes. I do work quite hard. I am a
career woman, you know. Perhaps that shocks you.'

'My dear, a doctor is never shocked.' He smiled.
Suddenly he leaned past her and tapped the spine of a
venerable volume on the shelf by her shoulder. 'Rabelais.
He is not considered suitable reading for ladies. Men
who read him, these days, do so frequently because they
find him ribald and amusing. They misunderstand him.
Rabelais, too, was a doctor. He understood that our
bodies are created for simple, basic purposes, and this
is what dictates our physical lives and also the way in
which the world appears to us. Theologians would add
to that, but I am not a theologian, and I speak only of
the body and the mind. You think only your husband
suffers because he cannot make love to you, as he so
obviously wishes to do. But you, too, dear madame,

you suffer.' His bright old eyes fixed themselves on her pale face. 'It is not enough, if you want help, to admit that he has need of you. You must also face the fact that you have need of him. I think you have pretended that was not so.'

Alix said dully, 'Yes. But I know differently now.'

Berthier tapped the arms of his chair. 'You are a remarkable young woman! You have clarity of insight. You face the truth. That is the beginning of the way to success.' He paused. 'But it is a difficult path to tread. You have a long way to go yet, my dear.'

Paris was dry, but in the grip of a severe frost. The flat in the quiet boulevard was chilly and deserted, because Séraphine, the housekeeper, had gone to stay with a married daughter in Brittany over the Christmas period. Alix sought out the concierge, to see if something couldn't be done about the heating, and returned upstairs, rubbing her chilled hands, to find Jake pottering in the kitchen, making coffee. He seemed quite cheerful, whistling an old music-hall ballad , and rummaging in Séraphine's tidy cupboards. He seemed to have a weight off his mind, and Alix wondered whether it was because they were home again, or because he was ruthlessly suppressing the memory of their failure in his bed.

Yet she was pleased to see him happy, and her own spirits rose. They had been sadly depressed. The long drive had tired her, and the flat seemed so cold and unwelcoming, hardly a homecoming. Yet when they had established themselves in the salon with the steaming coffee-pot, she felt herself begin to relax, and to think it was, after all, rather nice to be home, just the two of them together. She had hardly reached this conclusion when the doorbell rang furiously.

Alix said resignedly, 'I'll go . . .' and went to open it.

Paul bounced in, dishevelled and with his overcoat unbuttoned and his hat in his hand. He barged uninvited into the salon, and, pushing his hair out of his eyes, demanded, 'Where have you two been? I've been trying to get hold of you for days! No one even answers the telephone.'

'Sit down, Paul,' Alix told him, and he flopped down in a chair, still in his overcoat, and looked hopefully at the coffee, so she fetched another cup. 'The concierge could have told you that we'd gone into the country for Christmas.'

'If, by concierge, you mean that potty old fellow downstairs, I wouldn't ask him anything. He doesn't tell you anything, anyway. Just says, "Not at home!" and slams the door in the caller's face. What on earth did you want to go into the country for?' Paul sounded genuinely amazed. 'At this time of year, for the love of charity?'

'Log fires, good cooking and peace and quiet,' Jake said, giving him a direct look.

It bounced off, like water from the proverbial duck's back. 'You mean me? You two need me. Vegetating in the country . . . Retiring to the seaside next, I shouldn't be surprised,' Paul said in disgust.

'What do you want, Paul?' Alix asked him. 'It can't have been so urgent, surely?'

Paul set down his cup carelessly on the edge of the chair, so that it rocked unsteadily and threatened to spill coffee over the upholstery. Alix rescued it in haste and put it on a table. 'You know, do you, what date it is? Hah, no, you don't!' he exclaimed in triumph at the expression on their faces. 'My dear children, it's New Year's Eve, and I've come to invite you to a party. You shall see in the New Year with me.'

There was frankly nothing Alix felt less like doing. 'Oh, Paul, we've driven back from the country, for goodness' sake! I'm tired.'

'You can rest for an hour or two. Everyone will be there; you have to come! I'm expecting at least a hundred people to turn up.'

'In your flat? Paul, it's impossible!'

'No, *chère* Alix, not in my flat. That's only my *pied-à-terre* here in Paris, strictly for clients and whores. At my house.' He grinned at them triumphantly, because he could see the amazement on their faces. 'Yes, children, I have a house—twenty kilometres outside Paris—and you can take the train. So there's no reason why you can't come. What's more, it's a damn sight warmer there than in here!' He rubbed his hands and shivered theatrically, glancing about the room.

'How long have you had the house?' Alix enquired, still puzzling over this new development.

'About five years. I bought it for a song as it was in a terrible state, really tumbledown. It's taken me the whole five years to get it right, but it's coming along, and by the time I retire, which I shall do when I'm too old to work or make love, it's there I shall go.'

'Convenient,' Jake said drily.

Paul retrieved his coffee-cup from the table where Alix had put it, and smiled slightly, not at them, but to himself. She felt a sinking feeling in the pit of her stomach. She knew Paul well, and recognised that private, cruel little smile. Something amused him, and she was horribly certain of the cause.

'Paul knows . . .' she thought. 'He knows about Jake—and me. He's been thinking it over, and he's worked it out for himself. He's guessed the truth.' Aloud, she said sharply, 'It's kind of you, Paul, but we really can't.'

'I'd like to go,' Jake said calmly.

There was a little silence. Then Paul put down his empty cup and scrambled to his feet in an untidy flurry of hair and clothes. 'Good! See you later on.'

When he had gone, Alix said resentfully, 'Why did you accept? You saw I didn't want to go. I'm tired.'

'It's New Year's Eve. What were you planning instead? To stay here, so that we could stare at each other until midnight and then retire to our solitary respective couches?'

She gave a little gasp, and stared at him in dismay. His tone was so brusque, unkind, and he looked so angry, that she felt as though he'd struck her. The cold truth crowded in on her and would not be silenced. It was what she had secretly feared might happen. He didn't want to be alone with her. Her company only served as a reminder of what couldn't be. We can't go to bed together, he was saying, so what the heck? We might as well go out and forget it all for a few hours in cheerful company.

She found herself mumbling, 'Yes, all right, if you want to go.'

He turned his head away from her, and looked marginally less aggressive, though still obstinate. 'You can wear that pink dress, the one with the bits hanging round it like a lot of handkerchiefs.'

'You mean the georgette one.' She knew the dress he meant. It was a salmon pink and set off her red hair. It was also cut daringly low at the bosom and plunged at the back. It was a showy, sexy sort of dress, bought in a mad moment and afterwards regretted.

Jake said, 'Sure, I like that one.'

Once Paul had astonished them by telling them he owned a country house, or at least a house in the *banlieu*, which counted for Parisians as country, Alix was prepared for anything. Even so, it surprised her. It stood in its own restricted grounds behind a high wall, an early nineteenth century, First Empire building, perhaps built by some entrepreneur who had grown fat on the war industries flourishing to the rear of the great Napoleonic campaigns—a supplier of material for uniforms or army remounts.

It was dark when they arrived and stepped out of the taxicab that had brought them from the local station, and so the exterior was not to be studied. But there were lights at all the windows, and a great cacophony of shrieking, chattering voices, dance-band music and chinking glasses wafted out on the cold night air. As they entered, a prim-looking maid in a black dress and white cap and apron appeared and took Alix's fur coat, and a manservant appeared like magic to minister to Jake. No doubt they had both been hired for the evening from the firm which had done the catering. But the impression was that the house was run with all the efficient organisation that Paul himself appeared to lack. But Alix had long suspected that Paul's Bohemian carelessness as to detail was an assumed front. He always knew exactly what he was doing, and always planned at least three moves ahead. She wasn't surprised to glimpse, through a half-open door, a chessboard ready set out for play on a table. Paul liked to move people around like pawns.

The rest of the house, as far as she could take notice as they were hustled into the throng, confirmed these impressions. Not here were to be seen the vulgarities of the *nouveau-riche* style he created for others. This house had been restored with love and care and taste. It was beautiful. Like the original entrepreneur who had built it in the first decade of the nineteenth century, Paul would one day turn his back on the sordid money-making and come to live here.

Alone? Alix frowned slightly. He was divorced. He had mistresses, but they came and went with bewildering rapidity. Juliette had vanished from the scene. But perhaps he had long-term plans, even about that. Possibly he already had in mind a permanent mistress for this lovely house.

Paul himself came pushing through the crowd towards them, looking handsome, disreputable, slightly flushed and perspiring. 'You found it, then. Alix, you look beautiful . . .' He kissed her cheek. 'Let me get you both a drink.'

'There are so many people here!' she exclaimed.

'Yes, I wish I knew who they all were . . . Hold on.' He touched her arm. 'See that fellow over there, black moustache, trying to put his hand on that girl's backside? It's Laroche, the armaments magnate. I'll take you across to meet him later. He's bought a place out at Neuilly, and he wants us to discuss renovating it.'

Even now, business came first. Alix could already guess the sort of thing Laroche would want. He had plenty of money and would like people to see it. Fur rugs and oil paintings would abound, huge dining tables, built-in bars and drink cabinets, gold bathroom taps—and everything painted in a confusing mix of colours.

Jake was already talking to someone, and a former client had recognised Alix and now bore down on her. The next hour was lost in a confusing chatter of voices and passing drinks. Supper broke up the assembly and sent them all scurrying to the dining-room. Somehow or other she had become detached from Jake again, and suddenly saw, to her horror, Paul guiding the arms manufacturer towards her. Laroche teetered up, obviously drunk, to be introduced. He bowed over her hand uncertainly and kissed it, an unpleasant experience, for he had moist red lips and reeked of brandy.

Paul, characteristically, had deserted her as soon as he'd made the introductions. Laroche began to talk expansively, touching her shoulder familiarly with his pudgy fingers and ogling her with bloodshot, prominent eyes. Revulsion swept over her, not just because of him, but at the whole gathering. The heat was overpowering, the fumes of wine filled the air, and the smell of food, laid out in a magnificent array on a long table, was rich and cloying. A sweating chef in his white hat was slicing pinkly moist pâté and wafer thin slices of ham. A display of glazed fruit gleamed and glowed like a great rose window of stained glass.

Nausea welled up in Alix's throat. She burst out, 'Excuse me!' and bolted unceremoniously out of the room, leaving Laroche, swaying and bemused, wondering where she'd gone.

In the hall it was quiet and deserted, and the air was cooler and smelled as clear as a mountain breeze after the stuffy atmosphere of the dining-room. Alix drew a deep breath and wiped her hand over her forehead. She didn't know where Jake was, and had no wish to plunge back into the crowd of revellers. She glanced around her. To go wandering around the host's house would be the height of discourtesy, but she had an impulse to see more of Paul's secret hideaway. She climbed the stairs, stopping at intervals to study the paintings that lined the staircase. Some of them were English, hunting scenes, and she wondered whether Paul had ever been in England. He certainly spoke excellent English. At the top of the stairs, two sets of doors led off an ante-room furnished with period furniture. Alix opened one set at random and walked into the room beyond.

Almost at once, she realised to her dismay that she was in Paul's bedroom. Various of his belongings were lying around, and cigarette stubs in the ashtray. She had intended to retire instantly, but on the wall there was a photograph, and she found herself drawn towards it.

A young man in flying leathers stood beside a biplane. Across the corner of the picture someone had written in ink, in French, 'July 1917'. The young pilot was leaning back against the fuselage, grinning cheerfully at the camera. It was Paul, in his war years, his air just as rakish and anarchic, but with the charm of youth still on it, which made all the difference. The photograph filled Alix with indescribable pain, because it seemed to represent all their yesterdays. That's how she had first known Jake, in uniform, a little younger, fit, happy to be flying, his world filled with action, excitement and danger.

'Well, this is a pleasant surprise,' Paul's voice said unexpectedly from behind her. 'I certainly didn't expect to find you here, waiting for me, Alix.'

She whirled round with a gasp. Paul was leaning in the doorway, a champagne glass in one hand and an open bottle of Heidsieck in the other. His black bow tie was unravelled and hung down on either side of his neck. He grinned at her impudently, a hardened, more mature and more cynical reflection of the young flier in the photograph.

'I'm sorry, Paul,' Alix stammered. 'I was wandering around the house. Inexcusable, I know, but professional curiosity, I suppose—and I was desperate to get away from that awful man Laroche. Why did you abandon me like that?'

'Ouf!' He looked pained. 'Don't spoil it! I thought this was a romantic rendez-vous.'

'I wasn't expecting you to come up here, and I stayed only to look at the photograph,' she retorted quickly.

He winked at her. 'Well, now I am here. So if it wasn't a romantic tryst, we can still make it into one.' He pushed himself lazily away from the door and came into the room, kicking the door closed behind him with his heel.

'Paul!' Alix said hastily, putting out a hand to ward him off. It occurred to her that he might just be drunk enough to essay a pass he wouldn't make in other circumstances, and she knew his character well enough to realise that, if he'd taken such a thing into his head, he wouldn't be dissuaded by a simple refusal.

'Don't look so alarmed,' he said reproachfully. 'I'm not going to rape you. With a house full of people? No fun in it, anyway. But together we could create enchantment!'

'Yes, the house is full of people, and one of them is my husband!' Alix reminded him bluntly.

'Ah, the virtuous wife . . . How tiresome.' Paul wandered across the room to stand by her and survey the photograph critically. 'I don't know why I kept that there,' he said softly, 'I don't want to remember those times. They were a living hell, from beginning to end. Being French, you see, it was far worse, for us, than for the others. Canadians, English, Americans, Australians, they were in a foreign land and foreign skies. But we fought over our own country. We could see it down there below us, blasted by the guns and torn up by the trenches, strangled by the wire . . .' He shrugged, and added more briskly, 'That was a good little machine, the Nieuport, though. I suppose that's why I keep the photo on the wall—for the machine. I was still flying that one at the end of the war; more holes in it than a sieve, but it flew like a dream. It responded to every touch like a woman in love.'

He turned away and went over to the bed. Depositing his glass and champagne bottle neatly on the sheepskin rug beside it, he took off his dinner jacket and dropped it on the floor and then threw himself down on his back, his hands behind his head and his feet creasing the quilted blue satin coverlet.

'What brought you up here?' Alix asked. She had been moved by what he'd said, and by something in his voice as he'd said it, which she had not heard from him before. She came to the foot of the bed and stared down at his sprawled form.

Paul glanced up beneath half-lowered eyelids, and she felt the scrutiny of his eyes as he studied her. It was a four-poster bed, and she stood with one arm raised and her hand grasping the corner-post in an unconsciously graceful attitude which, because he was a trained artist, put him in mind of the studio models. The soft lighting made her hair glow like the live coals at the heart of a fire.

'My guests are amusing each other, but boring me!' His look became more openly appraising. 'You're a very beautiful woman, Alix. You have everything a man could want.'

For a moment, she almost hated him for those words.

'When did you decide that? When you discovered I was what's vulgarly called "well off"?' she retorted promptly. She wasn't sure if he'd learned about the money she'd inherited from old Nat Morrell, but suspected that Blanche must have told him of it. Since the wedding, she had marked a subtle change in Paul's attitude towards her. That Jake had money, must, of course, be obvious to him.

He chuckled, unabashed. 'There's nothing vulgar about you, my dear, or me. We're artists, fine souls trapped in a society of barbarians. I've always thought you beautiful, and you're talented too, and a good business-woman!' Unexpectedly, he sat up and leaned his shirt-sleeved arms on his crooked knees. 'Together, Alix, as partners, we could do more than make love. We could make a fortune. What do you say?'

'I'm working for you now.'

'Pah!' Paul dismissed this with an expansive gesture. 'I mean, full-time, real partners, in everything.' He emphasised the last word slightly and raised his dark eyebrows questioningly.

'You are forgetting I'm married,' Alix said tautly.

'Divorce him. Marry me,' he returned simply.

'That's impertinent!' she snapped angrily, her green eyes darkening.

'You might as well,' Paul said gently. 'I do realise how it is, Alix dear. You and he—you don't do you? Or rather, *he* can't . . .'

'It's a temporary problem!' she said furiously, 'and none of your business.'

'I see. So love will conquer all, will it? He does still tell you every day that he loves you, I take it?'

Jake had never told her he loved her. The cruelty of Paul's words cut her to the heart.

Alix said quietly, 'You're a scoundrel, Paul. But what puzzles me about it is that a man like yourself—with that background,' she indicated the flying photograph, 'should have no sense of loyalty. I just don't understand. War-time comradeship must have meant something to you. Jake was a pilot. You even knew him slightly, during the war. Now you're trying to seduce his wife. Don't you find it wrong?'

He shrugged again. 'No. Lancelot was a flower of chivalry, but it didn't stop him casting an adulterous eye on Arthur's Queen Guinevere. And you, dear Alix, are a modern Guinevere. You're married, but it's not a marriage. You're not happy, neither is he. Don't pretend otherwise. Do you think *I* don't recognise the symptoms of a relationship cracking at the seams? Of course I do. I've been through it all myself.' Paul laughed with unexpected bitterness, and lay back again, staring up at the frilled canopy over the bed.

'My wife's family was an old Norman one. They traced their descent back to a half-brother of William the Bastard. I know the English call him "the Conqueror", but we French like to get things right. You know, there couldn't have been a village maiden left *virgo intacta* within travelling distance of old Robert the Devil's castle. My wife was extraordinarily proud of all that. Odd, really, because the slightest breath of modern-day scandal, and the whole family was horrified. If it happened in the eleventh century, it was all right. *I* didn't happen in the eleventh century, and I was just unacceptable.'

'Why did you marry her? Were you in love with her?' Alix asked curiously.

He frowned, considering that one carefully. 'No, not really. She was pretty, in a wishy-washy sort of way, with a touch of schoolgirlish charm.' He grimaced. 'She was a selfish, spoilt little cat underneath it all, of course. Anyway, I rather forgot myself. We went out for a walk, you see, and it came on to rain, and there was a convenient old barn . . .'

'Don't tell me,' Alix said resignedly. 'I can guess the rest of it.'

'Yes, I'm afraid so. Oh, I didn't force myself on her. She was quite willing, even enthusiastic! But there we were. Or, rather, there was her papa, in due course, demanding that I marry her, because of her condition.' Paul shrugged elegantly. 'So I did. They didn't want *me*, of course; they wanted respectability.'

'You got her . . . You have a child?' Alix stared at him incredulously.

'Oh yes, somewhere. I've never seen him. I told you they only wanted the marriage certificate and the wedding ring—just to avoid a scandal and to legitimise the child. The marriage itself lasted all of six weeks, then she went back to Papa and Maman. That wasn't my fault. I was twenty years old and quite looking forward to being a father. However, Papa came to see me and told me in no uncertain terms to get out of his daughter's life. He even paid me off, quite generously. With the money came detailed instructions, naturally.

"Take the money, my lad, get out of town, never come back, and don't ever try and claim the child!" '

'I'm sorry,' Alix said soberly. 'Because that's very sad, for you all—for the child, his mother and for you.'

'Don't grieve, dear Alix. It happens all the time, more often than you think. She was a spoiled brat, as I told you. I dare say I'd have left her, anyway, eventually.'

'Well, I'm not leaving Jake!' Alix said sharply. 'Nor am I going to betray him. Certainly not with you! You should be ashamed even to think of deceiving someone like Jake, who has gone through so much!'

'Don't talk to me about the war!' Paul said, his voice suddenly harsh. 'Things were different then. *We* were different then. Younger, more naïve. You could even say "stupid". We believed what they told us—and we were fools!' He turned his head to one side so that his eyes met hers. 'War taught me one thing, Alix, and it wasn't comradeship. It was *"sauve qui peut"*—every man for himself, kill or be killed. Do you know how many good friends I saw die? Shot down, burnt alive, posted missing, which means that even their own mothers never knew what happened to their children . . . And you dare to talk to me of loyalty? *We* were the ones who were betrayed! And do you think those fat cattle downstairs, guzzling my food and drink and disporting their plump bodies to the music—do you think they give a damn for that sacrifice now? They've put up the monuments, paid for the Masses, tidied up the graves, and now they're only interested in enjoying themselves.'

Alix said, very seriously, 'That's a cynical view, Paul, and it's a mistaken one.'

'I'm wrong?' He smiled at her now, and rolled over on to his side, pushing himself up on one elbow. 'Too hard-bitten? Come on, come here and teach me otherwise.' He patted the satin coverlet invitingly.

'*No*, and you don't really think I would!' Alix frowned,

and added, less certainly, 'You don't believe it, do you, Paul? You don't truly think I might?'

'Why not? You might as well. What do the English say? Might as well be hung for a sheep as a lamb? Jake will have missed you by now. He'll look around and see you've gone from downstairs. The next thing he'll do is to look for *me*, and he'll see I'm gone, too. He'll put two and two together, and he'll come up with eight. Jake thinks you're up here in bed with me now, Alix. Put your money on it. He's not going to believe you when you go downstairs and deny it, so . . .' He grinned at her mischievously. 'You've nothing to lose, Alix, so come on, I promise you a very enjoyable time.'

'I'm going downstairs now!' Alix said sharply. She turned in a swirl of pink georgette and walked purposefully to the door.

Paul slid off the bed with the rapidity of a striking rattlesnake, crossing the room before she had a chance to even realise her danger, and barring her escape. He grasped her shoulder roughly.

'Don't be so damn prudish, Alix! Who cares any more? There are over a hundred people here tonight, and not a faithful husband or a loyal wife amongst them! His hands slid down to grasp her bare arms, and he pulled her towards him and bent his head to kiss her.

Alix lifted her hand and slapped his face, hard. He recoiled before the blow, which echoed in the room, and stared at her, his dark hair falling in disarray, and the marks of her fingers imprinted clearly on his cheek in four red stripes. For a terrible moment, when she realised what she'd done, she panicked, afraid of him. But he didn't react in the violent way she had expected.

He took his hands away from her and said softly, 'You didn't need to do that, Alix.'

'You're drunk, Paul!' she returned unevenly. 'Let me past.'

He spread his hands out in a disarmingly innocent gesture of surrender. 'Dear Madame Sherwood, you are as free as a bird, a beautiful pink flamingo.' He opened the bedroom door for her and stood aside to allow her to pass.

Alix hesitated, and walked by him into the ante-room beyond. Behind her, his voice said quietly, 'I'm not drunk, Alix, and I can wait.'

She whirled round with a gasp of anger, and saw his dishevelled figure in the doorway. At the sight of her anger, he pulled a wry face at her and said unexpectedly, 'I threw my wedding ring into the river. What do you plan to do with yours?'

'Keep on wearing it,' she said calmly.

He grimaced then, so comically, that, for all her anger, she almost laughed at his unrepentant, mischievous expression. Yet, at the same time, she felt a pain in her heart for that other Paul—gone now beyond recall—the young man dismissed by his aristocratic, spoilt wife and her family, and hurling his wedding ring into the water. What the failed marriage had begun, the war had completed. It had all made Paul into what he was now, and he couldn't change.

All thoughts of Paul were thrust aside as soon as she rejoined the merry throng downstairs. He had been right, and Jake *had* missed her. He was sitting alone in one corner, his grey eyes searching the packed room anxiously. Alix pushed her way ruthlessly through the throng and sat down beside him, knowing she looked untidy and upset, her hair disarranged and her make-up smudged. The shoulder-straps of the pink dress were twisted awry, and she tugged at them nervously, trying to straighten them.

Jake said nothing, either in greeting or comment, but

his eyes watched her flushed face as he waited for her to speak.

Alix said fiercely, '*No*, I haven't!'

'I didn't ask,' Jake said mildly, 'And I wasn't going to.'

'But that's how you first met me, wasn't it? I was blundering about in a garden trying to slip out of a party and up to Robbie's room. Now you think I've done it again.'

'Did you?' he asked evenly.

Alix felt her cheeks burn and the tears sting at her eyelids. '*No*, I told you! I was wandering around upstairs out of curiosity, and bumped into Paul. Yes, he did make a very mild sort of pass, but only because he's drunk. He didn't insist, and there was nothing to it.'

Someone shouted, 'It's five minutes to midnight!' Someone else pushed a glass of champagne into her unwilling hand. There was a strange, silent moment whilst everyone listened, breath held, until a clock could be heard striking the hour. As the twelfth stroke faded, bedlam broke loose. People were yelling on all sides, and the band was trying to play in hopeless competition. Coloured paper streamers were flying through the air like tracer fire.

'It's 1921,' Jake said unsmilingly. 'Happy new year, Mrs Sherwood!' He leaned towards her and kissed her cheek.

Alix flung her arms round his neck and burying her face in his shoulder, burst into tears. 'Let's go home, Jake. Let's go back to Paris—now!'

'Sure,' he said quietly. 'Anything you want, Alix.' Above her bent head, his gaze crossed the crowded room and rested on Daquin's debonair and rakish figure standing by the door, one arm round the shoulders of an attractive brunette. 'Anything you want . . .' Jake repeated.

The coloured paper streamers, blue, red and yellow, fluttered down and covered them in a tangled cat's-cradle of interwoven strands.

CHAPTER FOURTEEN

IN FEBRUARY, a routine visit to the specialist to check on his progress brought Jake unexpected news. The surgeon had decided that the pain in the hip was largely caused by fragments of floating bone, a residue of the original injury. An operation to remove them would present no problem, the specialist said, and the benefits would be considerable. He took off his half-moon spectacles and set them carefully on the top of his desk. He wore a wing collar and a frock-coat, and Alix suspected that he dyed his hair.

The thought of going back into hospital, yet again, and another period of convalescence, struck Jake hard. But he agreed—although Alix knew he didn't want to go through with it. However, the pain had become so bad recently that, as Jake put it sourly, 'I've no confounded choice!' So he was booked into a private clinic near Vincennes, and the specialist himself was going to operate.

'I believe we may be optimistic, Madame Sherwood,' the man said blandly. He had an irritating way of talking to her as though she were five years old and incapable of understanding the slightest medical explanation. All the time he was talking he smiled at her in a kindly way, as to an idiot, and twined his soft white fingers in and out of one another, smoothly, as if, in his mind, he tied a complicated knot. The pale sunlight fell on his improbably russet hair and was extinguished as if snuffed out.

No sooner had all this been arranged than a telegram

arrived unexpectedly from Gerard in England.

'What's up?' Jake asked quickly, seeing Alix's face change as she read it.

'Aunt Ethel died,' Alix said incredulously. She sat down abruptly on the nearest chair, and added, 'I can't believe it. She was always such a healthy woman. She wasn't young, of course, but I can never recall her being ill for a single day.'

'Creaking doors last the longest,' Jake said, 'Like me. When's the funeral?

'Tuesday—but I can't go over for it. That's the day you go into the clinic.'

Jake limped across to where she sat and stooped over her, putting his hands on her shoulders. Alix looked up at him.

'Listen, Alix,' he said quietly, 'you should go—and I want you to go. Your aunt was good to you. She brought you up. Gerard will appreciate your going to England for his mother's funeral. She was a nice lady. I remember her well. Besides, I don't need you here— No, wait!' He raised his voice slightly to forestall the protest forming on her lips, and because he could see the hurt in her green eyes at his rejection of her support at this time. He tried not to sound impatient as he said, 'That's not how it is, Alix. I'm not sending you away. But I'd rather you didn't . . . Oh, heck, I just don't want you to see me in a hospital bed! Understand, for pity's sake, please!'

'Yes, I understand,' Alix said gently.

He smiled at her a little crookedly, and for the first time since their failed attempt at lovemaking when staying with Monique, he kissed her on the mouth. His lips had a warm, vibrant touch that sent a quiver running through her entire body. 'I'm hell to live with, Alix, I know. But I did warn you.'

Alix felt the tears filling her eyes. 'It doesn't matter,

Jake, truly.'

'Well, it matters to *me*. I'm sorry, I wish . . . I wish it were different,' Jake told her, his voice brusque.

She reached up her arms and twisted them round his neck. 'I love you, Jake; that's why I'm here,' she told him earnestly. She had made a mistake.

'Yes, sure,' he said enigmatically. He detached himself from her and straightened up. 'You'd better go and telegraph Gerard that you'll be coming to the funeral.'

Mrs Daventry had been a long-time resident of the neighbourhood and had had many friends. Even so, Alix was surprised at the number of people who turned out on a cold, grey, frosty February day to attend the funeral. The ground was so hard in the churchyard that she wondered how the gravedigger had managed to hack out the trench that stood empty and waiting, decorously draped with green baize. The previous night had been marked by a heavy frost, and even now, at nearly lunchtime, the white hoar-frost still clung to the branches of the trees and trimmed the surrounding graves and tombstones with silver.

Alix had not noticed Robbie in the church, because she had been seated in the front pew with Gerard and Jennie. But as she turned away from the graveside she saw him standing alone at the back of the crowd. Gerard was busy receiving condolences, shaking hands with a long line of sympathetic black-clad figures. She walked across the frozen ground to Robbie and took his hands in her gloved ones, and squeezed his fingers affectionately.

'Hullo, Alix,' he said. 'Nice to see you. Wish it could be on a happier occasion.' He stooped and kissed her on the cheek in a brotherly way.

He looked a little older and had put on a little weight which, together with his heavy winter overcoat, made him a stockier figure than he had been. He'd also grown a blond moustache, which suited him. But he presented a reassuring, familiar sight in the bleak surroundings.

'It's good of you to come, Robbie. Aunt Ethel always thought a lot of you,' Alix said with undisguised pleasure.

He smiled ruefully. 'She was one of the few people who did! I'm in the neighbourhood, visiting my own mother. She's over seventy, you know, but pretty active. She's not here today because of the cold. I'm sort of representing her.'

A chill wind blew across the open churchyard, and by mutual unspoken consent they turned and walked away from the graveside throng with arms linked, back towards the church. How strange it was, Alix thought, but they seemed so much closer now then during their engagement, at ease with one another now that the pretence was done.

Inside the building it was warmer, but not very much so. It was empty now, and there was a heavy scent of flowers in the air, and melted candle-wax. Robbie walked down the aisle and stopped before the brass plaque commemorating his brother. It was beautifully polished, like burnished gold.

'Mother comes down here once a month, never fails, and polishes it,' Robbie said. 'She's never got over Phil's loss, you know. She never liked me very much. Well, I suppose you don't *have* to like your children. I don't mean that she wasn't always very fair, but I knew, even when I was in the nursery, that it was Phil she cared for. His old bedroom's never been touched. It's just as he left it after our last leave together. There's a dried-out packet of cigarettes up there, and a *Boys' Annual* he had for his tenth birthday in 1904—and a photograph of Harriet Bingley. *She's* doing well on the stage these days, did you know? Her name has been linked with a Member of the Aristocracy!' He declared the last words with a rhetorical flourish.

Alix put her hand on his arm, and he turned his head and smiled at her a little sadly. 'I was fond of Phil, too,' he said. 'Everyone liked him. He was a better man than I, in every way. He should have come back. He'd have made something of his life. Not like me.'

'Your wife isn't with you, visiting Lady Harris?'

Robbie grinned with a touch of his old, impish charm. 'Lord, no! Mother can't stand Edith, and *vice versa*! Mother says Edith has very obscure origins! Actually, Edith was on the stage at one time, years ago, as a dancer.'

'Are you happy with her, Robbie?'

He shrugged. 'It's all right—as a marriage. Edith does what she likes. It's her money, after all. He who pays the piper, calls the tune, as the proverb has it. So Edith makes all the decisions. I often feel I'm living in Edith's house—which I am, of course—but as a sort of piece of furniture, like the rest of it. I'm not a totally inactive piece, like a table, but more like a gramophone, which actually does do something if you want it to. I perform in the bedroom; that's my role.'

'You're not even fond of her?' Alix asked in some dismay.

'Yes, in a way. She's a decent sort, you know, underneath all that mascara and chic. I can't say she isn't generous with the pocket money, because she is. She's had a tough life.' Robbie paused and frowned, then he said seriously, 'Yes, I am really quite fond of her. I think she's fond of me—in the way women do get fond of lapdogs.'

They had walked out into the porch, and now sat down on a bench by the wall beneath the notice-board with its appeals for the mission field and flower rota lists. Robbie gave her another impish look, and said, 'I don't know how you'll take this—because Gerry told me that you work for Paul Daquin—but one of the worst things I have to put up with is the décor of that house.'

'You don't mean that Daquin did it?' Alix gasped, astonished.

'Yes. Edith brought him over to England to do it specially, because someone told her he was all the rage in Paris. It's atrocious. It's all frills and little cushions and muslins . . . It's the sort of thing that is meant to look feminine, but which isn't really.' Robbie paused and considered. 'In that way, it's rather like Edith herself, I suppose. Maybe Daquin got it right, at that.'

'I know some of the work he does is frightful—but people like it. It's what they want,' Alix said apologetically.

'What they *want*,' said Robbie with deep feeling, 'is their heads examined! You should try *living* in one of his décors, Alix, as I do.'

'His own house, you know, isn't a bit like that.' She told him about Paul's house and the care he'd taken restoring it. 'But he doesn't care about the clients. He just does whatever they want. It's prostituting his talent, he says, but they pay him awfully well for it.'

'Good luck to the fellow,' Robbie said grimly, adding in a change of tone, 'How's Jake?'

Alix told him about the operation and Robbie nodded and said, 'Poor chap. He's been through a lot. I might be in Paris at the end of next month. Perhaps I could call and see you both?'

'Would you, Robbie? Jake would like that very much. Here, I'll write down the address.'

'I'll be on my own,' Robbie said, as he tucked the slip of paper away in his jacket pocket. 'Edith's going down to Monte Carlo, to play the tables. She doesn't like to have me around when she does that.'

'Why not?'

Robbie gave her an odd bitter little look. 'She doesn't only play the tables . . .'

'You mean . . . other men?' Alix stared at him in disbelief. 'Surely not?'

'Oh, yes. She's tactful—she doesn't do it when I'm around. It's not that I bore her, or anything. It's her way of letting me see she hasn't given up her independence. She's still her own woman, and she wants me to know it. It also serves to remind me that I can be replaced.'

'And what about you?' Alix asked bluntly. 'Suppose you did the same?'

'I'd be out on my ear within ten minutes of her hearing about it!' Robbie stared reflectively at a dusty vase of dead flowers in a niche. 'Money does odd things to people. I used to think it would be nice to be rich. But Edith is a sort of prisoner of hers. Because she pays the bills, she can't think anyone wants anything from her except money. I think I'm the only person she's known for years who actually *likes* her.' Robbie hunched his shoulders and went on wryly, 'Of course I like the money, too!' He turned a candid gaze on Alix. 'But if she lost it all, tomorrow, I'd still stick by her. People think she's hard, but I know she's rather vulnerable.'

'She doesn't deserve you,' Alix said fervently.

'Maybe I just got what *I* deserved!' Robbie said thoughtfully. 'But she's what I need, too. I'm a weak person, Alix. I need someone to organise me. It used to annoy Jake, because he was always a strong personality. Edith is a lot like Jake. She started with nothing but determination to get off the bottom of the heap, and she made it to the top of the ladder by sheer grit. I admire her for it. I'd never have managed that, left to my own devices. Without Edith, I'd probably be selling insurance policies now, door to door. Jake has that same drive inside him. He'll never give up, and no matter what troubles he's having just now, he'll get over them somehow. Jake's a fighter: what's more, he's a winner.'

Later that day, when the funeral lunch was over and the mourners had left, Alix climbed the stairs to the top of the house, to the attic that had once been her studio. The door creaked as she pushed it open and stale air struck her nostrils. No one, now, came up here, no one used the room which had been exclusively hers. Cobwebs hung in the rafters and the skylight was grimy. The easel still stood at the far end, empty. A lingering smell of paint hung in the air, and the woodwork exuded turpentime and old ghosts.

Alix walked across the bare floor, her footsteps echoing loudly in the emptiness. Her old painting-smock still hung on a nail, and she stretched out her hand and touched it. As she did, there was a footfall and a creak of floorboards, and Gerard appeared on the threshold. He stood there irresolutely, as if waiting to be invited in.

'Come in, Gerry,' Alix said, adding sadly, 'It is your house now, after all.'

He came in slowly and lowered himself ponderously into the old, overstuffed armchair in which, once upon a time, he'd sat and watched her work. 'It was your home too, Alix,' he said seriously, 'and it still is—if you want to come back to it.'

She perched on a little stool beneath the grey light falling through the sky-light and surveyed him. 'What you mean, Gerry love, is "Is my marriage breaking up?" '

'Is it?' he asked bluntly.

Alix said, 'Not yet!' with a challenging look in her green eyes.

Gerard's reply was 'Humph!' and 'I'm still a solicitor, you know. If you want advice . . .'

'On a divorce? Never!' she interrupted him crisply. 'I'll never leave Jake.' She took the battle to his camp by asking, 'How is your marriage? Are you and Jennie happy?'

Gerard nodded decisively and said, 'Yes!' in a very firm voice which brooked no argument.

'Are you hoping for children?' It was rather a personal question, but she was family, after all, and one of them—either Gerard or herself—had better produce offspring or the entire clan would disappear in one generation. The way things were, she wasn't likely to be having any babies. Jake wanted a child, though; Berthier had said so.

Gerard was fidgeting about in the armchair and pulling strands of black horsehair out of a hole in the bulbous arm. 'Perhaps, in a year or two. We've been living here with Mother, and while she was alive it would hardly have been fair to bring a young child into the house with all the upset and baby paraphernalia—perambulators and nursemaid and so on.'

Alix glanced about the empty studio and observed, 'This would have made a nice bed-sitting room for a nursemaid.'

'No!' Gerard burst out fiercely. 'This is *your* room. No one comes up here.' He blushed a fiery red at her surprised expression, and added awkwardly, '*I* come up here sometimes when I'm in the house on my own. I don't feel alone up here, somehow. It's always as if you were here as well.' He drew a deep breath. 'Well, as regards children, there's Jennie's career to consider, don't forget. She's pretty busy. Mother could never understand it—a woman having a career. She kept asking, "why?" in a puzzled way. She liked Jennie enormously and they got along like a house on fire, but

Mother never could understand what drives Jennie. But, then, Mother never understood your going to Paris. Neither did I.' He glanced up. 'We're going to America in the summer, Jennie and I. Jennie's on some committee keen to study the effects of Prohibition.'

'Heavens, she's not going on the teetotal band-wagon, is she?' Alix exclaimed.

Gerard grinned briefly. 'I don't think my evening whisky and soda is under threat yet. I'm quite keen to make the trip, and I believe the sea-crossing is very pleasant. I'm not so keen on talking to congressmen about keeping the nation sober.'

'Jennie should talk to Jake about it,' Alix said. 'He thinks it's crazy. He read in an English newspaper that someone wanted to bring it in here, because "if we empty the pubs, we'll empty the prisons". Jake says Prohibition hasn't emptied the jails in the States. It's filled them with a different kind of crook—black-marketeers and moonshine boys, as he calls them. The police are so busy checking on places slipping trusted customers whisky in a teacup that they have no time left to chase after real criminals. Jake says people are distilling liquor themselves out of everything from potatoes to feed-corn, in their barns and garages, and they end up blind, stupid and paralysed from drinking it.'

'Lord,' said Gerard, impressed by this catalogue of woes. 'Keep him away from Jennie!'

There was no need for him to tell her that. Jennie and Jake had never hit it off, and never would. Alix was sorry about it, but knew that the clash of personalities involved couldn't be settled. Jennie, in her own quiet way, was as determined as Jake was. What's more, she was what Jake called 'a do-gooding woman', and he couldn't stand them.

Gerard asked, quite unexpectedly, 'Is he kind to you, Alix?'

She could have lied, but not to Gerard. She answered

honestly, 'He doesn't mean to be unkind, but he suffers a lot of pain, and gets short-tempered at times. He's always sorry afterwards. We have high hopes of this operation he's undergoing now. The specialist has promised it will help.'

Alix stared up at the dusty skylight above her head. Jake was facing the surgeon's knife again, and doing it without her. He had not wanted her there, but she knew she had to go back, today. A faint droning could be heard in the high distance. An aeroplane was going over. A flying machine had caused Jake to come to Europe and into her life. A crash in a flying machine had kept them apart.

The operation was a greater success than either of them had hoped. For once, the specialist had been right. Within two or three weeks Jake was hobbling round the apartment, still lame, but for the first time since the crash in 1918, out of pain.

The difference it made to him was extraordinary. Alix realised fully only now just how draining continual pain is to the sufferer, constantly wearing away at the system. It frays the nerves, destroys the ability to sleep and saps the concentration. Now, free of it after three long years, Jake even began to talk about driving the Sizaire again.

'Why the heck shouldn't I? Don't fuss so, Alix. If I get tired, I stop—it's as simple as that.'

'My chauffeuring not good enough for you?' she asked, trying to make light of the worries assailing her. He was going to overdo it, she felt it in her bones. He was going to overstrain the newly-healed hip and put himself back again on that couch, where he'd spent so many hours in frustrated immobility.

'You're a real demon at the wheel,' he said, grinning at her, and tousling her red curls roughly, so that she protested and dodged out of his way. He looked so happy at the thought of getting behind the wheel once more that she hadn't the heart to say anything further against the idea. He could see the concern in her green eyes, however, and his cheerfulness evaporated. Fixing her with a direct, uncompromising look of his grey eyes, he said truculently, 'Listen, ma'am, I'm not a child! You treat me like a baby learning to walk. I did all these things before, you know, and I'll do them again.'

'Yes, I know, but take it slowly, can't you? You're skipping around like a spring lamb, for goodness' sake!'

'Frightened I'll get away from you?' The grey eyes mocked her slightly.

Alix said resentfully, 'That's unfair, Jake.'

'Sure it is,' he agreed, and smiled briefly at her, to make amends. 'You know I didn't think you'd stick it out this long.'

Alix turned a surprised gaze on him, and asked, 'What?'

'Oh, this crazy marriage we have, which isn't one. I thought, well, five or six weeks, and you'd get tired of playing Florence Nightingale.'

Florence Nightingale. Did he, then, class her together with Jennie as a do-gooder of the kind which irritated him so? Something akin to fear touched Alix's heart as she watched him limp across to the sideboard and unstopper the brandy decanter.

Over his shoulder he said, 'Alix, I want to be honest with you. Don't think I don't appreciate all you've done, are still doing, for me. But, frankly, I was hoping you would have tired of playing Florence by now. You know I never wanted this—this sort of situation. It's nice to have you around, but I managed pretty well without you. You're just wasting your life here with me. This operation has made things a lot easier for me. I hope I'll drive the Sizaire again, but even that fellow with the false hairpiece, or whatever, can't work a miracle. It's no use fooling ourselves. I'm still a long

way from being what I was, or what I'd want to be.
I'm still a cripple, and I'll always be lame. You don't
need me. You need someone—different.'

'You know it hurts me, don't you, Jake.' Alix said
quietly. 'When you talk like that. Do you really think
that's what I'm doing? Playing at Florence Nightingale?'

'Well, aren't you?' The grey eyes looked into hers in
that direct way which seemed to read to the bottom of
her heart.

Alix flushed. 'A little, perhaps, but I wouldn't do it
for anyone but you.'

'So why, dear lady with the lamp, do it for me?'

Alix longed to say, 'Because I love you', but she had
tried telling him that, and it was always a mistake. Any
open gesture of affection from her was either brushed
away by him, or froze him into a bristling, self-protecting
entity like a rolled-up hedgehog.

There was a wall between them, and try as she might,
she couldn't breach it. Just recently, it even seemed to
have gained another layer of bricks.

These days, she felt as though he expected something
of her, but she didn't know what. Once or twice she
had looked up unexpectedly and caught him staring at
her moodily. It was as if he subjected her to a veiled
interrogation and wanted some sort of admission. She
couldn't quite make out what it was—but it dated from
the New Year's party at Paul's. That much was clear.

Spring came to Paris, and worked the magic spell it
always did over the city. The gardeners were to be seen
working busily in the parks, and the flowerbeds suddenly
became alive with spring bulbs. The children reappeared,
as if they had been released from a winter prison, and
ran laughing through the trees, jumping and waving
with arms and legs liberated from woolly gloves and
stockings.

The spring also brought Paul back into their lives.
After the New Year they'd been little of him, partly

because he'd gone off to Switzerland to ski in the entourage of a lady much featured in society magazines. Besides, Alix had not had time to work for him. But now he reappeared, looking tanned and fit, and with a fund of racy stories and society gossip. He began to call at the flat, somehow accepted as a friend of them both. Sometimes he came with a folder of sketches he wanted to discuss with Alix, which was his way, she knew, of tempting her back to work. He would spread them out with a fine lack of respect for other people's furniture and domestic privacy, and expound at length, speaking rapid, colloquial French which Alix found hard to follow, so that she had to concentrate hard on what he was doing and saying. When this happened, Jake sat by and listened in silence. He probably didn't understand all that was being said, but he watched Alix—and he watched Daquin—with a steady, appraising scrutiny that made her uneasy. Occasionally she would look up and catch the gaze of those level, shrewd grey eyes, and wonder just what he was thinking.

But Paul seemed anxious to include Jake in the conversation, and so, after an hour disputing colour schemes, he would push aside the papers, break into fluent English, and begin to talk to him. It was inevitable that the two men should talk of the only interest they had in common—aeroplanes. Flying reminiscences and technical details filled the air until the conversation turned on flying machines and aviation, and nothing else.

Alix became more and more unhappy, and not just because she was of necessity excluded from this dialogue between two enthusiasts of flight. She could see the effect it was having on Jake, the restlessness which entered his manner when he talked of flying, and the enthusiasm which lit up his eyes.

Then, one day, she came home to find Paul's red Hispano-Suiza parked outside the block of flats in midafternoon. It was surrounded by a crowd of curious little boys in school blouses. Paul was sitting upstairs in a haze of cigarette smoke expounding on the beauties of an old war-time fighter biplane he had bought,

'You can pick those machines up for next to nothing, these days. Europe is littered with them, left from the war. Most need work done on them. This one I have is an English machine, a Camel. I'm keeping it out at the flying club.' He gesticulated wildly as he spoke with Gallic enthusiasm, his black hair falling over his forehead. He had his socks on inside-out.

Jake said, 'I was flying a Camel when I was shot down.'

'I know. I want you to come out and see the machine, Jake. You know the type well, so you can advise me.' Paul leaned forward urgently.

The conversation sank into technical detail and continued for another hour. Alix threw open the balcony windows to let out the stale, smoky air, and went out on to the balcony. Below, the Hispano-Suiza had lost its throng of admirers, summoned to their respective homes by *le goûter*. The street was empty, sunny, quiet. She leaned her arms on the parapet and tried to shut out the murmur of voices coming from the salon. A movement struck her ear. Paul was taking his leave at last.

Alix, making a great effort to conceal her anger before Jake, offered to show Paul to the door, and under this pretext, followed him out on to the staircase landing. As they waited for the lift to come up from the bottom, Paul glanced at her with a touch of defiance in his face. He knew she was angry, and with him.

As the lift whirred towards them, she suddenly burst out furiously, 'What do you think you're playing at, Paul? Why on earth are you doing this to Jake?'

'Doing what?' he returned aggressively. 'Talking about

something he likes to talk about?' He shook an admonitory finger at her. 'Listen to me, Alix, you're far too possessive about him, did you know? You know it now, because I'm telling you. You're like a dragon—even if you're the prettiest dragon I've come across. You don't want him to see anyone, talk to anyone, have any life apart from you.'

'That's not true!' she gasped, horrified at the picture he painted.

'It is true. Let the man be himself. If he wants to talk to me about flying machines, he doesn't need your permission.'

'He's a sick man . . .' she began.

But Paul interrupted her, and said sharply, 'He's a flying man! Once a flying man, always a flying man. If you don't understand it, Alix, keep quiet. But don't interfere. He won't thank you for it.'

He jerked open the lift door, and it clanked away down. Alix stalked back into the flat. Jake was out on the balcony, enjoying the warm spring sunshine before it cooled and faded away in early evening. He was staring moodily up into the drifting clouds.

From the windows, Alix said anxiously, 'Jake?'

He turned his head at the sound of her voice. 'What's the matter?'

The words stuck in her throat. Alix turned on her heel and ran back into the salon. She threw herself down on the sofa and and thrust her clenched fist against her mouth to stop the words spilling out in sudden rebellion. Jake came limping in from the balcony, and demanded angrily, 'What's wrong now? Don't tell me; I can guess! You don't like my discussing flying with Daquin. You've never liked the idea of flying. You didn't like it when Robbie was a pilot, and you sure as hell didn't like my being a pilot! Listen, Alix,' He stomped awkwardly across to her and stooping down, gasped her shoulder and snarled, 'I was a flying man when you first met me, and I'm still a pilot. I may be grounded temporarily, but I'll fly again. I have to!'

'*Why?*' Alix shouted at him, the words winging around the room.

Jake sat down at the other end of the sofa and made an obvious effort to calm down. He spread out his hands, and said, 'Try and understand, will you?' He held up his hand to stop her interrupting, and frowning earnestly, went on passionately, 'You don't know what it's like, up there in the sky, all alone. It's a feeling of— of total liberty. It's not just exciting, or exhilarating— it's being free of the earth at last. It's what man has always dreamed of being since ancient times, since Icarus flew up to the sun on his waxen wings! Once in the air, you want to stay there for ever, to go on flying and flying . . .'

The enthusiasm in his voice died away, and more soberly, he added, 'When I flew over the trenches, I used to look down at those poor devils half buried alive in the mud down there with the rats and the dead men, and I knew that they and I were not fighting the same war. You see, that's where we were different, not just myself, but Robbie and Daquin, and all the others. We were like gladiators. We faced our foe openly, up in the sky, man to man. Down there they were shelling an enemy they couldn't even see, even if he was sometimes only yards away, or else they charged out "over the top", insanely, like lemmings to destruction, in an indiscriminate mass. But we knew our opponent. He was one man, like any one of us. We didn't hate him. We respected him. We shared his passion for the air. He was an aviator like any of us. We wanted to show him we were better aviators than he was, and he was trying to do the same; more rivalry than emnity.'

'I have *tried* to understand,' Alix said wretchedly.

His eyes met hers steadily. 'Then you must see why I have to fly again, Alix. Right now, I feel as though everything has been taken from me. I'm nothing any more, just a shell. I don't have anything.'

Alix said, in a small voice. 'You have *me.*'

But he shook his head. 'No I don't—not in the way I'd want. I want to fly, Alix. It means more to me than anything else in the world. If I could fly again, I'd know I could do anything. I'd be, again, what I was before.'

'So that's it, is it?' Alix demanded tightly, goaded beyond endurance. 'You don't care about me. You don't care what it does to me—if it tears me apart with worry or makes me feel I'm just an awkward obstacle in your path. When I first met you, during the war, I found you obstinate, ill-mannered, conceited and selfish! And you haven't changed, Jake Sherwood, not one bit!'

'I didn't ask you to come here and live with me,' Jake said coldly. 'That was all your idea. I went along with it because it was what *you* wanted. That wasn't being selfish, that was trying to please *you*. But, lady, you're kind of hard to please! Since we're being so frank and outspoken all of a sudden, let me remind you that when I first met *you*, in England, you were a thoroughly spoiled, very pretty and quite useless little rich girl. You had dear old Gerard hanging on your every word and following you about like a devoted spaniel. Much good it did him! He wasn't what you wanted, so he got pushed to one side. The same went for Robbie. He ended up on the scrap-heap, too. Now, I may not be just the way you want, Alix, but I'm neither Gerard nor Robbie. I don't wait around to be dismissed. If you don't like it here, you can pack your bags and walk right out of that door! That was our agreement, remember? You promised me, when you'd had enough, you'd say so, and we would call its quits. So, if you've had enough now, this is the time to say it.'

'How can you do this to me?' she cried out in horror, unable to believe her ears.

'You're doing it to yourself,' Jake said unkindly. He leaned back on the sofa. 'I think you should get back to work. Daquin wants your help. He's got some project in mind he wants you to work on. Why don't you go over to his studio and see what he's planning.'

It was as though he were giving her to Paul. Because he wanted to be rid of her? Because he really meant all the cruel and dreadful things he'd said? 'No,' Alix thought numbly, 'because he thinks it's what *I* want. Jake thinks Paul is my lover. He's believed it since the New Year—and there's nothing I can do about it.'

For a moment, the notion left her too appalled to think clearly. What had she done to make him think such a thing? Then, slowly, she began to see it as he saw it. She was a woman alone. True, Jake was there under the same roof, but he wasn't in the same bed, and that was what mattered. He'd never tried to make love to her since that terrible failed evening in the country. Perhaps he hated himself for his failure, and perhaps he also had begun to hate her, as she had feared he would. He wanted to justify that hatred; he wanted something she had said or done that would justify his resentment. Her association with Daquin had been more than enough. She had been both blind and stupid, incredibly stupid. How could she ever have imagined that Paul could continue to play any part in her life without such an obvious suspicion forming not only in Jake's mind, but probably in the mind of everyone who knew them?

Alix stared despairingly at Jake's lean, handsome, unyielding profile. He'd always been an uncompromising man; 'touchy,' Gerard had called it. When she had first met him, and it seemed such an age ago, way back in that war-time summer, he'd stood out at the

Harrises' party as a clear oddity, a man who didn't belong. He hadn't understood the sort of people they were, and he hadn't much liked them. Nor had they understood or much liked him. So he'd taken himself off alone to the empty dining-room and the brandy. Then, mischievous Fate had sent her stumbling into his arms and his life in a dark garden. He couldn't really have known what to make of her. That seemingly so self-assured man had been really at a loss. She should have tried to explain herself to him, but she hadn't, and now it was possibly too late.

Alix realised she was twisting her fingers nervously together, turning the gold wedding band round and round, and clasped them tightly to control them. 'Jake?' He glanced up at her, his face cold and unfriendly, but she took a deep breath and went on resolutely, though her voice sounded husky and unnatural and shook despite her efforts. 'We've only ever worked together, Paul and I. We've never slept together. I wouldn't deceive you in that way, and you have no reason—you have no *right*—to think that I would.'

'Wealthy married ladies with time on their hands spend their afternoons with their dressmakers or with their lovers, isn't that so? It's what I've always been led to believe.' His grey eyes glittered at her, full of hostility.

'I don't have time on my hands. I'm a working artist!' Alix cried out forcefully. 'And I'm your wife!'

'You're not my *wife!*' He leaned forward and grasped her arm. 'You never have been, and you never will be!'

'Because you won't try!' she countered, her voice trembling with emotion. 'We shouldn't be sitting here, arguing—we should be in that bedroom, trying to make a reality of our marriage!'

'I told you I'm not going through that again!' Jake said savagely. 'If that's what you want, go to Daquin or some other boudoir athlete like him! I'm not stopping you! But don't stay here and torment *me!*' He grabbed at his walking-stick and using it to push himself up from the sofa, struggled to his feet and stumbled towards her. His face was twisted in anger, and in that moment she was truly frightened of him.

'Damn you, Alix, why don't you *go?*' he shouted. He caught at her shoulder and gripped it so hard that she cried out as his fingers passed into her flesh. 'Do you think I'm blind? Do you think I'm stupid? Do you think I can't read Daquin's mind? I've sat here, and I've watched him watch you. Every time he looks at you, he sees you naked. So why don't you just go and show him . . . show him what he's so anxious to get his hands on? Why wait?' His fingers closed on the material of her dress and ripped it away in a violent wrench. 'Go and take your clothes off for *him*: there's no damn use in your doing it for me!'

'Jake!' she cried, trying to free herself.

But he hardly seemed to know what he was doing any more. He swore at her, cursing her and calling her dreadful names. His hands tore at her dress and at her underwear, his fingernails scratching long red lines on her skin until she managed to break free and take refuge on the further side of the room. Jake leaned back against the sofa arm for support, panting and sweating.

In the ensuing silence, Alix, gathering up the tatters of her clothing, said in a loud, determined tone, 'I'm not going, Jake, and you'll never drive me away!'

He closed his eyes and turned his head aside. After a moment, he said hoarsely, 'Listen, Alix, and listen carefully. I may be your husband in name only, but I'm not prepared to see you use that name to make a fool of me!'

'I'm going to see Paul!' Alix forgot about her dress. 'I'll tell him I'm not going back to work—and that he isn't to come here any more!'

'*No!*' Jake pushed himself away from the supporting sofa and limped towards her. 'No, Alix, wait . . . You don't have to do that.' He seemed to become aware for the first time of the scarlet streaks on her skin where his nails had scored the flesh, and she saw him wince. He rubbed his hand over his perspiring forehead, and muttered thickly, 'You've a growing career, and you've worked for it. I don't want you to give it up—not for me. You're a good designer. I let things boil up inside me. I don't want to take all you've achieved here away from you. Look, I need some time to think things out. Let's not talk about it any more, not just now?'

'This isn't something that is going to go away, Jake!' Alix cried out. 'You'll go on thinking the same thing, and I'll know it's there, in your mind . . .'

'Later, Alix, not now!' he broke in. He passed the back of his hand across his mouth and muttered, 'I'm sorry I shouted at you . . . I'm a difficult blighter, I know, who likes to get his own way.'

He sounded weary, as if tired by a long struggle and near to defeat. She felt so much love and longing for him then that she could have wept. But she forced back the tears because they would only have increased his feeling of guilt, the last thing she wanted. But Alix put her arms round him and whispered, 'I'll always be here, Jake—and it doesn't matter, really, if . . .'

'Yes, yes,' he interrupted. 'I know.' The words had a hollow, empty ring, and she released him and watched him limp back across the room. At the door, he turned and said quietly, 'Perhaps I'm the one who should have gone, taken his leave, long ago. I cheated Death in that crash, and I've paid the penalty ever since. Maybe the time has come to settle the final account.'

CHAPTER FIFTEEN

APRIL HAD turned into May, and Paul took Alix out to lunch with Laroche to discuss final details of the refurbishing of the house the arms manufacturer had bought. Paul had had the contract in his pocket for weeks, and there was no doubt the work would be done. But Laroche had confused ideas as to what he wanted, and had rejected a whole series of proposed schemes, offering instead a number of ideas so preposterous that even Paul rebelled and refused to consider them, saying his reputation was at stake.

He'd finally decided on a scheme put together by Alix and Paul in a combined effort one evening at the flat, under Jake's cool, observing eye. With all the delays, the work now loomed as a matter of urgency. Laroche wanted it finished in six weeks, and was no longer disposed to haggle and query every point. They beat out the last details over lunch, and when Laroche finally took farewell of them, agreement had been reached at last.

'Not before time!' Paul said sourly, but with relief, when Laroche had left. He signalled to the waiter to bring him some cognac.

Alix, refusing another drink, said, 'I really don't like that man, Paul. I don't want to deal with him. I'll do the work, but you must discuss it with him and see it's carried out.'

'If you like,' Paul said, shrugging. 'So long as it's completed on time.'

The restaurant was emptying. It was well into early

afternoon, and the boulevards were busy with spring visitors to the city, and window-shoppers. Alix watched the crowds hurry past the restaurant, and then turned to Paul, who was still sifting through his notes.

'Paul? Jake tells me that your aeroplane is in first-class order now. The mechanics have done a great job on it, he says.'

'You can be sure they have. They've had me breathing down their necks! I'm not paying for some young oaf to lean against the fuselage with an oily rag in his hand and do sweet nothing. The engine was playing up—but I think the problem's sorted out.'

Alix moved her wine-glass around in careful circles on the tablecloth. 'Now that you don't need Jake's advice about it, I wish—I wish you wouldn't take him out to the flying club so often. It makes him restless. You know he'd love to fly again, and he can't.'

'He watches me. I've taken the machine up a couple of times.' A faraway look briefly entered Paul's dark eyes. 'It handles like a dream; a baby could fly it.' He glanced at her. 'Look, I know how Jake feels. I'm a pilot, too. I know how I'd feel. I can't stop the man taking an interest in the machine, and his advice has been invaluable. All the mechanics at the flying club put together haven't half of Jake's knowledge. You worry too much. Alix. It's not doing him any harm.'

'I wish I knew why you've involved him like this,' she said fretfully.

Paul pushed the notes into a briefcase and leaning across the table, took hold of her hand. 'I like you both. I know you think I'm a selfish pig who cares only for himself. There aren't many other people I care about, I admit, but you and Jake happen to be two of them. Possibly the *only* two—so there!'

'You use people,' Alix said bluntly. 'I wouldn't like to think you were using me or Jake.'

'I'm using your ideas.' He tapped the briefcase.

'Yes, but you pay me for those. I'm more worried about what you take and don't pay for. The day Jake and I were married, you went off with Blanche.' She saw a wary flicker in his eyes. 'Did you go bed with her?'

'Yes,' Paul said frankly.

'I wish you hadn't. I've known her for years, and I suppose, now Gerry and Jennie are married, Blanche is a sort of connection by marriage of mine. You are a rotter, Paul.'

'Look,' he said, patting her hand, 'I was full of champagne, and so was she. Some drinks go to the head. Champagne goes to the loins. It's not my fault.'

'Nothing ever is, according to you! Well, I should be grateful you don't lie about it, anyway.'

'Would I lie to you?' Paul asked, and lifted her hand to his lips. 'To anyone else, but never to you, Alix, I swear.'

He kissed her fingers. No one looking into his earnest dark eyes would have doubted his sincerity.

But Alix doubted him, moved by an obscure instinct which had its roots in self-preservation. This was a man who had once asked her to divorce Jake, for his sake. He'd been a little drunk at the time, and drink often led to wild talk, but it also acted as a release. Many a man, when drunk, had admitted to secrets he'd kept carefully hidden when sober.

She accompanied Paul out of the restaurant, and blinking in the sunlight, allowed him to hand her up into the Hispano-Suiza. They drove back to the studio and climbed up the staircase together in silence. It was Theda Bara's afternoon off, and the whole studio was suite and deserted. Theda Bara's real name was Josette, and Alix made a conscious effort to call her by it, but Paul always called her by the nickname he'd given her, and it was hard not to do the same.

Paul began to read the jottings on the note-pad the secretary had left for him—calls received that morning, queries from clients and requests for appointments. Alix took off her hat and fluffed up her hair in the mirror. She was looking tired these days. Perhaps a holiday would help. Jake would go to St Tropez or Monte Carlo, if asked. But what on earth would they do there? The casinos held no attraction for her, or the faintly raffish society. Wealthy people spending money. Two days, and she'd be screaming to come back to Paris and work. She turned from the mirror. The suite had been closed up since Theda Bara had left at twelve-thirty, and it was warm and stuffy. She took off the jacket of her business costume and hung it on a hanger behind the door. The lunch had been heavy and she felt sleepy, not in the least disposed to work.

Paul tossed down the notepad. 'What's up?' Before she could answer, he went on, 'You don't have to tell me, I know. Things aren't progressing any better in the bedroom department between you and Jake, are they?'

'Look, Paul,' Alix began patiently, 'It's nothing to do . . .'

He walked across before she could finish and put his hands gently on her shoulders. 'Yes, it *does* have to do with me. I told you—I like you both. Alix, sometimes the truth hurts, but the truth in this case is that you and Jake are bad for each other. You'd be much better off, both of you, if you parted. You're just torturing each other, can't you see?'

'No!' she retorted fiercely. 'I've told you so before.!'

'Yes, I know you did. And I was more than a little drunk at the time and said all the wrong things . . . Or perhaps they were the right things? We'd make good partners, Alix. I've asked you this before, some time back, so you've had more than enough time to think it over. I'm still waiting for an answer.'

'And it's still "No".' Alix felt a stab of remorse. She was being unfair to Paul. It was he who had discovered her as a commercial artist and promoted her work. He was offering her a partnership in a thriving concern, and it required serious consideration, out of common decency. But he wanted another kind of partnership with it—and that was out of the question.

'Jake had an idea, too,' she said. 'He wants to create a passenger air company. He believes air travel will be what everyone wants in the future.'

Paul frowned, considering this. 'He's probably right, but he can do it without you. *I* need you, Alix. This whole business needs you.' He indicated the surrounding office. 'And I need you myself, for reasons of my own.' He smiled slightly, the message of what he wanted clearly written in his dark eyes.

When Alix shook her head, his hands, on her shoulders, tightened their grip and he went on urgently, 'You can't go on sleeping alone. It's inhuman! He's no right to expect it. Alix, you need me!' His hands slid down her arms and he drew her closer to him. His voice was husky, and there was a faint scent of brandy on his breath. The office was warm in the afternoon sunshine, and a fly buzzed lazily against the closed window.

Alix's head was beginning to swim. She didn't like to drink at lunchtime and normally avoided it, but today, because of Laroche, she'd been persuaded to two or three glasses of wine and a post-prandial liqueur. The mix of Bordeaux and Benedictine, on top of an excellent meal, was having its effect. Tiredness and depression added to the mixture. She was lonely, and discouraged, and wanted someone's help and understanding. Like a child starved of affection, she was ready to turn to anyone, and Paul, whispering in her ear, his hand caressing her breast through her flimsy georgette blouse, offered sympathy and concern and a kind of comfort.

She muttered, 'Don't, Paul . . .' ineffectually, but her muscles seemed too weak to resist him, turned to water, and she allowed him to lead her to the velvet-covered chaise-longue in the corner of his office, which had probably been the scene of many an amorous adventure.

The cushions gave beneath their combined weight. Paul was breathing heavily, his hand, slipped beneath her skirt, pressing on her bare thigh above her garter. In a matter of moments, she thought drowsily, it won't matter . . .

There was a loud crash from the outer office as the main door to the studio suite was slammed by someone who had entered. Theda Bara's youthful tones could be heard calling loudly, 'It's only me, Monsieur Daquin! I left my evening shoes. I picked them up from the cobblers' this morning on my way to work, and went off to lunch and clean forgot them. I'm going dancing tonight with my fiancé . . .'

'Damn!' Paul growled ferociously. He jumped to his feet and, tucking in his shirt as he went, strode out to forestall the girl. Alix heard their voices through the door, Paul's sharp, and the girl's cheerful and unconcerned.

Sanity returned to her with a shock, as if she had been suddenly deluged with icy water. She scrambled up and refastened her blouse with trembling fingers. Fate had taken a hand, stepping in and saving her from a disastrous and irreparable mistake. By the time Paul had got rid of Theda Bara and returned, Alix had tidied her hair and stood by the desk, calm and composed.

A glance sufficed to tell him he'd lost his chance. He grimaced and said, 'Confounded girl! I hope that young oaf she's going to marry turns out to be a wife-beater.'

'I'm sorry, Paul,' Alix said. 'I don't know what came

over me. It was inexcusable.'

'You don't need to make any excuses to *me,*' he said, wryly. 'I know exactly what came over both of us. It's called human nature.'

'No—it's called drinking too much and losing sight of reality. For us to embark on some sort of squalid *affaire* would be—ridiculous!'

'It might be many things, Alix,' he said, 'but never ridiculous.' He picked up the folder from the desk. 'Well? Do we work?'

The conservatory at the Frobishers' house was hardly worthy of comparison with the splendid edifices full of potted palms and intertwined vines that graced the homes of the wealthy. It was more in the nature of a dusty glass lean-to at the back of the house, and the only plants in it consisted of a row of pots containing geranium cuttings and a spindly fuchsia, prone to white-fly.

Nevertheless, when the sun shone in of an afternoon, it was warm and pleasant and Maisie Frobisher liked to take her afternoon cup of tea there, if she was alone. She was often alone these days. Since Jennie had married and left, Blanche had taken to going off on her own and was vague when questioned as to how she spent her time. This afternoon, however, she had gone respectably to neighbours to play Bridge. Mrs Frobisher had watched her trip away, elegant in a new blue afternoon dress much hung about with the strings of beads which were coming into fashion, and felt her spirits rise with the hope that she might—even at this late date—get Blanche 'off her hands'.

Maisie knew the world and wasn't a fool. The new blue dress must have cost far more than Blanche's modest dress allowance permitted. Then there were the beads and other accessories, and the fashionable new shingled hair-cut. Some man, probably married, picked up the bill. She only hoped Blanche had enough sense to be discreet about it. She was still only twenty-nine, and Maisie knew that at Bridge this afternoon she would be partnering Dr Cummins, whose wife had died two years before. He was fifty-two, balding, and had an irritating, braying laugh. But he was the senior partner in his practice and was reputed to be 'hanging out for a wife'. He owned a solid red-brick house with a tennis-court, and recently had exchanged his pony and trap for a Ford motor-car. He employed two indoor and an outdoor staff, not including the boy whose job it was to wash the motor-car. Thus the doctor was a fairly good catch, by any reckoning, certainly for a girl who would see thirty next birthday, had neither fortune nor family to recommend her, and over whose reputation the faintest of clouds was beginning to form.

There was a clatter, and an untidy fourteen-year-old girl, the latest in a long line of such maids employed in the Frobisher home, arrived with the tea-tray. Ellen's lank hair escaped from beneath her cap, despite the fact that, like the rest of the uniform, it was too big for her undernourished frame. She set down her burden and asked dubiously, 'That all right for you, mum?'

Maisie sighed. There was no cake, but the girl had cut a plate of sandwiches. The bread was very thick and the filling very thin, and Ellen had, yet again, forgotten to cut off the crusts. The girl would have to go. It was bad enough that the child looked like a scarecrow, but being served up doorsteps fit for a navvy's lunch-box was the last straw. Maisie dismissed her, helped herself to the least solid sandwich, and settled back to look at her scrap-book, which she only really enjoyed doing alone.

Most of all, she liked looking at the fashions of twenty-five or thirty years earlier. Her thin white fingers touched a sepia photograph. The Grecian bend. Nothing so elegant now. Girls didn't wear proper corsets any more. Even women whose figures needed a good deal of strapping in didn't wear real stays. The old stays, with whalebone ribs, they were the thing. Girls didn't wear any proper underwear, no proper bloomers, only jersey-silk knickers that were hardly respectable, and a peculiar new-fangled garment called a brassière. It was composed, as far as Maisie could see, of nothing but a wisp of silk and lace, and it was anyone's guess what it was supposed to do.

The sound of voices fell on her ear, and Ellen reappeared with a further clatter of the door and announced, 'It's Mrs Daventry, mum, come ter see yer.'

Maisie closed the scrap-book hurriedly, and thrust it under a cushion as Jennie came in. She presented her faded cheek for a brief kiss, and observed, 'I didn't expect you, dear.'

'I was passing.' Jennie sat down and took off her felt hat.

Maisie eyed her married daughter with something like mystification. She'd never understood her awkward, gawky, intelligent offspring, and as for what Gerard Daventry had seen in Jennie to make him prefer her to Blanche, that was something totally beyond her comprehension. She stared now in some exasperation at Jennie's plain navy costume with its mannish cut and her sensible shoes. The girl wore no make-up, and no jewellery apart from her engagement solitaire and wedding ring.

'You look a frump!' said Maisie aloud, not unkindly, but in a sort of maternal despair.

'Thank you, Mother. Where's Blanche?'

Ellen reappeared with an extra cup and set it down, beaming. 'There y'are. I thought you'd want a cup of tea as well, Shall I cut some more of them sandwiches?'

Both ladies declined this offer and Ellen clattered

away. She was a noisy girl.

With some optimism in her voice, Maisie informed Jennie that Blanche was playing Bridge at the Watsons', and partnering Dr Cummins. 'I really think he likes Blanche, and he's very comfortably situated.'

'You make the poor man sound like a suburban villa,' Jennie objected. 'If Blanche is setting her cap at Algy Cummins, she'd better mind her p's and q's.'

Maisie bridled and rose to the defence of her favourite. 'Don't you go criticising your sister. You could take a leaf from her book, with profit. Only look at yourself!'

'Mother, I've been at the meeting of a working committee . . .'

Maisie interrupted her vigorously. 'You get more like that daft old Emma Frobisher every day. You'll end up like her, too—with nothing but good causes in your life. I don't know how you ever managed to get Gerard away from poor Blanche, but you won't keep him like that.' She saw her daughter's cheeks redden angrily, and went on, 'Now just listen to me, Jennifer! Not that you ever did, not even when you were little. But you'd do well to mark what I say now. You're very lucky to find yourself married to Gerard. He's a good man, and, Lord knows,' Maisie said with feeling, 'there aren't too many of them! But hooking a man is nothing compared with what it takes to *keep* him. Perhaps Gerard didn't want poor Blanche, but *you* weren't exactly his first choice. He wanted Alix Morrell, that red-headed girl you were so friendly with, and she's his cousin as well. She went off with someone else, but she's still around. She was back here only a month or two ago, for the funeral. You've got a choice to make, my girl! You can have this high-faluting career of yours. Standing for parliament! Humph!' Maisie snorted. 'Or you can have your marriage. But you're going to find it hard to have both. What's Gerard doing while you're out at all these

meetings? Who's at home to welcome him when he gets
in at the end of the day? Not *you*! You're sitting on
some committee made up of women wearing costumes
like that one, I don't doubt—and hats like that one!'
Maisie pointed a scornful finger at the offending article.

'You don't understand, Mother, and I'm not going
to argue with you.' Jennie got up and crammed the
offending hat defiantly back on her head.

'I understand, madam, that it's not all in books!'
Maisie snapped.

Jennie stared at her in some surprise. 'Jake said
that . . .' she told the puzzled Maisie, but didn't explain.

When Jennie got home, she saw, from the hatstand,
that Gerard was back already. She had really intended
to be home before him today. But the meeting had run
on, taken up with some irrelevant point of order, and
for the third time this week she arrived home after him.
She ought not to have stopped by to see Mother. It had
been a wasted and acerbic visit, in any case. It had been
made worse because Mrs Frobisher had not said
anything which Jennie had not already begun to think
in her heart.

Now she asked the parlourmaid where the master
was, and was told that he had gone upstairs. 'To the
attic', the maid thought.

To Alix's old studio. Jennie knew Gerard went up
there when she was away from home. The scent of his
pipe tobacco lingered, betraying him, and the servants
knew to take his whisky and soda up there if he wasn't
in the drawing-room.

Jennie stood irresolutely in the hall, and then began
to climb the stairs. On the first landing, she stopped to
survey her reflection in the mirror. She wasn't pretty,
and she never had been. It was something she'd always
accepted. She had the brains, and Blanche the beauty.

Alix had managed to combine both. Jennie had never been jealous of Alix, but it did seem unfair. She patted her hair and continued on her upward climb.

Gerard was sitting in the old armchair, whisky and soda in hand, and apparently doing nothing but stare at Alix's old painting-smock hanging behind the door. He looked up in some surprise when Jennie appeared, and said, 'Hullo, old girl, I didn't know you were back.'

Some men called their wives by endearing names. 'Old girl' made her sound like a milk-float horse. Jennie said, a little awkwardly, 'I'm sorry I'm late, Gerry. I called in at Mother's.' She sat down on the little stool on which—had she known it—Alix had sat the last time she had been in here. Jennie said soberly, 'You come up here to be with her, don't you, Gerry?'

She blessed him for not pretending to misunderstand. Gerard rubbed his index finger over his moustache and said reflectively, 'It's more than that. Coming up here seems to roll back the years. They were happy days, before the war came and changed it all. We were all young. I remember Alix daubing away up here with her paints, and I was swotting for exams . . . We were all—very innocent.'

Jennie said quickly. 'I've been thinking about that American trip. They don't really need me. If you'd rather not go, Gerry, we can stay at home—or take a holiday trip together, just the two of us.'

Gerard eyed her shrewdly. 'And what's brought this on, eh?'

'I can't be Alix,' Jennie said doggedly, 'but I do love you, Gerry. Sometimes it may look as though I love my career more, but I don't really.'

Gerard put down his whisky and soda on the floor by the chair. 'I know that,' he said gently. He stood up and came across to her, large, solid and dependable. He pinched her cheek, as she looked up at him anxiously.

'Listen, Jen—you're my wife, and you're that because I wanted to marry you, just as you were and are. If I'd wanted someone else, I'd have gone looking for someone else. Yes, I'm fond of Alix, very fond of her. I was, when I was younger, rather more than that for a while. But we could never have made it work as husband and wife. Alix was already sensible enough to see that, and I came to see it eventually. She has got what she wanted in Sherwood, and I've got what I want in you. And nothing anyone else says matters a damn.' He put his arm round her shoulders and squeezed them.

Jennie leant her head against his chest and whispered, 'I do want us to be a family, Gerry.'

'Alix said this room would make a good bed-sitting room for a nursemaid,' Gerry told her. 'Before you came in, just now, I was thinking about that. Maybe it would, at that.'

'I appreciate your seeing me, Mrs Frobisher,' Dr Cummins said in his slightly squeaky voice.

'Goodness me, Doctor,' Maisie purred. 'You're more than welcome—being a friend of dear Blanche, as you are.' She touched her henna-ed hair and tried not to let her elation show in her face. At last—at long last—she was going to get Blanche off her hands. When he had asked to speak to her privately on a matter concerning her daughter, it had been too wonderful almost to believe. She's been obliged to fortify herself with a small brandy—in fact, two or three.

The poor man was looking distinctly ill-at-ease now, perched on the edge of the faded chintz-covered chair. Maisie smiled at him encouragingly. Before the wedding, she was thinking, her mind running on pleasantly, she'd have to get new chair-covers . . .

' . . . as a doctor,' he was saying, and Maisie recalled herself to matters in hand with a jerk. 'I have not been able to help but notice, the signs are all there, you see . . .'

Maisie frowned.

'I have long been interested in the work of Dr Freud, of Vienna.'

Maisie stared blankly. He was rambling on, talking of symptoms, treatment, of Blanche being young enough to hope for perfectly successful results . . . Slowly, horribly, it dawned on her that he was *not* asking for Blanche's hand in marriage. He was saying, incredibly, that her cherished daughter was ill.

Maisie's thin fingers gripped the arms of her chair so that the rings bit into the flesh. 'Dr Cummins, you must be mistaken. Blanche is a perfectly healthy girl! What on earth could be wrong with her?' Her voice grew increasingly aggressive, not only in disappointment, but in real anger. He was criticising her darling. The wretched man was daring to criticise Blanche! Sitting there, with his squeaky voice and balding dome, and trying to make out that Blanche was ill! A sudden fear touched Maisie's heart.

'What's *wrong* with her?' she almost shouted.

Dr Cummins licked his dry lips nervously and wondered how Mrs Frobisher would react to the word 'schizophrenia'. With incomprehension, most likely. Not, thought Cummins gloomily, that schizophrenia was the word he'd have chosen first. 'Nymphomania' came more readily to mind.

He cleared his throat. 'Dear Mrs Frobisher, don't be alarmed. Today, thank goodness, we are ceasing to be superstitious about mental illness. Now I know of a very reputable clinic . . .'

Maisie screamed. She flew at him, scratching at his eyes, and a wealth of viperish, obscene vocabulary from her distant Whitechapel youth came welling up and bursting forth. Not Blanche, not Blanche . . .!

He stumbled away, putting up both hands to shield himself, and somehow found the door. His fingers grappled wildly with the handle, and he ran down the hall and out of the front door, down the path and into the sanctuary of the open street.

Alix and Jake had not discussed Paul again, and since she was still working with him, it was impossible to forbid him to come to the flat. Jake liked to talk aeroplanes, and despite her plea to Paul, he was still going out to the flying club with him, visits that left him tense and unable to settle for hours afterwards. He would return, to wander restlessly about the flat, unable to settle to anything, not to business correspondence, or even to his piano. Alix didn't care to argue with him about it, and so was forced to watch as the restlessness and frustration built up in him, and the improvement in his health and spirits resulting from the successful operation was all undone.

In addition, he had gained a way with him which was almost secretive, and quite unlike his normal frank self. Purely by chance, she found out that he had paid several visits to his French lawyers without telling her. She was both alarmed and disturbed by the knowledge. Was he seeking a legal separation? Surely not without telling her? Business connected with one of the companies he controlled? Again, why should he not tell her about it? She'd acted as his secretary for some time. Now everything seemed to have been taken out of her hands and put into those of the legal men.

Alix sat by the balcony windows one fine afternoon and pretended to be busy fixing a new sheet of paper to her easel, while all the time surreptitiously watching him get ready to go out. He'd seemed even more quiet these last two or three days, as though he had something dwelling on his mind. She knew he was going out to the flying club, and watched him put his cigarettes in his pocket and check his wristwatch.

'It's no use my asking you not to go, I suppose?' Alix abandoned the easel and came to perch on the arm of the sofa.

'No.' Jake glanced across at her. She looked like a dejected child. Her face was devoid of make-up and her red curls were untidy and tumbled, so that he felt a sudden urge to stretch out his hand and set them to rights. Her green eyes glowed with that emerald hue which meant she was deeply upset.

If he could take her in his arms, it would make it all right. He could comfort her, caress her smooth skin, kiss her . . . and then?

He still wanted her, and he couldn't go on living this nightmare. This wanting and yearning and not possessing, which ate into his being. It had been bad enough before, but recently it was worse, because although he longed to believe her when she denied it, he could not quite rid himself of the suspicion that, in her despair, she had turned to another.

Jake didn't blame her. He couldn't hate her for it. It was his responsibility, his alone. Ever since he had first set eyes on her she had been the cornerstone of his life—and that stone was about to be kicked away. But this was not the time to be selfish. What mattered was Alix, and her future. Over these past few months he had borrowed her life from her, and it was time to give it back.

'You are a beautiful woman, Alix,' he said softly. 'I never met anyone like you.'

It was a long time since he had spoken to her so gently, and the antagonism that had existed between them for some time seemed to have drifted aside like a slowly dispelling mist.

'You were always different, too,' she said. 'You

changed my world, Jake. Whatever I am now, you made me.'

He smiled and shook his head. 'No,' he contradicted her, but not unkindly. 'A world different from mine made you what you are. I found you in that other world, and I should have left you there.' He stretched out his hand at last and touched her auburn curls. 'I always wanted to look after you. You made me feel that way. But you don't need me now; not any more.' He took his hand away. 'I know you've been wondering what the heck I've been doing, spending so much time with lawyers. But I want you to know that everything is in order. You could run it all without too much trouble, if I weren't around for any reason.' Jake hunched his broad shoulders and added a little defensively, 'I've wanted to say, before now, that I'm sorry if I've made you miserable, one way and another. That was never my intention.'

An odd feeling swept over Alix, as if a breeze blew over her, which was impossible, because the balcony windows were shut. 'All couples have their disagreements,' she said slowly. 'I married you because I wanted to be with you, and I have been with you, so it can't have been bad.'

Jake cupped his hands round her chin and tipped her face up towards his. 'No. It's been good. You came along when I needed you, Alix. To have you around for these past months, well, that's been more than something special for me. I wish—I wish we could have had more time with each other, earlier on. Who knows? We could have made something together, if only for a little time. It's funny how you never have as much time as you think you have. If people knew how little time they had, they wouldn't waste it. I wouldn't have hesitated, *then*. I'd have carried you off in the Sizaire out into the country somewhere, and made love to you under the trees. But I didn't, and we didn't . . .'

Alix said ruefully, 'You should have asked.'

'You would have said "Yes"?' The grey eyes regarded her interrogatively.

She coloured and felt her cheeks burning. 'I might have done.'

He gave a little snort of amusement. 'See what I mean? How we waste our chances! I read a poem once, by a fellow writing to his girl, a couple of hundred years ago. I guess people felt the same way then as they do now. He talked about "time's winged chariot", and that appealed to me, because I was a flying man and thought of myself as a sort of winged charioteer. But he had the same lack of time as I had, only he realised it.'

'Andrew Marvell,' Alix said. 'I remember that poem. We read it at school.'

'No one read poetry in the school I went to—not unless he wanted to get beaten up! I found my first book of poetry on a barrow among a lot of old clothes and odd shoes. It was in a back street, and they were immigrants buying and selling. They probably hadn't enough English to know what the book was, and I've no idea how the stall-holder came by it. But he handled it with such respect, and treated me with such respect when I bought it, because he thought I was an educated man. Well, I took it home and read it all, although some of it I didn't like too much. But Marvell had a way of getting to the heart of things. He wrote something else, about Charles the First, I think it was, and said, "He nothing common did, or mean". You know, if people could say that about *me* when I'm gone, I'd be pretty satisfied, at that.'

He smiled then down at her again, and bent his head and kissed her. There was a warmth on his lips and his embrace that had been missing from their relationship for so long, and which took her back to those lost war years, and a stolen kiss, unexpected, unlooked-for, and her first real lesson in love—real love.

Alix clung to him, knowing there could never be anyone but Jake for her, no matter what circumstances bound them, and that there never had been anyone like him from the very beginning. She felt that strange, tingling excitement run through her, and the old, sad longing. They were not one, perhaps, in the flesh, but they were one, in the spirit.

An impatient toot from the street below drifted in through the open balcony windows. 'Daquin!' Jake said, releasing her. He glanced through the windows at the patch of blue sky above the Parisian rooftops. 'A fine day. A day for flying.'

'Paul doesn't need you there!' she began, but he was already on his way.

At the door he paused, and looking back, said quickly, 'Goodbye, Alix. I meant what I said just now. It's been a good time.'

Again that feeling swept over her. She couldn't identify it at first, but when he had gone, she began to wonder if it wasn't fear.

Left alone in the flat, a tension built up in her which made it impossible to concentrate on anything or even to sit still. She began to prowl round restlessly from room to room, and finally found herself in Jake's bedroom.

She seldom went in there, and never when he was in it. She sat down now on the edge of the bed and surveyed it almost intently, as if it would tell her something about him and answer some riddle. But all it seemed to do was to remind her that he came from a different world from hers, and she had not yet found an entry to it. The books were mostly on the subject of engineering, interspersed with biographies and a few books on art. The one she had given him for Christmas lay on the bedside table, with a marker in the pages as if he'd been reading it in bed.

Alix knew he read a great deal after going to bed, often long into the night. She had seen the light shining beneath the door and heard the rustle of the turning pages. She didn't know if he stayed awake because of the pain or because of that recurring dream—or whether he was just one of those people who need very little sleep.

Her eyes fell on his jacket, which he had left hanging on the corner of a chair. She got up and retrieved it with housewifely concern for neatness. She pulled open the wardrobe door to take out a hanger. It was as she settled the coat on the hanger that she realised there was something tucked down in the inside breast-pocket. Through the lining, it felt like a piece of folded card. She had no intention of going through his pockets; such a thing normally would not even have occurred to her. But the curious feeling had not left her, and she was impelled to push her fingers into the pocket and extract the folded paper. It looked old, as though it had been carried for a long time, perhaps years, in a succession of jacket pockets like this one, and this was only the latest home for what looked like some kind of souvenir. It had been once been white, but was now yellowed, and the folds so firmly creased they would never come out. She took it to the dressing-table and flattened it out as much as possible. Then she frowned, puzzled. It was a menu, in English, of a London restaurant, a war-time menu, as the date printed at the top told her. There seemed no obvious reason on earth why Jake should carry a menu around, and for years.

She turned the piece of printed card over idly. There, on the back, in Robbie's handwriting, stood Mrs Daventry's address, and beneath it, in faded, almost illegible pencil, a street map. Now she recognised it at

last. The years rolled back, and she and Robbie sat
again in a West End restaurant with Jake and the tipsy,
peroxided Tilly, in a cloud of cigarette smoke from
Tilly's Abdullas. Robbie explained again to Jake how
to reach the Daventrys' house the next day to collect
Alix and bring her to the station. In her mind's eye, she
again saw Jake taking the card, folding it, and stuffing
it casually into the pocket of his RFC uniform. He had
carried it ever since. He must have had it on him when
he was shot down. She refolded it carefully and replaced
it in his pocket, then put the jacket back on the chair
as it had been, and left the room. It was his secret,
something he had not wanted her to know. But it hurt
her, that he had not wanted her to know.

There was a ring at the doorbell, and Alix heard
Séraphine's voice repeating something loudly, as though
to someone who had difficulty in understanding her.
Alix went quickly to the hall, and gave a cry of delight.

'Robbie! Oh, do come in. Why didn't you let us
know? Jake's gone—gone out, and I know he would
have stayed if he'd known you were coming. You will
wait, won't you, till he comes back?'

She ushered him into the salon, where he sat down
in one of the comfortable armchairs and looked about
him with approval.

'This is more like it! It looks like someone's home,
not a tart's boudoir.' He grinned at her cheerfully. 'I've
put Edith on the train for the Côte d'Azur, with enough
luggage for a State Visit and a down-at-heel Russian
prince for an escort. She'll pick up his losses at the
tables, give him a gold cigarette-case for his services,
and then ditch the poor chap.' Robbie chuckled. 'The
thing about Edith, bless her, is that I know I can trust
her—not to be faithful, but to be consistent!' He spread
out his arms. 'So I'm at liberty to amuse myself in
Paris. Tell me what you've been doing since we met.'

Someone to confide in was what she had lacked most during these last weeks, and Alix found herself pouring it all out to Robbie—Paul, the biplane, the trips to the flying club, and the effect it was all having on Jake.

'Hmm,' Robbie said thoughtfully. He stretched out his legs and regarded the toes of his two-tone shoes. 'I can't see what you can do to stop it, Alix. Daquin's right, in his way. Jake *is* a flying man, and once it's in the blood . . . I remember how he hated being grounded by the weather, during the war. Sometimes he'd prowl around the Mess, sometimes he'd pretend to sleep, but it was only pretence. At the first sign of the fog lifting, or whatever the problem had been, he was sprinting towards the machines. He couldn't wait to be airborne.'

'But it's different now, Robbie, because he can't handle a machine himself, and listening to Paul makes him so wretched and frustrated and unhappy! Something bad will come out of it all, it must! Pressure just can't go on building itself up inside a person like that. No human being can withstand it indefinitely . . .'

'Now hold on, Alix,' Robbie said firmly, calming her by his level tone. He made a placatory gesture with his hands, palm downwards. 'I have a feeling I've come into the middle of this story somewhere. What's Daquin's angle? Surely he must see the effect that his talk of flying and these visits to the club have on Jake?'

Alix heaved a deep sigh and rubbed her fingers through her hair so that the curls fluffed up in a higgledy-piggledy manner, and Robbie grinned briefly. 'I don't know, Robbie,' she said, and her tone took the grin from his face. 'Perhaps I'm just afraid to think about it. Paul . . .'

She broke off, and Robbie leaned forward. 'Come on, Alix. Old friends as we are, if you can't tell me, whom can you tell?'

'Oh, Robbie, you can't imagine how glad I am that

you're here! You see, Jake doesn't know this, but Paul has some crazy idea that I might divorce Jake—and marry him.'

'Oh?' Robbie said softly. 'Does he, now? And what gave Paul that idea?'

Alix flushed angrily. 'Not *me*! I didn't—if that's what you mean! You don't know Paul. He—He thinks and calculates and plans all the time. Outwardly, he's very Bohemian, devil-may-care, but inside he's like a machine, ticking away, working things out.'

Robbie lay back and folded his arms, staring at her speculatively. 'Look here, Alix,' he said bluntly, 'Edith doesn't have to *tell* me when she's playing around. I *know*. If you've been playing around with Daquin, you can bet that Jake knows! Don't glare at me like that, my precious. I'm a friend. At least, be honest with *me*.'

'I am being honest with you, Robbie,' she told him quietly. 'I haven't slept with Paul. I don't want to. Sometimes I don't even like him much. But I know Jake isn't sure. When Paul is here to discuss colour schemes and so on, Jake sits on that sofa and watches and listens. I know what he's thinking. He thinks Paul is my lover. Perhaps, even though I hate to admit this even to myself, most of all to myself, Jake thinks I would go to Paul if I could just bring myself to leave him.'

With gentle persistence, Robbie said, 'Jake has to have some reason for suspecting it, even if he's wrong, and *especially* if he's wrong. Come on, Alix, what is it?'

Alix got up and walked nervously to the window, twisting her hands. Outside the sky was blue and clear, a fine day for flying, just as Jake said. 'Jake has one bedroom; I have another,' she said dully. 'That's how it is, and always has been. All the terrible things that happened to him during the war have left a sort of mental scar. When he crashed, the last crash, he thought he was going to burn. He didn't, but it—it sort of locked up his mind. Since then, he's never . . .' she faltered, 'he's never . . .' The words trailed away.

'Good God!' Robbie said softly. He whistled a long-drawn-out descending note through his teeth.

There was a silence. Alix felt something akin to relief that their secret was out at last. She turned round to face Robbie and said, almost briskly, though it rang false, telling Robbie that she was very near to cracking up, 'So, you see, Jake thinks I might be better off with another man. I'm sure he knows Paul would like me to seek an annulment, and Jake's persuaded himself it's what I'd really like, too.'

Robbie sat up with an abruptness that made her jump. 'Sit down, Alix, and let me get you a drink. Don't argue, sweetie, just do it!' He pointed at her chair.

Alix sat down and rather unwillingly accepted the stiff Scotch he pushed into her hand.

'All right,' he said. 'Now let's take it all very carefully, and slowly, from the beginning. Jake and you are living together, but not as man and wife. Does Daquin realise this?'

'Yes,' Alix said harshly. 'He does. He guessed. He's clever. That's what makes me afraid of him.'

'Hold on; you're getting worked up again. Don't hang grimly on to that whisky. Drink it!'

Alix said mutinously, 'I don't like whisky.'

'Too bad. Drink it anyway. So Daquin knows the score, and he thinks it lets him in with a very good chance. But if you make it clear to him that he's off-limits, hell, Alix—there's nothing the fellow can do. Tell him to go and take a swim in the Seine. Preferably with a brick tied round his neck!'

But Alix was staring at him, and something in her face sent a prickle of fear running up Robbie's spine. 'What's up?' he asked quickly.

'Yes—there *is* something Paul can do!' Alix burst out. She set down the untasted whisky glass so that it clattered and spilled on the table-top. 'Yes, there *is*! Don't you see, Robbie? Paul can work on Jake, keep talking about flying, take him out to the club, make him feel worse and worse, until in the end . . .'

She broke off, and Robbie demanded 'Until what, for pity's sake?'

Alix looked towards the window and the fragment of blue sky trapped between the roof tops and the frame. 'Until, in the end, Jake tries to fly again. *That's* what he meant! That's why he's spent so much time with his lawyers!'

Robbie was gazing at her in incomprehension, and she jumped up and tugged at his sleeve. 'Robbie, we must get out to the flying club and stop him, stop *them*! Jake means to take Paul's machine up—I *know* it. Oh, how could I be so stupid, so dense?' She clenched her fists in agony. 'I let him go. I should have guessed. Robbie—Jake will be killed, and Paul knows it! Paul's worked for this, wanted this—he means to get rid of Jake, and Jake is obligingly playing his game!'

'Jake isn't so stupid!' Robbie objected sharply.

'Robbie,' Alix said quietly, 'Jake told me once that if ever he had a meaningless marriage, like the one my parents had and he and I have, he'd blow his brains out. Well, loaded revolvers aren't Jake's way. Jake's a flying man, and that's the way he's chosen to go.'

'*No!*' Robbie took her shoulders and gripped them. '*No* pilot crashes on purpose! Perhaps Jake *may* have some such muddle-headed idea in his mind if and when he takes that machine up, but once up there, in the sky, training and instinct take over. He'll fly that damn thing, and he'll land it—safely!'

'You're forgetting Paul,' she said in a low, hard voice. 'Paul doesn't leave things to chance like that. The other day, at lunch, he let slip something about having trouble with the engine. He covered up quickly, saying it was all right now. But—supposing it isn't?' Her green eyes, dark with fear, fixed themselves on Robbie's face. 'Supposing it isn't, Robbie?'

CHAPTER SIXTEEN

ROBBIE WAS shaking his head, refusing to accept what she said, but he was worried, his face deathly pale. 'Now, take it easy, Alix!' he said hoarsely. 'Perhaps your friend Paul is a shrewd, unscrupulous businessman and a moral rat. It doesn't make him a murderer, and that's what you're accusing him of being—or intending to become. He's a war time pilot, and no flying man sends another one up to his death deliberately.'

'I haven't got the time to argue with you,' Alix flung over her shoulder at him as she pulled on her coat. 'I'm taking the Sizaire and going out to the flying club. You can come, if you want.'

'Of course I'm coming,' he said with alacrity. 'Where's the motor?'

'Garaged near by. I think there's enough fuel in the tank.'

The short distance to the garage two streets away might have been miles, it seemed to take them so long to get there. It was the sort of mad journey like a nightmare, made at a run towards an unattainable goal. So many thoughts whirled wildly in Alix's head, as she pushed her way past startled pedestrians on the pavements and darted heedlessly across the intersections. Robbie, hastening along beside her, did his best to keep up and save them both from collision. One single great truth was emblazoned in white-hot letters before Alix's eyes. She knew why he'd done this.

'Oh, Jake,' she repeated over and over again in her tormented mind. 'This isn't what I want!'

'Best let me drive,' Robbie suggested breathlessly, as they reached the garage at last. 'You're too overwrought.'

'No!' she said crisply. 'You don't know the way, and you aren't used to Paris traffic.'

'Just take it slowly, and don't get us arrested by some officious gendarme, that's all!' he pleaded, scrambling into the seat beside her.

His words were snatched from his mouth as they roared out into the street and rattled away over the cobbles. Robbie noticed with some relief that she was a good driver, and reflected grimly that it was just as well, in the circumstances. She was taking the corners at reckless speed, and ignoring the instrument-readings on the dashboard in order to watch the road. With the Sizaire, it wasn't easy to keep an eye on the speed-gauge, and Robbie watched the needle creep round with gloomy foreboding.

Now that they were roaring through the suburbs, the traffic lessened, and Robbie felt less impelled to close his eyes and pray. All the same, he was beginning to think that the trip was worse than any encounter with the wretched Hun, any day.

'We're never going to get there at all if you go on driving like a lunatic,' he yelled into her ear.

Alix slowed down reluctantly.

'You're sure about Daquin, are you?' Robbie asked after a moment or two.

'As sure as I am of anything!' she replied curtly.

Robbie hunched his shoulders unhappily, and muttered, 'Rum business!'

Before the club-house, the red Hispano-Suiza stood unattended in solitary splendour. Alix's heart sank as she drew the Sizaire to a grinding halt in a squeal of brakes and a shower of gravel and scrambled out, together with Robbie.

As they looked about them, the scene was deceptively peaceful. In fact, the whole place seemed deserted. After the hustle and bustle of central Paris, here it was quiet and cool in the spring sunlight. The new green leaves rustled slightly on the trees behind them in the gentle breeze. The only other perceptible sound was the drone of a biplane high in the scudding clouds above their heads. Robbie shaded his eyes with his hands and squinted up into the sky.

'Camel,' he said. 'An old war-time one. Our squadron flew those.'

'That's Paul's,' Alix muttered. She ran round the corner of the club-house to the edge of the airfield, Robbie close behind her, his feet thumping heavily on the gravel. A solitary figure was leaning on a fence, smoking a cigarette, relaxed and nonchalant. He glanced over his shoulder as they came up, and looked mildly surprised.

'Hallo, Alix, what's brought you out here?'

'Where's Jake?' Alix demanded fiercely, ignoring Paul's question and not bothering to greet him.

But Paul, in turn, ignored her question to gesture towards Robbie with his smouldering cigarette and ask suspiciously, 'Who's that?'

'A friend, of mine and Jake's. *Paul*, tell me where Jake is!' she repeated in increasing anger and trepidation.

Paul raised his dark eyebrows, quite unperturbed, and made a faint jerk of his head skywards. 'Up there.'

All three of them stood in silence, and gazed up and at the distant machine turning gracefully against the pattern of sky and cloud.

Through dry lips, Alix whispered in horror, 'You had no right . . .'

'Look, Alix,' Paul interrupted calmly, 'I didn't force

the man into the machine at gunpoint. He *wanted* to fly. It would have been difficult for me to stop him.'

His whole manner was such that, had she not known him better, she would have sworn he was sincere. But she did know Paul better.

'You know the odds against his landing that machine!'

A shadow passed over Paul's handsome, cynical countenance, and his mouth hardened. He threw away the half-smoked cigarette. 'He's lame, he's awkward, he's a little rusty—but he was a war-time ace. I knew his reputation, even then. Jake Sherwood, he was a legend. That machine belongs to me; I paid good money for it. Do you think I want it smashed up? I have confidence in him, why can't you?'

He seemed to consider this answer, made in English, sufficient, and half turned away from her, digging in his pocket for his cigarette-case. He had just found it, when Alix grasped his arm with such unexpected strength and fury that he dropped the case on the turf, where it burst open, spilling his Turkish cigarettes across the grass.

'I don't want one of your self-justifying explanations, Paul!' she told him, her eyes blazing. 'I want to know what chance Jake has of getting that machine back safely!'

'Every chance!' Paul snapped vehemently. 'Good grief, Alix! I wouldn't have let him take it up if I hadn't every confidence in him, just like I said.'

'And in the engine?' she asked coolly.

She saw the truth then in his eyes, a flicker, like a shutter half-opening on a window, to be slammed shut at once, a glimpse into the mind of the man.

'The engine has been playing up,' he admitted, his voice elaborately casual. 'But the mechanics have repaired it. I cleared it with them this morning.'

'You'd better be right, old son,' Robbie said softly, speaking for the first time. 'Or you'll have a lot of explaining to do and make your explanations good ones, because I'm a flying man too, and I'll know which questions to ask.'

Paul whirled round angrily, his mouth open to reply, but, at the sight of Robbie's expression, changed his mind, shrugged, and turned back in silence. He stooped and retrieved his cigarette-case, and two or three cigarettes that hadn't broken, and lit one. His hand shook very slightly, but whether from nerves or in anger, Alix couldn't have said.

Above their heads, the biplane was circling for the last time over the aerodrome, losing height and coming in to land. Beside Alix, Robbie put his arm round her comfortingly. 'Hold on, my dear. All's not lost, you know. He's a heck of a fine pilot, and seems to be managing pretty well up there. He *had* to do it, you know, to show to himself, as well as to us, that he can still fly. He was always as obstinate as a mule.'

The breeze caught at Alix's auburn hair, ruffling it. 'No,' she said almost inaudibly. 'He wants to set me at liberty, like a caged creature. Jake thinks that if only he weren't there I'd make a different, new life—probably with . . .' She hesitated, then she pointed a finger at Paul and said loudly, in a voice redolent with scorn, 'With that *animal*! As if I ever would!'

What Paul, white-faced at her words, might have replied was not to be known. A sudden coughing noise and splutter from above caught the attention of all three of them. The engine roared into renewed life, coughed and fell silent again.

'Fuel's not getting through . . .' Robbie muttered. 'He can glide . . .' He licked a finger and held it up into the breeze and muttered, 'Damn, he's coming in from the wrong direction, the wind will catch the tail!'

Paul stepped back behind them, but neither paid any attention to him as he began to walk quickly away

towards the club-house. The biplane seemed frighten-
ingly low now, and they could see the head and shoulders
of the pilot in the cockpit as he fought with the controls.

The machine banked, lurching, and resumed an even
keel. Alix thought she could hear the beating of her
own heart as it tried to break out of her chest. All at
once the plane descended, a menacing dark shape like
a great bird of prey swooping down on them. They
could hear the wind rushing past the fuselage and
singing in the wires.

'Oh damn!' Robbie repeated in a flat, expressionless
voice, 'He's not going to make it. He's going to crash.'

To Alix's fascinated and horrified gaze, everything
seemed to happen very slowly, as if a piece of cinema
film were slowed down. The biplane was coming ever
closer, lower and lower, at first weaving from side to
side drunkenly before beginning to twist like a falling
sycamore seed. Suddenly the action seemed to accel-
erate, and from agonising slowness became terrifying
speed. The machine plummeted, striking the ground. It
bounced, just once, was caught by the wind and was
flung up into the air and over, like a child's paper dart.
There was a loud crack of splintered wood and one pair
of wings sheered off neatly, as if cut by a giant pair of
scissors, and the machine came to rest, upside-down, a
mangled skeleton of what it had once been.

But long before this Robbie had begun to move,
leaping over the low fence that bounded the perimeter
of the aerodrome, and sprinting towards the wrecked
machine. A young mechanic had appeared from
somewhere and was running towards them. Alix ducked
under the fence, kicked off her shoes, and raced across
the turf towards the crumpled Camel.

'Get back!' Robbie yelled at her, as she panted up to
the wreckage. He pushed her forcibly away. 'Ruddy
thing can go up at any minute!'

'Jake!' she gasped.

In the wreckage, a half-visible form stirred and a faint voice said, 'Oh, heck! Give me a hand, can't you?'

'Hang on, old chap,' Robbie called. 'We'll soon have you out.' He turned to the young mechanic and began to try, by gestures, to show him what he wanted him to do. Alix sniffed. On the air came a faint, pervasive stench of fuel.

'No . . .' she whispered.

At that moment, something impelled her to turn her head. In the distance, over by the club-house, Paul stood watching them. Seeing Alix look towards him, the lone spectator turned away and began to walk briskly from the scene. Alix began to run back from the wreckage towards his retreating figure, shouting, 'Paul! For goodness' sake! It's leaking!'

He turned back at her voice and hesitated, then, suddenly making up his mind, ran forward, jumped athletically over the fence and sprinted towards the wreckage.

From the edge of the field, Alix watched in frozen immobility as the three men tore their way through the tangled struts and wires, scraping their hands raw, in a feverish race against time. At last they dragged a body out, his heels trailing across the turf. But, as they got clear of the wreck, the figure began to move and could be heard protesting forcibly as he was carried across the field between them and set down in the shadow of the club-house.

Alix ran across, forced her way between them, and dropped on her knees beside him, heedless of the sharp gravel cutting into her skin. He'd hit his head, splitting the skin open, and blood poured freely down his face in a grotesque and horrifying mask. But he seemed oblivious of it. 'I did it!' he kept repeating in elation. 'I did it! Alix?'

'Oh, *Jake*!' she exclaimed in mingled relief and frustration. She flung both arms round him tightly, pressing his injured head to her bosom, blood staining her coat and hands.

He twisted his head in her embrace and peered up at her triumphantly. 'I told you I could . . .' He broke off and squinted into the haze of dirt, sweat and blood. 'Lord—is that you, Robbie?'

'You are a ruddy idiot,' Robbie said wearily, by way of acknowledgement. 'Don't you ever bloody learn?'

Jake grinned up at him, his teeth gleaming white in the mask of grime. 'Not me, I'm a flying man, remember?'

They had forgotten Paul. He had stepped away from the group and stood watching, as Alix hugged Jake to her. Then he glanced over his shoulder to the wrecked Camel, and suddenly vaulted over the fence and ran back towards it.

'Where the devil is he going?' Robbie exclaimed, looking up. 'He should keep away from that wreckage. What's he doing?'

Paul had reached the wreck and stopped a few feet away. He dragged the last of his damaged Turkish cigarettes from his pocket, lit it with quick, sure fingers and drew on it.

'He can't *smoke*—near *that*!' Robbie croaked in amazement and horror.

But Paul, as always, seemed to know exactly what he was doing. He took the cigarette from his mouth, examined the end to make sure it was burning well, and then leant forward and tossed the glowing stub into the tangle of wood and wire. Then he ran like the wind away from the wreckage, fleeing for his very life.

He got clear not a moment too soon. There was a dull 'crump' and then a 'swoosh', as a ball of orange and red flames roared crackling into the air. Alix and

Jake on the ground, and Robbie and the French mechanic standing, watched stupefied as the fire destroyed the last of the machine and a pall of dense, pungent black smoke formed over it and began to drift skyward like a great black exclamation-mark.

Paul had reached the perimeter fence, panting and sweating, and vaulted neatly over it. He pushed back his tumbled black hair with both hands, and walked straight past them, without a glance or sign of their presence, round the corner of the club-house.

No one spoke a word. In the silence, against the dull crackle of the burning wreck, they heard the purr of the Hispano-Suiza, and the crunch of the gravel as it was driven away.

'I do *not* need a doctor!' Jake yelled for the tenth time. 'For crying out loud—Robbie, tell her, will you, man?'

'She's right,' Robbie said firmly. 'You've had an almighty crack on the head. Not that it's likely to have done any damage, not to that thick skull! But it could need a stitch in it, and you're probably concussed. Best see the M.O.'

'I'm not concussed! Do I look like a man who's concussed? Do I sound like one?' Jake struggled up on the sofa and pushed away their helping hands vigorously.

'Ignore him,' Robbie said to Alix, 'and get hold of the medical chap, I should.'

They had driven Jake back to the flat and manhandled him into the lift between them, protesting, swearing and yet so elated that Robbie had observed it would have taken lead boots to keep his feet on the ground.

'Tea!' said Robbie now. 'That's the stuff. I don't mean drawing-room tea, the sort of thing they dish out with cucumber sandwiches. I mean Forces' tea. I'll go and brew up.'

He trotted off into the kitchen and could be heard involving himself in the intricacies of his personal tea-making ritual.

'I don't drink tea!' Jake shouted, and then said 'Ouch!' and groaned as the effort sent a jagged stab of pain through his head. He watched Alix ordering Séraphine to call the doctor, grumbling crossly, 'I do not need a doctor!'

'I'm sure he'll come anyway.' She surveyed his rumpled, dirt-streaked figure and exclaimed reproachfully, 'Oh, Jake, how *could* you?'

The grey eyes met hers evenly. 'I had to do it,' he said quietly, 'and I did it.'

'Yes, you did.' Alix smoothed back his tousled hair from the clotted blood on his brow. 'The doctor can't see you like that. I'll go and get some water.'

She arrived with the water and a cloth as Robbie arrived with the tea in a large mug.

'This is worse than crashing,' their patient informed them, as Alix dabbed at the dried blood and caked dust on his face and tried to wash the wound without setting it bleeding again, and Robbie spooned sugar generously into the steaming 'tea' and stirred it round rapidly so that it formed a sudsy whirlpool.

Robbie pushed the mug into Jake's hand and sat down. 'Listen, you chump! I call to see you after a gap of years, and I find you indulging in aerial acrobatics. A man of your age, too!' He grinned.

'Shut up!' Jake growled. He sipped at the tea, and grimaced. 'What's in this devil's brew?'

'Tea, sugar, some condensed milk I found in the cupboard, and brandy.'

'It tastes like nothing on earth!'

'Speaking of which,' Robbie said, 'I thought, for a moment back there, we were going to have to send for a padre, not the doc.'

'Engine cut out—Ow!' This was caused by Alix prodding unwisely at the cut on his brow. 'What's the matter with you two? Why not just leave me in the wreckage? Why drag me out just to poison me and torture me?'

'Out of our deep affection for you,' Robbie said. 'Silly b—' He remembered Alix and bit back what he was going to say. 'Idiot,' he amended, more mildly.

'You don't give concussed patients alcohol,' Alix said dubiously, eyeing the tea.

Both men looked up at her. 'You do in the RFC!' they said in unison.

The doctor came, ordered his patient to bed, but declared that, as far as he could see, no serious damage had been done. The cut on his head looked worse than it was, as did the rapidly blackening eye. In a week, the bruises would be fading. The cut would take a little longer to heal and would almost certainly leave a scar, but not, he said portentously, 'of significance'.

When the doctor had gone, Robbie prepared to take his own leave. He pulled on his overcoat and hovered unhappily in the hall. 'This fellow—Daquin—you'll have to watch out for him. We can't *prove* anything, you know. The blighter was quick-witted enough to destroy the aeroplane and all the evidence. That engine is nothing but a blackened, twisted lump of metal now.'

'Proof doesn't matter, Robbie,' Alix said firmly. 'I *know*, and Paul realises I do. It's enough.'

Robbie looked far from satisfied as they went out of the flat, and jabbed at the button to call up the lift.

'It's engaged,' Alix said, noticing the little red light. 'Someone is coming up. Just wait a tick.'

'Doesn't matter.' Robbie pulled on his cap. 'I'll run down the stairs. It's only a couple of flights.' He kissed her on the cheek. 'Take care, Alix, and good luck with our invalid. I'll call on you tomorrow.' He clattered away down the stairs and was lost to sight round the bend at the mezzanine.

Alix turned to go back into the flat, but as she did so, the lift, which had been purring upwards towards her, came to a jolting, rattling halt. The door of the iron cage clashed open and Paul stepped out to face her. He was the last person she had expected to see, and astonishment kept her rooted to the spot, when what she knew she should do was to dart into the flat and slam the door in his face. He looked pale and tense, his dark eyes watchful and his whole manner defensive, his hands thrust deep into his coat pockets. He said nothing, but waited for her to speak first.

'What are *you* doing here?' Alix demanded in a low, angry voice, her green eyes snapping at him. 'How dare you show your face to *me*?'

A scarlet flush touched Paul's pale cheekbones. 'I came to ask how Jake was.' He hunched his shoulders and, looking away from her, muttered, 'And to say I'm sorry.'

'Sorry? *Sorry!*' She could hardly believe her ears. Did he honestly imagine that a bout of disarming candour would rescue him from this scrape, as it had done from so many others?

'Yes, sorry!' Paul shouted at her with unexpected ferocity. His voice echoed hollowly in the stairwell.

'How could you do it?' Alix asked him, at a loss to understand his treachery. 'I would never have dreamt that even you, Paul, could have sunk to such a thing.'

'I wanted you,' he said forlornly, sounding like a child dispossessed of a favourite toy. 'He was in the way. I thought, without him, you might, eventually, turn to me.'

'You should have known that couldn't possibly happen, with or without Jake! I couldn't ever love you,

Paul. But I did, once, like you—and now . . .' She surveyed him, and added quietly, 'I feel nothing but contempt for you.'

He flinched. 'I feel much that way about myself. I'm not proud of what I did.'

'At least you don't deny it! Robbie said you burned that aeroplane to destroy any evidence. Did you?'

'No!' he said savagely. 'Your friend Robbie can think what he likes! I set fire to the machine because of what I did—because it was probably the worst thing I ever did, and it represented all the worst in me. I wanted to destroy it, and all the evil with it!' He looked and sounded truly wretched. 'Believe me or not, as you like, it's true, I swear.'

'Yes, I believe you,' Alix said slowly, watching his face. She wanted to believe he *was* telling the truth, but she could no longer truly believe in anything he told her. 'I can never work with you again, Paul. You know that, of course.'

He nodded. 'Yes. A pity. We worked well together. I'll miss you. You don't mind my using your designs for Laroche's house?' When she inclined her head briefly, he added, 'I'll pay you what I owe, through the bank. We needn't meet.'

He took her fingers and held them for a moment. She didn't protest, but she could see in his eyes how his mind was working. The relief was still there, but impudence had joined it and the vanity which, after all, was the underlying streak in his whole, flawed character. He'd talked himself out of another scrape successfully and was beginning to feel pleased with himself for having been so clever. This time, he'd come nearer to hurting himself than he'd ever done before—but he'd learned nothing from the perilous lesson.

Alix thought, 'It's not cleverness that he has, it's

cunning. In other ways he really is a stupid and pathetic man.'

But it no longer mattered to her whether he thought he'd got away with it or not. Sooner or later Paul's schemes would come unstuck. She wouldn't be around to see it, but she didn't care.

He'd been about to say something else to her, but perhaps he read her thoughts in her face. He flushed slightly and for a moment looked uncertain, as if the cold touch of truth had brushed his shoulder. He dropped her hand, nodded briefly to her, and stepped back into the waiting cage of the lift. It clanked away, carrying him out of her life.

The shutters had been closed in Jake's room, and when he opened his eyes, it was to find himself in semi-darkness. He squinted at the illuminated dial of his wristwatch and saw it was just before five o'clock, so he supposed the doctor had given him a mild sedative and he'd slept for a brief spell. Yet the adrenalin pumping through his veins was still such that even a sleeping-pill couldn't quell it. He was wide awake, elated, every nerve in his body a-tingle, as if it throbbed with a new life coursing through every fibre.

Automatically, as a man who had been through many crashes as an aviator, Jake checked that he could move his arms and legs and roll his head from side to side without pain. He wasn't hurt. His exploring fingers touched the puffed skin around his left eye and, gingerly, the gash on his head. He must look a mess, though. He lay back on the pillow and closed his eyes again.

Lying here, alone, it seemed as if he lived again that other crash that had abruptly terminated his war. He remembered crying out Alix's name, the talisman that had kept him in the land of the living. That image of Alix standing on the bright side of the frontier between life and death had never left him. For Alix, he had clung on, struggled back. For such a long time he had seemed to have fought that agonising battle for nothing, but now it was different. The victory which had so long eluded him, was his—there to take.

Now, in this quiet, dark Parisian bedroom, Jake muttered again, 'Alix?' and opened his eyes to see her pale face with its aureole of auburn hair watching him with concerned green eyes. Only this time it was real, and not his delirium.

He asked, 'Where have you been?'

Alix knew that his question meant: What had stopped her taking up that part of his life which was meant for her. She whispered, 'I was always there.'

Jake nodded, and grimaced slightly because it tugged at the gash on his forehead.

Alix smiled at him hesitantly. It was a beauty of a black eye, and the lurid gash was puffing up into a sizeable bump, yet there was such animation in his features that they seemed almost transfigured. He was watching her, his grey eyes lit by a strange light, as if this was not the Jake with whom she'd lived these past months but a different man, reborn, yet looking out at her through the same pair of eyes.

He pushed himself up on one elbow on the crumpled pillows, the sheet sliding away from his naked torso. Perspiration gleamed in the hollows of his collarbones, and the muscles of his chest and arms were taut and twitched, as if containing a turbulent store of unexploded energy.

A sudden panic swept over Alix as she realised how nearly they had escaped a final, fatal parting. She felt again a stab of the terrible agony that had enveloped her heart when she had seen the Camel twisting and turning in the blue sky, far above her head, and had known that Jake fought for his salvation, alone in victory or defeat.

'You were going to leave me behind,' she whispered, appalled, her voice sounding bewildered, like that of a lost and frightened child. Then, in an upsurge of searing pain, she cried out, 'How *could* you try such a reckless, such a—a *stupid* escapade? What should I do, without *you*?'

'I always made you angry,' Jake said huskily. 'Come here, and I'll make you forget your anger . . .'

He leaned forward and caught her face in his hands. As his mouth closed over hers, he pushed her back to the pillows beside him and rolled over, pinning her beneath his weight, and crushing her down on the bed. Instinctively, deprived of breath, she fought against the superior strength of that lean, muscular body which kept her trapped and the mouth which held hers prisoner, forcing it open, his tongue flickering past her teeth. Her own struggles conspired against her, awakening her body to a responding animal passion so that it no longer twisted against his, but with his, in a slowly gathering rhythm. Alix's hands caught desperately at his shoulders, her fingertips digging into the lean flesh and feeling the bunching of the muscles and sinews beneath.

Jake muttered something she could not quite catch. His left hand thrust fiercely against her breast, tearing the buttons out of the buttonholes on her fragile silk blouse. His fingers closed on the soft flesh so tightly that she gave a little cry of distress, and his hand relaxed its pressure a little, and he whispered, 'No, not anger, *excitement!*'

Alix confessed, 'Yes—Yes, you always made me feel like this . . . When I first knew you, I wanted to fight it and I couldn't . . .' She gave a little sob, turning in his arms.

'Don't fight it.' His fingers moved swiftly and surely,

divesting her of her clothing, the garments dropped one by one on the floor with a soft, seductive rustling until her naked form lay beside his, shimmering palely in the half-light, the damp bare flesh of their two bodies moulding together wherever it touched.

His powerful outline stooped over her and he kissed her breasts and her stomach, his fingers running along the length of her thighs, until she moaned and whispered apprehensively, 'Jake?'

'It's all right,' he told her, his voice hoarse and coming in breathless, urgent, broken phrases. 'The nightmare is over, and I woke up. I'm free . . . I know I can do any damn thing I want, and what I want most is you . . .'

She answered so quietly that it was like a whisper on a breeze, 'And I want you, Jake.'

She saw him smile, a smile of tenderness, of understanding and of love, so that they had no more need of words. He lay back and held out his arms towards her, and she put her hands on his shoulders and lowered herself across his loins.

Jake threw his arms about her, catching her slim, pliant, soft body against his firm, muscular one. She heard him whisper, 'Now,' as he became a part of her very being and they were no longer two people but one, a single creation, caught in a moment of ecstasy.

The setting sun found a chink in the blind, and a sudden ray of golden light fell into the darkened room across their entwined bodies, as Jake muttered a little sound between a gasp and a groan and relaxed in her arms. The golden beam, with its burden of dancing dust-particles, travelled slowly across the room, forsaking the man and the woman still bound together in their completed act of love.

Jake stirred and murmured into her ear, 'I love you. I always loved you. I know that nothing I've ever done could mean as much to me as being able to say, "You are my wife—I am your husband." '

Alix put up her hand to touch his cheek and whispered softly: 'You always were . . .'

Jake muttered, 'Alix,' and pressed himself against her, his fingers twisting themselves into a curl of her auburn hair, trapping her as his mouth sought out hers urgently.

A clock was ticking in the corner of the room, its insistent even click beating out a soft pulsating rhythm like a heartbeat. Alix wondered if Jake could feel her heart throbbing against his chest, the life force of her body adapting itself to the rhythm of his.

When they broke apart, he said unexpectedly in a quiet voice, 'That flight—I knew the machine was handling badly as soon as I took it up. I could have landed straight away with no problem. But I had to take the chance. You do understand, don't you, darling?'

She nodded, nestling her cheek against the warm, damp skin of his chest. His fingertips stroked the outline of her ear, making her shiver.

'I always wanted to be the best, Alix, and to have the best—design the best motor-car, be the best flier, even when I was convalescent and learned to play that goddam piano, I said, "Heck, if I'm going to be any kind of pianist, I'm going to be a good one . . ." But you were the best thing that ever happened to me, Alix. I don't know what I ever did to deserve you—I always was a selfish blighter. But once I'd met you, nothing I'd done meant anything any more, or could mean anything, without you. I was like the fellow in the scriptures who found a pearl of great price and traded everything to have it. You're my pearl of great price, Alix, and if I had to risk my life to possess you, then that's what I did—because without you, I'm nothing.'

Alix cupped her hands gently round his face. 'You are my life,' she told him softly, 'And my life, all of me, is yours.'

BRIGHT SMILES, *DARK* SECRETS.

Model Kristi Johanssen moves in a glittering world, a far cry from her small town upbringing.

She carries with her the horrific secret of physical abuse in childhood. Engaged to Philip, a top plastic surgeon, Kristi finds her secret a barrier between them.

Gareth, Philip's reclusive ex-film star brother, has the magnetism to overcome her fears.

But doesn't he possess a secret darker than her own?

Available July. Price £3.50

W**O**RLDWIDE

Available from Boots, Martins, John Menzies, W.H. Smith, Woolworths and other paperback stockists.

Conscience, scandal and desire.

A dynamic story of a woman whose integrity, both personal and professional, is compromised by the intrigue that surrounds her.

Against a background of corrupt Chinese government officials, the CIA and a high powered international art scandal, Lindsay Danner becomes the perfect pawn in a deadly game. Only ex-CIA hit man Catlin can ensure she succeeds… and lives.

Together they find a love which will unite them and overcome the impossible odds they face.

Available May. Price £3.50

W✪RLDWIDE

Available from Boots, Martins, John Menzies, W.H. Smith, Woolworths and other paperback stockists.

 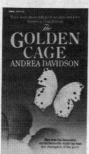 

Variety and the spice of life.

Adventure, intrigue, action and fantasy set in exotic locations from China to Antigua.

These Worldwide novels offer a variety of styles and tastes as different as the individual authors.

Choose from the harsh realities of civil war to the pure fantasy of the world of film, and succumb to the charms of our many talented authors.

There is a wide selection of contemporary and historical settings to cater for your every mood.

W🌐RLDWIDE